# Bi-Satisfied

*Nikki-Michelle*

www.urbanbooks.net

Urban Books, LLC
97 N 18th Street
Wyandanch, NY 11798

ISBN 13: 978-1-62286-709-7
ISBN 10: 1-62286-709-2

First Trade Paperback Printing September 2015
Printed in the United States of America

10 9 8 7 6 5 4 3 2 1

*This is a work of fiction. Any references or similarities to actual events, real people, living or dead, or to real locales are intended to give the novel a sense of reality. Any similarity in other names, characters, places, and incidents is entirely coincidental.*

Distributed by Kensington Publishing Corp.
Submit Orders to:
Customer Service
400 Hahn Road
Westminster, MD 21157-4627
Phone: 1-800-733-3000
Fax: 1-800-659-2436

# Acknowledgments

It has been a long but pleasantly enjoyable ride on the author train for me. First, I'd like to thank Brenda Hampton, the best agent in the world. You saw and continue to see in me what I couldn't. You took a chance on me. For that you will always have a place in my heart. Kai Leakes, no matter how we fight, you always stick around. We're soul mates. Deal with it.

When I first started, I introduced the world to Chyanne, Aric, Gabriel, Jamie, and the crew. This time I want to take you guys on a different ride, a different kind of love. Meet David, Summer, and Michael, three people who will show you love through different lenses. These characters grabbed a hold of me and wouldn't let go. I couldn't eat or sleep until they'd had their say. It took me a little over thirty days to finish the first draft of this story, and I can't wait to share it with you.

So, enjoy the ride and know that true love comes without conditions.

# Summer

Life had always been a conundrum to me. Ever since I found out I was adopted, I had been confused about life. I didn't know where I belonged. Didn't know who I belonged to. Didn't know my mother or my father. There were times when I had no desire to know them and times when I wished I did. Sometimes I wanted to know what it was like to feel a mother's love or a father's pride, but alas, I had never felt that. I mean, my foster parents had done the best they could, but I was the only black child in a house full of white people. Needless to say, things didn't always go the way they should have gone.

When I was twelve, my seventeen-year-old foster brother decided I was old enough to fuck, so he snuck into my bedroom and made it so. Pressing a pillow over my face, and damn near smothering me to death, he took my virginity. All I remembered was the smell of cigarettes, his blond hair, and his blue eyes before he decided he couldn't look at me anymore. Once the pillow was over my face, he used his pencil dick and humped me until he was content. Yeah, what he did was wrong, but his penis was so small and thin that he didn't even break my hymen. Was I still disgusted? Yes.

I didn't know what it meant to have my hymen broken until I had sex with my first black boyfriend. That was another story in itself, but I was going to tell it, too, one day. I'd been fascinated with sex ever since I'd seen my foster parents doing it on their boat. We'd lived on Lake

Spivey, a very posh, upscale neighborhood in metro Atlanta, and everyone there had had a boat and boating dock to go along with their mini mansion. I was twelve, and I happened to be going for a swim when I saw my foster dad drilling into my foster mom like he was using his dick to drill for gold. Her head was thrown back, her mouth was half open, her eyes were closed, and she was saying the nastiest things she could.

Mind you, my parents were devout Christians. Demanded that we got up to go to church on Sunday and that we didn't leave until Tuesday. I hadn't even known Christian people *had* sex, with the way my foster parents preached hellfire and brimstone. My foster parents were good-looking white people, the kind you expected to see in Beverly Hills, on Rodeo Drive. My father was an all-American white boy. From his perfectly cut blond hair to his gym-perfected six-pack, he was who you brought home to your white mama and daddy. My mom reminded me of Angelina Jolie. She was sexy like that.

I remembered watching as my dad pumped and worked his hips. Sweat drenched his brows as his ass cheeks clenched. I stood there in awe, wondering what the white stuff was that was coming from my mom's pussy and coating his manhood.

"Fuck me in my ass, John," she pleaded.

That was when things got a bit more interesting.

"Clarissa, thought you were saving that for me," I heard another male's voice say, and I got closer to the boat's window to see who it was.

It was one of the deacons from our church. He was as naked as he'd been on the day he was born. In his hand was his johnson, and he was stroking it like it pained him.

"Let him finish, Jim. I want to see Clarissa orgasm like before," said another woman in the room.

My twelve-year-old mouth fell open when I saw Deacon Jim's wife straddling a chair, her legs open as she played with her pink, hairless pussy. She was biting down on her bottom lip, one hand was vigorously tapping against her clitoris, and the other was massaging her breasts. I stood there, transfixed by what my twelve-year-old mind couldn't process. It felt like hours passed as I stood there and watched. My mother finally turned over, dipped her back, and begged my foster father to give her what she wanted.

They had been passing a bottle around with the letters *K* and *Y* on it. At the time, I had no idea what it was. Still, I watched in silence as my father poured some down the crack of my mom's lackluster rear end. First, he used his fingers to please her anally. Talked to her. Told her to relax and assured her that he would be gentle. I watched as she cooed under his touch and words. And then I watched as he ever so slowly slid his salmon-colored dick into her ass. Truthfully, it looked painful, but my foster mom was into it, and so were the deacon and his wife.

"That's right, John. Fuck her harder," the deacon's wife coaxed. "She likes it hard like that. Isn't that right, Clarissa?"

"Yes. Fuck, yes. Oh God, yes, John. Fuck me in the name of the Father."

John pumped as hard as he could once.

"The Son . . ."

John did it harder still and deeper this time.

"And the Holy Spirit."

My father was focused. His skin was ruddy in color as he gave her all she could handle and then some. I thought for sure he would come too as liquid ran down my foster mother's leg. I looked on in awe as the deacon and his wife dropped down to their knees and started to lap up whatever that was that had come out of her. I thought I'd seen it all when they both started to eat my mom's twat as my dad continued to ram his dick inside her anally.

But no, those Christians had another surprise for me. They all fucked one another in that small room on our boat, and when I said all, I meant all. I thought my eyes would pop out when my father took the same position as my mother. Deacon Jim grabbed that bottle of K-Y and poured some on John's backside. As Deacon Jim entered my father from the rear, that was the first time I'd ever seen a look of pure pleasure on a man's face. Both my mother and the deacon's wife lay on the bed in front of them, in the sixty-nine position, watching as their husbands screwed one another.

"Damn, Summer. I've been standing at this office door, talking to you, for five minutes already, and you've yet to even acknowledge me."

I jerked away from my thoughts of that day and gazed into the eyes of my best friend, David Hall. I smiled at the man. He was the most beautiful shade of chocolate you'd ever want to see on a man. His teeth showed that he never missed a dentist's appointment. Thin locks were pulled back in a ponytail on his head. His catlike brown eyes twinkled with mischief, as they always did. He was dressed like he was one of those preppy boys from Harvard, but the broad shoulders, the down South, Georgia boy swagger, and the deep voice told you it was more likely that he'd come from Morehouse. The man was fine. Everything any woman in her right mind would want. There was one problem for me: he was bisexual. That would forever kept him in the friend zone.

David was also one of my bosses. I worked in his law firm, as a paralegal to one of his partners. In fact, it was David who had gotten me the job.

"I'm so sorry, David. So sorry," I said as I chuckled. "I was in my head again. Was thinking about my foster parents," I admitted honestly.

He smiled, then walked in and sat in front of my desk. "Ah, the bisexual Christians who liked to have orgies with different members of the church," he commented, then chuckled.

He knew all about my folks because I'd told him. That was one of the reasons he and I had become such good friends. The one thing we had in common was the fact that neither of us knew where we came from. I'd been blessed with rich foster parents, while David had been cursed with being thrown from one group home to another. Still, he had made it out alive and had been able to make something of himself in the process.

I laughed. "Yes, I still think back to when I saw them on that boat."

"Sounds like some shit you should write in a book."

"Who'd believe me?"

"You'd be surprised. If *Fifty Shades of Bullshit* can make the *NYT* Best Sellers list, then I'm certain *Sixty-Nine Shades of Freaking in the Church* would make it," he commented casually as he laid a folder on my desk.

I laughed. "Leave my folks alone. They taught me a lot."

He chuckled again, crossed his left leg over the right, and looked at me. "I bet they did. Like how to—"

I laughed, cutting him off. I jumped up to close the door to my office, all the while holding my finger up to my lips, telling him to be quiet.

"Why do I have to be quiet in a law office I'm a partner in?" he joked, feigning ignorance.

"Because you know how nosy people are around here. The last thing I need is my parents' freaky sex life on blast."

David and I laughed about the whole thing for a few minutes more before I addressed the real reason he was there again. Although David was laughing and talking like nothing was bothering him, I'd known my best friend long enough to know something was wrong. He took his glasses off and sat them on top of his head, then rubbed the corners of his eyes with his thumb and index finger.

"Want to talk about it?" I asked him. I kicked my heels off and sat sideways on his lap. He was the only man I could sit that way with and know he wouldn't try anything that would force me to punch him in the nuts.

"Michael called me. He's coming to visit," he said.

"Michael? Your best friend from New York Michael?"

He nodded.

I wrapped an arm around my best friend's neck and shrugged. "Okay, and why do you act as if this is a bad thing?"

"I haven't seen him in years. Almost ten, to be exact."

"You've never told me why, and I've asked many times."

David had told me about Michael. They'd been best friends back in college, but then they'd parted ways. He'd never really delved into the details of the demise of their friendship. I had often asked him if Michael knew he was bisexual, and he had never answered that question for me. He would always say that it was complicated and that he didn't feel like explaining it at the time.

"Things happen between people, and some of those things you can never take back. I did something to him the last time we saw one another, and it didn't end so well."

"Well, is he gay? Did you fuck him and not call the next day?" I asked these questions in a joking manner, but I really wanted to know.

David chuckled. "No, he's not gay."

"Did you sleep with his woman?"

"Something like that."

"Jesus, David, you're a greedy bastard."

He chuckled again. "He was hurt after what I did. Didn't speak to me for a long time, no matter how many times I apologized."

"Did he love the woman you stuck your happy stick in?"

David nodded. "Loved her very much. Loved her so much that he even married her."

My eyes widened, and I leaned back to get a better look at David. "Oh God, tell me you didn't sleep with her while they were married."

He gave a light smile. "Yeah, I did. So sue me."

"Sue you? I can see why he hasn't spoken to you in ten years, with that attitude."

"I said we haven't seen one another in almost ten years. Through mutual friends we found each other again on Facebook. And as corny as this shit is about to sound, I did send the man an apology again through Facebook, since that was the only way I could communicate with him."

"Did he respond?"

"Yeah, he did. Accepted my apology."

"Okay, so I don't understand why his coming here has you all bent out of shape, or so it appears."

"Ever had that one person that you would damn near sell your soul to have?" he asked.

I stared at my best friend, looked him in his eyes as he did the same to me. Let those unspoken words settle between us. Hell, yeah, I knew what that feeling was like, but I digressed.

"But, wait, you screwed his wife," I said.

"Yes, I did."

"And you want him too?"

He nodded. "Always have."

"Damn. For real? But you said he's not gay."

"He isn't."

"And he has a wife."

"I know."

"I'm not about to let you do this down-low shit. Granted, Atlanta is known for it, but I'm not about to—"

David sighed and tapped my backside, signaling me to get off his lap. I did and then watched the very masculine male in front of me stand. David stood five-eleven to my five-seven. I gazed up at him quietly.

"You don't ever have to worry about that with me, Summer. You know that shit. I don't get down like that. Don't fuck with the niggas who do. Still, a man can hope, right?"

"I guess . . ."

I studied my best friend as he studied me, and I wondered what made him tick. Granted, for a long while, I had had a crush on David. Even after he'd told me he was bisexual. I knew I would never be able to cross over the romance line with him, but I still liked him. Now, I stood there wondering why a man as fine as he was didn't find a woman like me attractive. Would it be so hard for him actually to have feelings for me like he did for Michael?

David cast a glance out my office window and then looked back down at me with a smirk on his face. He was reading me. Silently reading the pages of my book, and I hated it. Hated when he could look at me and see what I was thinking.

He shrugged and then slid his hands in the pockets of his designer dress slacks. "All you had to do was say yes."

# David

All she'd ever had to do was say yes, but I knew she wouldn't. That was just the way Summer was. Like I knew how many freckles lined her almond-colored face, I knew that she was into me in ways she didn't want to be known. Had known it since the day we met eight years before. I was a thirty-eight-year-old bisexual male and was damn proud of it. I didn't have a problem with my sexuality. Other people did. I didn't have a problem with being sexual with a man or a woman. For as long as I could remember, it had come natural to me. I could love men and women. I'd never had a totally successful relationship with a man, but I couldn't say I had a clean track record with women, either.

My encounters with men had been mostly for sexual gratification. There had been a few men who I had had an emotional attachment to, but I had been quick to withdraw from any one of them who had got too attached to me. With women, I'd had some good relationships and some bad ones. Most of them couldn't handle the fact that I was bisexual. Didn't think a man like me could be faithful to them, because I'd had sex with men before. So these days, I stayed to myself. Had sex with a man here, made love to a woman there, but there was never anything serious.

Summer could have been the one, but as with most women, my sexuality scared her. And that was fine with me. She still respected me as a man and a friend. I loved her for that.

"W-what?" she stammered, pretending she hadn't heard what I'd said.

"All you had to do was say yes," I repeated.

"Yes? What are you talking about, David? Yes to what?"

"I know that look, Summer. I've seen it enough times to know what you're thinking."

She shook her head and then turned her eyes away from me. "Whatever, David," she said and then moved behind her desk to pick up the folder I'd put there. "So when is Michael coming again?" she asked, taking a seat.

"Should be here next week."

"Are you going to tell him you have a man crush on him?" Although she was smiling and joking, I could see that hint of jealously behind her eyelids. Could see the fact that she felt some type of way.

"Whatever, Summer. I came to tell you because I want you to meet him," I told her.

She raised both her brows, then screwed up her face. "Why in hell do I need to meet him?"

"Because both of you are good friends of mine."

"And?"

"And because I know if you're there, he may not jump stupid."

"I mean, if there is so much tension, then why even meet up?"

"Because he wants to squash the beef."

"Not if you're worried about him getting in your ass." She smirked. "No pun intended."

I had to chuckle at that. She was trying to be funny. I took in her appearance. Let my eyes drink in her thick, caramel, toned thighs, which were being showcased by a skirt that stopped a few inches above her knees. Summer was the kind of thick that only a down South, country black man could appreciate.

"I'm the giver. Never the taker," I told her.

She rolled her doe-like eyes. "Whatever. Anyway, if you need me to, then I'll meet the dude." Her response was so lackluster.

"You don't have to sound so enthused."

"Trust me," she said with a chuckle, "I'm not."

"Hater."

"Asshole."

"You mad?"

"Fuck you."

"When?"

"Never."

"Your loss."

"Get out of my office, David."

I walked behind her desk, forced her chair around so she was facing me, and stood between her legs. "Make me," I dared her.

The sexual tension between Summer and me had always been thick. Since the day she'd walked into Lenox Square, she'd stood out to me. She had walked in like she owned the place, but she had looked like she bought her clothes at a thrift shop. She hadn't looked like she belonged with the pseudo-wealthy and hood rich people milling about. It was well known in the A that Lenox was more like a gay club and the place where people who lived in the hood shopped to prove to the world that they had money to blow. I'd been at Brooks Brothers that day, being fitted for a suit for a wedding. I'd seen her pass by the window and had to stop her.

She reminded me of a plus-sized Tracee Ellis Ross, and she had a Chrisette Michele disposition about her. She didn't care that people stared at her ripped jeans, which hung low on her hips. Didn't give a damn that they ogled her D-cup breasts through her fashionably ripped shirt. Wasn't even bothered that her stomach wasn't necessarily flat enough for her to be showcasing it the way she was. She just didn't give a damn. Summer wore no makeup, and her freckles made her all the more unique. She had her bushy hair back in a ponytail, which bounced as she walked.

She was looking for a job. Had a degree that would allow her to be a paralegal, but couldn't find any work in the economy. I let her pass by the store the first time without saying anything, but I couldn't allow her to pass me by a second time. I stopped her, asked her to go on a date with me. She took my card and told me she would think about it. Took her three weeks to send me a text. When she did, we set up a date to meet at Sambuca. It was a jazz club back then. Later it closed down. We talked over good food, wine, and music. I got to know her. Told her up front that I was a bisexual black man. She friend zoned me before the date was done.

The one thing that made me want to keep her in my life as a friend, though, was the fact that she didn't judge me. Didn't flinch when I told her my sexual preferences. She took my hand and thanked me for being honest with her. It was then that I knew she was special. She taught me that not all black women saw me as an abomination and as an affront to what was supposed to be a natural occurrence between men and women. Later on she told me that her father was bisexual and her mother was cool with it. So I guess it had been instilled in her that men like me were still human, albeit a different breed. She and I formed a friendship that night was wrapped in her thoughts of *What if?* and my hope that she'd give me one chance.

It never happened. I pulled my glasses back down on my face as I looked down at her now in her office. Her chest slowly heaved as she gazed back up at me.

"Not . . . not about to play this game with you, David," she said softly.

"Why does it have to be a game?" I asked her.

"You just sat there and all but told me you're lusting after your best male friend to the point of torture."

"You're overexaggerating."

"And you're in denial."

I placed my hands on the arms of her chair and caged her in as I leaned over her. She inhaled and exhaled. Licked her lips, then quirked a brow.

"So are you," I told her. I put my lips close to hers. Gazed into those walnut-colored eyes and dared her to do what she was afraid to do. Wanted her to so badly my dick moved around in my boxer briefs, as if it was the negative end to her positive one. I moved my hand from the arms of the chair, placed them on her thighs. I slid them up to the danger zone and waited for her to tell me to stop. When she didn't, I slid them up farther as my lips got closer to hers.

"David . . . ," she called out to me.

I knew she felt the electricity that passed between us, because I felt it to. It trickled down my arms and forced my hands to tighten on her thighs.

"All you have to do is say yes," I coaxed her.

I'd give anything for her to say yes. For some reason, I felt like I had something to prove to Summer. Needed to show her that a man like me could satisfy her. I needed that woman to look past the insecurities she felt because I was a bisexual male and allow me to love her body like she'd never known a man to do.

But she never said yes. Like before, she didn't say yes now. A knock on her office door brought us back to reality. I pretended that the folder, which she'd dropped back down on her desk, was of great importance and demanded that she get it back to me in a timely fashion as I exited her office.

***

Later on that evening, after I had gone to the gym and had showered, I was sitting in my place, lounging around, when my cell rang. I looked at the caller ID and saw that it was Michael calling. I thumbed my nose as I picked up the phone after muting the TV and stared at it for a moment. In a few days he and I would be face-to-face. I'd come face-to-face with the one who got away, among other things.

"What's up?" I greeted.

"Not much. You busy? Got any plans for the night?" he asked off the cuff. His voice got to me. It settled in the pit of my stomach and made the muscles there clench hard.

"Not that I know of. Summer might drop by, but that's it."

"You do now. My flight lands at nine thirty."

"Wait, what?" I asked as I looked at the designer watch on my left wrist. "You aren't supposed to be here until next week."

"Change of plans. I'll be there tonight. Is that going to be a problem?"

I shook my head, as if he could see me. "Nah. See you when you get here."

There was silence, but neither one of us hung up the phone. That unfinished business between us had settled in the room like the elephant it was.

"Think you can handle me being there? No bullshit like the last time?" he finally asked.

"We were younger then. I'm a grown man now."

He chuckled, and I found myself opening and closing my fist to stave off the jittery feeling he was giving me.

"Yeah. We'll see. And I'll finally get to meet the famous Summer. Does she know about me?"

I sighed. "She knows you're my best friend, who's married, with children. She knows about the shit that happened between us."

"All of it?"

"What I wanted her to know."

"Same ole David, huh?" he asked and chuckled sarcastically. "Telling half-truths to make whole lies."

"Fuck off, Michael." I sighed. "How are Sadi and the kids?" I asked so we wouldn't fall into the same routine of rehashing old shit.

"They're good. MJ turned nine last week and is almost half my height already. Gemma is ten going on fifteen. Getting on my damn nerves. Like her mother."

"But you love them. That's all that matters."

"Glad you finally figured that out," he said. I sighed and mumbled under my breath as he continued. "Fuck off, David. See you when I get there. Make sure you bring Summer. Saw that picture you posted of you two on Facebook. She's pretty. Juicy backside."

It was my turn to chuckle sarcastically. "Trouble in your man-made paradise?"

Michael was a wolf in sheep's clothing. Sadi thought that nigga shit gold and pissed rainbows. He could do no wrong in her eyes. Part of that might have been her guilt over the stolen night she and I had shared together. The other part might have been the fact that he'd never cheated on her, and he took care of her and the kids like any husband and father should. Actually, knowing Michael, I was sure he went above and beyond for his family. So the fact that he was eyeballing Summer let me know something was going on in fairy-tale land.

"Nope. Just wanted to see if she was that thick in person. Want to count those freckles up close and personal too," he admitted.

I rolled my shoulders and cleared my throat. Was feeling some type of way. The fact that he knew I liked Summer wasn't lost on me. He was intentionally trying to ruffle my feathers.

"Have a safe flight."

He laughed. "You mad? Sounds like you're mad."

"Fuck you, Michael."

"Maybe . . . maybe not."

I felt the sweat beads forming on my head. I was happy when he was the first to hang up the phone. His last statement did something to me. Took me back to almost eleven years ago, when shit started to go downhill for me and my best friend. I'd lied to Summer earlier today . . . in a sense. Michael didn't consider himself a gay male. So when she'd asked me that, I could honestly answer no. He didn't like labels, but he would answer yes to being bisexual before he would to being gay. In fact, he hated to be called gay or bisexual. But it was his right to be called whatever he wanted to answer to. I couldn't be mad at that.

What I could be mad and annoyed about was the fact that out of the blue he had decided to visit, and now he was going to show up way before his original date. That annoyed me. That told me that something else was going on with him. I knew my best friend. I knew he wasn't showing up just because, so I was already on pins and needles. But it had been ten years since I'd seen the one who had got away. I needed to see him face-to-face. Needed to clear the air on a lot of shit. I hoped this time it didn't end with one of us in jail.

Love did that to people. Made them act out in ways they wouldn't normally, especially when that love was thrown back in their face. I knew what made women and men snap. I'd been there. I'd been on the receiving end of loving someone, and in the end I had found out that I was the only one that deeply in love. Shit was never the same after that, and it always ended badly. At least for me . . . shit always ended badly.

I stood with my phone still in my hand and walked to the bar in my kitchen. Grabbed the Jim Beam Devil's Cut whiskey and downed a few shots. Needed the burn to get my head together. Found myself taking about four more shots before I dialed Summer.

I heard Beyoncé in the background before she spoke up. Summer was breathing hard. "Talk fast. In the middle of cardio," she breathed out.

"You busy after?" I asked her.

"Why? You cooking? You owe me steak and potatoes with steamed vegetables."

She was huffing and puffing. I could almost taste the sweat coming off her skin. I loved to see her sweat. Anytime we worked out together, I was always amazed by her stamina, just as I'd been the first time I saw her jogging. It had changed my mind about the stereotype of plus-sized women not being able to exercise.

"Nah, but Michael decided he was going to fly in tonight, so I wanted to know if you were up for meeting him."

She grunted a bit as Beyoncé asked her driver to roll up the partition. "Is he fine?"

"He is."

"He gay?"

"Told you no."

"Can I fuck him? It's been a while, David. Like about two years."

"Didn't and doesn't have to be."

"I'm not fucking you. You like the same thing I do."

I almost told her that Michael did too, but I caught myself. That wasn't my truth to expose.

"So you won't have sex with a single bisexual male, but you'll be a married man's mistress?"

"Yeah. And?" she asked, as if I'd offended her.

"What part of the game is that?"

"The part I don't mind playing."

"Black women got the game backward. You'll go out there and fall in love with a man with a family, but you'll turn your nose up at a man like me. I'm perfectly single."

"You like your men how I like mine," she said.

For some reason, she was starting to annoy me. I heard Michael's voice in my head, talking about wanting to count her freckles up close. My teeth ground as images in my mind of their bodies grinding together unnerved me.

"Kiss my ass, Summer. You're so full of shit," I said, with a laugh laced with irritation. "Keep ignoring the fact that I like my women a certain way too."

"Not doing this with you, David," she said.

"Obviously."

"What time?"

"What?"

She sighed. "What time is he flying in?"

"Said his flight lands at nine thirty."

"And where are we meeting him?"

I put the whiskey away and walked over to lean against the island in the middle of my gourmet kitchen. The polished wooden floor was cold under my feet. Made me kick myself for not turning on the flooring's heating system.

"I don't know. Maybe I'll tell him to meet us at Strip in Atlantic Station," I answered.

There was silence on the other end of the phone. "You mad at me?" Summer asked me.

I lied with ease. "No."

"You lie, David."

"Whatever."

"I'm sorry."

"I know."

"Forgive me?"

"Whatever."

That was the way our friendship worked. She would say something slick about my sexual preferences, almost as if she was mad about it. We'd get snippy with one another. She'd apologize. I'd accept. Things would go back to normal with us.

# Summer

I hated when David was upset, annoyed, or anything with me. I knew sometimes my mouth would say shit before my mind could catch up with me. But he was still my friend. Sometimes I hated that all I saw David as was a greedy man who had to have his cake and eat it too. I didn't want him to be attracted to men and women. I wanted him to want only me, a woman. *Shut up.* I knew how stupid I sounded. Especially since we'd never even explored the option of a relationship. Yes, the sexual tension was so thick, we could practically eye fuck one another into orgasms, but I wanted it to be more than that.

In some strange sense, I was jealous of all the men he'd loved and been with sexually. I was jealous of how primal in his sexuality I knew he could be. I knew any man that he'd laid dick to was more than satisfied. I felt inadequate. Felt like I wasn't enough for him. Felt like even if I gave in to my sexual curiosity, he would still need something that I couldn't give him. Therefore, I stayed safely in our friend zone. Content on at least having him in a way that I knew I would be adequate enough to satisfy him.

I pulled the denim shorts over my ripped tights and then pulled the oversize gray sweater over my head. I loved the way the sweater fell over my left shoulder. I quickly stepped into my calf-high army boots but did not bother to tie them. I dressed in a way that reflected my personality outside of work. I was somewhere between a hippie and female Black Panther in heart. I didn't bother to put my hair in a ponytail. Just let it fall where it may. I grabbed my keys, phone, and purse and headed out the door. David was punctual. If I was late, it would ruin our whole night, because he would be pissed about it.

It didn't take me long to get to Strip. As usual, the house was packed, but David had gotten us a booth that was tucked away on the first level. In the black chairs around the shiny square red tabletops sat black, brown, and white people, and they were either gay, straight, bisexual, or other. The ambiance of the place said it was hip. The dim lighting was punctuated by the faux candles that stood glowing in the middle of the tables. Live music was blasting from the DJ booth upstairs. Most of the chicks in the place had three-hundred-dollar weaves and brand-name purses and shoes, and they wore enough makeup to keep MAC in business forever. I'd never been into the hype of having name-brand everything. I was perfectly okay with shopping at Wal-Mart, Target, Conway, and occasionally Macy's. Didn't need to spend all my money to fit in with society.

Eyes turned to look at me as I walked through the place to get to my best friend. Probably because it was nice and cold outside, yet I had decided that short shorts and tights would be my attire for the evening. I had on a leather coat, with a scarf around my neck, but I hated the heat. So the night wind and the air was my kind of hype. I saw David as he looked up and spotted me. He'd been texting on his phone. My heart almost stopped at the sight of him. He would always stand out among men.

His chocolate skin glowed in the vague lighting. Eyes sparkled behind his designer eyeglasses. He had on a black turtleneck that strained against the muscles in his chest and arms. The dress slacks he had on sat right on his hips. I already knew his shoe game was on point. He wouldn't ever dress in anything less than the best. It was who he was. His locks sat back in a thin headband. But it was his smile . . . His smile was what made my heart beat. Dimples placed evenly on either side of his cheeks lured me in.

He stood as I got closer to the booth. Both men and women took in his good looks. My smile faltered. *Fuck Atlanta for being the gay mecca, the down-low capital. Fuck the whole damn city,* I thought. The women who ogled him never bothered me, but the males . . . *Fuck every openly gay and undercover gay male who is staring at him like they want him to screw them straight. Fuck 'em.* Still, I smiled back at my best friend. Grinned when he left the booth and held his arms open for me as a greeting. David didn't hug me like I was his friend. He hugged me like I was his woman. His spicy, earthy, masculine scent made me melt into him.

"Damn, you smell good," his deep voice rumbled against my ear.

"That's funny. I was about to say the same to you," I said with a giggle.

We were good. The things I'd said to him earlier had faded away. He hugged me for a long time. His hands traveled down my back . . . stopped. I knew he wanted desperately to give me an ass grab, but he didn't allow himself. My ass had been a blessing and a curse, depending on how you looked at it. I kept squats in my exercise routine because I loved my ass. Finally, he pulled away. I looked at the table of feminine gay males sitting in front of us and sneered a sneer of triumph, knowing in reality that I felt it was they who were winning. One looked at me and flippantly rolled his eyes. I didn't care.

David allowed me to unzip my coat and then helped me out of it before ushering me to the booth to sit. He laid my coat on the seat next to us as he slid in next to me.

"You're looking good," he said, complimenting me.

"Thank you, and so are you."

"You're going to catch a cold that's going to put you on your ass."

I chuckled, then asked to have a sip of his water before responding. "I know, but you know I love the cold. This is perfect weather for me."

He smiled. Sipped on the same straw I had and then looked around. "See how all those men were staring at that ass, though?"

I always laughed when we fell into our way of teasing one another. There we were, two professionals who sometimes spoke as if we had only just graduated from high school.

"Nobody is looking at me when everyone is fixated on you," I said and slyly nodded to the table full of flamboyantly gay males who couldn't stop looking at David.

He looked over at them and then back at me with a scowl. David didn't care for effeminate males. They weren't his type of hype.

"I don't understand that shit," he commented, with his lips turned down into a frown. "If I wanted a woman, I'd be with one. When I want a man, I want a man," he said.

We'd had that conversation before. Nothing turned him off more than feminine males. He liked his men the same way I liked mine. We stopped talking for a moment so the waiter could take my order, or so I thought.

"I already ordered for you," David told me.

I watched as the waiter placed a glass of Riesling in front of me and the Sushi Boat for Four. Sake was David's choice of drink. I smiled. He knew me so well.

"So, we're not waiting on Michael to eat?" I asked after we had blessed the food.

He shook his head, one arm wrapped around me. "Nah."

To the people looking on, we probably looked like lovers instead of best friends, especially as we shared the B-52 roll. He fed me. I fed him. We forwent the silverware and used our fingers. When his tongue brushed against my fingers, my pussy vibrated. I inhaled and exhaled slowly. I smiled because he smirked. He'd felt that jolt of energy between us too.

"Say yes," he whispered, daring me. "One time . . . say yes."

I rolled my shoulders, sipped my wine, but I didn't say yes.

I said, "No."

All he did was laugh.

We were well into our sushi when David's phone rang.

"What's up?" he answered as he wiped his mouth with the black cloth napkin. "Nah, we're in here. First floor. In the booth in the center . . . What? No, you have to pay to park. . . . Follow the signs to find the parking deck. . . ."

"Tell him if he parks on the first level, it's only six bucks for six hours," I said, trying to be a part of the conversation. Whenever David talked to men, I felt intimidated . . . inadequate.

"He's good," David said to me, then got back on his phone. "A'ight. Give me a second." David hung up his phone and then slid out of the booth.

"Where you going?" I asked him.

"Going to meet him so he won't get lost trying to find us."

"It's not that hard to find this place if he parks on level one. Just tell him to come up the escalators—"

"Summer," David said to stop me.

"What?"

"Can I go get my friend and bring him back?" he asked with a smile.

Shrugging, I said, "I guess."

He leaned down to kiss my lips—something we did from time to time—and then walked off. I sat there for a moment, taking in the music and my surroundings. Place was as crowded as usual on a Friday. My nerves were jittery, for some reason. So I asked the waitress to tell David I'd gone to the bathroom if he happened to make it back to the booth before I did. The bathroom at Strip looked like a one-bedroom apartment. An oversize mirror took up the wall to the left. A rectangular sink with four faucets sat to the right, and the stalls were big enough to hold at least four people each.

I handled my business with the toilet bowl man, washed my hands, and decided to add a little lip gloss to my lips. I made sure the shorts I had on weren't riding too far up my crack, and then walked back out. As soon as I did, all heads turned to look at me. The gay males at the table in front of the booth all looked me up and down. I looked over and saw that David had sat back down. As soon as the other patrons moved out of my way, I was able to see that someone—I assumed it was Michael—was sitting with him.

I didn't know what I'd expected Michael to look like. Wait, I was lying. I had expected him, had wanted him, to be ugly as sin, but that wasn't what he actually looked like. He stood. He was still in his double-breasted trench coat. The coat was open, and I saw that he was wearing wing-tip dress shoes, chocolate-brown dress slacks, and a baby-blue button-down, which was in stark contrast to his milk chocolate skin. *Jesus be some panty liners,* I thought. My thong got real uncomfortable as it slid around due to the wetness invading my private parts. Michael was still standing as I approached, and David jumped to his feet when he saw me. Michael might have lived up north, but he was still cognizant of his Southern roots. Neither man would sit when a lady in their company entered the room.

Michael was taller than David. A low-cut Caesar with deep waves adorned his head. His hair had been tapered and razor shaped to perfection. There was no facial hair, and his lips . . . dear God, his lips were so damn thick and plush that I found myself wanting to kiss him on sight. David tilted his head as he watched me. He knew me. Knew I was a sucker for what Michael represented. He was a married man, and I had a track record of sleeping with married men. They weren't my problem. We'd fuck, and then I could send them back home for their wives to deal with. *So sue me.* Being with another woman's man wasn't beneath me.

"Michael, this is Summer. Summer, this is Michael, another good friend of mine," David said after I'd finally reached the table.

For a second I didn't even know what to say. I was tongue-tied. There I was, with the sexiest black men—men, period—in the place. I was intent on taking Michael's hand to shake it, but he pulled me into a hug, which sent me reeling. The man smelled like he bathed with African black soap, and I noticed some other fragrance, which I couldn't identify. It was so natural that I had to sniff him again to lock the smell in my nostrils.

"Nice to meet you, Summer," Michael said as he pulled back from the hug. "I've heard a lot about you."

I smiled and finally found my voice. "It's nice to finally meet you as well. I can say I've heard a lot about you too."

He smiled. A Colgate smile had nothing on David's and Michael's smiles. David moved over so I could slide into the booth. The two of them sat down, flanking me. I looked like a piece of caramel sandwiched between two pieces of chocolate. I was their Milky Way Simply Caramel bar.

The waiter came over and took Michael's drink order, a Guinness Extra Stout, but he refrained from ordering food for the moment.

"So, Summer, how'd you end up on the arm of this one?" he asked and then stood again to take his coat off.

So call me a perverted cunt, but the print, the bulge in that man's pants made me lick my lips. I took a sip of my wine and glanced around to see if anyone else saw what I saw. Apparently, a few men and women did, because all their eyes had zoomed in on it.

I cleared my throat and then looked over at him as he sat back down. On one side of me, David's thigh rubbed against mine. On the other side, Michael's thigh did the same. I had a fever.

"I was an unemployed chick walking through Lenox Square."

"Why Lenox Square, if you were unemployed?" Michael asked.

"Was looking for work."

"David told me you have two degrees. Why the mall for a job?"

"Nobody was calling me back. So I dumbed down my résumé and started looking into retail."

"Did you get a job there?" Michael asked.

I shook my head. "Didn't have to. I went on a date with David, and he offered me a job the next day."

Michael quirked a brow and did a slight head tilt. The way he smirked told me what he was thinking.

"I didn't fuck him to get this job, if that's what you're thinking. But I'm not above it."

Michael laughed. "You're funny, Summer."

I turned to look at David, to see why he wasn't saying anything. He was watching me and Michael with an amused expression on his face.

"I know. David tells me all the time," I said to Michael. "You okay?" I asked David.

David nodded. "I'm good."

"You sure? You ain't saying much."

"Just letting you two talk."

"You don't want to catch up with your friend?" I asked.

"I've known the asshole long enough," David quipped, then gave Michael the once-over and grunted. "Nothing's changed."

Michael gave a hearty chuckle and thanked the waiter, who had just sat his beer down. After we assured him that we didn't need anything else, the waiter walked away with a smile.

"Hater has never been a good job reference, bruh," Michael quipped back. "So you always spend the night at his house, playing Twister in booty shorts?" he asked me out of the blue.

He must have seen that photo of me and David on Facebook. That was one thing I hated. I knew Michael could see me on Facebook, but because you had to be his friend to see anything about him, I wasn't able to do the same snooping as he was. Trust me, I'd tried.

There was something about the way those two were not talking that got to me. I'd asked David if he had fucked Michael, and he had said no. But there was some tension in the air that I could feel.

Still, I answered his question. "Most times. David likes to look at my ass. I like to give him my ass to look at. What better way than a game of Twister?" I put a piece of sushi in my mouth as David laughed. After I swallowed the sushi, I turned to face Michael. "You done grilling me now or nah?" I asked.

Michael laughed too. "I wanted to see if you were hell, like he said you were. He always talks about you, so I wanted to see the woman, the myth, the enigma myself. Those are all words he has used to describe you."

I could see the sincerity in his eyes. I saw the way he looked at his best friend, and I noticed they both chuckled the same way. Maybe David's quietness was due to the fact that he was allowing us to talk, and not to some other shit, as I had been thinking. I smiled and offered Michael some sushi. I didn't know him well enough to be feeding him with my fingers, so I pulled the utensils from the black cloth napkin. Placed a few pieces of sushi on a small plate for him and then slid the plate to him. Then I turned back to offer David some with my fingers. I loved that piece of intimacy he and I shared. It was the closest thing I had had to a relationship with a man in two years. I didn't pull back when he pulled me closer to him.

As the night went on, the three of us talked about different things. Talked about the Falcons lackluster football season, along with the Giants. Talked about politics and religion. I was surprised to learn that Michael wasn't a fan of President Obama. Wasn't surprised that despite that fact, he still hadn't voted for Romney in the elections. I laughed when he told us he had voted for Roseanne Barr. I erupted in stomach-churning laughter when he told me about the shit he and David had gotten into back in college. He talked about the foursome he and David had had with two sisters, one of whom had happened to get her period and didn't know it. Michael had thought she was just that sopping wet. He had pulled his fingers out of her fire and had had bloody digits. He'd been so turned off that he'd walked out of the room.

"Did you at least wash your hands?" I asked, screwing up my face.

Michael shrugged. "Man, look, I don't even know. Can't remember. Just know I started calling the shawty Carrie afterward."

"She tried to fight him in the hall of the hotel the next day because he called her that shit," David said, chiming in as he laughed.

I laughed again. This was all very comical to me. Michael had turned out to be a cool guy. I liked his laugh. His personality was A1, but it was the impeccable way he carried himself that made him stand out as a king among men. When he stood to go to restroom and strolled away from the booth, he commanded attention. With one hand in his pocket and a walk that put Denzel to shame, he was the star of that show. He'd stolen the spotlight from David.

I took my new glass of wine to my mouth and turned my head to look at David, only to find that he had watched me watch Michael.

"Good to see you remembered I'm here with you," he said.

"Huh?"

"Yeah."

"What are you talking about?"

"Just saying, you've been all on his dick since he got here."

I had to chuckle at that. "Sounds like you're feeling some type of way because you can't get on it. You mad, bruh?" I asked, to be funny. He gave me a look that said he wasn't amused. "Oh, God, David, you can't be serious."

He shrugged, then said, "It's cool. Making an observation. You'd rather be a home wrecker than an honest woman, huh? Okay. Got it."

"Wait. What?"

"If you throw it at that nigga, he's going to catch it, then toss you back in the dugout."

"So now I'm throwing my pussy at him?"

"Calls it like I sees it," he commented casually.

"You're such a dick, David."

"Eight inches of it when I'm in a zone. Nine if the pussy's good."

I punched him in his arm as hard as I could. He snatched me by the back of my hair and then brought my face directly to his.

We had an audience. I could see people watching from my peripheral. I knew if I took it there, David would too.

# David

"Let me go, David!" Summer demanded.

I didn't want to, though. Her lips were so close to mine that all I had to do was kiss her. All I had to do was suck her bottom lip into my mouth, like I was tempted to do. Yeah, she and I kissed each other on the lips all the time, but that was more of a friendly notion. The way I wanted to kiss her now had nothing to do with being friendly. I could feel her chest slowly rising, like there was pressure on it. The cat and mouse between us was at its breaking point. I knew people were watching. All eyes were on us, but I blocked them out. Didn't care that they were eager to see what was going on and what would happen next. They didn't know if I was abusing her or if we were a couple who enjoyed a little roughhousing with our displays of affection.

"Not letting you go anywhere," I told her.

I gazed deep into the abyss of her eyes. Counted those freckles up close and then placed my lips gently against hers. Heard a few gasps from those around us when my other hand gripped her left breast as my tongue invaded her mouth. She gasped herself. She stopped breathing for a moment, so I remembered to breathe for both of us. I'd never been on this side of intimacy with her, and yet I knew what she liked. I knew she liked the firm grip of my hand in her hair. Could tell that the way my other hand squeezed her breast to the point of pain was about to be her undoing.

But it was her kiss . . . the way she moaned and leaned into me when her tongue danced with mine that took me under. I'd never felt her . . . I'd never tasted her the way I was in that moment. She'd accused me of being jealous, of being mad that she was all on another man's dick, with me right there. That was the way we were. She would get jealous, I would become envious, and still . . . we were just friends.

I was jealous. Didn't like to see her give another man the attention that had been reserved only for me. Even when she had been with other men, she had reserved the kind of attention she'd given to Michael only for me. Yes, I was jealous. Jealous of the way both of them were into one another. I could see what was to come a mile away. Michael was feeling her. He didn't really say a lot to me, because there were still things to resolve between us. I wanted her. I wanted him. I wanted us . . . all at once. But I knew it would never happen. Could never happen.

I knew when Michael had invaded our personal space again. Smelled the scent that belonged only to him. That smell of Egyptian musk, black soap, and hemp shea butter. It was a scent one could never forget. I knew she'd smelled him too. She'd been alerted by the earthy, musky scent that only Michael carried. I was very familiar with his scent.

Summer pulled back from the kiss. She hung her head, laid her hands on my chest as she caught her breath. I loosened the grip on her hair. Started to massage her scalp as I held her close to me. I knew she was embarrassed that we had put on a show. I looked over at Michael, who was standing near the table full of flamboyant males, who were looking him up and down before turning their attention back to me and Summer. He had a glass of amber-colored liquor in his hand, his eyes on me. Summer already had my dick alive. The primitive look in Michael's eyes spoke of times past, when he and I had shared secrets.

He stopped looking at me long enough to nod at Summer. I'd been so fixated on him that I hadn't noticed that she'd noticed me observing him. She looked from him to me, then back to him. She picked up on what I didn't want her to know. Before I could stop her, she shoved me away, grabbed her purse and coat, and then made a beeline for the exit.

"You should have told her," Michael said to me after I'd slid out of the booth to go after her.

"Told her what?" I asked with a bit of annoyance in my voice.

"More than what you wanted her to know."

For a long while we stared one another down. Then Michael chuckled, walked over to the booth, and sat down. I rushed outside, into the winter's cold, to chase after Summer. I had left my coat behind, having forgotten the season in all the excitement. I remembered her telling me to tell Michael about parking on level one, and so I rushed down the escalator. I bumped into a few people on my way down, but I didn't give a damn.

"Aye, nigga! Watch where you going!" some idiot who was trying to impress a hood rat yelled behind me.

He didn't want it. Lawyer or not, I had grown up in one of the A's toughest boys' homes, and it had bred an entity he didn't want to rumble with. I ignored him, though. Didn't have time to embarrass him in front of his woman. I let him keep his pride so his girl could have a story to tell her girls about how crazy her *nigga* was. I stopped in the middle of a walkway and spun around, having no idea where to look for my best friend. I snatched my phone and pushed one.

She was the only person I had on speed dial.

She sent me to voice mail.

I tried back and back and back and back and back. Each time I got her voice mail. I cursed inwardly and continued my search of level one, hoping she hadn't left yet. A horn blared, headlights flashed at me, and I barely dodged this black Charger. It would have hit me, but the person behind the wheel hit the brakes. Someone yelled at me to watch out. The driver's shocked expression told me she hadn't been trying to hit me. I slammed my hand down on the hood of the car in a fit of aggression, rushed around to the driver's side, and snatched the door open. I leaned in and put the car in park. The woman behind the wheel screamed, kicked, and punched at me when I pulled her out of her car.

"Stop!" I yelled at her as she swung wildly.

Her uninhibited naturally sandy brown and blond hair swung around her face. She kept swinging at me. Yelled at me to leave her alone, but I wouldn't. Between her swings, I grabbed both sides of her face and made her kiss me again. We had another kind of audience. It was made up of the kind who walked on by and onlookers who didn't mind seeing what they thought was a couple fight and then fuck, hopefully.

I didn't care about any of them. Only wanted to keep the kiss going. Wanted Summer to feel what she was doing to me. I knew she could feel the swell of my manhood on her stomach, but I needed her to feel what went unspoken in that kiss too. She fought me. Refused to open her mouth until my tongue touched her lips, urged her to open up and accept what I was offering. Her tears of confusion made a salty balm over our lips.

She still didn't say yes, but she didn't say no, either. Our tongues touched and tangoed aggressively. Horns blared behind her car, but we didn't care. My hands slid underneath her sweater to caress her waist. I loved the fact that her waist had enough meat for me to pull on, hold on to as I held her.

We had to move. I knew we had to move, but I didn't want to break the kiss, for fear of her running again. So I took the initiative. I moved her out of the way. Got in the driver's seat of her whip, adjusted the seat, and told her to get in. She hesitated, but then she saw the line behind us and rushed around to get into her car. I pulled off, drove around until we found a spot that gave us some kind of privacy. I parked her car, and for a while we sat there in loud silence.

"Thought you said Michael wasn't gay," she finally said.

She wouldn't look at me. Arms folded across her ample chest, she looked out the passenger-side window.

"He isn't," I said.

"Don't lie to me, David."

"I'm not lying. He doesn't identify as gay."

She whipped her head around to look at me. "So what is he?"

"You have to ask him that."

"Did you fuck him?"

I pulled the leather tie from my locks and ran a hand through them. My glasses seemed to strain my eyes. I pulled them off. Used my thumb and index finger to rub my eyes before putting my glasses back on.

She was still looking at me. I could see her shaking her head. "You lied to me," she said.

I could feel annoyance creeping up my spine. I shrugged and asked, "Why do you even care, Summer? We aren't together."

"So. We don't lie to one another. Thought we were better than that."

I chuckled. There wasn't shit funny, but my agitation made me chuckle. "You always do this, Summer. You want the perks of being in a relationship, *minus* the relationship, the man, and the sex."

"So did you fuck him?" she asked again, as if she hadn't heard anything I'd said.

"No."

It happened so quickly that I didn't see it coming. The burning sensation in my face alerted me to the fact that I'd been slapped. My glasses fell down between the seats. Before I knew it, we had turned into something we weren't. I yanked her across the seat as much as the Charger would allow me. Her back fell onto my legs, and I hemmed her in as I glared down at her.

"Why the fuck are we even doing this?" I yelled in her face. "We're not even together. So what's the purpose of you acting like we are?"

Her face was ruddy. Her freckles always showed more when she was angry. Her eyes watered, but she wasn't crying. "Why would you have me sitting there with him like that?" she asked.

"There is nothing going on with me and Michael. Nothing at all."

"But there used to be, right?"

"I'm not . . . Summer, please stop, okay? Just stop. We're fighting, and for what? Because you—"

She cut me off. "Just tell me, David. I want to know."

"This is stupid," I said as I let her go.

She sat up. I opened the door and stepped out of the car. It took me a minute to find my glasses, but I did. Summer got out of the car and walked around to where I was. We didn't say anything. She looked up at me while running a hand through her hair. People milled about. Loud music blasted as cars entered and exited the parking deck. The nightlife in Atlantic Station was in full effect.

Summer said, "Why is it stupid? Because you don't want to tell me? You've never been this closed off about anything or anyone before. So that lets me know that something more has gone on than what you told me."

"Yes."

"Yes, what?"

"Yes, it's stupid because I don't want to tell you, and yes, a long time ago, something happened with me and Michael that goes beyond me fucking his wife. Satisfied now?"

"Why couldn't you tell me that the first time I asked?"

"Because maybe I didn't want to, Summer. Maybe I didn't want to rehash those old demons . . . open Pandora's box."

She didn't say anything right away. She stood there, shaking her head and mumbling to herself before she spoke up. "This is why we can't ever be together. Why we can never, ever be together."

"Why? Because I have a past?" I asked.

"Because I'm always going to wonder about shit like this."

"Those are your insecurities."

To be honest, she'd shown me a side of her that had me rethinking crossing any line and having something other than a friendship with her. I didn't like where she had taken us. I didn't do the whole "throwing hands at one another" thing. That wasn't my kind of hype. I didn't feel like talking anymore. Wasn't in the mood to answer any more questions, so I told her to get in her car and go home. Normally, I would wait for her to get in her car, and then I would buckle her in and kiss her on the forehead. I wasn't in the mood for any of that. I walked off before she even got in the car.

"David," she called behind me.

I had half a mind to keep walking, but that thing . . . that thing I had for her deep down inside made me turn around to look at her.

"Yeah?"

"Do you love him?"

"Not anymore."

"Are you going home alone?"

I shrugged. "I don't know, Summer."

She looked down at the ground like life had been sucked out of her. "Oh," was all she said before she slowly slid into the front seat of her car.

I turned and walked back to the restaurant. Michael was still sitting there. He was talking to a woman who was none the wiser about who he really was. She was pretty enough, but I could tell by her body language that she was no match for Michael's advances. She looked like she was practically coming where she sat as Michael stroked a finger against her cheek. He saw me approaching the booth and cut his conversation short.

"Where's Summer?" he asked.

"Gone."

"You good?"

"I'm great," I lied. "Let me take care of the check, and we can get out of here."

"Already done," he said, pointing to the thirty-dollar tip and the receipt on the table. "Summer chilling with you tonight?"

I knew he was asking so he could find out what had gone down between us.

"No."

"You two have a fight?"

"Nope."

"You may as well go ahead and be with her. You two already act like you are together. Why not make that shit official?"

"Some shit ain't meant to be," I said as I looked directly at him.

"You fight like a married couple, talk like best friends, and flirt like first loves, so obviously it is meant to be."

I didn't respond to that. I grunted and remained silent.

Not too much else was said between us as we gathered our coats and headed for the exit. Once we figured out where the other had parked, we made our way to the same area in which Summer and I had just had our fight. We stood next to his rented platinum BMW and talked.

"What's the real reason you're here, Michael?" I finally asked him.

"Needed to get some shit off my chest," he answered honestly.

"Ten years later?"

"Took you that long to give me a sincere apology for the stunt you pulled."

"I did apologize before."

"Your idea of an apology went something like, 'I'm sorry I fucked your wife, but you made me do it.'"

I couldn't deny the fact that he was right. "I was a different person back then."

"And you're changed now?"

I nodded. "Yeah."

"I can't tell."

"You don't know the new me."

"I know the old you, and that's good enough."

"You know the man I used to be, not the man I've become."

He shrugged nonchalantly. "If you say so. You fucked Sadi to get back at me."

"I fucked Sadi to show you that you were loyal to her, but she wasn't as loyal to you."

"Why did that matter to you, though?"

"You know why. I fucking loved you, man. And you threw that shit away like it was nothing."

"I told you from the beginning not to fall in love with me. I was never going to be with you the way you wanted me to."

I slid my hands into the pockets of my slacks and thought about the days when Michael and I used to sneak away and grab hotel rooms so that we could fuck to our hearts' content. Now that I looked back, I realized that was all it was. I was making love. He was fucking.

"Yeah, you made that pretty clear when you ran off and got married without telling me," I said.

"You knew I was with Sadi. It shouldn't have come as a surprise."

As we talked, I took in his appearance again. You couldn't help but be attracted to the man he was. Michael was a man's man. He knew how to touch you during the act of coitus and make you feel like the world belonged at your feet. He wasn't all that affectionate. When it came to sex between the two of us, it had always been heated, hedonistic, and primal. Michael reminded me of the serpent in the Garden of Eden.

As he stood there, both of us staring into the other's eyes, reliving times it was best not to try to re-create, I felt the tip of my dick leak in remembrance. I could tell by the way he smirked that he was remembering too. So it didn't surprise me when he leaned in for a kiss. I didn't deny him. It had been a minute since I'd kissed a man. There'd been plenty of fucking sessions, but no kissing. Kissing was intimate. Reserved only for those I intended to share more than sex with.

Our kiss was different than the one I had shared with Summer. My kiss with Summer was something I couldn't explain. The kisses I'd shared with her earlier felt as though they'd been dipped in the thought of *What if?* The kiss with Michael was laced with poison. I was drowning in the knowledge of what I knew could be our undoing. Funny thing was, neither of us touched when we kissed. Just let our lips lead our tongues to the promised land. I groaned. He gave something as guttural and then pulled back as he adjusted his dick and I did the same with mine.

For a while we stood there as the cold wind molested us.

"Girl, these niggas in Atlanta be gay as fuck," we heard a woman say as loudly as she could. "You see them two big, masculine-ass mafuckers kissing? I done seen it all. This shit right here is why the fuck I will never date a nigga in Atlanta," she said, venting, like she didn't care that we heard her.

Her girls laughed and egged her on.

"That's some nasty shit," another one said.

"Fucking faggots," one more added, chiming in.

The ringleader said, "And that son of a bitch has on a wedding ring. If I knew his wife, I'd blow this nigga's spot all up."

We both looked at the women. A group of beautiful, but angry, black women. Truth be told, they probably had a right to be. The world had turned against them. The media was obsessed with their bodies, looks, hair. . . . The black men of Twitter, YouTube, and Facebook had told them that they were no good. That they were just angry, bitter, materialistic, fat bitches. Books on down-low brothers had made them think all black men were gay. Angry was the least they should be.

Michael and I chuckled. Things like that had never bothered us. Back in college, we had prided ourselves on the fact that we gave women a choice. Neither of us had let a woman think she was getting anything other than what we were. Most times, once we told women we were bisexual, they would turn their noses up and run off in disgust, but we still didn't stop being honest . . . until Sadi showed up.

"I'd fuck you into a coma right now," Michael said to me. He'd never been one to mince words.

I laughed. "Always the giver . . ."

"Never the taker," he said, finishing my sentence for me.

As bad as I wanted to stop by a drugstore and grab an extra pack of Magnums, I wouldn't. Summer was on my brain, and Michael had a wife and kids back home. I wouldn't turn into one of those niggas we despised. Wouldn't go on some down-low tryst with him because he and I wanted to fuck one another and give in to erogenous needs.

"Going home to Summer?" he asked me as he unlocked his rental with the remote key.

"Summer has her own place," I answered.

"Still didn't answer my question, though."

And I wouldn't. I hugged him—we held the hug a little longer than we should have—and then headed to my car. I sent Summer a text along the way.

# Summer

Not going home. Wait up for me.

I looked at my phone, then at the time on the clock. Almost one o'clock. David's text had woken me up from my drunken stupor. I'd come home, embarrassed about the way I'd carried on. Maybe he and I didn't need to remain friends. Shit was too volatile. Feelings were getting involved, and I was starting to act like a crazy bitch on her period.

I got up from the couch and stumbled to the bathroom. In the mirror, I saw scratches on my neck and chest, along with bruises, from our fight in my car. I couldn't believe I had acted like that, like he was my man and I had a right to be mad about what he'd done in his past. David had been putting up with my shit for years, and I didn't know why. I had called my mother when I got in, but she had cursed me out and had told me to take my drunk ass to bed. Then I'd called my sister Hannah, and she had pretty much told me the same thing. I knew not to call my brother Samson. He would not only curse me out but would also block my number so I wouldn't call him when I was drunk again. He'd done it before.

Out of our big foster family, my foster mom, my foster sister Hannah, and my foster brother Samson were the closest. They loved me, dirty drawers and all. I paid my water bill to the toilet bowl man and slowly made my way back to the couch. I was going to try to clean up the mess I'd made, but I didn't feel like it. I kept looking at the time, praying David wouldn't be too mad when he got to me. Was also praying he would hurry up, so I could lie back down.

By the time he got there, I'd fallen back asleep, and it took him calling my phone to wake me up. It was a little after two when I opened my front door.

"Where you been?" I asked him. "What took you so long?"

I was still afraid that maybe Michael had been the recipient of his loving.

He held his arms open. "Went home to shower and change. Grabbed some food, too," he answered. I saw he had on sweats and a T-shirt. His locks were back in a ponytail. "You been drinking?" His words came out more like he was stating the obvious rather than posing a question.

"Had a few more glasses of wine when I got home," I told him.

I moved to the side and let him walk in. He had food in his hand. IHOP. I hadn't eaten anything all day other than the sushi. The breakfast food smelled good, but I was too emotional to eat. He walked into my kitchen, flipped the lights on, and put his keys and his phone on the marble countertop. I folded my arms and leaned against the doorpost as he moved around my kitchen like he owned it. He went to the cabinet and pulled out red and black square plates.

"You hungry?" he asked without looking at me.

"Yeah, kind of," I answered.

I didn't know if I could really stomach any food, but I wanted to be near him.

"Steak omelet or country omelet?"

"Steak."

"Grits?"

"You get cheese?"

"Of course I did, Summer."

He answered me like I was getting on his nerves. Like I should have known that he knew I wouldn't eat my grits without cheese.

"Yeah, grits."

I watched as he took the food from the carryout containers and placed it on the plates. He took the plates to the glass table in my dining room. Came back and grabbed two glasses and filled them up with orange juice before taking them back to the table. He took the time to clean up the small mess he'd made. David had always been a clean man. He didn't have OCD, but you would never catch his home messy. Once he had set the drinks by the food, he pulled my chair out and held a hand out for me.

I was kicking myself in the ass. Almost wanted to cry, because David had a way of using his silence to speak for him. He wouldn't say anything to me. Most of the time he wouldn't even argue back. He would let me show my ass, and he would still treat me the same as he'd always done. I didn't know what to make of that. It bothered me a lot. I walked over, took his hand, and sat down in the chair. He made sure I was comfortable before he sat down. After he blessed the food, we ate in silence. More like he ate. I couldn't bring myself to eat more than a few spoonfuls of grits.

"David—"

He cut me off. "No. Don't apologize, because you're just going to do it again. We're going to do it again . . . be in this place. So stop apologizing," he said firmly.

"I promise, I didn't mean to go there."

"Go where?" he asked, looking up at me.

"I didn't mean to hit you."

"Sure."

"I'm serious."

He shrugged and went back to eating. Cut into his pancakes as his silence and nonchalance cut into me. Finally, he said, "So am I. It's what we do."

"No, it isn't. We've never . . . I've never hit you, and you've never lied to me."

"Not what I'm talking about." He chewed slowly, then looked back up at me. "We do this thing, this shit where we act like we're in a relationship, but we're not. We go out together. We sleep in the same beds. Hide how deep our friendship really is while at work. Look at me. You pretty much gave me your ass to kiss tonight, and what the fuck am I doing? Sitting in your house, catering to you. So, I get it now. You don't want a man. You want somebody to play with. Hence the reason why you're always fucking married men."

My eye twitched. His words stung. The anger and malice there made me grind my teeth. I told him, "That was low, David. Real fucking low."

He stared at me head-on, his eyes never leaving mine. "That's the truth, Summer. Does it hurt?"

"I don't . . . I'm not always fucking married men."

"Bullshit. You used to look at every single man in the room until you found a man with a wedding band, and all bets were off."

"Not t-true," I stammered. "Sometimes it happened that way."

"Yeah, I guess the same way you slipped, tripped, and landed on their dicks."

"So you see me as a whore, then?"

He didn't answer me. Looked back down at his plate and began to eat.

"Wow. Tell me how you really feel, then," I said sarcastically.

Pushing away from the table, I stood. I walked out of the room and headed upstairs to my bedroom. I slammed my door behind me and sat on my bed. For a while all I could do was look around aimlessly as David's words attacked me over and over again in my head.

*You don't want a man. You want somebody to play with.*

I *did* want a man. Just didn't want one who was sexually attracted to other men.

*You don't want a man. You want somebody to play with. Hence the reason why you're always fucking married men.*

His words clawed at my insides. Made me place my head between my legs to stifle a scream. Truth be told, he was right. Married men were safer. I didn't have to worry about any attachments. Didn't have to worry about whether they would love me, then leave me. Both of us had the same agenda. We could fuck, get those rocks off, and then get dressed and leave without saying good-bye. No soliloquies of affection. No "I miss yous." No "I love yous." Just wet pussy and hard dick finding gratification.

My room needed to be cleaned. A bottle of sweet red wine sat on the nightstand next to my bed. I leaned back, scooped the bottle up, and pulled the cork out. I took a full swig. Drank way more than I should have. Clothes lay all around my room, having been thrown on the floor haphazardly. My bed hadn't been made in about a week. I needed to do laundry. Clean underwear, thongs, boy shorts, and the like were all around. Shoes had been strewn about.

I heard my Bose speakers come alive within the walls of my home. The smooth sounds of Marvin Gaye serenaded me as he told me he wanted me and needed me to want him too. David was talking to me again without speaking to me. I took the wine bottle to the bathroom with me. I stripped naked and turned my shower on. Stepped into the carved stone shower stall with the square-shaped showerhead and let the water drown out what my heart and mind were yelling at me. I tried to ignore the fact that my body was betraying me, had always betrayed me when it came to David.

"Out of all the men . . . ," I mumbled to myself.

As much as I tried to drown out the song in the shower, Marvin's words still crept in like a thief in the night and stole my reprieve. David had the song on repeat as I washed myself with honeysuckle and mint body wash. I stayed in the shower for as long as I could. My fingers and toes started to wrinkle. Didn't know how long I'd been in there. I got out of the shower and, still wet, walked out of the bathroom to find my room had been cleaned. Bed made, shoes placed neatly back on my shoe rack. Underwear put back where it was supposed to be. Laundry basket had disappeared. Clothes put away. I ran a hand through my wet hair and turned to find David standing behind me.

"Shit! Y-you scared m-me," I stuttered.

He didn't say anything. He looked down at me as his locks swept across his T-shirt. I had a towel wrapped around me. Water trickled down my body. My hair was dripping wet. I wiggled my fingers and toes. I wanted to kiss him again. Wanted to see if before had all been because of the atmosphere and the mood we were in, or if what I had felt was real. I didn't want to lose David. No, he wasn't my man, but he was the only man who had been a constant in my life besides my foster father.

We both knew what our looks implied. I closed the gap between us as he walked farther into the room. His eyes were heady. Alcohol and fatigue gave him the look of being high. I wanted to kiss him, but he dropped his head against mine and cupped the back of my neck with one of his hands. The other hand grabbed one of mine. We'd been fighting the inevitable for years. I could feel him swelling through his sweats. Smelled the mint on his breath, which told me he'd just brushed his teeth. Yes, he had toiletries at my place. Had clothes too, and a pillow on the other side of my bed.

I let the towel go. Felt it slide down my naked body and hit the floor. With my free hand, I found my way underneath his shirt. His breath caught; his abs quivered as he tried to maintain control. I tilted my head up . . . had to catch my breath as our lips stopped short of kissing. We both knew that if we went there, there would be no turning back. He pulled back a bit, looked down into my eyes.

"Say it," he asked me.

"You already know," I answered.

"I want you to say it."

I was so afraid . . . so damn scared to say that three-letter word. I took his mouth, hard. Kissed him like the wanton whore he thought me to be. My kiss was not gentle, as his had been. My kiss was animalistic. I tore at his shirt. Backed him up. Slammed his back against the wall. I was in control. I loved the fact that even though David was a dominant male, he gave me that moment of control. That kiss, the way he was returning, it was poetic. Every time I sucked on his lips, his tongue rewarded me with a heated exchange of equal forcefulness. His teeth pulled at my bottom lip as my hand slipped into his pants.

He growled low in his throat when I held him tightly, gave him a slow, long stroke to make him grow larger. There was no better aphrodisiac for a woman than to feel a man grow in the palm of her hand all because she had willed him to do so. I stroked him, kissed him, bit his neck, and his hands explored worlds he'd never gotten a chance to before now. One hand slipped between my legs. I was so wet that he didn't have to travel deep to find the puddle.

"Damn, Summer," he croaked out.

I gave in to the feeling. Forgot about the fact that he was a switch-hitter. Didn't let that bother me in the moment. I just gave in . . . enjoyed the feel of his fingers sliding between my lips while his thumb stroked my clitoris. He stroked me while I milked him. I let my fingers play in his pre-cum. Saturated the mushroom head of his dick with his own excitement, just as he did his fingers with my juices.

Once the foreplay was too much to bear, he picked me up, guided me back to my bed, and gently laid me down. Pulling off what remained of his T-shirt, he shifted his weight on the bed as he caged me between his muscled arms. He took a moment to look me in the eye again before using his mouth to show both my breasts equal attention. I'd never had a man pay attention to my nipples the way he was doing. He suckled one into his mouth while using his hands to massage my baby feeders. From one nipple to the next, he suckled. He bit down with enough pressure to cause me blinding excitement.

Marvin kept singing to us. Kept us caught up in the moment, so we couldn't hear our own thoughts. The music was our drug while David's long tongue slid down my chest to my stomach. He took time to pay my belly button some attention. Went on to place kisses on both sides of the creases in my pelvis.

"Shit . . . David," I managed to mutter.

My back was arched and my toes were curled in anticipation of what he was about to do. He kissed around my slick, hairless mound, teasing me. My clit ached. Pussy swelled, yearning for what I knew was to come. He placed tongue kisses against my inner thighs, and just when I thought he was about to place his face between my thighs, he moved back over. Tongued all around my pussy, then blew on my clit, making me shiver in eagerness.

I went to grab his locks. Wanted to guide his face to where I wanted . . . where I needed his lips to be. He gripped my hands. Did it so fast that it almost scared me. I looked down at him as he came back up. I could see his dick tenting his sweats. I had to watch out for that curve when the time came.

He looked me in the eye as he licked his lips. "Say it," he demanded.

"David . . . please." My thighs were shaking, practically quaking, because I needed that release.

"Say it, Summer. Say yes."

I wanted to, but I couldn't. If I said yes, I'd be saying yes to opening myself up to love. I'd be saying yes to more than sex. David was already in my mind and my spirit. If I said yes, I'd be allowing him inside my body and my soul as well. I couldn't do that. Couldn't be with a man whom I would never be enough for. I could be a lot of things for him, but I could never be a man. He was watching me. He knew me. Knew that I wouldn't tell him what he so desperately needed to hear. His lips balled, and I thought he was going to leave me unfulfilled.

Instead, he dropped to his knees. His mouth . . . lips . . . tongue zoomed in on my pussy in a primal fit of sexual rage. He rolled his tongue up and down my slit, occasionally flicking it against my clit. His mouth covered my pussy, licking and sucking on those parts that made me a woman. I wanted to touch him, but he wouldn't let my hands go. My back arched when he used his tongue to fuck me. My hips bucked and my teeth ground when he sucked and tongued my clitoris. My breaths came out in spurts.

"Fuckkk," I groaned. I sang a Song of Solomon all in the name of David.

It was coming. I knew I was coming. Felt those muscles clench in the bottom of my stomach. Felt that rush of adrenaline taking me on a natural high.

I screamed, "Oh, shit . . ." Then I yelled his name. "David . . ." Needed religion. *Dear God . . .*

I made an ugly face. The "come" face, which made me forget I was human. I was having the kind of orgasm that transformed me into something else . . . another entity altogether. He released my hands to fight to get me to release my thighs, which were clamped around his head. He finally pried them open. Splayed them as wide as he wanted them. Not once did he stop licking, sucking, drinking, slurping, dining on me.

I became greedy. Grabbed a handful of locks on both sides of his head and ground my hips up and down his face. He gave a guttural groan. Moved his face in sync with my hips. Cupped his hands underneath my ass while I rode his face to another orgasm. By the time I realized that I'd had enough, I was on the verge of blacking out.

# David

She was out. Had fallen asleep with her legs hanging off the bed. A few moments after I'd brought her to climax, I'd come up and kissed her lips softly until she could get her breathing under control. She was asleep before she knew it. I got up, licked my lips, which still carried her taste, and then scooped her up and placed her in the bed the right way. Her body was limp, and heavier because of it.

Once I moved her, she lay spread-eagle as she slept. I went to the bathroom and washed her juices off my face and neck. Grabbed her Johnson & Johnson so I could stroke out the nut she had left me with. I could still taste the sweetness of her come. Summer ate Greek yogurt like she had an addiction. So it was no wonder that she smelled like water and tasted like honey. The live, active cultures in the yogurt helped to take care of her feminine parts. Those things, along with the fruit she ate daily, mostly pineapples, kiwis, and bananas, made for a tasty treat.

I walked downstairs to make sure her air was on. Although it was cold as shit outside, Summer needed the air on, or she wouldn't rest well. Had learned that about her early on. Since I didn't plan on going home, I grabbed blankets from her laundry room and made myself at home on her sofa.

I'd cleaned up the mess she'd made down here, in addition to her bedroom. Summer's parents had spoiled her. They hadn't insisted she do her chores when she was a child; therefore, she procrastinated when it came to doing them now. I looked around her townhome and knew her mother had decorated it for her. Black art decorated the walls. Pictures of different tribes in Africa, along with the earth-toned color scheme, indicated that her foster mother wanted her to keep in touch with her roots. In the center of the hardwood floor in the front room was a chocolate rug with circles of different colors in it. Built-in bookshelves on one side of the room were filled with works by black authors, such as Zane, Eric Jerome Dickey, K'wan, Brenda Hampton, Brenda Jackson, Francis Ray, and L. A. Banks. On the bookshelves on the other side of the room, you saw works by Langston Hughes, Zora Neale Hurston, Terry McMillan, Alice Walker, and others.

While she was an avid reader, Summer wasn't domestic. She wasn't filthy, but she sure wasn't Suzy Homemaker, either. If she and I ever explored the road of a relationship, I already knew some of those domestic things would fall on me. I didn't mind it at all. As a kid, I used to clean to keep from going upside the heads of niggas who thought I was soft because I was quiet. I had to show quite a few of them that I was the exact opposite.

Just then my phone beeped and vibrated. I picked it up to see that Michael had texted me. My eyes shifted toward the stairs. I wouldn't do that to her. Wouldn't talk to a man whom I had those kinds of feelings for while I was under her roof, especially not after the sexual intimacy we'd shared.

As bad as I had wanted to dip inside her, I couldn't. First of all, she had passed out. Probably from the alcohol and the orgasm. Second of all, she hadn't said yes. I needed her to say yes. I wanted her to want me the way I wanted her. Not to mention, there were other things we needed to address before we went down that road.

You must be asleep or at Summer's home. Came
by your place and you weren't there.

I chuckled at that text. There was a reason I had left
my place and had come to Summer's place. Michael was a
hard man to say no to. I was no fool. I'd warned Summer
about him, and then I'd taken my own advice.

Another text came through.

You owe me one last time. You took that away
from me, so you owe me.

I put the phone down and settled myself on the couch.
He was right. I had taken the last time we were supposed
to hook up away from him. I hadn't felt there was a need
for us to go there again. Not to mention all the drama that
had been going on with us, thanks to me fucking Sadi.
Nah, there hadn't been a need for it.

With these thoughts swirling in my head, I drifted off
to sleep. I woke up just before the sun broke through the
clouds to find myself covered with a warm body. Still
naked, Summer had crawled over me and had laid her
head on my chest, her legs around my waist. She'd fallen
asleep that way. It felt good to have her there. I was cold
as fuck. I knew she'd taken the cover off because she
was hot. I gave a lazy smile as I looked down at her. My
Summer didn't like the heat she oftentimes produced.
My phone beeped again. I went to adjust my glasses and
realized that she had taken them off. She was always
fussing about me sleeping with them on.

I picked up the phone, strained to see through the
fuzziness that Michael was asking us to meet him for
breakfast later. I dropped the phone back on the table,
wrapped Summer and myself in a light blanket, and fell
back to sleep.

\*\*\*

"I don't want to go to breakfast with him," Summer snapped when I told her.

We were in her front room as I got dressed. I had taken a seat so I could pull my socks on. Summer was standing against the wall across from me with a look on her face that said she wasn't too thrilled about us going to meet Michael. The night before she had been all into him. Then she had found out that he and I had been more than friends once upon a time.

"I would like to," I responded.

"Why?"

"Because he's my friend, and he came to town to visit me. I'd like to spend a little time with him."

Summer stared at me. Gave me a look that said something between "You're lying" and "I don't trust you." She was still naked. We'd showered together. No words had been spoken about what had happened hours earlier. She had wanted to return the favor. She had got down on her knees in the shower and had given me what she'd deprived me of when she passed out. I'd had head from men and women, some of the best, but Summer . . . Summer didn't give head. Summer gave fellatio.

There was an art to giving fellatio. All that tantric shit she liked to read about had been put on display for the first time with me. She had made love to my dick with her mouth. Had praised it with her tongue as she'd French-kissed the head of it. She'd tickled the little ridge around the base of my head with her tongue. Alternated licking and sucking the head, until she caught me by surprise and swallowed my whole dick. No gags. No choking. Just swallowed, hummed, and massaged my balls until my toes were throwing gang signs. She did that until she felt me swell in her throat, and then she pulled back. I was coated with her slick saliva. The long, thick veins in my dick were pulsating so hard, it ached. She lifted me in her hand and stroked as she sloppily sucked my scrotum.

I was amazed at what she could do with her mouth. For a second, I got mad that she'd probably given that kind of pleasure to other men. Summer did what she did so well when it came to the art of fellatio that she turned herself on. She had an orgasm while she was pleasing me. There was something about this that was appealing not only physically but also mentally. She was nasty with it too. Begged me to fuck her face when she dropped her hands. She didn't really have to say it, since I had already grabbed two fistfuls of her hair and had started to stroke in and out of her mouth. Didn't take me long to come after that. She swallowed down any chance of us having kids.

"Well, I'm not going," she huffed, bringing me back to the present.

I sighed and stood. "You sure?"

"Positive."

"I would like you to come."

"I would like you not to . . . at least not with him."

"I'm not fucking Michael."

"Sure," she responded sassily.

"We're really going to do this again, huh?" I asked her, knowing she was still feeling a bit angry and confused about the way she had acted last night.

She didn't say anything right away. "Guess I'll see you later, then," she finally mumbled.

"Summer," I called behind her as she walked away. "Summer. So you're going to walk away from me like that?"

Her bedroom door slamming behind her was my answer. I finished getting dressed in silence. I still had a few things at her place, so I wouldn't have to rush home and then back. I'd sent Michael a text telling him that both of us would be there for breakfast. He'd find me one person short when I showed up. I tried talking to Summer again, but she ignored me. Wouldn't even open her door.

Thirty minutes later, I was sitting inside Highland Bakery on Highland Avenue. The usual early morning Saturday crowd had gathered. If you didn't get there early, you were subjected to a long line that wrapped around the block. Luckily for me, Michael was already inside when I got there. I made more than a few people angry when I bypassed the line and headed inside. I could here there muffled grumbling as I went. I spotted Michael as soon as I walked in. He was on the phone and was sitting at the end of a long wooden bench, which was more like a banquette, right near the hostess stand. I could tell he was expecting Summer by the way he looked behind me to see if she was there. She wasn't. I made my way through the long line of the people standing at the register and then over to him. He ended the phone call as I sat down across from him.

"Where's the lady?" he asked me.

"She decided she didn't want breakfast," I lied.

"Ah, I see," he said with a slick smirk. "You good this morning?"

"Never better. You?"

"Would be better if I had been with you and Summer last night, I'm sure."

I chuckled and adjusted my pants. "Not too much happened."

"I'm quite sure it was enough to put that stupid-ass grin on your face, though."

"You'll never know."

It was his turn to chuckle. "Very overprotective of her, I see."

"Nah. Just cautious about you."

"It's you she should be cautious about, no?" he asked and then took a sip of his coffee.

"Why me?"

"You're the sneaky one."

"I've always been honest with her. There is nothing about me she doesn't know."

"Except when it comes to me, right?"

I shook my head and leaned back a bit in my chair. "She knows about that now too."

"Oh, I see."

He looked around the place a bit. Flashed that million-dollar smile at a few women. Ignored the obviously gay males. We both spotted a few not so obvious gay men. One in a gold and purple Greek jacket couldn't stop staring at us. For as hard as he pretended to be, I bet he could take dick like a pro. We gave head nods and predatory smiles. Then we both looked back at one another and laughed.

"Nothing's changed with you, Michael," I told him.

"You're still the same, David," he responded.

It felt good to be in that moment with him. Things had been a whole lot tenser the night before. I felt relaxed now. I didn't know why. Maybe it had something to do with what Summer and I had shared. It could have been the fact that he and I needed that bit of calm to fix what had been broken between us.

"In some senses. Hard to find dudes these days who are serious about their health and their status," I said.

"I feel you. You up on that, though?"

"What? Who? Him?" I asked, nodding my head in the Q-Dog's direction.

"Naw, man. Your status. You know your status?"

"Always, my man. Nothing's changed about that. I keep my dick clean."

He nodded.

I asked, "What about you?"

"Always."

"Why, if you ain't cheating on Sadi?"

He'd walked right into that one. He knew it and laughed about it.

"I've never cheated on her. May have slipped, tripped, and accidently landed in some pussy, which I had to fight and struggle my way out of until I nutted, but I ain't ever cheated, my nigga," he explained, throwing slang in at the end that reminded me of us before the college degrees.

I cracked up laughing at my boy. That was Michael. He would always be right, even when he was wrong.

"So you fucking around on her?" I asked.

"You heard what I said."

"Men too?"

"Nah. Never that. Not on my wife," he said, looking at me with that slick smirk. "Unless it's you."

My heart slammed against my rib cage. Flashbacks of those hotel room stays played in 3-D before my eyes. We stared at each other in silence for a long while.

"We don't want to travel down that road," I finally said.

"Oh, but I do," he assured me.

"Not doing that shit. You're married to a woman who doesn't know shit about that side of you. We're not those kinds of niggas, remember?" I told him.

He licked his lips and leaned forward. "We're still not. You're safe. I know I can trust you this time around. You won't tell. You won't talk. You're not a walking STD. Safe."

The corner of my upper lip twitched. "Fuck you, Michael."

"Trying to."

"You came all the way here to see if we could fuck?"

He turned his lips down, gave a slight shrug. "Among other things," he said and leaned back. "We did need to talk. I missed you . . . a bit. Missed the friends and lovers we used to be."

As bad as I wanted to believe him, something in me called bullshit. Something else was going on that he wasn't telling me about.

"I call bullshit, bruh."

"Call it what you want. I'm just telling you what's going on in my head."

"No."

"No, what?"

"Not doing that to your wife and kids. Find another *safe* haven to fall into."

Underneath the table, where no one could see, he placed his hand on my thigh. The muscles in my legs tensed. Dick stirred around in my boxer briefs. He knew what he was doing. Dangled that piece of forbidden fruit like the snake-ass nigga he was, and dared me to take a bite.

"You know you want to," he said to me.

"Maybe so, but I've learned not to always do what my dick tells me to."

"More than your dick and body want this, David. Why deny it? You miss that connection we both had. It's still there, and I know you feel it. It can't be denied. Give in to it. We walk that thin gray line one more time, and then it's over," he said, tempting me.

"That's the problem. It will never be that simple. It never has with us."

"Things are different now. I have a wife and kids back home. Can't be wild, reckless Mike anymore."

I quirked a brow. What the hell did he call what he was doing, then? His hand was still on my thigh. Massaging it with a firmness that had me placing a hand over my dick to quell the sudden need to release the kraken. I rubbed a hand across the back of my neck. Reached under the table to move his hand. At least I tried to, but he grabbed my wrist. I grabbed his in return. Two dominate males vying for that control. We had a lock on one another, the way warriors greeted each other with a handshake. The smirk left his face, and what was there was pure, adulterated temptation.

A shadow was cast over us. For a while I felt like his wife had caught us. Thought maybe she had followed her husband to Atlanta to see what he was really up to and had caught us both with our hands in a different kind of cookie jar. But no, his wife wasn't looming over us. The threat of a summer torrential downpour of rain was, though.

# Summer

He wasn't answering his phone. My nerves were on edge. Why in the hell wouldn't he answer his phone? For as long as David and I had been friends, he'd never ignored my calls. Even if he was in a meeting, he would answer his phone. Put it on speaker so I could hear what was going on. It was his way of letting me know he saw me, wasn't ignoring me, but couldn't talk at the moment. I would hang up and text an apology for calling in the middle of business. He would text me back, telling me we would talk as soon as he was done. He'd spoiled me.

So I couldn't understand why when he was with Michael, he wouldn't answer the phone. I knew where they were. He'd told me before he left. I hopped up, threw on a dress that was way too thin for the weather, put on some wedge sneakers, and grabbed my coat. I drove like I was nervous about the reason he wasn't able to answer his phone. Almost rear-ended someone while sending David text messages, pissed that he wasn't answering me. By the time I made it to Highland Bakery in Old Fourth Ward, I was jittery. I felt like I was walking on a cloud as I floated to the door.

I saw them holding hands under the table, though it was more like they had locked wrists, and I wondered if anyone had been paying attention. I paid close attention to the male in the purple and gold Greek letter jacket, who seemed to be fixated on the two of them. When I approached them, David looked up at me like he had been caught stealing.

"You're not answering your phone," was all I said to him.

He moved his hand from underneath the table, touched his slack pockets, and checked his jacket pockets. Then both he and Michael stood, still being the Southern gentlemen they were.

"I must have left it in my truck," David said to me. "I put it on the charger and forgot to grab it."

I hated that it seemed as if he had been so anxious to get to Michael that he had forgotten his phone. I felt Michael watching me, but I refused to look at him. No matter how much heat I felt while in his presence, I wouldn't make eye contact with that man. Whether I wanted to admit it or not, he was finer than sin. Those waves on his head were perfect. He had on a pair of tan wing-tip dress shoes, khaki slacks, which strained against the muscles in his thighs when he sat back down, and a royal purple sweater that showcased all the time he spent in the gym. The way he was dressed, and that all-knowing smile he possessed, annoyed me. Not because of anything other than the fact that he looked too damn good dressed and looking that way.

I kept my eyes locked on David, which wasn't all that much better. He too sat there looking like *GQ* should be calling. Those eyes and dimples called out to me. Those lips . . . When he licked his lips, I remembered what it felt like to have them on me. I almost . . . My legs almost gave out from under me.

I cleared my throat. David knew why I was really there, but he wouldn't say anything in front of Michael. Wouldn't embarrass me like I did him the night before. I was jealous. I had wanted to see if he had snuck off somewhere with Michael and had given in to the obvious attraction I knew was lingering between them.

"Nice of you to join us," Michael said from the sidelines.

I made the mistake of turning to look at him. Jesus, why did I look at him? For the first time, in the natural light of the day, I noticed the color of his eyes. The color of honey lured me in like a moth to a flame. His dark skin and those honey-colored eyes forced my breathing to slow down. He noticed the visible change in me brought about by my newfound awareness, smirked, and then patted the spot beside him on the bench, offering me a seat. I wanted to sit beside David, but he was in the chair across from Michael. There was no empty chair beside him. Someone had taken it. The greedy-ass people of Old Fourth Ward had forced me to sit next to Michael by default. I looked at David. He nodded. I slowly took the seat being offered.

"Hungry?" Michael asked me.

I glanced at David, then back at his other best friend. "A little." Michael's scent was so mesmerizing that I wiped away the invisible sweat on my forehead.

"I ordered peanut butter French toast," Michael informed me.

"Never tried it."

"You'll like it. Trust me."

"If you say so."

He chuckled. "I do."

"I'm going to run to my truck and get my phone," David said, chiming in.

Michael nodded. I looked at David. It was rare that he went anywhere without his phone, especially when he was working a case. Someone could call at any time to let him in on new leads or to give him the names of possible witnesses he could call to the stand.

"You going to be okay?" David asked me.

I nodded. "Yeah."

Once David was gone, Michael sipped his coffee. Placed an arm behind me on the wooden bench as he studied me.

"Why do I get the feeling you don't like me as much as you did last night?" he asked after placing his coffee mug back on the table.

I gave a side eye and asked him, "What ever gave you that idea?"

"That mean side eye. And the fact that David finally told you the truth about us."

"He said you're not gay. Am I missing something?" I asked.

Since he'd opened the jack-in-the-box and shaken the eight ball, I was going to ask all the questions I could. I wanted to know what it was about the man that would make David hide their relationship from me. I glanced around at the crowd. Saw every race of people ATL had to offer. The low buzz of the other patrons didn't seem to bother us, as we sat in our own world. I saw women gawking at Michael. They had eye fucked David, too, before he went outside, but it was Michael who demanded their attention just by being there. He sat there, looking regal. Back straight, shoulders broad. Sat like a true pharaoh. The pheromones he exuded were mind-numbing.

Michael cast a glance in my direction. "I'm not gay."

"You have sex with men."

"And women."

"You're gay," I insisted.

"I'm not. Don't label me. I hate labels."

"It's not a label. It's what you are."

"How the fuck you going to tell me who or what I am? I don't answer to that label because you call me that."

He was getting annoyed. I'd pushed a button I didn't know existed. Some of the jealousy I was feeling started to turn into malice. I smirked.

"So what should I call you? Confused?" I asked to see how far I could push him.

He moved his arm from behind me, rubbed his big hands together, and leaned to the side to look at me.

"Do you call David confused?"

"David knows what he wants."

He shrugged nonchalantly. "Did you ask him?"

"I don't have to. He knows what he wants."

"Are you sure?"

"Positive."

"And what does he want?"

I wouldn't answer that question. If I answered that, then I would probably have to admit that David wanted both of us. Although he tried to play it cool, I could see the attraction between the two of them. It angered me, because I knew I couldn't do anything about that. I would never be able to compete with that.

"We both know what he wants, right, Summer?" he asked me.

"Whatever, Michael."

"I like the way you say my name. Say it again," he demanded.

I gazed up into his eyes and inhaled his scent again. Worst thing I could have ever done. His tongue snaked out to lick his lips as they curved into a smile.

For a long while we stared at one another. I thought I'd pissed him off. Thought I'd gotten under his skin, but then he laughed. Laughed loud enough that people looked at us to see what was funny.

"You're funny, Summer, and you're trouble. You're beautiful, funny, sexy, and trouble," he said, then took another sip of his coffee, all the while keeping his eyes on me. "David, you didn't tell me Summer was this much trouble," he said, looking behind me.

I turned to see David walking back over to us. David thumbed his nose as he sat down, and glanced from me to Michael. David laid his phone on the table.

"Why do you say she's trouble?" he asked Michael.

"Look at her," he responded. "Any woman packing this much heat is trouble. No worries, though. I've always loved getting into trouble. . . ."

Michael let the end of his sentence trail off as he looked from me to David and then back to me. The insinuation was clear. He was so sure of himself that he'd already laid claim to my sex without even asking. The heat in his gaze was enough to knock the panties right off me. I could tell by the way David was observing us that he was trying to figure out what had gone down in his brief absence.

He didn't get the chance to find out. The food arrived, and although Michael and I still did a little back-and-forth throughout breakfast, it wasn't as bad as it could have been. After we were done with breakfast, Michael talked us into seeing a movie at the AMC Southlake 24. Driving in separate cars there gave me time to simmer down after my little quarrel with Michael.

Couldn't remember what the movie was about. I was with two men who I happened to be sexually attracted to. To one more so than the other, but that was only because I didn't want to get to know the other one on that level, or at least that was what I told myself. We all had time to talk before the movie started. First, we grabbed snacks, drinks, and popcorn. All of mine were courtesy of Michael and David. They refused to let me pay for anything while I was in their presence. I was used to this with David. Thought it was nice of Michael, since he didn't know me all that well.

"Consider it a peace offering," he said to me as we walked to theater in which our film was playing. "I'm not confused. Not gay. I'm me. I'm a man who happens to like both men and women. Can you live with that?" he asked me as we walked behind David, who was on the phone.

I stopped and looked up at him. "Did you come all this way just to have sex with David?"

"And what if I did?"

"Is he open to it?"

"Ask him."

"If he was, would you? Even with a wife at home?"

He shrugged. "Depends on the mood."

I looked at David, who'd finally noticed that we'd stopped. He was still on the phone, talking to one of the partners at the firm, but his eyes were planted firmly on us.

"What does that mean?" I asked, looking back at Michael.

He gave me the once-over, which made my inner thighs moist. "Can I have you too?"

"What?"

"You heard me. I'm a man who knows what he wants. I won't have him if I can't have you too."

I chuckled. My cheeks were flushed, I was sure. "You don't know me."

"I know I like what I see, Freckles. That's what I'll call you from now on . . . Freckles. Told David I want to count your freckles up close," Michael said.

He closed the small gap between us and brushed a smooth finger over my freckles. I licked my lips to wet them. Took a sip of the large Sprite in my hand to wet my throat. I looked at David. I couldn't read him. Didn't know what he was thinking. I didn't want to make him mad. I knew that. I was so busy trying to gauge David's reaction that when Michael turned my attention back to him, lifted my chin, and placed his lips against mine, I almost dropped the popcorn and the Sprite.

*Shit. Damn. Oh . . . my . . . God.*

My vocabulary had become limited. Michael's lips were as soft as I thought they would be. I got lost in that man's kiss. The way his lips overtook mine had me moaning, and I didn't even know it. Was too afraid to think about who kissed better. Didn't want to. I wanted to pull away but couldn't. The more I tried to stop, the deeper he took the kiss. My nipples pushed against the fabric of my bra. I didn't move, for fear that my arousal would run down my leg. I was having an orgasm while standing in the hallway of a movie theater.

"Damn, bruh," I heard someone say as he passed us.

Heard a few female giggles. "God damn, he kissing the shit outta her," one woman said.

"Wish a nigga would kiss me like that," another said.

A third woman remarked, "They may as well go home and start fucking. . . ."

People laughed, and someone else said, "Them niggas ain't 'bout to make it home. I'ma go in whatever movie theater they going in."

No matter what they said, Michael didn't pull away from the kiss. In fact, it seemed as if having an audience riled him up more. I dropped the popcorn and the drink. Needed my hands. Had to place them somewhere on him when he pulled me closer to him. One of his hands gripped my ass, while the other played in the back of my hair. I had to use one of my hands to keep the back of my dress down.

That motherfucker kissed me until my lips went numb. When he pulled back, I was left panting . . . watching him . . . waiting on him to do it again . . . wanting him. . . .

I felt sorry for his wife at that moment. I couldn't be his wife. To know that your husband possessed that much sexual prowess had to be bad for a woman's mental health. She had to know what she had at home. Had to know he was a beautiful liar. The devil. Temptation in the flesh.

"Say yes," Michael said to me.

"Huh?"

Michael had said it, but it was David's voice I'd heard. He had asked the same thing of me that David had countless times before.

*Oh, shit. David.* I looked to my right and saw that David was no longer on the phone. He was watching us, arms folded across his chest, with an unreadable expression on his face. He walked toward us, which caused some sort of fear in me. The people watching us came to a stop. It was clear they thought some shit was about to go down. I did too. I was breathing rapidly as David approached me. Nope. We weren't together, but I'd crossed a line, I knew.

But David didn't flip out. He took my hand in his, pulled me away from the mess I'd made of the popcorn and soda.

"Oh, shit. Shawty pimping," some female claimed.

"Damn, son," another remarked.

"The shit you see in the A, my nigga," a third female said.

We ignored them all. I could say I was a bit embarrassed. Didn't know what to think or feel. All I knew was my pussy needed handling. Michael stopped David before we walked away. He whispered something in his ear that caused David to cut his eyes at me. He gave me the once-over but said nothing. Nodded once at Michael and kept walking. I glanced back over my shoulder to see Michael cleaning the mess I had made. Then Michael caught up with us, and he and my best friend walked hand in hand into the theater.

All of that happened before the movie even started. David and I sat silently through the trailers. Michael left and then came back in with fresh popcorn and Sprite. We all sat at the very back of the theater, which was good. Michael sat on one side of me, while David sat on the other.

"Your pussy's wet, huh?" David asked me out of the blue.

I didn't answer him. Was taken aback by the abruptness of the question coming from him.

"You're sitting like a woman with a wet pussy," he continued.

I had been fidgeting around in my seat. Couldn't get comfortable, because of the very thing he'd alluded to. Most women would have probably felt bad about even being sexually attracted to two men at once. Me, not so much. I'd never been afraid of my sexuality, because Clarissa Kennedy hadn't allowed me or any of my sisters to be. She felt as if women had the right to be as sexually liberated as men. Mom had taught us that as long as we were responsible when it came to sex, we could do whatever we wanted.

"You're mad at me for letting Michael kiss me?" I asked him.

"Oh, he kissed you, huh?" he asked sarcastically.

"Yeah, you saw him. I was watching you, and he kissed me."

David grunted as he kept looking at the movie screen as the lights dimmed. We were talking loud enough for Michael to hear, but he didn't seem to care. He was on his phone. I assumed he was talking to his wife, since he asked about his kids. David didn't say anything else. He focused on the movie. Michael was asking his wife about her day at work. I was the oddball out.

I stood, did a little jig so that my thong would act right. Had a good mind to go to the bathroom and rid myself of it. But I sat back down. Caught Michael watching my ass while I bounced around. I heard him ask his wife if she missed him. I saw a big smile on his face. I looked at David. Still no reaction from him. I crossed my legs and uncrossed them. Leaned against the back of the chair in front of me, then sat back again.

David looked at me from the corner of his eye. Leaned to the side, with his thumb and index finger looking as if they were cradling his chin. Michael grabbed my hand and placed it on his dick. I had a good mind to snatch my hand back, but he wouldn't let me. He told his wife how much he missed her while using my hand to massage his dick.

I was so turned on that it threatened to drive me crazy. Needed a release that those two men held me in the palms of their hands. I felt heat when David leaned toward me. I almost moaned out loud when his tongue licked the vein in my neck, and then he used his lips to suck down on it and finish me off. David's hand crept between my thighs as he kissed my neck. His fingers slipped inside me with ease. I wasn't wearing any underwear, I finally remembered. That was why I had had to hold the back of my dress down when Michael palmed my ass. That thong I thought I had on was a figment of my imagination. My pussy was so swollen with desire that it felt as if something was straining against my vaginal lips. David fingered me, massaged my clitoris with the pad of his thumb, all the while telling me how much he wanted me in my ear.

"He made you come," David said to me. "You let him make you come. Took me eight years to make you come for me. Took him less than forty-eight hours," he mumbled against my ear.

The heat from his breath and the way his teeth grazed my ear worked me over. Made my hips roll in my seat. The moment was erotic. Seductive. But I heard the clear tone of jealousy in David's voice.

"I'm sorry," I said, apologizing to David. "Hmm," I moaned, biting down on my lips.

"Shhh," Michael whispered in my other ear.

I guessed he'd hung up with the wife. He unzipped his slacks. Slipped my hand into his boxer briefs and allowed me to feel the long thickness that he kept there.

"Jesus," I whispered.

Michael's hand joined David's between my thighs. David removed his fingers. They were soaked with my come. Two of Michael's fingers took their place. His fingers were thicker than David's. David's were longer, but Michael's fingers were thicker. My knees rose as my back arched, and I clawed at David's shirt. Gripped Michael's dick tighter in my hand. He groaned low. Swelled more in my hand, and I felt his pre-excitement leak over my fingertips.

David brought his come-laden fingers to my mouth. Smeared my arousal on my lips like gloss, then kissed me. His tongue traced the outline of my lips, forcing me to suck the tip. He pulled the top of my dress down, causing my breasts to spill forward. While he cupped the left one in his hand, Michael's mouth sucked on the right one as he aggressively finger fucked me. Both of them drank from me. They worked as a team. When one sucked my nipples, the other ravished the rest of my breasts. When I saw their tongues touch . . .

Something happened in that moment. I was ashamed of what happened to me in that moment. Their tongues touched. As they kissed my nipples, I kept seeing their tongues touch. My head fell back. I was in complete ecstasy. There was something intoxicatingly erotic and dangerously satisfying about this moment.

The base of Michael's palm gave my clit all the stimulation it could handle. He removed his index finger. Kept his middle finger inside, stroking my G-spot.

I thought I would slobber when David's middle finger joined his. Good God, they were both fingering me. My G-spot was swelling. Pussy was queefing, but no sound came out. Those muscles in my stomach tightened, as if I was doing an ab workout. There was something overtaking me that I'd never had happen before. It felt as if I had a strong urge to release. I wanted to be afraid of that feeling, but knowing what it was—since I had seen it on videos, had read up on it— I gave in. Before I could warn them, I squirted all over the seat and their fingers.

"Damn," they said in unison as they removed their fingers.

Michael ran a dry hand down his face while looking at his other hand, which was dripping wet, and then he laughed low. David gazed into my eyes when they finally opened. He kissed me softly. I couldn't catch my breath. He had to breathe for me. So his mouth covered mine, and he kissed me until I could inhale.

# Summer

I adjusted Michael's shirt on me. Rolled up the sleeves and then placed the belt I'd had on with my dress around my waist. I'd splashed water all over my dress and the seat in the movie theater. Michael had had to go to his rental and grab the extra dress shirt he had. It had been simple enough for me to make it look like a tunic dress. I had to make sure the wind didn't decide to put my goods on display.

I walked out of the bathroom of the AMC Southlake 24 movie theater and saw that they were standing there, waiting for me. They'd been having a conversation, which stopped when they saw me. Didn't know if they didn't want me to hear what they were talking about or if they stopped talking so that they could take in the sight of me. My soiled dress was in my purse. A part of me wanted to be embarrassed, but another part of me said, *Fuck it.*

I'd had the ultimate orgasm without a dick penetrating me. Most women couldn't even achieve an orgasm from oral sex, and I'd experienced it with just fingers, nipple stimulation, and the heat of the moment.

David was the first to walk over to me. "You good?" he asked.

I nodded. "Yeah. I think I have some biker shorts in my gym bag in the car. I can slide those on and be okay until I get back home," I said to him.

"Okay. Did we overstep our boundaries?"

I laughed softly. "No."

Michael walked up behind us, placed a hand on the small of my back. "That was pretty impressive shit, Freckles. Never had a woman show me that side of things. You do that often?" he asked me unabashedly.

"No. First time."

"For real?" David asked.

"For real," I replied, shifting my weight from one foot to the other. "Never had that happen to me before. Gave me a head rush."

"It gave my head something too," Michael commented.

"He just jacked his dick in a bathroom stall," David said.

"Had to. Was going to have blue balls if I didn't," Michael responded.

Michael was staring at me like I was his next meal. His gaze was predaceous. I'd awakened the beast in him. He was on the hunt.

"You tired? Want to go home?" David asked me.

"Are you coming with me?" I said.

"Was going to hang with Michael for a few."

"Can I come, or is this a guy only thing?" I asked.

David shrugged. "Depends."

"On what?"

"Are you coming because you want to hang with us just because, or are you coming because . . ."

"Because I want to make sure you don't fuck him?" I said, finishing his question.

He nodded. "Is that why you want to come?"

"Partially," I answered honestly.

David smiled at me. He'd always been a fan of my honesty. He'd said it was one of the things that made him more attracted to me.

"Want me to trail you home so you can drop your car off?" he asked as he took my hand.

I nodded. David and I always held hands. It had become second nature to us. Had happened with ease once we started hanging out regularly. This time Michael was the odd man out. He walked behind us while we approached the exit. David held the door open for me. Walked out behind me, then held the door for Michael as a courtesy. David and I walked hand in hand while Michael spoke with his wife again. This time Michael wasn't all smiles. He was agitated. I didn't know why. Didn't matter to me, though. That was her problem. I smiled up at David as we walked to row seven, where my car was parked.

"You mad at me?" I asked him.

He looked around the parking lot. Families were out. A little girl ran between us because her father was chasing her. He yelled at her not to do that again, but the little girl didn't care. She was in joy land as her mother joined the chase. In that moment I wondered what my mother and father had looked like. Wondered if my father had been a married man, and my mother his mistress. Could being attracted to married men be hereditary?

"Why would I be mad?" David asked, bringing me back to reality.

"Because of Michael. I let him do what he did to me. I touched his dick too."

"Did you like it?"

"Like what?"

"Touching his dick."

"It was nice . . . real nice. But yours has a curve. I wanna see it up close again."

David laughed. So did I. I was fascinated by the slight curve in David's dick.

"Did you like his kiss?" he asked me.

I wasn't going to lie. "I did."

"You had an orgasm while he kissed you."

We spotted my Charger, and I hit the button on my remote for the automated locks on the car. My headlights flashed, indicating that the driver-side door was unlocked. I looked behind me and saw that Michael had stopped a few paces back. This time it was he who watched me and David intently. A gust of wind came through, blowing the shirt up. David opened my car door and told me to get inside. I did.

"I know. I never had that happen before," I admitted. "Michael gives a different kind of kiss."

David kneeled down in front of me. He placed butterfly kisses on my thighs before responding. "I know."

"You've kissed him?"

"Of course."

Since he's been here?"

"Yes, Summer."

"He kiss better than me?"

"Summer."

"Does he?"

David looked at me. "You tell me."

I sighed. Hated to admit that Michael's kiss was something like a phenomenon. "He fucked my mouth with his mouth. Made me come with a kiss. I hate that shit."

He chuckled. "He has that kind of power."

"Think I can ever kiss you like that?"

"Yes."

I gave a big cheesy smile. I was looking for David's approval and acceptance of what I'd done. David brought his lips to mine again. I knew my kiss had nothing on Michael's. Still, I tried, anyway. Afterward, David went to his car, and Michael headed to his rental. They both followed me home.

Once I got home, I thought that since I was there, it was best to clean myself up better. I took a quick shower, while David and Michael talked about politics. Michael hated that his insurance premium had gone up because of the Affordable Care Act, better known as Obamacare. David was all for everyone being able to afford health care. They had a healthy debate about it while I washed up.

After showering, I came downstairs with nothing covering me but my bath sheet. I walked in on them kissing. I remembered what I'd felt when I saw their tongues touch in the movie theater. There was something shamefully appealing about what I was witnessing. Two dominate males locked in a kiss. I'd never seen anything like that up close and personal. Again, my womanhood flooded with desire. I couldn't explain what I felt as I watched those two kiss. I had never thought I'd be turned on by two men being intimate. It was strange because they didn't touch one another like they had done with me. But the kiss was so primitive that it piqued my curiosity. I wanted to get closer to their erotica. Their kiss had no value other than to stimulate my sexual desire.

I rushed back upstairs. Grabbed my Hitachi wand—Mr. Hitachi was the name I'd given it— plugged it in, and fell back on my bed. I needed a release so badly that I didn't even check to see that I had closed the door all the way behind me. I discarded the towel. Used my fingers to spread my lips and put the vibrating sex toy against my clitoris. My eyes rolled back in my head. God, I needed a release. Another one. Needed to come again so badly, it pissed me off when Mr. Hitachi wasn't getting me there fast enough. Usually, he would get me off in a matter of seconds. But not in that moment.

I put the wand on the highest speed. This maximized the vibrations, but it still didn't get me off fast enough. Shit felt good, but not as good as when Michael had kissed me . . . not as good as when they both had brought me to a squirting orgasm.

"Fuck!" I yelled out in frustration.

I needed that release again. I didn't even notice the two males at the door, watching me. The door to my room slowly crept open. Without an invitation, Michael walked in. He watched me with no shame. Rubbed his dick through his slacks as he did so. David stayed at the door, waiting for me to give him permission to enter.

"You're so much fucking trouble, Summer," Michael said to me. "So fucking sexual. Like, do you realize how many men would kill to know that they had brought a woman to a squirting orgasm from fingers and kissing alone?" he asked.

"He's smitten with you now, baby," David said.

He'd called me baby. He'd never called me that before. I kept my eyes on David. I was aware of Michael in the room. But I kept my eyes on David. There was something going on between us in that moment that I could readily explain. That magnetic pull to him was stronger than ever.

"My wife doesn't even squirt," Michael admitted.

It was as if he was amazed by my ability to ejaculate fluid from my female parts when I had an orgasm. I was amazed at it myself. I wanted to experience it again.

David licked his lips. I could see he wanted me. I wanted him too. Was tired of playing the what-if game.

"Michael wants to eat your pussy," he told me. Mr. Hitachi was still stimulating me as Michael unbuttoned the top of his shirt. "Can he eat you out?"

I turned my head and looked at David. "I don't know. Can he?"

David shook his head. "No."

I was disappointed more than shocked by his answer. If Michael could eat pussy the way he could kiss, I was done for. I wanted to experience that shit like I'd never wanted to experience anything else. Still, I didn't want to make David feel any kind of way.

"Well, if you don't want him to, then no . . . ," I said.

David walked over to the bed and took the wand from my hand.

"No, baby. I need that back," I whined as I tried to grab it from his hand.

He tossed it on the bed, above my head, and crawled between my legs. Only his clothes stopped him from penetrating me. He kissed me, and his hands roamed over my body. His big hands squeezed and palmed my breasts, like he was captivated by the fluffiness of them. He pulled his glasses off so I could look directly into the torture behind his eyes. He was fighting his own demons. We were in our own Garden of Eden.

I cast a glance at Michael. His eyes were locked on us. In the heady, hedonistic den of his mind, he was plotting. I could tell by the way he watched me and David. He wanted in but didn't want to force his way in. He was going to make us take a bite of that forbidden fruit without even having to dangle it in front of us. A slow smirk spread across his face as he locked eyes with me.

"If he does, you can't have an orgasm," David said to me. He used his hand to cup my chin, bringing my attention back to him. He knew that what he was asking was impossible. That was the same man who had brought me to an orgasm by kissing. No way he wouldn't be able to do the same if he put his mouth between my legs.

"If he is able to perform the act of cunnilingus the way he performed the act of kissing, I'm going to disappoint you," I admitted to David.

"The act of what?" Michael asked from across the room.

"Cunnilingus," David and I repeated in unison. "The act of performing oral sex on a woman."

I smiled at the way we had said that. David hadn't really said anything that most people didn't know, that is, except Michael. But it was the way he curved his lips into a slick smile and gazed at me while he spoke that was unique. Getting your point across sexually without being crass was a big thing for me. It turned me on when he could use terms other than "eating pussy." David had always turned me on mentally. That mental stimulation was what made me crave him. He was a force to be reckoned with not only in the courtroom but also in the bedroom. He had mastered the art of making love to a woman mentally.

"Is that the politically correct term or something?" Michael asked. "Why not just say, 'Eating pussy'?"

David chuckled. The way Michael had said, 'Eating pussy,' was soothing, too. Don't get me wrong. Being crass was a great thing, but you had to know when to be tactless. Michael's timing was on. It turned me on too, for some reason. The abrasiveness of the phrase tickled my yoni. David was my mental stimulation. Got that fire in me blazing. Michael threw the gasoline on it.

I spoke up. "It's more appealing for me mentally to refer to it as cunnilingus."

"Sounds like an STD," Michael said.

I laughed low.

Michael spoke up again. "I'd much rather perform the act of eating your pussy."

I turned my attention back to David and asked his permission again. "I would like that too."

"No," David said.

"Do you give head?" Michael asked, acting as if David's answer didn't bother him.

"She performs fellatio," David answered for me.

Michael squinted. "Say what?"

"She doesn't give head. What she does is more. She doesn't just slobber, spit, and suck. She makes love to your lingam with her mouth."

My back arched as David talked. He'd been listening when we talked about tantric sex.

"Lingam, huh? Not dick, but lingam," Michael mused and nodded. I found it comical that he knew what *lingam* meant but not *cunnilingus*. "She's trouble, David."

David shrugged, kissed me once more, and then stood. Grabbed his glasses as he took in the sight of my body for a long while before responding. "Doesn't matter. I've always liked getting into trouble."

# David

## Seduction . . .

Summer was seducing me. That was the only thing I could think of as I watched her. She was on the dance floor with Michael. Both of them were working their hips in ways that let you know they had island in their blood. I wasn't too sure about Summer, but I knew the island in Michael was on full display. He was grinding and winding his hips behind Summer's backside like he had been born to do it. Made any hip thrusting and gyrating that Chris Brown was known for seem juvenile.

The rest of the people in the secret, dimly lit club stopped dancing to watch them. Women looked at Summer as if she had violated some code of womanhood by being that wanton in public. There were women in the building whose bodies rivaled those of video vixens. They still had nothing on her. Summer was voluptuous. She wore every bit of her size sixteen with pride. Threw that fat ass and her thick hips around like she had no worries. Michael was in a zone. Hypnotized by her shapely rump and surprised at the way she worked with him. I could tell by the way he was biting down on his bottom lip and was keeping his gaze fixed on her. He was controlling their movements with one hand wrapped around her waist.

My ex-lover and my possible future ex-lover tried to get a sexual healing through dancing. The way Michael was tuned in to her, you could tell he was begging her to heal him. I watched on in silence as I sipped my poison for the evening. Wondered what it would be like to have them both naked in a room with me alone. I knew what it felt like to be with Michael that way, but I had no idea how deep Summer could go once I dipped in her love. As if they knew what I'd been thinking, both of them looked over at me. Summer's back was to Michael as they swayed to the beat.

Summer's eyes didn't say yes . . . but they didn't say no, either. Curiosity hung in the air around her. After what Michael had done to her in that movie theater, she carried this look of curiosity in her eyes. Curiosity was going to kill her cat. Satisfaction would be eager to revive it. I watched them both with equal intensity until the song faded out. A few people clapped as the two of them left the dance floor. Michael's dick was hard. I could see it trying to free itself from behind the zipper of his slacks.

They both walked over with smiles on their faces. For a few moments, they stood in front of our table, smiling, talking, and sensually eyeing one another. I was invisible to them. Michael excused himself to go to the bathroom. Probably to rub one out again. I'd never seen a woman get to him the way Summer had . . . not even Sadi. That part alone should have warned me that trouble was on the way. I ignored the warning signs, though. I was too caught up watching the way their bodies moved in sync with one another.

"I'm hungry," Summer said to me as she eased my drink from my hand. "You hungry?" she asked me after she took a sip.

"I could eat something," I answered.

I didn't mean for my words to come out like that, but the insinuation behind them and the way she blushed at my words made me smirk. She flagged down a passing waitress. Ordered fifty wings, a basket of fries, and Sprites for the three of us.

"Does Michael eat hot wings?" Summer asked me. She was including him in things now. Just that quick two was company, and three . . . It wasn't a crowd yet.

"Lemon pepper," I told her.

She asked the waitress to make half the wing order to Michael's liking. Things had changed within a matter of hours between the three of us. Michael wanted Summer. I wanted Summer. I wanted Michael. Michael wanted me. Neither of us knew what Summer wanted. After the conversation at her house about cunnilingus and fellatio, I had told Summer that she had to get dressed, or we were all going to cross a line from which there would be no return.

"This place is nice," she said once she finished ordering food for us. "How long have you known about it?" she asked.

I glanced around the club again. It was packed to capacity. They couldn't let anyone else in, or the fire marshal would shut it down. It wasn't that big to begin with. Small and intimate. Perfect setting for what took place once the doors were locked. Bowls of condoms in different colors sat out in the open. Lubricants, whips, chains, handcuffs, whatever you were into, were provided. Beds lined the walls, but tonight wasn't the night they could be used. You could do anything you wanted to do out in the open tonight except have actual intercourse. Only the bar stools, booths, tables, and lounge chairs could be used tonight, unless, of course, you went to one of the private rooms.

"Since college."

She looked around the place. Saw couples of every orientation milling about, and her gears started turning. "You've never brought me here before," she said.

"Didn't think you would like it."

"But you brought me here now." Her fingers were tapping the table. I could tell she wanted to ask a question that she really didn't want to know the answer to.

"Sometimes, no matter how comfortable some of us are with our sexuality, we still need a place where we can mingle without the constant stares and the judgments about who we are. We need a place to be free of all of that," I said to her.

"And this is it? This is like a safe haven, then?"

"Give or take a word."

We both watched as a couple sat at a table with a flamboyantly gay male. The matching wedding bands told us they were married. The woman whispered in the gay male's ear, while her husband looked around nervously. The gay male smiled at the man once the woman had finished. Summer looked on as he took the husband's hand and led him to a back room.

Summer looked at me. "This a hookup spot?"

"Give or take a word."

"You ever hook up with anybody here?"

I shook my head. "No. I don't get ass and slang dick with random people."

"Michael?"

"No."

"You two used to come here a lot?"

"Yes."

"To get away?"

"To get away."

She stared at me for a long time. Those freckles danced around her cheeks under the lights. She batted her long lashes as we watched one another. She had cornrowed her hair back into two big braids. The style brought out those high cheekbones she had. Thigh-high boots with six-inch heels adorned her feet. A teal minidress that barely contained all she had to offer was her attire. The bottom of it stopped below her ass, cupping it as a lover would. Her breasts were on full display for the world to see.

She sidled up to me. Laid a delicate hand on my cheek and smiled somewhat. She was trying. Trying hard to accept that part of who I was. Trying not to be jealous of the men in the room, including the one strolling back our way from the men's room. Michael stopped and flirted with a few women in the place. Summer grunted and rolled her eyes. I knew what she was feeling. I felt it every time she and Michael touched.

"You and Michael—" she began but then stopped.

"Me and Michael what?" I asked her.

"You two always share women?"

"We have on more than one occasion."

"So there's nothing special about it or about the women you've shared?"

I finished off my drink. Signaled to the waitress for another. She smiled and winked at me. Summer sighed and folded her arms across her ample chest. I smiled at her and pulled her close to me. She was jealous. Had always been. I didn't know why she felt the need to be. I only had eyes for her. But she was asking questions, showing interest. That was a good thing. I didn't answer her question verbally. Held her close to me and stared down languidly into her brown eyes. The liquor had me a little lit, but not to the point of inebriation.

We had been at the club for a little over an hour. Had danced together and separately. Had let the dim lighting and the erotic ambiance of the place get us higher in lust than we should have been. Both of us had decided to ignore the fact that Michael was married. I held her like she belonged to me. In my mind she did. I didn't want to share, but I had learned long ago that when it came to Michael, I always had to share. One way or another, with him, I had to share.

"We had sex with women together. Shared one or four. They didn't have to be special to get sex. We were in it for instant gratification," I told her.

"What about men? You two share men too?"

"Once or five times."

Her breathing deepened, and she looked away again. Looked at Michael as he flirted with some woman who looked as if she belonged at Magic City on Mondays. She got quiet. Didn't ask me anything else. A few minutes later our wings came. Summer and I sat down to eat.

She fed me a few, and then I had had enough. While she sucked the hot wing sauce from her fingers, I slipped my hand underneath her dress. Eased her lace thong to the side and played in her sex. She was wet. Clit was firm. I wanted her badly. Needed to touch her, because I had to be sure it was all real. Had to make sure Summer was in an underground sex club/safe haven and was allowing me to finger fuck her underneath the table as she ate hot wings. Her walls quivered, which caused her PC muscles to grip my fingers in a choke hold. She stopped eating when my two fingers strummed her core bud. Took a moment to drop her head and call on the Son of God.

I hated when she hid her face from me. I wanted to see her climax. Wanted to see if she gave me that same ugly come face as she had before. There was something so uninhibited and primal about the way she made that face. I looked across the room to see Michael watching us. He could read my body language. Knew I was stirring the pot. I pulled my fingers from Summer's love, then licked each one as if syrup dripped from it. Michael rolled his shoulders. Whatever Ms. Magic City Monday was talking about got lost in translation when he walked off and made his way back to the table.

Summer looked up as he sat next to her, and wiped her fingers with the Wet-Naps. She'd ordered wings for him, but when he tried to get one, she moved the basket. He tried to kiss her, and she turned her head. Gave that kiss to me. I accepted it with no problem. She was showing her displeasure with him. Turned her back to him to show her contempt for him, which was the result of him not giving her his full attention. Summer was spoiled. She felt entitled. It would do him some good to remember that.

Michael chuckled, then leaned forward and clasped his hands together on the table. "It's like that?" he asked her.

She cast a glance at him over her shoulder. "You say something?" she asked flippantly.

It was my turn to chuckle then. "She's spoiled, bruh," I told him.

"Yeah?" he asked while looking her up and down. She had crossed one leg over the other as she leaned into me, so he got a full side view of her ass and thighs. He couldn't keep his eyes off of either. "I'll remember that next time," he finally added.

Summer grunted her response. Slipped her hand into my slacks and held me in her hand. I loved when she did that shit. Made me feel like I belonged to her. She snaked her tongue out and licked my top lip, then bit my bottom one. The alcohol couldn't get me intoxicated, but Summer was taking my blood level way past the legal limit. She licked my chin and let her teeth graze me there. Bit down into my neck firmly, but gently enough to give me that pain and pleasure I longed for. My head fell back from my desire and arousal. Like I knew her, she knew me.

Eight years . . . eight fucking years I'd waited . . . just so I had to share.

My eyes opened when I felt Michael slide up behind her. He wouldn't be denied. His big hand gripped and massaged her backside. Michael rubbed up and down her thighs as he placed kisses against her shoulders. As if he'd said, "Open sesame," her legs slowly spread. He was quick to take the opening. Slid his hands between her thighs, like her pussy belonged to him. The waitress walked over and sat my drink on the table. She couldn't take her eyes off my dick. Summer had pulled it out and had started to stroke it like it was hers to do with what she pleased.

Her eyes were closed. Her head had fallen back because Michael was fingering her love and sucking her left breast. While her head was thrown back, she couldn't pay attention to his hand, which was leaving her wet pussy and making its way over to my hard dick. She tensed. Stopped stroking when she felt his hand join hers. I took my drink to the head. Summer looked down. Michael never looked up. His hand was wrapped around hers, and he used her hand to stroke my manhood.

I twisted my neck from side to side. Had to roll my shoulders. The shirt I had on seemed to be getting smaller in size. I slid forward a bit on the seat. Needed to get comfortable. I was tense. Summer's heated gaze was on me now. She was looking me right in the eyes. She looked confused. Nervous. Unsure of what was going on, what was about to happen. Michael still had her hand and was jacking me off while sucking her breasts like a feeding infant.

"Want to stop?" I found the words to ask her. Yeah, the whole thing had me in a zone, but none of it mattered if she was uncomfortable.

She slowly shook her head. Michael raised his head, looked over at me while he continued to use her hand to pleasure me.

"Let me eat her pussy, David," he practically pleaded.

"No," David told him.

He made a clicking sound with his lips. "Ask her if she wants me to."

"No."

"Ask her." He talked while one of his hands slid back between her legs and the other continued to hold her hand and stroke me.

I licked my lips, trying to get my breathing under control. Summer's eyes were at half-mast, but she could see me. I could tell she wanted it. Didn't want to ask her, because I knew she would say yes. I was being possessive and selfish. Didn't want another nigga to get what I'd been working so hard to have, no matter who it was.

Still, I asked, "Do you want him to eat your pussy?"

"Yes."

"Are you going to come?"

"I . . . I don't know," she answered.

"I'm going to be mad if you do."

"Okay," she said.

I looked at Michael. Didn't want to, but I gave him permission. We had an audience. People had gathered around discreetly and were watching. Michael dropped to his knees with ease. When that nigga's tongue snaked out to its full length, half the women and the men in the room gasped. Summer's eyes widened. She wasn't expecting the length and thickness of his kitty licker. No woman ever was. As soon as his tongue flattened and licked her from back to front, she shivered. A sound erupted from her that gave the impression that she was about to speak in tongues. Her legs spread wider on their own. He didn't have to open them. She was spread-eagle for him.

I looked on as he spread her lips with his tongue. Became a voyeur with the rest of the room as he lapped at her vaginal entrance and then traveled up to her clit. He flicked the tip of his tongue back and forth so quick, it looked like a serpent's tongue.

"Ayeee," Summer cried like she was Spanish.

She was making that ugly come face for him. He ran his tongue between her inner and outer lips. Fucked her pussy with his tongue. In and out, around and around. Every time he did that tongue-flicking thing, she gripped my dick tighter. He made her stroke harder while he stiffened his tongue. Flicked here and there, but kept going back to her clit. Rubbed his face in her pretty pussy.

Summer's head was turning from side to side. Her back was arching, bowing forward, then backward. She was baring her teeth. She couldn't take the tongue-lashing he was giving her. Her clit was fully exposed; her pearl at full peak. Michael pulled back, let his tongue extend past his chin—he was showing off for his audience—then licked Summer from her center and closed his lips around her vaginal lips until he got to her clitoris. Pulled that pink morsel into his mouth and sucked gently . . . at first. I leaned forward. Quickly inserted my index and ring fingers into her. I stroked slowly . . . at first. Michael sucked hard. I pushed my fingers in and out of her harder. Michael sucked faster. I stroked faster. Tapped that beautiful G-spot until it looked as if she was crying.

"Ah, God, David! Oh, my God . . . ," she all but yelled.

We tag teamed her. While he focused on the organ made strictly for her pleasure, I focused on a spot to intensify it. Michael still had her hand in his and was still jacking my dick. Shit was intoxicatingly mind-numbing. I could feel myself about to explode, but I wouldn't. Not yet. Not until she did. In a matter of seconds, before my thoughts had even been formulated, I snatched my fingers from her love and watched her drown Michael in her come.

"Shit!" he yelled and jumped back in shock.

She kept squirting. Looked like she was about to cry. People around the room whispered aggressively. Talked about what had happened. They wanted to experience what she had.

Michael ran a hand down his face. Summer's body kept erupting. That didn't stop that greedy nigga, though. He went back in for more. Kept eating her out until she couldn't take any more. Once she caught her breath, she looked over at me. She couldn't breathe, like always. Only this time she didn't give me a chance to breathe for her. She dropped her head in my lap. She removed her hand from Michael's. Made him hold my dick while she sucked me off. Coated my dick in warm saliva while using his hand as a placeholder. Then she used his hand to stroke me while she blew me.

I was somewhere between oblivion and torture.

"Fuck," I groaned.

It was my turn to make the ugly come face, especially when she felt my head swell. She knew it was the signal for my climax. Summer took me to the back of her throat, and I released like a geyser. I had to grab her head. My hips bucked, and I was afraid I was going to choke her, but she didn't let up. My ass cheeks were clenched, and I'd lifted myself a few inches from the seat.

"Summer . . . baby . . . ," I growled low.

She got my meaning. I'd already turned into a punk in front of my boy. She wouldn't make me turn into a bitch any further, like she'd done in the shower. She sat up. Looked around and was ashamed that people were staring. She was struggling to breathe, but so was I. So I couldn't breathe for her. Michael did it for me. He removed his hand from my dick and took her mouth. Kissed her to the point that she was damn near another orgasm.

A few minutes later, after we'd gotten ourselves together as best we could, Summer wearing my dress shirt wrapped around her waist because she'd soaked another dress, we did our walk of shame out of our den of iniquity. The night air slapped us all as soon as we walked out the double doors. The wind acted as the hand of God, chastising us for fornicating and committing adultery.

Summer had spaghetti legs. She stumbled and almost fell. Both Michael and I caught her arms. She giggled nervously. We laughed at her. She tried to walk again, only to stumble again. I scooped her into my arms and walked for her. Michael's phone kept ringing. Sadi wanted to know where her husband was.

"Hello," he answered. His voice was deep enough that he sounded as if he was asleep, but he wasn't. He was stimulated sexually, so his voice had dropped an octave. I remembered that voice. Remembered how he sounded late at night, when the getting was good.

I let him handle talking to his wife as I got Summer to my truck. She wrapped her arms around my neck. Laid her head on my shoulder and relaxed.

"You let him make you come again," I told her.

"*You* made me come," she replied.

"His mouth was on you."

"Your fingers were in me. I called out one man's name."

That hadn't been lost on me. He'd been giving her more pleasure than she could handle, but not once had she called his name. She'd called mine, though. I kissed her lips as I carried her. She smiled.

"Tomorrow. I fly out tomorrow," Michael was saying as he walked up to us.

I was putting Summer in the front seat. I buckled her seat belt and was about to shut the door when she pulled me back down to kiss her. I was just as eager to return the kiss. She moaned loudly. Grabbed my dick through my pants and rubbed it aggressively. She was hot and bothered. I needed to get her home.

# Summer

Trojan Magnums, I was allergic to those. He knew that. So we tried Durex XL. We stopped at a local CVS, and the three of us examined the different brands of condoms together as we held hands. David held my right hand. Michael held my left. People stared at us openly. Wondered what the hell we were about to get into and why we were brazen enough to broadcast it. We didn't care. At least I knew I didn't. All I cared about was feeling David, and possibly Michael, inside me. For that, we needed protection.

Michael was playing in my hair, taking my two corn-rows out, as David continued to examine the condoms. Michael kissed my neck. Said he had to touch me in some way. Promised he couldn't keep his hands off me. While David asked a random store clerk who was passing by if Durex condoms were really extra-large, Michael kept kissing me. People kept watching. We still didn't care. While Michael paid for the condoms, David whispered in my ear. Told me he wanted to fuck me hard, make love to me gently, and have sex with me passionately all at the same time. I giggled like a schoolgirl. I wanted him to do all of those things too.

The Durex XLs didn't fit. Too small. David said they felt more like LifeStyles condoms. He was thick. Dick was thicker than a full-grown cucumber. So damn copious. He was annoyed. I was frustrated. Sexually so. We didn't want to go back out and take the time to find an XL condom that fit.

Rain had started to fall. My kind of weather. The rain mixed with the cold was titillating for me. I opened my window a bit. Liked the way a gust of cold air would creep under the sash from time to time and join in. The air wrapped us in a cocoon that no one could penetrate.

"We need protection," David told me.

I responded, "I know."

"Can't do it without it."

"Have to be safe and responsible."

"Yeah . . ."

He was between my legs, naked. What a sight he was to behold when he was naked. Shoulders broad, chest sculpted, abs perfectly molded into six perfect packs, which led down to a V cut so flawless that I had to stare at it for moments. There, below that V, sat what made him anatomically male. That slight curve, though. I had to watch out for that curve.

There I lay, underneath my best friend, while his best friend watched from a chair across the room. Michael was naked too. He was lying back in my big chair, with a towel underneath him, as he manhandled his own dick. He needed two hands to do it. Something about Michael's hands turned me on. They were so big, he could palm one of my ass cheeks easily with only one of them. I enjoyed that. Even though his face was shielded by the shadows in the room, I knew he was watching us. He was breathing hard. Chest moving up and down. His abs constricting with each breath. Those calves and thighs of his were powerful. He was taller than David. Legs were longer. More muscle, more horsepower resided in those thighs.

David brought my attention back to him. The head of his dick was leveled at the entrance to my love.

"Status?" I said to him.

"Negative."

"You positive?"

"Positive it's a negative," he answered assuredly. Then he asked me, "Status?"

"Negative."

"You positive?"

"Positive it's a negative," I responded in kind.

I was so wet. So fucking wet. Past the point of rethinking what we were about to do. I took David's glasses off his face. Placed them over my eyes and wrapped my arms around his neck. He chuckled. I smiled. We had forgone the bed. We'd stopped at my oversize couch and let our clothes fall where they may.

My legs widened so he could fall deeper between them. The passion brewing between us had been a long time coming. So much so that when his head broke skin, both of us stopped breathing for a second. David almost lost control. I was caught off guard by how much he filled me up. Damn. He filled me up beyond capacity. I bit down on my lower lip, hissed, backed up a bit, and stared up at him. He followed me, sinking deeper and deeper into my love below as he did so. He kept his eyes on me. Affixed me to him so I could see and feel what I had been missing.

I had thought he would be gentle. Had thought he would ease me into taking all he had to offer, but no. David gave me all of him right away. More than I could stand. Sank so deep into me that before he gave me the first stroke, my eyes were widening due to the threat of an orgasm.

"Eight years, Summer. You made me wait eight damn years just so I would have to share you," he said. His eyes told me he was angry. He was holding on to that passion that he was anxious to express so that he could show me how angry he was.

"I'm so—"

"Don't apologize. Too late," he growled.

He pulled all the way out of me. Dipped his head to kiss me as he aggressively entered me again. When my tongue snaked out to meet his, he sucked it into his mouth, pulled back out, and then slowly eased back inside me. I was hot. On fire. Droplets of rain broke through the window screen. Splashed against his back, my face, thighs, breasts. As David worked his hips up and down like he was a professional dancer, he sucked my neck. Didn't forget about my ears. My ears were sensitive. A pleasure zone that many men had ignored. But not David. He paid both of them the same attention. He let his breath heat them up. Licked and nibbled as he made me act like I'd never before had the kind of sex he was giving me.

"Damn," Michael groaned from across the room.

Both David and I turned to look at him. Michael was in his own state of bliss. He got to watch both me and David in an orgasmic tailspin of coitus. Michael was coming. David never broke stroke as we both watched Michael struggle to keep his composure.

"You feel so good, David," I whispered in his ear. He grunted. I kept talking. Let my teeth nick his ear. "Damn, you feel so good. I hate this shit," I said.

"You feel even better, baby. So fucking tight and wet," he groaned low as he shut his eyes tightly, then opened them quickly, like he'd remembered he didn't want to miss anything.

My nails dug into his back. I cried out when he put a hump in back. He stopped making love to me and started to fuck me. Went deeper, harder, with just enough force to make me hyperventilate and convulse. His hips beat against mine like African drums. Worked in a rhythm that had him sweating. I worked my hips with him. Had to give it back as good as I was getting it. The muscles in his arms coiled underneath his skin as he caged me. Pushed my knees past my ears. Opened me up to him so he could feel the full depth of what I claimed I hated.

There was nothing between us. No barrier. He was swelling. Stretching my walls until they accommodated him. Giving me those nine inches he had bragged about the night before, because the pussy was good. I moaned a song of pain and pleasure. I didn't know which I wanted more, the pain or the pleasure. Both were so damn good to me. So fucking good to me. My moans encouraged him as he stroked deeper inside me with a sense of urgency. He was on a mission. I wanted to help him get there. My pussy would forever be stamped with the name David.

"Say it, Summer," he demanded in a voice not his own.

He was lost with me. He had gone off the love we were making. He was straining to hold on. Like he wanted me to know what I was doing to him. Had done to him.

"David . . . please . . . don't . . ." I didn't want to say it. He was going to make me say it. He was going to have his way one way or the other.

"Stop playing with me," he demanded as he blanketed my body with his. "Say. It."

His arms enclosed my thighs, spread my cheeks, and he got deeper. David was skilled. Too confident in those skills. He had played the game with me long enough. Now it was time for me to play by his rules. God, his rules were so damn hard. Shit, they were so hard. . . .

I heard Michael groan. It was something guttural that sounded like it had come from a big cat on the savanna of Africa. I focused my attention on Michael, as much of it as David would allow, long enough to see his creamy satisfaction oozing over his big hands. David got bolder. Dipped his head down to take on sucking both breasts, moving from one to the other, as he pumped like he was trying to get me hooked on him.

The sex David was giving me was anything but ideal. It went beyond what regular people thought of as sex. No, what David was giving me was years of pent-up aggression. Years of chasing this pussy. When he had finally got it, he'd pounced on it. Claimed me as his own. Pulled out, with my come coloring his dick like creamy glaze on a doughnut. Flipped me over onto my stomach and entered me again, forcefully. I roared out like an animal in the wild. He bit down on the back of my neck. Snarled, with a low rumble in his throat. He snatched the back of my hair and made me raise my head. The move made me arch perfectly into his hips. I raised my hips inches off the couch so I could throw my ass back into him.

"Ahhh, God! Fuck, yes! Yes, David, yes."

"Mine?" he asked.

It took me too long to answer. He rode me harder, deeper. I couldn't answer. My eyes had rolled to the back of my head. I was struggling to catch my breath. His tongue traveled down the base of my neck. The love we were making was brutal yet sensual. Animalistic yet beautiful. He had . . . He had me.

Michael stood, made his way halfway across the room until he was stopped in his tracks.

"No," David said with so much venom that it scared me.

Michael backed away. He wasn't invited this time around. David was claiming me as his own. Michael had no right to that part of us. The alpha male had showed his dominance, making Michael the beta. If he had come any closer, it was clear he would have become the omega.

David had claimed me. I was his and his alone.

"Mine?" he asked me again. His hands were gripping my waist so tight that his nails were breaking my skin. He was deep. Fucking me hard. Loving me long. Passionately having sex with me all at once.

I shivered. "Yes, David, yes. Yours. Jesus, it's yours!"

***

Hours later, rain was still beating down on the roof and against the windowpanes of my townhome. David lay asleep on his side of my bed. Michael had been on the other side before he got up to take his wife's phone call. They'd sandwiched me. We'd played another game of oral fixation. I'd given Michael the treatment I gave David in the club. I'd wanted to return the favor for what he had done to me. So I had wrapped my lips around the head of his manhood and had made his ass clench too. I'd placed butterfly kisses against those powerful thighs. Used my nails to rake up and down his inner thighs as I pleased him with my mouth.

Michael couldn't handle my mouth the way David could. His come had started to seep out long before I got to the high point of my oral presentation. I'd stroked his shaft with both my hands, then moved one to fondle his scrotum. Lifted that heavy sack and licked his perineum. That was one of the moves that had made David putty in the palms of my hands in the shower. I didn't give head. I performed the art of fellatio. Giving head took no skill. I took pride in sucking their dicks. It gave me pleasure to see these strong, powerful alpha males become so weak in those moments. His release came shooting out at me like a stream. I didn't swallow his seed, as I'd done with David. I was trying to save something for his wife.

I watched David as he slept. He always had on his glasses when he went to sleep. No matter what I said or how I fussed, he still slept in his glasses. I removed them from his face and placed them on the nightstand. The males in my home had eventually gone back downstairs to pick up their clothes from my front-room floor, which meant that I had to do the same, or David would fuss. Michael's clothes lay across the back of the chair in my bedroom, nice and neat. David's lay across the sitting stool in the corner, and were also neatly folded. My dress and shoes for the evening were still scattered about downstairs.

Rather than go downstairs and find my clothes, I continued to watch David as he slept. I was sure that Michael turned him on as much as I did. When he had realized Michael's hand was touching him with mine when we were in the club, his arousal had shot up another level. As much as I hated to admit it, something about that moment had given me a natural high. I had to be honest. Still, there was jealousy there. My phone beeped just then, informing me of the call I'd missed. I'd check it later.

I climbed out of bed and walked into the bathroom. Released the fluid that had my bladder aching. I washed my hands, my face. Brushed my teeth and wiped Michael's dried come off my chest with a warm, soapy towel. I walked back out to find David lying on his back, one arm thrown over his head and one hand on his dick. His chocolate body was the epitome of perfection. He lay there like an African god in the afterglow of our act of congress.

I could hear echoes of Michael's voice downstairs. Michael hadn't been back to his hotel room all day. I wondered if his wife had any clue as to what he was up to. Did her womanly intuition have her calling him like she had been? I looked back at David and imagined what it would be like to see him and Michael together. They were both so alpha, I found it hard to imagine either of them bent over, taking dick. David had told me repeatedly that he was always the giver and never the taker. Did that apply to the man downstairs too?

David had made me say yes. He'd made me say what he'd been trying to have me say for the past eight years. My mind kept flashing back to when he'd made Michael back up off me. Something about that had me wanting to be fucked again. I wanted David to do again what he'd done to me in that moment. He was so licentious that it was mesmerizing. I would give anything to see David's come face again. Moments before he released, he'd been the one in control. He'd wanted to see my face again. Had flipped me over and had kissed me as he slowed his strokes down. He had kissed me vigorously and then had pulled back. Had tried to hide his face between my neck and shoulder blades. It had felt like he was about to cheat me out of seeing the pleasure I could bring him.

*"Look at me, David. Please, baby, look at me. Let me see," I coaxed.*

*His arms were shaking as I felt his dick swell more. That curve in his dick, that slight curve, was my undoing. He'd used it to his advantage. He'd seen all my love faces. I wanted to see his. He slowly pulled his head up. He was weak. So damn feeble as he tried to hold on for as long as he could. There was something about the way he was looking at me. Something about the way he was pleading with me not to move. His hands held my hips still.*

*"Shit, baby." He held his breath.*

*I slowly rocked my hips.*

*"Summer!" His body jerked.*

*I lifted my hips and moved in sync with him.*

*"Ah, fuck, baby." He shut his eyes tight. His head fell back. Mouth was half open. "Fuck." He let go. Dropped his forehead against mine and went harder again. Deeper still. Faster and breathlessly, until I felt him paint my walls with his release.*

*It had all been so damn intense that he collapsed on top of me. I couldn't breathe for him, and he couldn't breathe for me. For a long while the three of us lay there. Michael in the chair. David between my thighs on the couch. My hands played in his locks until I fell asleep. I woke up a few minutes later and found myself being carried up the stairs to my room.*

That was where we all had been until Michael's phone woke me up.

I walked downstairs to find him standing in my kitchen, shirtless. His boxer briefs hugged the perfect globes of his tight ass. There was a long diagonal keloid going down his back. Like somebody had tried sliced him open before. The scar didn't take away from the brute strength that showed when he moved. The sinewy muscles in his back were on display, indicating the time he had spent in the gym. He was still on the phone with his wife as he ate grapes and drank a bottle of my Fiji water. He'd made himself at home in my place. He spilled some water on the counter and started to look around for something to wipe it up with.

I walked over to the sink, reached under it, and handed him a paper towel. He smiled at me. Eyed me hungrily. I was as naked as the day I was born. He was wearing only his boxer briefs. I wanted to see him naked. Had never seen him completely naked other than when he was touching himself while he watched me and David earlier. Even then most of his body had been covered by the shadows. I was so busy staring at the physical man he was that I barely heard my Bose speakers playing. I blushed at the way he eyed me.

I tried to walk away, and he stopped me. Grabbed my hand and gently pulled me to him. Jesus, he smelled good. Before, when I first met him, I had sniffed him slyly. This time, I did it shamelessly. Stood on my toes and sniffed his neck as I heard his wife's voice through the phone. He grunted low and chuckled.

"Mike, what are you doing?" she asked him.

He had her on speakerphone. "Nothing," he answered.

"Are you touching yourself? I'm sure you are. You're in love with your own dick," she said, then giggled.

He wrapped one arm around me. Grabbed one handful of my ass while popping a grape into his mouth. "Something like that," he answered.

Michael lowered his mouth to mine. Offered me a piece of his fruit. I kept my eyes on his as I accepted his offering. It was probably a mistake to do so. I probably shouldn't have taken a bite of that fruit from his lips. David was in my bed, sleeping. I started to feel like I was cheating on him. I wanted to pull back, but when Michael's lips touched mine, I started to crave the kiss he'd given me earlier. Wanted to see blinding lights behind my eyelids again as he kissed me.

"Stop playing with yourself," his wife said. "When you come home, I'll do it for you."

I slipped my hand into his boxer briefs. He gave something akin to a guttural grumble. "Nah, I've started now. Gotta see it to the end."

His wife's voice was silky, almost like she tricked men into paying $5.99 a minute so they could get off on her voice alone. I hadn't fucked her husband . . . technically. The only thing he had penetrated on me was my mouth. He'd skillfully eaten my pussy. I was almost positive she wouldn't be happy about that. Still, there was something about the way we were in that moment that made me want to do more than technically have him penetrate me. Michael's dick didn't come with that slight curve that I was enamored with, but he was packing enough meat to do more than fill you to the rim. His dick came with a thickness that made it heavy in the palms of your hands.

Michael licked his lips and laid his phone on the island. He picked me up and sat me next to his phone before standing between my legs.

"You're such a fucking perv, Michael. You'll play with your dick just because you have one," his wife said. Although she laughed, there was something in her voice that said her husband touching himself annoyed her.

"It's mine. I like the way my dick feels in my hand, so I touch it."

"Ugh. My God. Do you have to be so freaking filthy all the time?" she asked.

Michael kissed me. Tongue traced the outside of my lips before he answered his wife. "I'm talking to my wife. Why can't I be as filthy as I want?"

"Maybe your wife doesn't want to be filthy all the time," his wife said.

He didn't respond right away. He sighed and exhaled loudly. Kind of like a teenage boy would if his mother chastised him about going down the wrong path. His wife didn't like the fact that he was a freak. It sounded as if he had to stifle or hide who he was when he was around her. I wondered if she'd always been that way. Wondered if she had been a prude when she'd fucked David too or if her prudery was reserved for her husband. As stupid as it sounded, I was jealous of her. I was mad that she had fucked the man I wanted . . . the one I was secretly in love with. I was going to fuck her husband like she'd fucked David.

I slid to the end of the island. Let my tongue trace over each of his nipples as my hand continued to play in his underwear. I let my tongue glide smoothly over his chocolate skin, relishing the taste of him. He was hard. Harder than he had been in the movie theater. He was looking at me like he wanted to show me another side of adultery. Like he wanted to show me what it was like to get him with all his sexual fortitude.

While I kissed him, one of his hands slipped between my legs. There was no fingering this time. He wanted to see if I was wet. I needed to be well lubricated to handle what he was packing. Like before with David, I had to be relaxed. Relaxed and well lubricated.

It had been two years. I had been feeling it in every muscle I owned ever since David had released me. My inner thighs, my hip bone, and the like felt as if I'd been doing squats for hours. Two years, no dick. It had been two days now, and I was about to be the recipient of a second satisfying dick. I welcomed it.

My heart skipped a beat when I heard David moving around upstairs. I didn't know if he would be okay with what Michael and I were doing without him.

"I didn't ask you to be. You asked me what I was doing, and I told you," Michael said to his wife.

"Well, play with your dick enough while you're in Atlanta so I won't have to walk in on you playing with it here," she fussed. "You do that crap way too much."

Her voice was no longer silky smooth. There was venom there, like she hated the fact that her husband was so in tune with his sexuality. Michael sidled up to the island, gripped my thighs. We both turned when we heard David walking down the stairs. When he entered the kitchen, I gasped at the way he looked. His locks swinging back and forth, he stalked closer to both of us. His eyes were alive. The look on his face told me he wanted more of me, needed more of me. While my eyes took in the man whom I loved past the point of being friends, though I hated to admit it, Michael discarded his underwear and eased his way inside me.

I couldn't help it. A moan escaped my lips that was so sensual, Michael had to place his tongue in my mouth to quiet me. I eased back, breaking the kiss he had used to silence me. I hissed as my hands gripped both sides of the island. The cool feeling of it, along with Michael's invasion of my inner walls, forced an arch to form in my back that was so deep, it hurt.

Michael answered his wife. "Don't worry. I will."

"Is that porn, Mike? You're watching disgusting whores and desperate men screw for a fee, right?" she nagged, the disgust clearly showing in her voice.

"If that's what you want to call it."

My eyes watched David as he watched us. I couldn't read him. I didn't know what he was thinking anymore, but I was happy when he walked forward and placed his lips on mine. He had to silence me. He was helping to cover up his friend's adulterous fuck session. Michael had placed his palm flat against my pelvis, and he was using the heel of his hand to press down as he worked his hips. The way he had danced earlier, moved his hips like he was born and bred in the Caribbean, proved that he could do it while naked too.

My legs started to shake. David's upper body covered me while he tongued me down. His hands were all over my breasts, massaging them, and then they slid down my stomach and to my clit to help his best friend out. He was seducing my senses with his touch. Still, I moaned into his mouth. My back arched farther, and my hips started to thrust back into Michael.

"And you're going to turn the volume up so I can hear it, huh?" his wife asked. "Good night, Mike," she said.

He didn't respond. Kept pumping into me like he was trying to make me his, and then he stopped. Stopped abruptly, like he hadn't been about to make me lose my mind. He stood between my thighs, dick inside me, pulsating. Anytime his dick thumped, my Kegel muscles responded in kind. He pulled out. Picked up his phone to make sure his wife was gone and then put his focus back on me. Used his head to thrust between the folds of my pussy, stimulating my clit more. He did that until I was sweating and practically begging him to fuck me. When he finally did give in to my request, he went in deep. Made me take all of him. Pressed his pelvic bone against my clitoris so that as he fucked me, my clit would feel that heated friction.

His wife had to be out of her damned mind not to appreciate the animal he was.

# David

We were locked in a perpetual war of lovemaking. The harder he fucked her, the harder I fucked him. There was jealousy laced with tension and sensual madness in each of my thrusts. Each time he made her moan, hiss, arch, and throw her pussy back at him, I buried myself deeper into him. Summer had come to me, had asked me to show her this side of me. She wanted to see me with Michael.

"You sure?" I'd asked her.

She'd nodded, but she had been nervous. I could tell. "Yeah. I want to see . . . you with him. I need to see it to accept it."

"You don't have to see it."

"I have to, David, trust me."

I had thumbed my bottom lip and glanced around the room. Michael was quiet. Had been quiet since the phone call with his wife and his escapade with Summer. He was listening, though. I could tell he was listening by the way he leaned forward and looked at us. We had all showered and were lounging around in Summer's front room. Music was playing, and we were basking in the afterglow of supernova sex.

"Can you handle it? If we go there, will you be able to handle it?" I asked her to be sure.

She shrugged. "I don't know, but I'm willing to at least try. I want to see. I saw how you reacted to him when he touched you in the club. I saw you two kiss. I handled it okay. I don't want to deny you the pleasure you've been giving me. I can handle it, David."

I was shocked. I wasn't expecting her to ask to see the other side of me. I looked back at Michael. There was no need for me to ask if he was willing. I knew he would be. I wanted to touch him. Wanted to be with him. Hadn't had a connection with any man the way he and I had connected. That was the way it had always been. When I had seen him strut across the Morehouse campus, he and I had connected.

I'd been trying to stick to my guns, to abstain, the whole time, being that he was married. Not so much that he was married, because at least if his wife had known about that side of him, I wouldn't feel like I was being the stereotypical down-low nigga who deceived women. Being reckless and adding to the negativity surrounding black men, homosexuality, and bisexuality. Yet I was willing to do anything for the woman standing in front of me. So I did it. Got into it, into Michael, like we had been back in college. Back in those hotel rooms, away from prying eyes and wondering minds.

She had seen Michael touching me, but she had never seen me touch him. I opened up, showed her that side of me. Kissed him, put my feelings into those kisses. Touched him as he touched me. I didn't hold back. I wanted her to see what she had asked for.

I'd asked her if she could handle. She couldn't. Not at first. I started slow. Gave it to her in increments, so as not to freak her out. Slipped my dick into Michael inch by inch so I could hear his low moan. Summer's breathing was slow. She inhaled and exhaled like it hurt for her to do so. As soon as my dick had slipped all the way into him, she gasped. I stopped. At least I wanted to stop, but I couldn't. Michael's groan, that primal shit that only he could give me, set me off. There was something about making another man, one as masculine as you, moan. There was nothing like it.

The fact that Michael still kept his mannishness while we were having sex had always been a turn-on. So this time was no different. I was into it, and so was he. He used the chair to balance himself as I worked behind him. He didn't bend over. Didn't put the same dip in his back that Summer would have if I had been loving her from behind. His hand was on his dick, and he was jerking himself off. I could see Summer fighting the many different emotions I was sure she was feeling. On her face was a plethora of emotions. There was a little bit of shock mixed with jealousy and anger, but there was also arousal. She hated that she felt as if she would never be enough for me. I could see she was feeling some type of way about the unmatched pleasure written across my face. I didn't hide it from her, either. I gave her what she had asked for.

She crossed her legs. Sat back in the other chair. Uncrossed her legs and leaned forward. Her left leg started to shake. She didn't know what to feel. Didn't know how to react. Michael said something vulgar to me. I responded in kind. Summer's eyes blinked rapidly, and her whole body started to shake. I bent my legs, sank deeper into Michael. He was sexy and in the throes of passion. A sheen of sweat covered his dark brown skin as the muscles rolled in his back. It was beautiful. The muscles in his ass looked the same. I felt beads of sweat form at my temples. Heavy breathing serenaded us.

I could feel that Michael hadn't been with other men the way he was with me. I was the only man he was a bottom for. The rest of the time he was the top, but for me . . . for me, he took dick. My dick. All of it. I threw my head back and gave in to that need to let my desire and satisfaction be heard.

Summer stood up abruptly. I thought she was headed for the exit. In fact, she did head to the door. I called out to her. So did Michael. I didn't want to force her to stay.

Didn't want her to leave, because I knew I was too deep into the moment to go after her. There was silence. The moment was tense until she closed the door. I didn't know what was about to happen. Had no idea what to expect. I just knew I didn't want her to leave.

She walked over to where we were. There was anger in her eyes. So much so that she slapped me and then slapped Michael harder. I wanted to reach out and grab her. Wanted to shake the shit out of her, because she'd told me she could handle it or least would try to. She wasn't handling it. I watched her as she forced herself between Michael and the chair. She stood there, eyeing him. Kept her eyes on him as he asked me to keep fucking him. I looked at her, but she wouldn't look at me. I wanted her to look at me, but she kept her eyes locked on him.

That angered me as I gave Michael what he had asked for. As I did so, he kissed her. Sucked on her neck and breasts. I could tell by the way Summer was biting her lower lip that he was getting to her. I fucked him, and he seduced her. Was coaxing her into the kind of threesome she hadn't wanted initially. Her eyelids fluttered when he lifted her from the floor and slowly entered her. He inched his way inside her like he had all the time in the world.

Then she looked at me. In her eyes was spite. She wanted me to feel what it was like to have the same man who brought me immense pleasure do the same to her. The more Michael moved in and out of her, the more my dick swelled as I moved in and out of him. Michael was losing control. . . . He was fucking Summer. . . . I was fucking him. . . . All three of us were fucking one another.

"Fuck, David," he roared at me, then bit down into Summer's neck.

Her head fell back, and she let go. Started throwing her pussy back at him while calling out his name over and over again. I was jealous. I fucked Michael like I was jealous. He sexed Summer like he had something to prove. He was working his hips and grinding with her like he was trying to make her forget about me.

We were locked in a perpetual war of lovemaking.

I could feel my head swell as I was about to explode. Michael rode Summer harder. He yelled that he was about to come. Summer begged him to come with her as she locked her eyes on me.

"Fuck me harder, and then come with me, Michael. Don't hold back. Let it all go, baby," she cooed at him, all the while keeping her eyes locked on me. "Fuck him harder, David. Make him come for me," she demanded of me. "Uh-huh. Oh, God, make him come for me, David," she said breathlessly. "Make . . . him . . ."

I gave her what she wanted. Threw dick to Michael that only a real man could take. I was at my apex, reaching that peak of utter delirium, when my world became foggy.

An alarm went off in my head. Why the hell was an alarm going off right when I was so close to climaxing?

"David?" a voice called out to me. "David, the alarm. Turn the alarm off," he said.

My eyes shot open. I slapped Summer's alarm until it quieted, and then looked around the room. One of my hands was on my dick and was soaked with my come, and the other was wrapped around Summer as she slept on my chest. It took me a minute to get my bearings. My vision was blurry. As always, Summer had taken my glasses off as I slept. I moved my arm from underneath Summer's head and grabbed my glasses from the nightstand and looked around. Michael was lying on the other side of her.

I looked at the clock after placing my arm back around her. Glaring boxed red numbers told me it was six thirty in the morning.

"Good dream, huh?" Michael asked me with a smirk on his face.

"Fuck you," I replied, glad the sheet was still covering my privates, although I was sure moisture could be seen on it, anyway.

"Trying to."

I cut my eyes over at him. He chuckled.

It had all been a dream. The three of us hadn't acted out that fantasy of a threesome. After the tryst in her kitchen, we had found our way to her bed again. Had sucked, licked, and had congress with one another until we couldn't keep our eyes open anymore.

"What time does your flight leave?" I asked him.

"Three thirty."

"What time are you trying to get back to your hotel room?"

He sat up and threw his legs over the side of the bed. His back inflated and deflated slowly. Something was on his mind. I looked at the keloid across his back, which stood out like an African tribal marking. He stood, and I took in the power in his back, ass, and thighs. My dick came to life in remembrance of what it had been like to penetrate all that power. I looked at the woman sleeping soundly in my arms.

She'd said yes. Finally. After eight years she'd said yes. But it was during sex. So, to me, that didn't count. I needed her to say yes while she was sober. Sex did to the brain what drugs and alcohol did to the brain. I needed her to be sober when she said yes to me again. Still, the fact that she had said yes would be enough for me right now.

"After breakfast," he said as he turned to me.

His dick was still semi-hard as he watched Summer, then looked at me. Remnants of her sticky come coated his thighs. We had lain there naked as we slept. We had played while we were naked too. Summer had looked on in curiosity as Michael and I had used our hands to play with the other's manhood until we both got off. The way she had squeezed her legs closed had told me that she, too, was turned on, but she had been too afraid to show it. Hadn't wanted to admit that having two males who were not afraid of their sexuality, as was the case with Michael and me, had turned her on.

"Everything good with you and Sadi back home?"

He tsk-tsked. Didn't answer me right away. He walked into the bathroom and released his bladder. Flushed the toilet and washed his hands.

"I don't know how to answer that," he said after he emerged from the bathroom and leaned against the doorpost. "Shit's been crazy for the past couple of years. Seems like every year she changes on me."

"What do you mean?"

"Shit, we used to have sex every day, sometimes twice, three times a day. Now, even if I try to eat her pussy, she acts as if the shit disgusts her."

"You think she's cheating?"

He shrugged. "I don't know. I'm sexually adventurous. I know that. I've introduced her to some things during our marriage that I thought she was cool with, but now it seems like anything I do sexually repulses her. I can't even touch my own dick without her saying something."

"Damn, that sounds like you're about to be close to the priesthood."

"Tell me about it. Hence the reason I slip, trip, and fall into pussy I have to struggle with until I bust a nut. "

"How often you cheating on her?"

He shrugged. "Started a couple of weeks ago. Girl who works at my shop in Staten Island. It's just sex, though. Want somebody who doesn't make me feel like sucking my dick is a chore they hate to do."

Michael looked at Summer as he finished his last statement. She stirred in my arms, as if she could subconsciously feel him staring at her. I knew he was remembering how she had performed fellatio on him. I gently laid her head down on the pillow and sat up. I yawned and stretched my back before looking back over at Michael. My eyes traveled from his feet up to his thighs, lingered at what made him a man. I took in his hands. Summer was in love with his hands. Kept saying she couldn't believe he was a mechanic, with hands as smooth as his were. She loved when he touched her. My right eye twitched. Eyes kept roaming over the abs we had constructed together and he had perfected even more over time, then moved up to his chiseled chest. I tilted my head and focused on his lips.

"I'm saying, though, if you're going to keep looking at me like you want—"

"Never said I didn't want to," I said, cutting him off. "Just not going to."

My dream replayed itself for me in that moment. Shit had been intense. Had felt real. Almost too real. I grabbed my shirt and wiped my come from my hands and thighs, then tossed it in Summer's laundry basket across the room.

"Door's always open," he replied, with that classic grin on his face.

I didn't respond as I chuckled and stood. I walked over to where he was so I could go into the bathroom. He moved when I got to the door, then stopped so that we stood adjacent to one another. The heat emanating from us was almost too much to bear. His hands grabbed my locks as he let his tongue trail my ear. Shit that always turned me on.

"I'm sure it is," I told him.

"Walk through it."

"Nah."

He chuckled. Kissed my neck and then my shoulder. I was tempted to take him up on that offer. The need to relive burying myself inside him almost rendered me senseless. When he went to kiss my cheek, I turned so he could catch my lips.

"You say no, but you play with fire," he said after the kiss was over.

I kissed him again. Let my tongue invade his mouth like he belonged to me. I wanted to kiss him long enough to do to him what he'd done to Summer in the movie theater. My hands cupped the back of his neck so I could take the kiss deeper. Needed to show him that I had indeed missed him. Wanted him. I could have gotten lost in that kiss, which was what he wanted. I could tell by the way his hand tugged at my locks. But I wasn't a fool.

I pulled back when he tried to deepen the kiss. "Because I know when to leave the kitchen," I said as I moved away from him and stepped into the bathroom. I stepped forward and smacked his muscled ass, then stepped back into the bathroom, winked at him with a lopsided grin of my own, and closed the door behind me. I locked it, too, just to be on the safe side.

I took care of what I needed to in the bathroom, hopped in the shower, and got dressed. Michael and I had discussed the issues surrounding his marriage. Had avoided the sexual tension between us all together. He was annoyed that I wouldn't take him down like he wanted. I was annoyed that he acted as if he couldn't comprehend my reason for not doing so.

By the time Summer made it down the stairs, I was ready to go for breakfast. No matter how Michael and I were feeling in the moment, we couldn't deny Summer's presence. She had her hair in that loose ponytail style I liked. Ripped skinny jeans and an oversize sweater comprised her outfit of choice, along with wine-colored combat boots that matched the color of her sweater. She stopped in front of me and kissed me. She kissed me anywhere her lips could get on my face. My eyes, lips, neck. Stuck her tongue back in my mouth and made me want to take her back upstairs and make her scream yes for me again.

She pulled back and smiled at me. She didn't kiss Michael, though. She asked him to palm her ass. Told him she craved the way his hands had massaged her breasts. She kissed me and wanted him to touch her. I looked on in silence as he made her body his playground. Then she stopped him.

"I need to eat because I'm weak," she said.

"Only takes five minutes for me to take care of that orgasm I know you want," Michael practically pleaded with her.

"Would take me only three," I told her, feeling competitive.

Michael growled. That nigga actually growled low in his throat as he looked at me while holding her waist from behind as she leaned forward against the island.

I walked over to Summer and kissed her lips softly. "Mine?" I asked her.

There was a heady look in her eyes. "Yours," she responded.

Michael kissed the back of her neck and released his hold on her. Once she had grabbed her purse, keys, and phone, we headed out.

We dined at Soulfood Bistro and Café near Underground Atlanta, a shopping district in Five Points. It was a quaint little place that was always crowded. The place was run by four generations of black women. They made the kind of food that only black women could put their special mark on and keep you coming back for more. From the homemade biscuits to the homemade maple syrup, you knew black women were in the kitchen.

Michael's wife called him again while we were eating. She didn't speak to him long, even though he tried to speak to her. She put the kids on the phone and then rushed him like he was aggravating her. I could see that it bothered him by the way he spoke to her. Sadi didn't seem to care, though. She wanted to get off the phone. Michael left his plate on the table and walked outside so he wouldn't cause a scene while he voiced his displeasure with the way she was treating him.

"Has she always been that way?" Summer asked me.

I shrugged. "I don't know."

"Has she always been afraid of sex?"

"I don't know."

"Was she as uptight with you?"

"Nope."

I really didn't want to talk about Sadi or the time she and I had sex. She had been something to do, a way for me to try to hurt the one who had hurt me. But Summer was curious. She wanted to know about the woman who was married to the man I used to love.

"So, she had no problem busting it open for you, but she won't do the same for her husband?" she asked.

"He said it started in the past few years."

"What does she do for a living?"

"She's a lawyer."

"Oh."

"Yeah."

"A lawyer and a mechanic. That's different. Odd and different," she commented, more so to herself than to me.

I was busy stuffing down my country ham and scrambled eggs. "Yeah," I finally responded.

"Michael went to school to be a mechanic?"

"Not at first."

She waited for me to elaborate, but I didn't. "Well, what was he going to be before a mechanic?" she asked.

"A lawyer."

She grunted, deep in thought, as she ate her red velvet pancakes. "How in the hell did he go from being a law student to a mechanic?" she asked a moment later.

"You have to ask him," I answered. I could feel myself getting irritated with her twenty-one questions about Michael.

She picked up on it. "Am I annoying you, David?"

I finally looked over at her. "A little bit."

She didn't respond. She finished her breakfast in silence from there on out. When Michael came back in, she talked to him. Asked him frankly why his wife wasn't comfortable with his sexual nature. He declined to answer.

# David

After breakfast was done, we decided to walk around Five Points for a bit and make a stop at Underground Atlanta. Some kind of way during the walk, one of Summer's hands ended up in mine and the other in Michael's. People stared openly at the plus-sized beauty with the two black men on her arms. We walked through Underground Atlanta, beneath the streets, where eclectic collided with eccentric, and yet all eyes were on us.

We stopped at the African Pride shop so Michael could purchase a few things that he couldn't find in New York sometimes. Mainly, he wanted the homemade body oils that the shop owner made with all organic ingredients. I grabbed some black soap for Summer. She liked the smell of it. Grabbed some incense for both of us. She saw a painting of a dark-skinned woman caught in the rapture of love and surrounded by two African warriors. I invested in my future and spent more dough on the painting for her.

Michael volunteered to take it back to my truck, but only because Sadi had called him and asked him if he was on his way to the airport. Suffice it to say, he wasn't. There would be another argument for him to endure, I was sure.

"You said yes to me last night. Did you mean it?" I asked Summer as we walked hand in hand to the Aroma Paradise Bar to get her some scented crystals.

"Yeah," she answered softly. Her answer didn't carry any weight, didn't affirm anything.

"It was during sex, so it doesn't count."

"What? Why?"

"Because you were high."

"On sex?"

"Yes. We all were. Sex has the same effect on the brain as drugs and alcohol." She laughed. I didn't. "I need you to say it when you're sober."

She picked up a scented crystal, sniffed, and put it back down. "So, essentially you're saying that you didn't believe me? You don't think I was coherent enough to mean that I was yours?"

"You told me your pussy was mine," I said as I made a purchase, not caring that the cashier at the Aroma Paradise Bar was staring, wide-eyed. "I was so deep inside you, I was breathing for you. You gave me your sex, but do I have you?"

Summer swallowed slowly and licked her lips. My words had gotten to her. "Really, David?"

"Seriously, Summer."

"I guess I could ask you which you were asking for."

"I was asking for you, all of you, which includes your sex." My hand cupped her love below. She inhaled in surprise. "Mind." I kissed her left temple, then her right. "Body." I placed my hands on her waist and pull her body close to mine. "Heart." I kissed her bare skin above her heart, a spot that her loose-fitting sweater didn't cover. "And soul," I said at last, wrapping my arms around her as I kissed the spot between her eyes.

"God, David. Why do you do this to me?" she asked as she looked up at me.

"Do what, Summer? Ask you to let me love you?"

"Yes, when you know I'll never be enough."

I kept my composure. I knew there was a reason something inside me wouldn't let me be content with her saying yes the night before. I didn't say anything else while we waited for my items to be wrapped, as the cashier was all ears. Didn't want to expose our lives too much. I paid for the crystals and oils Summer wanted, and then we moved on.

"You feel you'll never be enough simply because I'm attracted to men as well as women, right?"

She widened her eyes and nodded. "Yeah, I feel like nothing I do can compete with that or complete you."

"I hate when you say that shit. You make it seem as if I'm a slave to my sexuality, which is insulting, and I'm not. If I'm with you, then I'm with you. Just because I'm bisexual doesn't mean I have to have a man and a woman at the same time or at all. It doesn't mean that I have to love both sexes equally at the same time, or I can't function. I don't have this overwhelming urge to carry on two relationships, one with a man and one with a woman, at once. I can be faithful to the person I'm with. I can be happy with one person."

"You say that, but I see what Michael does to you now. The sexual tension between you two is so strong that it rubs off on me."

"No, the sexual tension between you and me has always been there. Michael is the gasoline for the fire we make."

"And it's blazing."

I chuckled as we walked hand in hand. Underground Atlanta was filled with people, as usual on a Sunday. Hustlers and con artists alike were milling about. Everybody was trying to make a dollar or three. A Boney James wannabe was blowing away on his saxophone as walked through the throng of ATLiens. People had crowded around him to listen to his soulful display of jazz. They dropped a few dollars and coins in his hat to show how much they enjoyed him. Summer looked around in her purse and pulled out a couple of dollars to add to his take for the day.

"Scorching," I commented.

She was smiling a wide smile. "But, seriously, I see the love you still have for him in your eyes, even though you say you don't love him anymore."

"No, what you see is the fact that I still care for him . . . a lot."

"And if we get together, how will that affect how I feel and what we have?"

"It shouldn't affect you at all. I've been honest with you about all things involving Michael."

"Not at first," she said quickly.

"True, but I have been since he first got here. Give me that."

She studied me for a moment and then nodded. "Okay, I'll give you that."

"Thank you. I care about him deeply. But I'm not in love with him."

"How do you know?"

I stopped walking so she could look at me when I answered her. "Because I'm in love with someone else. It was love at first sight when I laid eyes on her in Lenox Square eight years ago. I just didn't know it then like I know it now."

She glanced away and then looked back up at me. She was speechless. Kept opening and closing her mouth, like she was a fish out of water. She was about to say something when my cell interrupted her.

"Yeah?" I answered.

"Where did you two go?" Michael asked. Irritation laced his voice.

"Follow the sound of the saxophone," I told him.

"A'ight."

I ended the call and looked back at Summer. She was watching the saxophonist play like he was making love to his instrument.

She finally turned to look at me. "You can't love me, David. I don't know who I am. Don't know where I come from. I'm flawed. A married man's whore, remember?"

I glanced up to see Michael heading toward us. Summer had reminded me of words not spoken but implied during our last argument.

"I'm sorry, Summer. I was angry."

"But you really feel that way about me, or it wouldn't have been said."

"I didn't say it."

"Okay, it wouldn't have been implied."

"You pissed me off, and I let my anger get the best of me. Even so, I'd feel the same love for you regardless."

She was quiet awhile. Gave a semi-smile when she saw Michael closing in on us. "Look, give me some time to think about it, okay? A little time to make sure my head is on straight before I make the decision, okay?"

I wanted to ask her how much time. Felt the need to question her as to why she needed time to think about letting a man love her openly and honestly. I wanted to know if she had asked all the married men she had slept with to give her time to decide if she was going to be their mistress or not. When Michael walked up to her and kissed her on the lips like he didn't have a wife at home, I wanted to ask her who I had to be to get reciprocity.

But I didn't ask her any of those things. Not in that moment.

"Shouldn't we be heading back to your hotel?" I asked Michael. I dropped Summer's hand. Pretended like I needed to clean my glasses when she looked at me. I didn't want to be angry in the moment, but I could feel the simmering fury riding me.

He looked at the watch on his arm and then shook his head. "I'll fly out in the morning," he said. "Already changed my flight."

"More trouble in paradise?" Summer asked, butting in.

Michael smiled down at her. "Nah. No trouble in my paradise right now."

Summer looked back at me. Her eyes were asking me if there was trouble in our paradise. There was for me, but I didn't want to ruin her day. So I held my hand out to her while Michael took her other hand, and we carried on.

We stayed in Underground Atlanta and Five Points until noon. Probably should have left sooner, but the thing with time was, when you were having fun, you lost track of it. Summer and Michael flirted like high school students. Sneaking kisses here. Stealing touches there. They disappeared behind a building for a few minutes, and Michael came out adjusting his khaki cargo shorts and wiping his mouth. That was after she and I had snuck behind that same building an hour or so before.

I'd been rough with her. Had taken her hard from behind. Had snatched her hair by the roots. Had clawed at her neck while I bit down and sucked on the other side. Like any dominant male, I had been marking my territory. I had to put my hand over her mouth when I got deeper and rougher. I had to make sure her singsongy moans didn't alert anyone to our stolen moment of sexual gratification. Her come oozed out and glazed my dick as I pumped my hips in and out of her.

"Don't make me wait too long," I told her while I dicked her down.

"Ugh, ah, shit, David!" she cried out.

"Promise me. . . ."

She hissed loudly. "I promise, I promise."

She sounded like a jungle cat. I fucked her like an animal. And when I was ready to climax, I made sure she felt me deep in the depth of her gut.

# Summer

I was wet. In a constant state of wetness. And it was all because of the two men on either side of me. I'd never been as turned on or as stimulated in all my life. I felt like a lush who had had too much at the bar and didn't know when enough was enough. Every chance I had, I was singing like Elle Varner, begging for a refill. My desperate pleas never went unanswered. My underwear and jeans had become a bit uncomfortable as the three of us shared a paper cone of praline pecans.

"This shit is going to give me cavities," Michael complained, but he didn't stop popping the pecans in his mouth.

We were walking through Kenny's Alley, looking for a spot to eat since Michael had gotten hungry again. Kenny's Alley was one of downtown Atlanta's best-kept secrets, although judging by the mass of people milling about, you wouldn't be able to tell. There was something in the alley for everyone's taste. From Irish pubs to urban nightlife to a Jamaican restaurant and lounge, you could find it all in Kenny's Alley.

Michael settled on Caribbean food, while I was focused on how quiet David had gotten. I knew he was upset about the conversation we'd had earlier. I didn't know what was wrong with me. I wanted to believe him when he said I'd be enough for him, but something in me wouldn't allow it.

"You're not talking to me again," I said as we settled at a table. "Are we okay?"

Michael chuckled as he eavesdropped, and then disappeared, on his way to the bathroom. I sat next to David and tried to see how much damage I'd done.

"We're fine, Summer. Same as we've always been," he answered.

"Doesn't sound like it."

He slowly cut his eyes over at me. "I'm cool."

I didn't want to push the issue, so I took his word for it. I laid my head on his shoulder and enjoyed being near him. What he and I had talked about was heavy on my mind. I had to admit that at times I wanted David more than I needed to breathe. I thought back to my foster parents. My mom and dad had a very loving and healthy relationship, and they both seemed happy. Still, I wondered what it was in my mother that had allowed her to be okay with him having sex with other men. I mean, they had had sex with other women too, but I had always wondered if she had had threesomes and foursomes with other men for herself or to please that other side of him.

"Is it different?" I asked David.

He was busy looking at his schedule for the week on his smartphone when he answered me. "Is what different?" he asked, with a glance up at me before returning his gaze to his phone.

"Being with men?"

He stopped scrolling with his finger and looked over at me. "What do you mean?"

"Does it feel the same?"

"What? The sex?"

"Everything. The sex. The love. The passion. Everything. Does it feel different?"

"Are you asking me this for a reason or just because you want to know?"

"Both. I need to know so I will know how to answer you, so I can be comfortable and secure."

"So if I said that sex or being in a relationship with men is better than when I'm with a woman, you'd tell me no?"

I swallowed and lifted my head. He was going to make this difficult for me. And that was not what I wanted. "David, look, I ask because I'm insecure when it comes to your sexuality. I feel very insecure knowing that if we get together, your attraction to men may be a problem for me. I don't want you to be in a relationship like that. You deserve better. You deserve someone who can love you, all of you, for who you are. I feel like I'm inadequate. I can be a lot of things for you and to you, but I can never be a man," I explained emphatically.

He inhaled hard. Exhaled just as hard and then gave me a hard stare. "Are you . . . ," he started to ask and then cleared his throat before continuing. "Do you ask any of the married men you sleep with questions about their sexuality or questions about their wives and children when you fall into affairs with them? What if I start to feel like I won't be enough for you? What if I start to feel like, because there isn't a ring on my finger, I won't have the same appeal as the married men you sleep with do?" he asked with a shrug. "Just asking. You know, for my security and all. So that I don't have to feel inadequate."

I hadn't expected him to go there. Hadn't expected that he would turn the tables on me and put me in the hot seat. Although a part of me wanted to be defensive, I knew that I'd probably pushed him to the point of annoyance and anger.

"David . . ."

"Let me guess. You must have told David how you really felt, and now you get to feel his wrath," Michael said as he intruded on our conversation.

I hadn't even seen him approaching us. And I was kind of annoyed that he had decided to walk into the middle of what David and I had been talking about. I turned from Michael and put my attention back on David, who seemed to be two seconds away from snapping. He gave Michael a look that I'd never seen from him as long as we'd known one another. David frowned, and his eyes turned to something akin to slits. His lips were turned down, like something stunk.

"And just what the fuck does this have to do with you?" David asked him.

Michael adjusted his cargo shorts, pulling them above his knees, before he took a seat across from us. "Nothing really, except I know what it's like to be on the receiving end of your anger when you can't handle the truth."

"Handle the truth? What do you know about that?" David asked.

From the time Michael had got to Atlanta until a few minutes before, there had been nothing but tension between us, sexual tension. Now I got to see a different kind of tension between the two men who had shown me what it felt like to have your body worshipped by earthbound gods.

Michael gave something of a smile and looked at me. "You have to get used to this, Freckles. David wants everyone to accept his true feelings at face value, but as soon as you tell him how you really feel, this is what you get. He can't accept rejection. Has never been able to accept rejection," Michael stated with a slick smile. "Good thing you don't have a husband, someone you really love," he added, then turned his attention back to David. "You won't have to worry about David fucking him to get back at you."

David chuckled low. Even though I could tell he was nowhere near amused, he kept chuckling. He laid his phone on the table and leaned forward. For a minute, I thought he was seconds away from hitting Michael.

"That's comical coming from a nigga who wouldn't know what love looked like if it was staring him in the face," he said as he gave Michael direct eye contact.

"I know I love my wife."

The way Michael said that indicated that something had been left unspoken. Just that quick, I was stuck in an ex-lovers' spat.

"Yeah, but does she love you? is the question," David retorted.

"That must be the question you always asked yourself when it came to me. Must have sucked like hell to know you loved me, but not to be sure if I loved you, huh?"

"You know, it's no wonder you two get along so well. Both of you are a piece of the same cloth. You think it's okay to take my feelings lightly. Play with me, then toss me to the side, like I don't count. Like I'm just something to do," David said as he grabbed his phone and stood.

Something Michael had said had rubbed him the wrong way. He'd already been upset with me, but Michael had thrown in that last straw and had broken the camel's back. I didn't even understand where Michael's anger had come from. Maybe it had something to do with the fact that he had been fighting with his wife. Maybe he and David still hadn't resolved those issues between them. I didn't know. All I knew was that I didn't want our day to end, and I didn't want David to leave.

"The bitch in you is starting to show," Michael threw back at David.

I threw daggers at Michael with my eyes as I snapped my head to look at him.

David shrugged. "Maybe it was the same bitch in me that was in your wife too."

Michael looked at me and then back at David with a slick smirk on his face. They were two alpha males locked in a battle of dominance over who was in whose pussy while they belonged to the other. David shook his head and then walked off.

"David, where're you going?" I asked as I rushed after him.

The man walked with a stride that made me remember the way he had stroked me into orgasmic oblivion. Even though it was clear he was angry, he kept his composure, which was another thing I loved to love about him.

I caught up with him and grabbed his arm.

He pulled his arm away from me. "I need to go before I do or say something I can't take back." He kissed my lips and walked away.

I was left standing there, trying to figure out how we had gone from having a great time to being enemies on an imaginary battlefield. That was love. Always a damn battlefield. You could easily step on an IED and not even know it until love had TKOed you.

I walked back over to Michael, who'd started eating his food, like he had no care in the world. I grabbed my purse and the Styrofoam carryout container of food that David and I had planned to share.

"Did I miss something?" I asked him.

He looked up at me as he licked his lips. On his plate were oxtails in heavy gravy, rice and beans, steamed cabbage, and plantains. Michael was sexy even when he ate. Even when he was being an asshole, his attractiveness couldn't be denied. His tongue ran across his bottom lip again, and I felt a stirring in my underwear.

"About what?" he asked nonchalantly.

"What was that? Why did you go hard at him like that?"

"Because David doesn't like to be told his shit stinks. He's Mr. Perfect, and everyone else is flawed. His flaw is thinking he doesn't have one. Get used to it. It's a trait he and my wife have in common."

I stood there and stared at Michael for a while. I wanted to ask him to elaborate, but my heart, mind, soul, and body were pulling me toward the man I'd known for eight years. I turned and walked away at a fast clip, hoping I could catch David before he drove off. Michael and I had ridden with David, so I suddenly wondered how Michael would get back to his hotel room.

I stopped in my tracks and swiveled around. "Hey," I yelled above the noise of the eatery to get Michael's attention.

He turned around. "Yeah?" he called.

"You coming?"

"Nah. I'm good."

"How will you get back to your room?"

"Taxi."

With that, he turned his attention back to finishing his food, and I hightailed it out of the place to find David. It was funny how life turned the tables on you. Two nights ago it had been David who had run through a parking deck, trying to find me. Now it was I who was rushing to a parking deck to find him. Thankfully, the karma gods weren't in too much of a mood to screw me over. David was just about to leave the parking deck as I was rushing in.

"Open the door!" I yelled as I knocked on the passenger-side window.

The wind had chilled me to the bone. Normally, it wouldn't be an issue for me, but for some reason, that day it was. For a moment, I thought David wasn't going to open the door. He was behind another car, waiting to turn. I knocked on the window again, feeling hopeless as people stared on. He wouldn't even look at me.

"David, please open the door. Look, I'm sorry," I pleaded, no longer giving a damn about making a spectacle of myself. The car in front of him pulled out, and I started to think that he was going to drive away and leave me there, looking the fool. "I'm cold, baby," I said.

He sat there, staring straight ahead. It was only when another horn blared behind him that he unlocked the door. I quickly hopped in, placed the food and my purse on the backseat, and buckled up. Normally, when he and I were out together, he would buckle me in. Make sure I was safe and secure. That was what I'd wanted him to do when I'd asked him those questions. I'd wanted him to buckle me into the relationship and make sure I was secure. I needed him to do that.

My birth parents hadn't done that. They hadn't given me that safety net I needed. I hadn't bonded with them. Instead, a white lady and her husband had seen something in a black child that made them love me as if they'd birthed me themselves.

We drove in silence. KISS 104.1 and Sasha the Diva kept us entertained. Bloodstone serenaded us, even though our natural high had been all but diminished. David's body language said he didn't want to be bothered. He was leaning away from me, his right hand on the steering wheel, while his left hand aimlessly stroked his chin.

"Can we at least talk?" I finally asked after he got on I-75.

"Not in the mood to talk," he answered.

"Not even if it's about what you asked me earlier?"

"No."

"David—"

"Summer," he said to me sternly. "I don't want to talk, all right?"

"Okay."

I'd never been one to make a man do what he didn't want to do. If he said he didn't want to talk, then I wouldn't make him. I kept quiet as we rode along. Maybe when we got back to my place or his, whichever one we were going to, he'd be in a better mood and we could talk.

My mind wandered back to Michael and how he would get back to his hotel room. I wondered if the three of us would get to share one another again. Pondered whether I would once more get to experience pleasure in ways unknown to many women. I glanced at David and wanted to see the look of unmitigated pleasurable torture on his face, all in the name of me. Wanted to make Michael growl and make those guttural groans again as he released. Then I wanted to have both of them stand erect as I kneeled between them and sucked my way back to the promised land, with all their children passing my esophagus to get to my belly.

Then I wanted David and me to talk candidly about what we both wanted from one another. I wanted him to tell me that I could be all he needed for forever and a day after never. I wanted to know if I could love such a man the way my mother had loved my father. Those were my thoughts as I laid my head on his shoulder after he'd leaned back toward me. He put his left hand on the wheel and his right one on his lap. I eased my hand underneath his just to have him touch me. When his hand closed around mine, I smiled.

I was awakened about thirty minutes later, as David parked in front of my townhome. I groggily got out of his truck and realized Michael's rental was still at my house. For some reason, I'd forgotten it was there. David had my purse and the food. I unlocked my door and expected him to walk in with me, but he didn't.

"Aren't you coming in?" I asked him after stifling a yawn.

"No. Going home. I need to be by myself for a minute."

I was disappointed with his answer. Actually, my feelings were hurt. "I made you mad again, huh?"

"You're just being you, Summer. I accept that," he said, handing me the plate of food and my purse. He kissed my lips softly, passionately, and held my waist as he did so, as if he really didn't want to leave. "I'll see you later," he said after he pulled away.

He left me standing there, feeling as if I was letting the secret to my future happiness get away.

For the next two or three hours, I lollygagged around my house, doing nothing. There was no David and no Michael. Just me and my thoughts. I tried to call David at least ten times, and not once did he answer. That was a first for us. He had never intentionally ignored my calls. I was starting to feel like something had changed between us. Was starting to feel hopeless and a little lovesick.

*Bang! Bang! Bang!*

Somewhere in my head someone was knocking on my door. I thought I was dreaming as I lay there on the couch, and it took me a minute to realize that someone was actually at my door. I sat up quickly, not caring that my equilibrium was off. I stumbled a bit like a wino would after having too much wine. I rushed to the door in hopes that David was there. He and I had fought and had had disagreements many times over the years, but he had never stayed away from me. He had always come back and we had always worked it out. I'd been hoping that this night would be no different.

I looked through the peephole and then opened the door.

"Hey," I said.

"May I come in?" he asked.

I moved to the side and let in the man standing at my door. He brushed past me, and his scent lingered behind him. No one would ever be able to forget the way he smelled. He'd changed clothes since I'd seen him last earlier in the day. Name-brand running shoes, sweats, and a thick T-shirt made up his attire, as if he was going to the gym. I homed in on the print in his pants. I couldn't help it, because the thickness of the print couldn't be denied. I closed my door and locked it, then slowly trailed behind him to my front room.

He took a seat on the couch I'd been lying on. I sat beside him. Both of us were enveloped in our thoughts and the loud silence in the room. My TV was on, but I'd muted it hours ago.

"It's cold as shit in here, Freckles," he told me. "You should turn your heat on."

I shrugged. "I don't like the heat."

The man who had come to my door wasn't David. David wouldn't have suggested I turn on the heat.

"How're you feeling?" he asked me.

"I don't know. Can't explain it."

"Have you talked to him?"

I shook my head. "No."

"Tried to call him?"

"Yes. You?"

Michael shook his head.

"You think he'll pick up if you call?" I asked.

It was his turn to shrug. "I don't know."

"Will you call him for me?"

"Nah. If he wanted to talk, he would call."

"Maybe it's me he doesn't want to talk to. Maybe if you call, he'll pick up." I was getting a little desperate.

"I'm not calling him, Freckles. When he wants to talk, he'll call."

I was quiet for a moment. I sighed, then stood to look out my window. I'd give anything to see that black-on-black 2014 Yukon XL Denali roll up in my driveway.

"May I see your phone?" I asked Michael as I sat back down.

"Why?"

"I want to see if he picks up when he sees your number."

"Freckles, let it go, baby girl," he told me.

"Just let me see your phone."

He stared at me for a long time and then passed his smartphone over. "Press number three," he said.

*Speed dial.* He had David on speed dial. That jealousy of him that I felt crept back into my bones like a late-night chill. I pressed three, like he had told me to, and waited.

One ring.

Two rings.

Three rings.

Four.

Then I got the automated voice telling me to leave a message. I passed Michael his phone. Tried to call David from my phone again, only to get the same voice-mail treatment.

# Summer

"Tell me about you and David."

Michael was on my floor, pushing his body up and down repeatedly as he counted aloud his progress. He was on his second round of rapid push-ups. The scar on his back was holding my attention. It had piqued my curiosity. I sat lotus-style in front of him as we talked. Since David wouldn't answer my calls, Michael and I were talking and keeping one another company. I'd gone to my room, but the silence had killed me, so I'd come back downstairs.

His right leg crossed behind the left one while he drew his body level to the floor and asked me, "What about us do you want to know?" His breathing was heavy but even as he continued his random round of exercise.

"How did this thing between the two of you start?"

The muscles in his back and arms coiled and rolled like steel cables. There was a light sheen of sweat on his back, which made his chocolate skin glisten in the dim lighting of my front room.

"Started out as just sex and then gradually turned into something else," he said as he pushed up and held it.

He blew out a bit of steam as he made eye contact with me, then looked at the print of womanhood on the short gym shorts I had changed into. He looked back up at me again. Then he went down, pushed back up, and balanced himself for several seconds again.

"Everything was cool at first," he continued. "We didn't hide our sexuality, but we didn't make a show out of it, either. There were hotel room stays. Lots of those. Sometimes just the two of us. Other times we'd meet a chick or chicks, take them back to the room, and have fun."

I butted in to ask, "Sexual?"

He nodded as he pushed up and down. Down, then up. "Sexual entertainment was what we specialized in. Sometimes there would be a dude we knew was bisexual but was trying to hide it. We'd invite him back to the room with us. Had fun that way. We were having fun. No recklessness, though. There was always protection. Kept our dicks clean, like we keep them clean now. I knew he had feelings for me, but I told him up front not to fall in love with me."

"Why?" I asked.

"Because I know me. I wasn't going to be with him the way he wanted me to. Sex with men for me is more about the pleasure I get from it. Nothing more."

"So you never cared about him?"

"I didn't say that. I cared. Just didn't love him like he did me."

"So where does your wife, Sadi, come in?"

He did another round of push-ups before he stood, grabbed his bottle of water from my bookcase, and took the bottle to his mouth. He leaned against the bookcase and answered, "Met Sadi one night at Morehouse. At a party one of my homeboys was throwing. Shit was like love at first sight, you know. I'd met a lot of women, but none that intrigued me the way she did. So I started talking to her. Got the notion that she was feeling me too. So we exchanged numbers that night. Started hanging out almost every day."

"Where did that leave David?"

"I stopped hanging with him as much. Started trying to build something with Sadi. Always wanted a wife and kids, you know," he said, then shrugged before sitting in front of me lotus-style.

We both sat there, backs erect, me watching him as he watched me.

"Did David know that?" I asked.

"Yeah, he knew. I'd told him that more than once. Guess he thought I was just talking, though. I mean, at first everything was cool and shit. I'd still see him from time to time."

"You two were still having sex?"

"Yeah, we still partook in that pleasure we shared."

"Why didn't you tell Sadi you were bi—" I was about to call him bisexual, then cut myself off, remembering he hated to be referred by that term. "Why didn't you tell her you were into dating guys too?"

"I didn't *date* guys. Had sex with them but never dated them."

"What do you call what you and David had?"

"Friends with benefits."

"Oh."

"Everything was cool. David didn't think I should hide that side of myself from her."

"Why did you?" I asked.

"That's a question I still ask myself every day. I don't know why, but shit was way too deep between her and me to confess it by then. She's the only woman that I've never disclosed my sexuality to. Maybe that's why God decided to get the last laugh."

"What do you mean?"

He cast his glance away from me for a second and then looked back at me. For the first time, I didn't see cocky, arrogant, "so sure of himself" Michael. That part of him had faded in that moment. It had happened so quickly that if I had blinked, I would have missed it.

Michael gave a lopsided grin. "Some shit I'll keep to myself for the time being, Freckles. Anyway, shit was cool, and then Sadi decided she wanted to get married, and by that, I mean elope. So that was what we did. We decided not to tell anyone, and we eloped."

"How did David find out?"

"Sadi told him."

"Why would she do that?"

"She ran into him while he was out a few days later. Told him herself. She didn't think I would mind, since I'd introduced him as my best friend."

"Damn . . . Is that when they fucked?"

Michael laughed. "Yeah."

"So she went from telling your best friend about your nuptials to fucking him in one breath? What kind of hillbilly, ghetto ho shit is that?"

I was being judgmental, and I knew it. Most people would have labeled me a ho for fucking two men at once, one whom I'd met a little less than seventy-two hours prior, but it wasn't about me. It was about the woman who had come between two best friends/lovers.

"Your guess is as good as mine, Freckles," Michael said as he pulled out his phone and started to scroll through it like he was looking for something.

"How did you find out?"

"David told me. Came to my apartment, with her pussy fresh on his lips. Her thong in his hand," he revealed.

I couldn't believe my David would do something like that. Not the David I'd gotten to know. Not the David I loved. The David I knew and loved wasn't an asshole.

"I can't believe he did that," I muttered in a low voice. "That was a bold move."

"That's the reason both of us ended up in jail."

"You fought him?"

"I tried to give that nigga a kick to the chest that rivaled some shit of a Spartan in a movie called *300*. Kicked him through my front door."

My eyes widened. I sat there, trying to imagine that fight. I imagined the two of them going at each other like male lions in a pride would when they were fighting over a female. Locked in a battle fit to be a fight to the death. I started to feel antsy at the thought of David letting Michael beat his ass. Even though David had clearly been in the wrong, I still didn't like the idea of somebody laying hands on him. *Look who's fucking talking,* I thought.

I looked at Michael, who had stopped scrolling through his phone. Whatever he had found, he was staring at it like it was an enigma to him.

"What happened then?" I asked.

"Then he got up and returned the favor. Some niggas there would say he got in my ass. I'd say it was a tie. That would be my story, and I would stick to it," he said with a chuckle, which made me smile. It took a big man to admit he had got his ass handed to him.

"What happened after you two got out of jail?"

"My wife had already passed the bar and had job offers out the ass in New York. She'd been begging me to move there, anyway. She bailed me out. A few months later, I paid my landlord, packed up, and got the fuck on with my life. About six months later, David found me. Gave me his version of an apology. I wasn't trying to hear it. Had a pregnant wife who was pissed that I had done three years of law school, only to buy my first auto shop to run."

"Well, yeah, that is crazy, Michael. Why go to law school just to be a mechanic?"

"My pops is a lawyer."

I gave him a look of confusion, wondering why that would be his answer. "And?"

Michael gave me a sobering look. "My pops is Jamaican. Him didn't tek kindly fi him male child being a batty bwoy."

His Caribbean dialect had snuck up on me. I didn't know he had it in him, but judging by the way I remembered him moving his hips on the dance floor and while he was knocking my back out, I could see it more clearly now.

"Always wanted his son to follow in his footsteps. Found out I liked men and women and tried to cut the gay part out of me," he continued.

My mind went to the scar on his back, and I gasped. "Your father did *that* to you?"

He nodded. "I was walking out of my parents' house after I'd told them the truth about me. Pops came chasing after me with a machete. Got me good, but Mom Dukes wasn't going to let him kill her only son, so she and my sisters grabbed him. They struggled to hold him back while my mama begged for me to leave. '*Just go!*' she kept screaming at me. David's crib was closer to me than Grady Hospital, so I drove there and passed out in my car in his driveway. Lucky for me, he had a chick over who was leaving, and she saw me. Her scream is the last thing I remember hearing. Woke up about a day later, stitched up in Grady."

"Oh, my God, Michael. I'm so sorry. . . ."

"Yeah, me too. Still didn't turn my old man in, though. Told the police some random person had attacked me from behind and I didn't see who'd done it."

I took a moment to take in the man. When you first met Michael, you thought all was well in his world. He walked with an air of superiority that made you think the world was his. But underneath all that bravado was a man who had silenced his demons. Had put the past under his feet and had walked away from it, as if it had never existed. I knew what that felt like. I knew what it was to have to silence the voices in your head in order to move on from the past.

"Do you keep in contact with your family now?" I asked him.

He shook his head somberly. "My youngest sister is the only one who really reaches out to me and my family these days. My mom will sporadically send a text to ask how I'm doing. To tell me that she's happy I married a woman and had children, and that despite my sinful illness, she'll always love me."

I rushed in to hug him. I felt the need to hold him. I closed my eyes and squeezed him tight as my fingers traced up and down the elongated scar. I thought about David. Wondered if his family had casted him out the same way Michael's family had done to him. David never talked about what he remembered of his parents, since he'd been in the system most of his childhood.

I sat there, holding Michael that way. He had said he didn't love David, but the first person he had run to when he needed someone the most was David. Same as me. I thought back to what he'd said earlier about Sadi and David having things in common. It seemed as if he'd gone out and found a female version of David . . . the same way that David had compared Michael and me. David had found a female version of Michael, it would seem. I let those thoughts drift off into the wind. Wouldn't even do that to myself. Wouldn't think about what it meant.

I pulled back from the hug, then laid my head against his. "You're a strong man, Michael."

He smirked as his hands roamed up and down my back, then settled on my ass and gave it a hard squeeze. "Most of the time," he confirmed. "You can't be holding a brother like this, though."

As he talked, his lips brushed against mine. I couldn't help the instant heat I felt in the pit of my stomach. As his big hand gripped my backside, his fingers brushed against my vaginal lips, stirring my desire. My lips had already swelled to the point where my clit was rubbing against the fabric of my shorts. He placed his lips against the swell of my breasts, and my nipples got even harder. Started to ache.

"Why not? Can't a girl show some compassion?"

"Yeah, she can," he answered, then let his eyes roam over my face.

His gaze was intense, heated. Like he was seeing through the very fabric of what made me a woman. For a minute I thought I had Michael figured out. We all had vices we used to get over the pain in our lives. Maybe his vice was sex. We'd quickly gone from talking about the issues that plagued his life to treading the waters of our hedonistic rituals of pleasure seeking.

I let out a deep breath. "Think David would be mad if we did this while he wasn't here?"

"I don't know. We can stop if you want to."

There it was. He'd given me an out, but as he expertly moved my shorts to the side so his fingers could slip inside me, I knew he was bluffing. My nails lightly scratched the surface of his back as I moaned low.

"You lie, Michael."

"I know, Freckles. Been wanting to see what it would feel like to have you ride my dick. Want to see if you can ride as good as you threw that pussy back at me in the kitchen."

Our eye contact was strong and direct. Those honey-colored hypnotizers were enticing me back into his world. His words aroused me. No, they had no couth to them, but I liked that. I liked that straightforwardness. I did want to fuck Michael. Wanted to fuck him again and again and again. I wanted to know what it felt like to have David take me from behind while Michael sucked on my clit. I had the urge to see if I could handle them both at once, one inside my vaginal walls, making me cream, and the other taking me somewhere I'd never been before as he slowly inched his way into my chocolate star. Michael and David made me that way. Made me want to do things I'd never done before. Touch what I'd never touched. See what I'd never seen.

I wanted that. The same way I wanted David to walk in and catch me and Michael in the act of coitus on my front-room floor. The same way I wanted him to join us and take me to another world. The same way I needed David to answer his phone and not be mad at me anymore. Oh . . . God . . . the same way I needed Michael not to ever stop sucking on my breasts as he was doing. He wrapped his long tongue around each nipple. Sucked and gently bit each sensitive morsel until he sucked my entire areola into his mouth.

All the while his other hand stopped fingering me to hurriedly release his dick from his sweats. Once he had removed it, I took it in my hands and gave it one slow stroke before rising and guiding him inside me. I owned Michael in that moment. I could tell by the way his eyes widened and he mouthed the word "wow" as my hips started to work slowly against him. He was mine. Not Sadi's. Not David's. Michael was mine. I owned him. I wanted to own David. Wanted to possess him.

I had to shake my head from side to side. Bit down on my bottom lip and praised every god there was for the magnificence that was his manhood. God, he hugged my walls. Stretched them to fit him snugly as I glided up and down his disco stick. I may not have known if I had any island in me or not, but I wanted to prove to him that my hips worked as well as his. I couldn't stop looking at his face. Couldn't get over the fact that as powerful a man as he was, he was putty in my hands at that moment.

So damn weak. Mouth at half-mast, stuck somewhere between the letter *O* and looking as if he was about to have a heart attack, I basked in that moment of glory.

"Fucking fuck, Freckles. Shit, baby. Wait. Shit. Wait. I don't want to come yet," he begged as he buried his face in my chest. I stopped, as he had requested. Only because I was selfish and didn't want him to come yet, either. "You do this shit to David?" he asked me in all seriousness.

I smiled slyly. Didn't answer him.

I rolled my back. Dipped my hips and gave him a slow wind and watched him lose his mind. He fell back against my couch, angst on his features. His position gave me better leverage. I squatted with ease while he was inside me. Those Kegel exercises were working overtime as I butterflied him to premature ejaculation. He made a face like he was in pain. Inhaled and exhaled like he was drowning and trying desperately to catch his last breath. Twitched like he'd been struck by electricity. Once the tides had rolled in and the waves had subsided, he focused his watery eyes back on me.

"Shit, Freckles. Fuck," he said as he looked up at me in a panic. "Did you come?"

I shook my head once. "No."

Although I hadn't had my orgasm, I wasn't even mad. For some reason, my pleasure came in seeing me break Michael down to his sex. I owned him with sex. Not with powerful words. Not with damaging emotions. Just sex. For a woman like me to do that to a man like Michael was a potent aphrodisiac.

He quickly flipped me over onto my back and swiftly entered me again. His dick was semi-hard, but it was enough to cause me great pleasure. He kissed my neck. Sucked and licked all around, making me moan a song of arousal. He didn't forget my ears. Like David, he didn't ignore my ears. I loved when they took the time to hit that pleasure zone. Michael devoured my breasts like he was ravished by the need to stimulate me that way, and all the while his hips worked with fervor. That simple missionary position caused his pelvis to give my clitoris direct stimulation. His dick was hardening again. Damn, he was getting so hard. I clawed and pulled at the pillows on the couch behind me. His hands held my waist to keep me from moving. He didn't want to run the risk of coming again before I did.

I loved that shit. Absolutely loved the way he isolated my hips so he could do all the work. I screamed out my satisfaction loudly. I didn't care who heard me. Michael stuck his tongue in my mouth and took the fire in the room up a notch. Slid one hand between us and put pressure on my core bud until I had no choice but to release my orgasm. He buried his face in my neck and muttered obscene vulgarities about how good my snatch was to him. Told me he hadn't had pussy as good as mine in all his life. Told me he wanted to see me squirt again. Wanted me to sit on his face and drown him in my love. He told me all of this as he grunted and groaned that Freckles was making him bust another nut so soon after the first one.

Once it was all over, he lay on top of me, breathing like he was having an asthma attack. I kept my arms and legs wrapped around him, a satisfied smile on my face. We lay there in silence and let our heavy breathing serenade us. I thought he was sleeping after a while, until he rolled over, pulled me to him so that we were spooning, and held me.

I was shocked when he asked me, "Think we should call him again?"

I wanted to call David. I did, but I knew I needed to get at least a few hours of sleep in before working in the morning. And I was weak. Too damn weak to move my arms to pick up the phone.

"He'll be at work in the morning," I said. "I miss him too."

"What time does he get to the office?"

"About seven."

"What time do you leave?"

"About six."

"Wake me up when you get up."

"Okay."

We were quiet again. I was in and out of a sleep state.

"You're trouble, Freckles," he said after a while.

"But you like getting into trouble."

He gave a weak chuckle. "Yeah, I do."

My phone rang about three or four times in the middle of the night. Each time I answered, no one said anything. I didn't bother looking at the caller ID and answered blindly each time as I'd been asleep. Michael turned the TV off after the fourth phone call. We both got up to pee. He grabbed some blankets, and we pulled pillows from the couch and placed them on the floor near the couch. We fell back to sleep, with satisfaction wafting over our bodies and with David on our brain.

# David

Two weeks had passed since our weekend rendezvous with Michael. Summer and I had fallen back into our same routine. I'd stayed mad at her for all of a couple of days, until she cornered me in my office and demanded I talk to her.

"So, how long are we going to do this?" she asked.

"Do what?" I asked her as I looked up from the files on my desk.

"How long are you going to make me pay for being honest?"

It was after hours. I'd been working late nights so I wouldn't be tempted to say, "Forget it all," and go back to the way things were. Her hair was in a lopsided ponytail. She looked as if she had just got done exercising and had decided to show up. She was in yoga pants and an oversize T-shirt. Dressed down, but beautiful nonetheless.

"For about as long as you continue to make me suffer for your insecurities."

"That's what you think I'm doing?"

"That's what it feels like."

"Well, I'm not. What if I told you I was trying to save you your sanity? If you know I'm insecure, then why want to be with me? You want to live your life, with me always questioning you about other men? You want to always have to check your phone, only to see me giving you ultimatums about who you can and can't hang out with? What kind of relationship would that be? We'd end up apart, because you'll get tired of that, and you'll want your freedom, your peace."

She had a point. I couldn't argue with it. No, I didn't want to live that way. Had done that in past relationships and didn't want to travel that road again. It always resulted in countless arguments, pointless explanations, and stressful fights. Dealing with an insecure mate was hell. The kind that I didn't want to live through again. Yet I couldn't stand the fact that it felt like I had to give up on love with the one woman I wanted, needed.

"There are always ways we can work around that," I told her. "That's what I'm trying to do now. Trying to get you to open yourself up to love without all the bullshit. You never gave me a chance, Summer. Never gave us a chance."

Summer looked around my office. Pretended to be interested in the degrees and accolades I had on the walls. There was one picture that held her attention. A picture of me and her. Whenever anyone looked at that picture of us, they always questioned why we weren't together. It was clear that we were happy together in that photo. Hot sand underneath our feet and happiness on our faces as we stood on a beach in Aruba.

She walked over to me. Took my pen from my hand, pushed my chair back, and straddled my lap. Summer placed her hand on my shoulders and breathed in deeply as she looked down at me. Her being that close evoked an instant chemical reaction in me. I leaned back as I watched her. I wondered what she was going to do. In her eyes I could see images of us dancing around. I saw myself as her husband. She as my wife. I saw our future in her eyes. Wondered if she saw the same.

She leaned down to kiss my lips, and I turned my head, letting her catch my cheek. I was still angry and annoyed with her all in the same breath. Although I wanted to hold her and kiss her, I knew I couldn't keep letting Summer play with me the way she did. I couldn't keep letting her think that it was okay to use my feelings like a toy that she could pick up and put down whenever she wanted. As bad as I wanted to lay her on my desk, rip away those yoga pants, and taste what I knew was sitting plump and juicy between her legs, I wouldn't. To hear her tell me no again, give me the lame excuse that she didn't feel as if she was all that I needed, was comical to me.

I needed a break. Needed a reprieve to get my head together. Summer was getting to me. She was starting to affect me, and not in the way I wanted her to. I'd spoiled Summer. Made her think my world revolved around hers. And it did in a sense. It was for that very reason that she thought it was okay for her to treat me the way she did. The very reason she assumed that I'd be forgiving so easily.

The woman who carried my heart in the palm of her hand was determined, though. She placed that kiss against my cheek like she didn't care that I'd turned my head. Gave light licks and nibbles to my jawline. My head started to swim as I thought about getting lost deep in her waves. I inhaled and exhaled deeply as I turned my eyes back to her.

"I know you're mad at me—" she began.

"No, I'm not," I said quickly, cutting her off.

"Then why this treatment of me?"

I wasn't going to answer that question again. I felt as if I was becoming repetitive. Didn't know how many more times I could tell her the answer to that question.

She didn't say anything for a while and then, "I miss you, David."

I had to be honest. Couldn't deny that I missed her too. "I know. I miss you too."

"So are you coming over once you're done here?"

She'd found a crack in my wall. Had known what she was doing when she walked in my office, looking and smelling like she did. I'd missed being around her so much that I'd gone to taking pages out of Michael's playbook. I'd started playing with my dick. Every night I'd gone home, remembering what it was to be so deep inside her, and I'd lost myself. I didn't know where she began and I ended. Just the thought of it in that moment was killing me. Summer was so sexually aware that it was hard for a man to let her go once things were supposed to be over. To mix her sexuality with her mental prowess was kryptonite in that moment for me. She had me, and she knew it. I didn't want to let her know how easy it was for her to get under my skin, though.

"No," I told her.

"Please."

"No."

She sighed, then laid her head on my shoulder. We sat that way for minutes. I could feel the heat from her desire and made the mistake of moving. That simple slip allowed her to feel what she was doing to me. She spread her legs wider and settled more onto my lap. The swell of my manhood pressed firmly against what made her a woman anatomically. Wasn't long before her soft lips found my neck. I opened and closed my left hand. Made a tight fist to release some tension. She let her tongue trail all the way up to the spot beneath my right earlobe.

"Let me make it up to you," she whispered in my ear. Her face was so close to mine that if someone had walked in, they would have assumed we were Siamese twins joined at the jaw.

I looked in her eyes. "Did you think about that when you were fucking Michael?"

She sat up and then gazed down at me with uncertainty. She'd told me about how she and Michael had fucked way into the night and in the early morning before he left. She'd been a little disappointed that she'd awakened to find him gone. He'd asked her to wake him, but she had woken up late, only to find that he'd left her. Typical Michael. He had got his fill, what he wanted, and then he was gone like a thief in the night. I took issue with what they had done, as crazy as it sounded. The jealousy I felt betrayed me.

"You wouldn't pick up the phone," was her answer.

"So that meant it was okay?"

"No. Didn't say that." She cast a glance down at her hands, then back up at me.

I didn't respond to her. Couldn't, because guilt had also taken up residence in me. I'd been pissed at Michael for fucking her too. I was jealous that I couldn't have him the way I wanted to, either. Was envious of how effortless it was for her to have him her way, and for him to have her his way. Didn't matter to either of them that he was a married man. That was the stigma attached to our sexuality. A woman could spread her legs for a married man, and the worst thing she would be called was a home wrecker or a whore. If a man cheated on his wife with another man, especially in the black community, then he was the reason HIV ran rampant in the black community. He was disgusting and nasty, and the world would never be forgiving to a down-low faggot.

It angered me that Michael had placed himself into that DL category. Why he did that with his wife was beyond me. I was jealous of the chemistry between him and Summer. Wanted to know what it meant to say, "Fuck all my morals," and to go there with him one more time. I wanted to, but his living a secret wasn't all I'd have to worry about if I did that. I'd have to worry about the woman sitting on my lap and how she would see me after the deed was done. I had all the restraints, and they had all the freedom. What part of the game was that?

"You think you can just come in here to say, 'I'm sorry,' and all will be well?" I asked Summer.

She contemplated her answer and then said, "I was hoping I could."

I frowned. "What?"

"I was hoping I could. Was hoping this time would be different. Since you've been ignoring me, I've had time to think."

I shrugged and asked, "And?"

"And I'm ready to answer you honestly."

I studied her curiously as I tilted my head. "And you think that will make me do what you want? What if I told you it was too late, Summer? Huh? What if I said I didn't care anymore?"

"I'd say you were lying."

"You want to take that bet?" I asked her honestly.

She swallowed slowly and then frowned a bit as she asked, "Are you serious?"

"I am."

"Then look me in my eyes and say so," she demanded as she placed her lips lightly against mine. "Tell me to my face."

I sat forward. Stared into those pretty brown eyes of hers. "It's too late. I don't care anymore," I said with finality.

She slowly sat back. Her face drained of all its color. I got satisfaction from that. It was damn good to know I could have that effect on her. Her eyes blinked rapidly, and then she stood. For a moment all she did was stare down at me as I gazed up at her. In eight years she'd never heard those words from me. For eight years we'd played this game. It had been a long time coming, or so I told myself. Her eyes glazed over with unshed tears when she turned, snatched up her purse, yanked my office door open, and stormed out.

I went home that night knowing that I'd lied not only to her, but also to myself. No matter what that woman did or said to me, I'd never not care about her or be done with her. I went in search of the only thing that completed me, like the night did the day, like yin did yang. Got to her house and used my key to let myself in. Found her lying in bed, with tears painting her cheeks. I didn't like to see her cry. Had seen her shed tears only when she talked about her foster father being in prison. I couldn't stand to see the hurt I'd caused her. Like all the other times, I went to her, and she welcomed me with open arms. I fell between her thighs naturally. She opened them for me just the same. It had taken me eight years to get her the way we were in that moment.

Even so, it was like the laws of attraction with us. Like attracted like. She attracted me. . . . I attracted her. And this was the universe's response.

So there we were. Back at her place. Both of us naked, with me on my back and her rolling her hips against mine. No woman or man I'd ever been with could move like Summer. She worked a man over like it was her purpose in life. Like she had been born to do it. She was into it like she wanted you to remember her long after you went back home to your wife.

I thought about Michael. As if she could read my mind, she gazed deep into my eyes and smiled. I lifted my hips to meet hers. Made her catch my thrust in a way that ensured she wouldn't be able to throw it back. She moaned hard, deep in her gut, and lolled forward. She rested her head against mine as I made her sing a continuing song of pleasure and pain. Tried to knock Michael from her head, as I was sure she'd tried to do plenty of times before.

She sat up again. Got her bearings after I slowed down my frantic thrusts. My hands cupped Summer's plentiful breasts while I screwed up my face and stared into her "I'm about to come" face. She was slowly rocking those thick hips, and then she moved up and down. Rose all the way up until I threatened to come out, then slowly dropped back down. She took all of me. Flinched when she knew she'd bitten off more than she could chew.

"You're going to hurt yourself," I whispered to her.

Her eyes rolled to the back of her head before she leaned forward to kiss me. "As long as it hurts this good, I don't care."

She hissed and then grunted. Dipped her head to kiss my neck, ears, nipples. She licked and sucked my nipples like she was showing me how she wanted me to return the favor. When she sat up, I did return the favor and then some. There were certain parts of Summer's body that turned her arousal up a notch more so than others. Certain parts that I could kiss or touch that would set fire to the love we made. Like when my hands gripped and squeezed her sides as my hips rose to meet hers. Or the way my hands traveled up to snatch and pull at her hair. Sometimes, my nails dug into the skin on her back. Made her arch so perfectly that I could feel when her womb quivered. The wetness between us was so consistent that it sang to us each time she moved.

Maxwell and Alicia serenaded us in the background. Felt as if they were singing our life story as our lovemaking swayed to the tune of the song. Like the singers in the song, we couldn't stay away from one another. "Like moths to a flame" didn't explain us. This thing . . . the thing we had was like staring head-on into the sun. No matter how it burned, no matter the damage, we couldn't stay away. I didn't hold back on letting her hear how she made me feel. My moans and groans, my sounds of satisfaction, blended in with hers.

Her teeth grazed her bottom lip as she studied my face. My heart swelled as it thumped in my chest. If you'd never experienced a natural high, then you wouldn't know what I was going through at that moment. It was like an out-of-body experience. Felt as if I was floating above us. That feeling excited me. Made me work harder to get her to the point of no return. We were loud. No fucks were given as to what her neighbors would think. She begged me to love her harder. Wanted us to release together. She said she needed that. Needed us to reach that climax together so she could get that high that only I could give her.

"Nobody has ever made me feel the way you do," she assured me.

"Not even him?" I asked her.

She knew who I was asking about. I'd seen the way those two reacted to one another. Knew the sexual chemistry there was explosive. He made her as wet as I did, if not wetter. So damn wet. She was practically leaking down her legs in that movie theater after he'd first kissed her. That was from his kiss alone. I knew that feeling. Knew what it was to kiss Michael and be ready to explode minutes later.

"Not even him," she said to me.

"Mine?" I asked her.

"Yours."

I quickly flipped her over so that she was back under me. My weight was on her as I lifted her legs over the creases of my arms and made her take all of me to the hilt. She absorbed every ounce of me. Didn't leave anything to the imagination. My mouth hurried to find hers as I swelled to the point that it ached. The muscles in my ass and in the backs of my thighs were working overtime as we made her bed rock. We made our own song with the rocking of her bed. I kissed her like I was starved for that kind of affection. Moved from her lips to her eyes, then back to her lips before finding her neck.

"Oh, God, David . . . I'm coming, baby," she told me softly.

"Yeah? Open your eyes, baby. Let me see you," I told her.

She did what I had asked. Summer was so beautiful when she made that ugly come face. I found my rhythm. Moved slow, smooth, and steady in and out of her. Looked down and saw the way her satisfaction coated my dick, and moved against her harder. That was my motivation. I wanted to keep her coming that way. I switched gears. Gave her daddy long strokes that made her gasp for air like she was drowning, then mean, short strokes that had her back arching and her body jerking like someone was reviving her with electricity.

As she gave in to that feeling of bliss . . . oblivion, she threw her hips at me. Matched my long strokes with her short ones. Opened her legs wide so I could keep hitting that spot she liked.

"Right there, David. Right there. Ah, yeah. Please don't stop, baby," she pleaded.

And I wouldn't. I wouldn't stop until I released. I released in her so hard that my guttural groan sounded like some shit that should have been on Animal Planet.

"Did you keep in contact with Michael's wife after she cheated with you?" Summer asked me out of the blue.

We lay basking in the afterglow of sex, thinking, *What now?* She'd thrown her right thigh on my right one, and she'd laid her head on my chest. There was some light touching between the two of us. The heavy rain falling outside had replaced the music that had come through the Bose speakers in the walls of her home.

I looked down at her and wondered where the hell that question had come from. "What?"

"Did you still talk to her after she screwed you?" There was something in her voice that I couldn't readily pick up on, but if I was a betting man, I'd say it was contempt for Sadi.

"Why?"

She shrugged and then glanced up at me. "Just want to know."

"She called me a few times after."

"You never called her?"

"No. What reason would I have to?"

"So you didn't like her at all?"

"Liked her enough to get what I wanted, but that was it."

"Oh."

"Why? Did Michael tell you otherwise?" I asked her.

"No. Was curious, is all."

I had to chuckle. Summer was as transparent as Saran Wrap. I'd seen that she and Michael were friends on Facebook now. He followed her on Instagram too. Nigga liked every picture he could find of her. I believed if he could have, he would've liked the pictures with her ass to the camera twice. He made slick comments to her. Ones with sexual innuendos in them that a regular person wouldn't notice if he or she was looking at them. But as a man who knew Michael almost better than he knew himself, I had picked up on it instantly.

I'd seen that she'd gone through his pictures too. Thing with Michael was, he didn't believe in sharing his family with the world. So there were only pictures of him showcasing his arrogance. A shirt off here, which meant he was flexing his prowess at the gym. Sweats hanging low in another picture, which obviously meant he was showcasing his abs and the print of his dick. Michael was into himself like that.

Sadi was on his friends list, but if you didn't know them, then you didn't know they were married, judging by his Facebook page, although she had pictures of Michael on her page. Neither of them would put their kids on their pages. Had always wanted to keep that part of their lives private. Sadi posted little words of affection on Michael's page, which he would respond to, but obviously, Summer couldn't see them, because she wasn't friends with Sadi.

I could look at Summer and tell that Michael had left an impression on her. She'd gone from disliking him, because of his connection to me, to being curious about his wife. Clear indication that he'd stirred that female competitiveness with other women within her. While she wondered about me and Michael's wife, I thought back to the disagreement we'd had while at Underground Atlanta. I shouldn't have snapped at her, but I'd been that angry and annoyed.

"You like Michael now, huh?" I asked her to take my mind off it.

"Not sure. I'm stuck somewhere between infatuation and being in lust."

I laughed. "I know the feeling."

"Has he called you?" she asked me.

"Yeah."

"You talk to him?"

"Once or twice."

She looked taken aback, like she was offended by my answer. "But you wouldn't talk to me?"

"And?"

Part of me was being honest with her. Another part of me enjoyed the fact that I could ruffle her feathers. There she was, telling me she was in lust with my ex-lover a few minutes after she and I had sexed one another into another realm.

"You don't see a problem with that, David?"

"No."

"What?"

"No," I repeated.

"Why?"

"I don't love him. His words don't hurt like yours do."

She chuckled and shook her head a bit. "Okay then."

"Have you talked to him?" I turned her question on her.

"We text."

"Oh, I see."

"What's that supposed to mean?"

"How often are you two texting?"

"Every other day. Sometimes more than once a day. Sometimes all day. He told me his wife has been giving him hell. Said he missed us and wanted to come back, but he couldn't, because of her."

I smiled wide. She had said the last part of her statement with such nastiness. As if she was mad his wife was demanding that he stay home.

"Guess you were texting him to get over not talking to me, huh?" I asked sarcastically.

She looked at me with a slight smirk. "Of course."

"I see. Guess I was talking to him to get over not speaking to you too."

"Whatever, David."

"Feeling's mutual, Summer, or should I call you Freckles?"

She screwed up her face at me but couldn't hide the blush the name Michael had given her. We lay there in silence for a bit. The rain kept falling harder and harder. Then thunder and lightning decided to join the chorus of rain She crawled over me. Straddled my lap and gazed into my eyes. For the longest time, she stared at me as she lay that way. She didn't make any moves. Didn't say anything. Just studied me.

My senses were aware and alert. My manhood could feel the heat of her womanly parts. I made that muscle jump underneath her. She moaned lightly, then smiled. I gave her one in return. The mood was set. Eroticism at its best. We were in a state of arousal and anticipation. We would attempt through whatever means to get there too.

# Summer

When David and I woke up the next morning, we were sluggish and fulfilled. We'd torn and ripped at one another all night long. I'd missed him over that two-week period. Didn't want to admit I'd become addicted to the way he sexed me. When I was away from him, I'd sat at home alone, and during those late nights I'd tried to use my Hitachi wand to get that feeling of pure bliss again. My magic wand hadn't worked, though. I couldn't work a spell powerful enough to reproduce the orgasms David had given me.

So, all through the night, we made up for the lost time. I was sore. So sore that I was barely walking. There were bruises on my inner thighs from when he had pushed my knees behind my ears. Bruises showed where he had licked, sucked, and bit on them. It looked as if I'd been battered and beaten on the insides of my thighs. But all the pain was so worth it in the end. I'd never known satisfaction the way I knew it with David.

We rose slowly. Showered sluggishly. And even though I was too sore to take any more, when he entered me from behind, slid between my slippery petals, and penetrated me until I could give only whimpers, instead of my usual moans, I knew what it was to have an out-of-body experience. Warm water beat down on us as we experienced nirvana again. God, he was all over me. Licked and kissed me everywhere, from the front to the back. David tickled my brown star with his tongue. Introduced me to another realm of pleasure when he let his thumb linger there while he pushed in and out of me slowly.

I'd lost my mind. Told him to give me more. Shivered when he used my wetness mixed with the water as lubricant to let his thumb slip slowly into me anally. He didn't give me the whole thing. Just enough for me to know what it was to feel pleasure that way. In that moment I wanted to do or say whatever he wanted me to. The way he smacked my ass and spread my cheeks took me up that elevator to heaven. *All aboard, ready or not.* David made me come so hard.

We stayed in that damn shower until the water chilled our bones and we couldn't stand it anymore. I attempted to cook breakfast, but David chased me through the house. Took me down in my front room and had breakfast his way. We were interrupted by a call from his partner, my boss. He wanted to know if David could take his place in court the following Monday. I took him down deep in the back of my throat as he took that phone call.

Licked his balls and made him stutter as he talked about a client possibly serving prison time for the aggravated assault charges brought against him. He spit out legal terms, while I spit on his dick. Spit on it and slurped it all back up. I made it nasty for him. Swallowed his whole manhood until he could feel my throat close when I swallowed. I did that humming thing he liked. Performed the act of fellatio so well, it made him hang up on his partner as he released that pent-up aggression. I kept sucking and sucking until he snatched me by the back of my hair and shoved me backward. I'd tried to suck all the life he had to give me and to leave only a husk of the man he'd been.

"Shit. Sorry," he muttered, trying to catch his breath. He looked like he was about to cry. That beautiful nut he released weakened him more. "I'm sorry, baby." His body jerked and twitched as his head lolled back. He licked his lips while trying to catch his breath. "I didn't . . . didn't mean to push you. . . . Sensitive . . ."

He was having trouble breathing. I smiled. Got up off my naked ass and walked over to kiss him. Breathed for him until he calmed down.

We finally got dressed. Headed to the Your Dekalb Farmers Market to pick up some fresh produce and other items for dinner. Walked through a sea of ethnicities and races to get fresh lobsters and crab legs. Grabbed some spinach pasta and ingredients for him to make his home-made Alfredo sauce. Walked over to the beef counter so he could get prime cuts of steak.

We hadn't done much talking the night before or during the morning. We'd been so lost in each other that we hadn't seemed to care about that question that lingered between us. My mind traveled back to when Michael had invaded our world.

I'd had David, and I'd had Michael. Those two had given me pleasure like I'd never known. Part of me wished Michael would fly back down to us. I wanted a little bit more of him before I said enough. So many thoughts were on my mind when it came to our threesome. I'd seen them touch one another before. The little things they did to one another turned me on. I'd never forget the way my body reacted when I saw their tongues touch for the first time while they lapped at my breasts.

But how did I, as a woman, get over those fears of allowing David to let go and experience what I knew he missed with Michael? Was it selfish of me to experience the unbridled satisfaction of my sexual exploration and leave David lacking? Was the fact that Michael was married the only reason David didn't travel down that road again?

"You should have worn a bigger coat," David said to me once he'd made sure I was safely buckled into my car.

David walked around to the passenger side and got in. He always fussed when I didn't wear the appropriate attire for winter. It was cold out. Most people were bundled up as if there was snow on the ground. I had on red tights, boots that resembled moccasins, and a light T-shirt, with only a hoodie as my cover.

"It's colder than Eskimo twat, and you out here in only a hoodie," he added, continuing to fuss.

He too was bundled up. Gloves, leather coat, skullcap, and all.

"I'm okay," I said to him as I backed out and then blended in with the traffic.

"That's not the point."

"Stop fussing."

"Wear a coat."

I shook my head and rolled my eyes as I pulled into traffic on East Ponce de Leon. I was quiet as David took phone calls. I texted my mother while at a stop light and told her I would call her later. My mind raced back to Michael again. I hadn't really got a chance to say good-bye to him. He had gotten up and had dressed before I even opened my eyes. Woke me only when he was on his way out the door so I could lock my door behind him. He had to get back home to his wife and kids. Didn't kiss me good-bye or give me hug. He rushed back to his hotel room to pack. David and I had been only a secret rendezvous for him. Something about that made me feel like we had been only something for him to do.

"I need the legal memo you did on the Johnson case once we get back to your place," David told me once he'd gotten off the phone.

"I haven't finished it yet," I said.

"Need it by tomorrow."

I glanced at him. "I won't be done by tomorrow."

"I need it by tomorrow," he repeated. When it came to work, he didn't show me any favors. Treated me like the rest of the hired helpers around the office.

"Okay," I responded.

Didn't want to make him go on a tangent about it, and he would. When it came to work and time, it was best to be on time and to do the work thoroughly, or he'd rip you a new asshole. I cruised down the expressway in silence as we headed back to my house. After he finished fooling with his phone, he slipped it in his phone jacket pocket and then placed his hand on my thigh. I smiled a bit at the warm, tingly feeling I felt in my private areas. When his hand eased upward until it nestled tightly between my thighs, I glanced at him.

His head was thrown back on the seat, as if he was sleeping, but he wasn't. "Pay attention to the road, Summer," he said to me.

"Kind of hard with your hand down there," I responded.

His head lolled to the side, and he opened his eyes and looked at me. "You trying to kill us?"

I looked back at the road, then quickly at him again. "It'd be your fault."

He smirked, rubbed his hand against me until I clenched involuntarily. My hands gripped the steering wheel hard.

"David, stop," I told him.

"Make me."

I exhaled loudly, blowing out steam, and tried to keep my focus on the road. "I don't have on any underwear. You're going to have me get out of the car with a wet spot on my tights."

All he did was chuckle. After a while he stopped. I decided to get us home quickly, before he made me kill us. My mind wandered back to Michael. I kept wondering what his wife looked like. Wondered if she looked better than me. I wanted to put a face to the voice of the woman who hated for her husband to touch himself. Wanted to know what it was about her that would make David lie with her so easily.

I drove the rest of the way back to my place with David's hand still resting peacefully on my sweet spot. Once we got in, David didn't have time to cook, since he had to familiarize himself with the case so he could be prepared for Monday. I prepared dinner for us, while he sat at the table and clicked away on his MacBook. After we ate, I took a seat at my home computer and finished the memorandum on the Johnson case, since I knew David wasn't joking about needing it by the next day.

I distracted him a few times. Sat on his lap and got a bit touchy-feely. He welcomed it for a while but then told me he had to get done, or he wouldn't be ready for court on Monday. I pouted. Reluctantly agreed to leave him be. I finished the legal memo. Hit PRINT and then decided to go shower. I messed around in my room, cleaned up a bit. Called my mom, like I'd told her I would.

"Summer? Hey, baby girl." My mom's voice came floating through the phone.

I looked at the clock and saw that it was almost seven in the evening. I'd been so caught up in David and Michael that I hadn't had a chance to talk to her. We'd send a text here and there, but we'd had no phone time. I missed her songbird-like voice.

"Hey, Mama. What are you up to?" I asked.

David stirred around downstairs. I could hear him on the phone as I talked with my mother.

"Oh, you know, preparing Sunday dinner for tomorrow. Were you busy?"

"No." I cleared my throat. "Not right now I'm not."

"Well, I haven't gotten a call from you since you called me drunk. Everything okay?"

"Yeah. Me and David—"

"You two were fighting again?"

"We weren't fighting."

"Well, what did you do this time, Summer?"

I sighed and rolled my eyes. My family loved David too. He'd been invited to many family dinners over the past eight years. "Mama, can't I have called you just because?" I asked.

"Not when you're drunk, Summer. You only call drunk when David is involved. So what happened?"

I didn't know if I wanted to rehash what had happened. Besides, it was over. We'd rectified the situation. No need to bring up old troubles.

"I'll tell you some other time," I said.

"Okay, honey. If you don't want to talk, then you don't have to. Don't hold it in if you need to get it out, okay?"

That was my mother. Ever the supportive spouse and parent. She would listen to whatever problems we came to her with. From the first time Hannah's period came to when my cherry had been popped, Mama had been all ears. Had never made us feel as if talking about sex was a bad thing. As much of an "old-time religion" Christian as she was, she had never made us feel like having sex would send us to hell.

"I know, Mama," I said with a smile.

"I talked to your father today."

My ears perked up. We hadn't heard from Dad in months. He would go through these phases where he wouldn't call us and wouldn't allow us to come visit him.

"How is he?" I asked anxiously.

"He's well, baby. He sent me a letter too, with pictures, new pictures. Isn't it funny that on the day he calls, I get a letter and pictures too? He must have sent them out earlier in the week or last week some time." She giggled like a schoolgirl. I heard pots and pans rattling around.

The spray of water coming on made it sound as if there was wind in the background.

I smiled at the fact that she was still very much in love with Dad. "Does he still look like Jax from *Sons of Anarchy?*"

Mama cackled. "You know he hated when you told him that. He says that white boy looks dirty."

We both laughed at my father's assessment. No matter how old my dad got, he kept getting younger, it seemed. My mama was almost ten years younger than he was, and she looked damn good for her age as well, but Dad looked a whole lot younger than she did.

"How's he holding up in there?"

"He just got out of Sol-Con for fighting again. That was why we hadn't heard from him in so long this time around. I thought he had gone into one of his moods again." Sol-Con was what my father called solitary confinement.

"Did he ask about me?"

"Of course he did, silly child. If he doesn't ask about any of the other children, he will always ask about you."

I could hear the emotion in her voice. She always got emotional when we talked about Daddy. We both got quiet.

A few moments later, I said, "Mama?"

She was breathing erratically, so I knew she was shedding tears. "Yes, Summer?"

"Is he going to say what the parole board wants to hear this time around?"

"Oh, dear God, I hope so, Summer. I truly hope so. I miss him so much, baby girl. I do. It was so hard after he went away. Trying to raise the rest of the kids without him. Getting you all through college. I miss my man so much. He was . . . is the best thing that ever happened to me."

Guilt tackled me in that moment. I stood from the bed and walked over to the window. Droplets of rain slid down the window as I imagined the tears falling down Mama's face. David was chuckling at something. He spoke loudly. He was talking to Michael. I'd heard when he uttered his name moments before. Told him to go fuck himself as he laughed.

"I'm sorry, Mama . . . ," I whispered.

"You did the right thing, Summer. You did. I wish you would have told sooner. Then the other children wouldn't have suffered. We tried so hard to provide a safe environment for you guys, but every once in a while a devil got through."

My thoughts traveled back to the foster brother who had raped and molested me. It had gone on until I was fifteen, and then he'd just stopped. He had lived with us while he was in college. I thought he had simply targeted me because I was the oddball in the family, the black sheep literally. That and the fact that he had caught me at the yacht that day I was watching my parents have sex. He had threatened to tell, and that had been enough to keep me quiet. And then, one night, I'd caught him doing it to one of the little girls. She wasn't black. She was white, like my other siblings. That had sparked something in me. There was nothing wrong with me. It was him. He just liked preying on children. I made a beeline to my parents and told them everything. Once I opened my mouth, three more of my foster brothers and sisters spoke up.

My dad was livid. Mama had to stop him from going to my brother's job to harm him. Took all of us crying and begging him to stay home for him not to do it. He finally agreed to stay home and calmed down before confronting that brother. And then, late that night, when we were all asleep, Dad snuck out of the house. A few hours later Mama got the phone call that he had shot and killed Bobby. Took a shotgun and blew a hole through his chest.

"I didn't know he would kill Bobby," I whispered.

"That perverted devil got exactly what he deserved, Summer. Don't you go blaming yourself for this again. John would probably do it all over again if he had to. No child deserves that pain. None. Took us years of therapy to get you, Celine, and the other children functional again. All those damn child services people in our home, like we were running some kind of perv camp," she fussed. She slammed pots and pans around as she did. I could hear the ruckus.

"Is Daddy going to let us come see him?" I asked as I wiped my tears away.

"No," she said in a huff. "Said we didn't need to see him all bruised up. Those goddamned racist Aryan Brotherhood assholes are giving him a hard time because he crosses color lines," she said with a chuckle. "You know how your father is. Ever the liberal hippie. He would have been a Black Panther if he could have gotten away with it."

I smiled. "Yeah, but prison is a whole new ball game. Different set of rules in there."

"I know. I told him not to get himself killed while in there. Wish he would let us see him."

"I wish he would too," I told her.

That was how Daddy was. He was ever a man's man. Even after I saw him with another man, nothing changed the image of him I had in my head. My parents had their sexual preferences, but they were still my parents. They protected me the most, because they felt they had to. I was one of only ten black children in my private school at the time. But Clarissa and John Kennedy made sure I wasn't treated any differently when it came to academics and extracurricular activities. They'd chew the whole administration out if they had to.

Although things changed when Daddy went to prison, we had enough money, so we didn't know the difference. Mama ran Daddy's boating and boat sales company until she couldn't do it without him anymore. She sold it, with his permission, and deposited another big check into our family's back account.

Mom kept talking but changed the subject. Brought the spotlight back on me and asked when I was coming for dinner. Told me to make sure David was with me when I did. That took my mind back to the question that I was soon going to have to answer when it came to me and David. I knew that sooner or later he would feel the need to ask me again. After the sex-induced haze wore off, he'd want his answer.

My mom and I talked for a few minutes more. Then she got off the phone so she could call Hannah. She said I'd called and reminded her that she needed to call the others. She was making her rounds, calling all her children to check in. I sat in my room for a moment. Needed to get my emotions in check. No matter what my mom had said, I would always feel like it was my fault a good man was in prison.

# Summer

I had to shake myself out of those thoughts. Didn't want to be depressed, like we all had been when Dad first went away. I walked back downstairs to find that David had ended his phone call with Michael. Wondered what they had talked about. Wanted to know if he'd asked David about me or if he had decided to come back to Atlanta to walk the road of adultery with us again. Decided to check my Facebook page. First person I saw when I logged on was Michael. He'd posted a new picture. Sweat dripped down his body, as if water had been thrown on him. His left hand was a fist as he flexed his arm. Tongue was hanging out of his mouth, making Gene Simmons's tongue look subpar. I crossed my legs and moved around in my desk chair. I remembered what that tongue could do. Thought back to how it had wrestled with my clitoris until it had won that fight.

*#Beast* was all the caption read underneath the picture. I would have clicked LIKE on the picture, but something told me not to. Scrolled through all the comments and laughed at how women had no shame throwing themselves at him. I kept staring into his eyes. Couldn't get over the golden honey color, which stood out in stark contrast to the dark chocolate complexion. Apparently, I wasn't the only one infatuated and in lust with him. His adoring female public talked about everything from the length of his tongue to what they wanted him to do with his big hands. I wondered if he'd had sex with any of the women who were obviously

willing to give him pussy. Saw a few gays in the mix too. Started to feel a bit of jealousy and closed the picture.

I needed a high to get over the conversation with my mom. I knew what junkies and alcoholics meant when they said the high took their minds off the pain. I swallowed hard. There was only one thing that could get me that high. I logged out of Facebook, then walked over to kiss David on his shoulder. He cast a quick glance at me and gave me a light smile. I moved his locks to the side and then kissed the back of his neck.

He grunted. "You're not going to let me finish this, are you?" he asked.

"Can't you take a break?"

"No."

I placed his hand against my sex so he could feel what I wanted. "You sure?"

He chuckled and turned around on the stool. "So staring at Michael gets you heated, and you come to me to put the fire out?"

"I wasn't staring," I said, defending myself. Even when I thought David wasn't watching, he was keeping his eyes on my every move.

"What do you call it?" he asked as he pulled me between his legs. He kept his hand on my sex. He was rubbing and stroking slightly.

"Was admiring the state-of-the-art gym behind him."

David chuckled. Pulled me closer, then slipped his hand underneath my nightshirt. I was already soaked. All he had to do was whip his johnson out, and I could guide him right to the promised land. "Yeah?" He let his fingers slip and slide between my folds.

"Shit," I murmured. "Yeah, fine landscaping, artwork in that gym."

"I know. Been on that land, doing the 'scaping,' plenty of times. I know every inch of that artwork," he responded.

I flinched. He slipped two of his fingers inside me. "I don't care."

"Yes, you do."

"I don't."

"Want to see me do it again?" he asked me.

I tilted my head and bit down on my bottom lip. "Say what?"

"Michael said he's thinking about coming back," he answered.

"When?" I asked.

"Tomorrow or the next day. He isn't too sure yet."

I didn't want to show my excitement, but I was sure he felt it. "You in lust with him too?" I asked David.

He gave me a lopsided grin. "Never fell out of lust with him."

David's thumb, soaked by my arousal, made figure eights around my clitoris. His middle finger loved me so good that my head fell back and my legs started to quiver.

"We can be in lust with him together," I whispered.

"We already are," he answered.

"We can show him what it feels like to have us lust after him together too." I eyed David cautiously. Needed to see if he was reading between the lines. Wanted to see if he was picking up what wasn't being said.

He didn't say anything at first. "Can you handle it?"

"What? The lust? Doing just fine now," I said with an air of confidence that I didn't really feel.

"The lust between him and me is a bit different. More powerful. Primal. Aggressive."

I knew what he was telling me. He was giving me a way out. Telling me that I didn't have to do this. Informing me that the energy was not the same between him and Michael as it was between him and me.

"I want to see it. Show me," I said.

He removed his fingers from inside me, stood from the bar stool. He took my hand as we walked to my couch. Made me stand in front of him while he sat on the edge.

"Take your shirt off," he told me.

I did without hesitation. "What are you about to do?"

He didn't answer. Just gazed up at me. Took in my facial features, then studied my breasts. My nipples hardened. Breasts swelled in the name of David. He held my hands as his eyes roamed my body like it was a work of art. Sometimes it wasn't about the sex. It was about the eroticism of the moment. It was in the look that he was giving. The way he licked his lips, then bit down on the bottom one told me what he was thinking. It caused my heart rate to jump a notch. I could feel the goose bumps rising on my flesh.

He finally moved one hand to touch my stomach. Let it trail upward to that place between my breasts, then brought it back down again. David placed kisses around my mound. He placed kisses down below, everywhere he could, but he never stopped touching me. Sometimes something as simple as a touch, that feeling of being sexually aroused, excited me more than anything. It was all about the connection I felt to him in that moment that had me shaking.

I was so into his touch that when his tongue touched my clitoris, I hissed and jumped back. He pulled me back to him. Placed his hands on my ass cheeks to hold me in place while he used his legs to spread mine. David buried his face between my thighs. French-kissed my pearl until I was making sounds I didn't recognize. As bad as I wanted to run away, I couldn't, because he wouldn't let me. He had me locked to him so he could eat to his heart's desire. My hands found his locks as my head fell back. I was feeling like I could have him stay there forever.

I was in a state of euphoria. Couldn't stop moaning, squirming, and rolling my hips against his face if I wanted to. David was greedy. Wouldn't give in to my pleas of not being able to take any more. He threw one of my legs over his shoulders and made me take all he had to give and then some. Women went mad after they got oral pleasure like this. Women lost their damned minds. Started going through phones. Demanding that the person giving never give that pleasure to another soul. Became possessive, as if they owned that person and the pleasure they gave.

I wondered if he had done this to Michael's wife. Michael had said her pussy had been on David's lips. Envy turned my eyes green as I thought about how many ways David must have had that woman. Must have been good to her. She'd kept calling him afterward. His lips must have made her forget the new husband she'd eloped with.

David dropped from the couch. Fell on his knees, like he was surrendering all his sins to me. After lapping at my lips, he let the tip of his tongue flick against my clitoris. Licked slowly against it before sucking it into his mouth. His hands never stopped touching me. Palming my ass, massaging it. Fondling my breasts. Moved his nails to dig down my back. He hummed against my clit, and the vibrations damn near crippled me.

It was then that he let me go. Before my orgasm took me to that deluxe apartment in the sky, he let me go. David stood up before he cupped both sides of my face and allowed me to taste what he had done to me. It always paid to keep a clean pussy. I loved the way I tasted and smelled. No musty odor. Just water and the sweet nectar of fruit juices. Aggressiveness laced his tongue. I returned what he gave me with fervor. I needed to come, but he held it in the palm of his hand. Wouldn't release it until he was ready. He pulled back and then looked down at me.

"I didn't come," I told him.

"I know. Didn't want you to," he said as he backed away.

"Where you going?"

"Be right back," he said to me.

"David . . ."

"Be right back."

He walked away and left me there. I felt like he'd taken my sanity with him. I needed that release. I was so close to the edge that it was almost paralyzing. I'd always been able to please myself. Had always been taught that it wasn't up to the man to give you an orgasm. A woman had to know her own body to get the pleasure she so desired, Clarissa Kennedy had taught me. I crawled onto my couch. Couldn't sit on the microfiber like I wanted to, since my wetness would stain it. I got on my knees, chest on the back of my couch. Ass poked out and back arched like David was behind me, giving me life through the strokes of his penis.

Used my left hand to touch myself. My eyes rolled in the back of my head as I did so. There she was. That beautiful orgasm I was chasing was in the distance. I worked my Kegels, tightened them, then released as I stroked my clit. I imagined David and Michael watching me. Imagined them stroking their arousals as I played in mine. Could hear them telling me nasty and vulgar things they wanted to do to me. My pleasure soaked my fingers.

I got at least half of my wish. David walked back into the room. I heard the noise of the movements he made. Turned my head to see he had moved one of my end tables to the center of the room. Had placed it in front of the couch. I watched him as I spit out vulgar words. Called on the Son of the Most High a few times as I released that first one. David brought his MacBook around. The camera was on, as I could see my backside on the screen.

"You're r-recording us?" I mumbled.

"Nah," he answered.

I watched as he pulled up Skype, pressed the CALL button, and seconds later Michael's face showed up on the screen.

"What up?" Michael answered.

He hadn't really taken in what was happening on his screen yet. David didn't respond. He moved out of the way, and there was a full moon view of my backside and wet desire. I listened as David's belt buckle clanked and rattled. His pants hit the floor, and he removed his boxer briefs.

"Hey, Michael," I said.

"Shit," was how he responded once he realized what was happening.

I heard his wife fussing at the kids in the background. Watched as his camera moved like it was tumbling across the floor. Michael was rushing away from his family. Had to move so he could watch his live, homemade porn in private. The room on his end went dark for a minute, and then light invaded the background again. He sat his laptop down. Adjusted it and tilted his head to the side.

"What the fuck y'all trying to do? Get me divorced?" he asked.

Sounded like attitude was in his voice, but I knew it was a front. Could tell by the way he was breathing and licking his lips. Michael was a freak in every sense of the word. He lived for shit like what we were doing. It gave him another reason to play with his dick. David walked over to the couch with stealth. Grabbed a handful of my hair and pulled it back. That move created the perfect arch and dip in my back. He eased inside me so slowly that all I could do was bare my teeth and groan like it was the only language I knew.

One of David's hands closed around my neck as he whispered low in my ear. "Tell him you think he should come back," he demanded.

He was so deep inside me that the emotional attachment I felt to him started to surface. He was stirring something in my soul with the way he was working me.

"Fuck, David, I love you," I blurted out before I could stop myself.

"I know," was how he responded. "You want him to come back?" he asked me.

"Yes," I whispered.

"Tell him," he demanded as he stroked me faster, going harder each time he sank back inside me.

We were in lust with Michael. Allowing our minds to wander and fall into thoughts of *Vorfreude* once again when it came to Michael. Dangerous game we were playing, and we both knew it.

"So y'all just gone do this in front of me? Knowing I can't be there to join in, huh?" Michael asked sarcastically.

"Get on a plane, Michael," I said with bated breath.

"Can't. Wife's like Sherlock around here," he said.

"Why?" I asked.

"I don't know." His head tilted, and he licked his lips. "Damn, Summer," Michael whispered, like he was fascinated with what he was seeing.

Every woman had that intuition, that gut feeling that told her the man she shared a home and bed with was up to no good. I was sure Sadi's womanly instincts had kicked in. They were telling her that Michael had gone to Atlanta and had done more than he told her he had.

David made me pay for Michael saying no. Bit down into that space between my neck and shoulder as he penetrated me to the point of pain. That slight curve was killing me, but the way the mushroom head of his arousal tapped against my spot was bringing me back to life.

"She isn't satisfying you, anyway," I said to Michael.

He was watching us but staring at me. His eyes never left mine as he looked on. "She gave me some when I came home," he answered lackadaisically.

"Yeah, but was it satisfying?"

I heard him chuckle.

"I made you run from this pussy," I bragged.

He stopped chuckling. "Wait. What?"

"You couldn't handle it. David handles this shit," I said as my legs started to shake. "David," I moaned. "David doesn't run from it."

Michael grunted. I could tell by the way he licked his lips and sat back in his chair that he was remembering how I'd owned him on my front-room floor. And I was coming all over David's thighs My come drenched his thighs, showing my satisfaction David stopped abruptly. Pulled away from me and moved from the camera's view. My head fell forward when he let my hair go. My body twitched as he stood to the side. He grabbed a throw from my love seat and then placed it on the couch. He sat, wide legged, dick still rigid with life. I knew what he wanted. I eased over, straddled his lap.

David was tense. He knew that in this position there was the potential that he too would succumb to the notion of coming before he was ready. I had to ease down on that thang. Couldn't just slap myself down on David's dick. It would rip my insides to hell if I did. David's arms caressed me as Michael still tried to recover from the fact that I'd challenged his manhood. David kissed me passionately. Our heads moved in sync. We kissed the way that lovers would as my hips started to rock slowly. His left leg bounced once or twice as he fisted his hands in my hair.

If I had had eyes in the back of my head, I would have seen that David was holding eye contact with Michael as he kissed me. There was something exciting to him about the fact that Michael was watching us. Watching me ride him. Watching him succumb to the power of my pussy. I would have seen that Michael had pulled out his male anatomy and had started to stroke it in slow motion. David was watching Michael. Michael was watching us. I saw only stars behind my eyelids.

I threw my head back and put an arch in my back as I rolled my hips. My orgasmic song blended with Michael's primal grunts and David's frantic thrusts.

"Get on the plane, Michael," I urged him.

"Make me," he shot back. He was still angry that I'd called his male prowess into question.

David's breathing got deeper. As he rocked his hips in tune with me, I lifted my backside and gave a slow bounce, which made him growl. Made him throw his head back, mouth at half-mast.

"Shit, baby . . . Summer. Shit," he said, praising me. Then he whispered, "Wait."

I gave in to what he wanted. Waited until he could control his urge to release that tension building in his groin. I could feel him swell and grow inside me. There was a slow burn traveling up and down my spine. One that forced me to start to roll my hips slowly again. I looked down into David's face, and for a while, it was just he and I. No Michael being a voyeur on the camera behind us. Just me and the man who was killing me softly.

He was sweating. Glasses still on his face. I removed them and tossed them to the side of us. Stopped fucking him and started to love him. I slowly kissed his lips. Traced the outline of them with my tongue. When his tongue snaked out, instead of letting it inside my mouth, I sucked on it. His body tensed, then relaxed. I loved when his nails dug into the skin on my back.

He slowly started to work his hips underneath me again. The right corner of his upper lip started to twitch as he bit down on his bottom one. Those chocolate eyes danced and swayed with me. Hypnotized me and wouldn't let me go. I picked up the speed of my hips. Made sure he could feel me when I took him in and out of my body. His head lolled back. Hips bucked underneath me, and I knew I had him where I wanted him.

"Come for me," I told him.

He shut his eyes tight as he called my name over and over again. I tightened my muscles around him so I could feel the throbbing of his dick as he climaxed. I demanded he open his eyes. I kept eye contact with him. Made him look at me as we both experienced nirvana together.

# David

Monday rolled around and found everything in a tail-spin. Court was a circus. My client decided to threaten his wife in open court. Told her that next time he would kill her. That asshole made my job a whole lot harder than it had to be. As punishment, I didn't object when the judge held him in contempt and threw him in jail.

Then the weather called for snow, and everyone in Atlanta lost their minds as they flooded the streets to get to the grocery store and buy as much milk, bread, cereal, canned foods, and eggs as possible. Didn't get a chance to see Summer before court, because my partner, her boss, kept her busy.

I missed her. Thought about the weekend we'd shared. It had been like getting to know all over again the woman I'd known for the past eight years. We'd talked. We'd had a body party with one another. We'd got naked, painted one another with body paint, then rolled around on a canvas in her basement. We'd done things that we hadn't done before, like talk about the parents we never really knew. Both of us had always wondered what it would be like to be loved by birth parents. I'd always thought Summer was lucky. At least she had her foster parents. The Kennedys loved Summer like they had birthed her. Loved her to the point that one of them killed the foster son who had been sexually molesting her. Yeah, she was the lucky one, still. I had had group homes and sexual predators for guardians. She'd tried to get me to speak more about the sexual predator part, but I'd refused. It was something I'd never mentioned to her before, and another thing we had in common.

I cruised through the rest of the workday without incident. Saw Summer in passing. Cornered her in her office and locked the door behind me. Touched and kissed on her for a good twenty minutes, until she had to get back to work. Stuck my hand under her skirt and let my fingers dance in her love. I got on my knees and took her to heaven with my lips and tongue. Lapped at her love like I was famished and she was the only thing that could sate me. Did all that like we were lovers instead of friends. By the time five o'clock rolled around, I wanted to head home and relax for a bit. Had been at Summer's place the whole weekend, so it would be good to rest in my own bed for a few hours. The day had other plans, though.

My phone rang as soon as I walked into my home.

"Hello?" I answered, already knowing who it was.

"You still at work?" he asked me.

"No. Just getting home."

"I'm in Atlanta. Had some business to handle."

My eye twitched. Body got a chill at the thought of what would happen this time around. Thought about what Summer and I had agreed to. We were exploring sexual gratification with a married man. I'd agreed to become one of the niggas I despised. All for Summer. I would do anything to make her happy.

"And?" I responded.

"You two up for some company?"

I thumbed my nose, then put my briefcase on the table as I walked through the foyer and headed upstairs to my bedroom. "Summer's still at work."

"Does that mean you're busy?"

I inhaled as I tugged at my necktie to pull it off. "Not really. Just got home. Going to shower. Grab a few hours of sleep, until Summer gets off."

"You two always hang together like this?" he asked.

"Most times."

"Best friends in every sense of the word, huh?"

"Pretty much."

"I'm headed back to my hotel. Wanted to know if I could see you. Maybe grab a quick bite to eat."

Traffic was loud in his background. The people in Atlanta couldn't drive if their lives depended on it. I could hear KISS 104.1 playing on his radio as horns blared. I glanced at the clock and wondered what time Summer would be getting home.

"I can come to you if you want to chill at home. Can stop and grab something on the way," he suggested.

Michael knew what he was doing. Always knew, when he was trying to have things go his way, just what to say and do. While I may have been about to cross that thin gray line, I wouldn't let him come to my home. Wouldn't let him inside these walls. These walls couldn't be tainted by the treachery I was sure to help him commit.

"No. You can't come here. I'll meet you, though," I told him.

He chuckled low. It traveled down to my dick and made it spring to life. "So, I can't come to your crib, huh?" he asked.

"Nah. Not a good idea."

"Why not?"

"It's just not. You want to meet up or no?" I asked him so he wouldn't keep questioning me about it.

I looked around my bedroom. The pink-colored body pillow that lay on the other side of my bed showed where Summer slept whenever she came over. Looked at my dresser and saw things there that said she had a place in my space, as I had in hers. That little game we played was a funny one. On my bedroom wall was the same picture of us that I had in my office. Smiling faces and happier times.

"Yeah, it's cool. How long before you're dressed and headed out?" he asked.

I looked at the Movado watch on my arm. "About an hour. Where you trying to meet?"

"I'm at the InterContinental in Buckhead. There is a restaurant there. We can meet up there."

"A'ight. See you in about an hour or so."

I hung up with Michael and headed to the shower. Needed to wash away the stress of the day and relax. After I was done, I texted Summer to let her know where I was going, knowing she was in a meeting and wouldn't be able to answer her phone. After I oiled myself down, I put on a pair of designer jeans, a nice black button-down shirt, and black loafers. Pulled my locks back into a ponytail and headed out.

Got through traffic on I-75 and 400. Made it to the InterContinental without incident. I called up to Michael's room and told him to meet me downstairs, at the Bourbon Bar. While I waited for him, I watched as someone rolled cigars near the bar in the lobby. Watched as the concierge rolled in luggage and guests smiled and milled about. The ambiance of the place was reminiscent of a lounge, with small tables and sofas. I grabbed a seat at the bar and ordered two old-fashioneds, which was a regular glass of bourbon that the bartender put his or her own twist on.

It didn't take Michael long to come down. I slid him his drink when he sat on the bar stool next to me, which was more like a chair. He too was in jeans and loafers. Only he was wearing a black sweater that fit snug against his frame. His hair was groomed to perfection, the only way Michael would wear it. His scent followed him, as usual. I couldn't deny that instant need to reopen old doors. As usual, his eyes told he was up to no good. We ignored the obvious stares coming our way.

"I'm surprised Sadi let you out of the house," I said to him.

"Had to go ahead and decide to purchase that auto shop down here that I wanted," he told me. "Used that as my excuse to get away."

"She buy that?"

He shrugged. "Probably not, but my shops bring in more money than her lucrative law career, so she's not going to object."

Michael had several auto shops. They were located in New York, Jersey, Boston, and Connecticut, as well as in DC, Maryland, and Virginia, or the DMV, as most called them. We all may have thought he was nuts to walk away from law school into the world of grease, oil, and auto parts, but he had proved us all wrong and had stayed at the top of his game as a profitable businessman.

I took a sip of my drink and then responded. "So she doesn't like the fact that you're a mechanic, but she will spend the money that comes with it."

He gave a lopsided smile. "You know how she is."

"No, I don't, actually. How're the kids?"

The smile left his face, and he took a long swig of his drink. "They're okay," was all he said.

That was unusual for him. Michael loved doting on his kids. They were his pride and joy. So the fact that he balked at the opportunity to talk about them told me something else was wrong.

"Everything okay?" I asked him.

"Yeah. Thinking about some shit that Sadi and I have to talk about when I get back."

"About the kids?"

"Among other things."

"Want to talk about it?"

"Not really," he said, then took his drink to his mouth. "How you and the troublemaker, Ms. Freckles?" he asked with a smirk.

I smiled. "We're good."

"Judging by what I saw on camera, I'd say so. Last I knew, seemed like we'd pissed you off enough for you to ignore both of our phone calls."

"I was pissed off. I didn't feel like talking about it then. Don't want to talk now—"

"It's not always about what you want, David. That's your problem," Michael said to me. "You never listen when someone is trying to relay how they feel to you. You hear it, but you don't listen."

I sighed and signaled to the waiter for another drink. I didn't really come to meet him to rehash old shit that it didn't seem like we were ever going to squash. I asked him sarcastically, "So, we're about to do this here and now?"

"Look, on some real shit, I came here to rectify the situation between us. But the last time I was here, that weekend turned into some shit I wasn't expecting. I mean, I enjoyed the hell out of it, but I don't feel I did what I set out to do," he explained.

"When I apologized to you last time, I meant that. There was no bullshit that time. What I did was fucked up, but at the time it was all I had left," I told him honestly.

I'd been a man in love with a man who would never love me. I should have believed him when he told me he wouldn't the first time.

"I admit that I could have told you about the two of us getting married, but no matter what the fuck I said to you, you were still going to feel and think the way David wanted to feel and think. I told you I was in love with Sadi. Told you I wanted to be with her and build a family with her."

"Meanwhile, we were still fucking around."

"Because I was trying not to up and leave you hanging."

"But you did in the end, anyway."

"After you fucked my wife."

I thumbed my nose as I said, "I had figured we could put the thing that happened with me and Sadi behind us, but obviously, you're still feeling some kind of way about it."

"I'm not feeling *some kind of way,* David. That was . . . is my wife. You did it to hurt me, for no other reason than me wanting to be with her and not you. Then, not only did I have to live with that, I had to deal with knowing she betrayed me so easily. What you did fucked with me for a long time, and it's hard to get over something that's been staring me in the face for the past ten years."

"What do you want from me, Michael?" I asked with a shrug. "All I can do is give you an apology. I can't take that shit back."

People had turned to look in our direction, because my voice had risen a notch higher than I'd intended it to. Last thing I wanted to do was cause a scene in this place. I'd been around when some shit went down in a place like this. I once saw a dude with locks walk in and take a bar stool to another man's face. I knew that if Michael and I got too heated, it had the potential to be dangerous, as we'd come to blows many times before. It was one of the things—another was him being married—that kept me from having sex with him. I knew if I crossed that line again with him, it had the potential to lead down a tumultuous road.

I settled our tab. We grabbed our drinks to go and headed up to his room. It would be safer for us to have that conversation there. No need for us to talk about it in a public setting, anyway. That was the excuse I told myself as we hopped on the elevator and headed up to the presidential suite. Took the tension to his room. I took my drink and sat on the sofa in front of the fireplace in the living room. He walked into the bedroom, while I texted Summer to see where she was.

Wasn't surprised when she called me back right away. "You're still at the hotel with Michael?" she asked.

"Yeah."

"How long will you be there?" she asked.

I looked up to see Michael walk out of the bedroom. He had removed his sweater and had on only his jeans. No shoes. No socks. He was showcasing the body he spent so much time in the gym perfecting. He walked into the living room, and I watched as he placed something on a nearby table. He had his drink in his hand as he sat down across from me. He leaned back casually and watched me talk to Summer.

That heat, that sexual attraction that had brought us together in the first place, settled in between him and me. He smirked. I cast my gaze in another direction.

"I don't know," I told Summer.

"That's not an answer, David."

"You know where I am. If I'm not back at the time you want, come get me," I told her.

There was a long pause on the other end of the line before she hung up.

"Was that trouble calling?" Michael asked me.

"Yeah. Look, if we're going to try to at least remain friends, I don't want this shit with Sadi to keep coming between us," I told him.

"Going to be real hard for it not to, David," he said after he took a drink, then hissed. "You have no idea how what you did started to change the dynamics of my marriage after a while. Sadi doesn't even fucking know I know she fucked you," he confessed.

I frowned and sat back. Had to adjust my dick. I couldn't even refute the fact that I wanted Michael in the worst way. Still, I wouldn't even be able to go there with him if we didn't settle this shit.

"How'd you manage that?" I ask him.

"Manage what?"

"Not letting her know you know."

"I just never said anything. That would have opened another can of worms. She would have started asking too many questions about the other reasons for my anger," he said and chuckled.

"That's what happens when we're not completely honest about who we are. What other reasons would there be, anyway? You never loved me. So we know that wasn't a reason."

He tilted his head to the side and smiled languidly. That smile was the one that got me on day one. That same smile had lured the many men and women we'd shared during our time together. That smile and his eyes. Everybody had always been infatuated with his honey-colored eyes.

*My dimples. His eyes. The dynamic duo.*

He must have been thinking on the same wavelength as me, because we fell into a conversation about the days of old. Laughed about how we had snagged men and women with ease. The issue of Sadi and what I had done was a nonissue for the moment. He got up, called room service, and ordered a bottle of bourbon, to be sent up to the room. A few minutes later room service delivered it. Between shots of bourbon and talk of how Summer could work her pussy muscles better than any woman he'd ever come across, Sadi was forgotten about altogether.

I knew where things were headed when I got up to leave and he stopped me. I wanted to stay and continue to talk to him, because it was the most in depth and honest we'd been about the whole issue between us, but I needed to get to Summer. I tried to say my good-byes to him. Wasn't prepared when he stopped me from walking past him and placed a kiss on my lips. He kissed me like he wanted me to remember what we used to have. When our tongues touched, that spark of electricity that we always generated came to life, stirring something in the pit of my stomach.

That kiss came with an intensity intended to make me throw caution to the wind. There was passion in that kiss that told me that he had been deprived of the kind of chemistry we shared. I almost got lost in the way his lips felt pressed against mine. I pulled back, though. Fought with my inner demons for a minute as his eyes dared me to cross that line. Take that dive off the cliff of sanity, like he and I had done so many times before. Most people used drugs and alcohol as their vices. Michael and I had learned to use sex.

I didn't stop him when he came in for another kiss. I quickly stepped out of my loafers. My desire was already pressing against the zipper of my jeans, so when he went for my belt buckle, I helped him along the way. My shirt came next as I snaked an arm around his waist and pulled him closer to me. Michael had a body designed for pleasure. His ass would make any man or woman weep. I groped one cheek as our tongues danced to our own tune. He tugged at my jeans. I helped rid him of his, along with his boxer briefs. When he hooked his finger inside my boxer briefs and yanked them down, my manhood sprang out. Bobbed and weaved like it was ready for the fight.

I backed him up until his back slammed against the wall. Caged him between my arms as I kissed his neck, ears, lips . . . let my tongue trace his jawline while he returned the favor. The mood was set. Our bodies perspired and had a sheen of lust that could be seen and felt only by us. Chest to chest. We both knew what was coming next. I growled low in my throat. Moaned when he ran his teeth over that spot between my neck and shoulder. My hands gripped his waist as his hands slid down my back and squeezed my backside.

He pulled my locks from the ponytail holder as I gazed into his eyes. The curve of Michael's ass was magnificent, I thought as one hand came around to grope it again. That primal part of me wanted to bury myself in it and not come out until he begged me to. But I knew he never would. Michael was the only man to take every inch of me. I missed that. Wanted the thrill and excitement of seeing myself slip slowly inside him and watching him take me in with ease, as only he could.

There was pressure building. The need to get inside him was mounting.

Michael smirked. "If I didn't know any better, I would say you missed us and want this as bad as I do."

I took his hand and placed it on my dick. "Worry about that. Nothing else."

I rotated my fingers, encouraging him to turn and face the wall. Once he did so, I closed the gap. I was breathing down his neck. Michael had never taken dick from any other man but me. Two alpha males had met on the campus of Morehouse. One of us had had to cave. He'd lost that bet in the end. Had had to take all this dick and be fine with that. When we'd been with other men, I'd relished the way we fucked them. I got immense pleasure in seeing the way Michael fucked other men. He was so uninhibited. Took no prisoners.

Both of us hated for any male to lose his masculinity while we fucked him. We got off on having a man take our dick downs. Those grunts, groans, moans, strangled sounds of pain and pleasure turned us into animals. Predatory, like wolves in the wild, we would become. We would watch each other while fucking other men. Gave them all the dick they could take and then some. Got off on having a masculine male on his knees, taking our dicks to the back of his throat. Then relished the fact that once they left, it would be the two of us again, going at one another in ways that no other men could satisfy us.

Then there were the women. The women we tag teamed together were never the same. We had stalkers after we let women go. Had women show up at our jobs and school, demanding to know why we had never called them again or insisting we fuck them once more. Ate pussy like it was a pie-eating contest. Rolled our hips in sync while we loved up on women. High-fived, tagged, then switched. Took women down to their bare minimum sexually. Made 'em speak in tongues and cry out to the heavens that we had to stop fucking them the way we did, when they knew they didn't really mean it. We were out of control. Didn't know how to stop. Didn't want to. Dental dams, boxes and boxes of condoms, and trips to the health department to get those status checks were what we did.

We lived recklessly, most would say. We didn't give a damn as long as we stayed safe. That was our motto. If we stayed safe, we could fuck any man or woman we wanted. And that was what we did.

I kissed his shoulder blades as I used my hand to guide my dick between his cheeks. No penetration yet. Just stimulation to get him going. Michael's hands fisted against the wall as his breathing deepened. Back expanded as he took deep breaths.

"You want it?" I asked him. "Tell me you want it."

"You know I want it, nigga. Stop playing."

I let my tongue trail from the top of his spine all the way down to that dip in his back before the lobes of his muscled ass called out to me. I placed kisses on each cheek. Watched the muscles flex, then smacked his tight backside. Snaked my tongue out and licked around each lobe. I grabbed the oil that he had placed on the table next to the wall earlier. Poured the warm lubricant down his back and watched it glide between his cheeks. His chocolate skin glistened as I massaged the oil into his back. Sinewy muscles coiled in his back like steel cables.

Took my dick in my hand and aimed my head at his back entrance. Let my head sit there before I slipped slowly inside him. The sound of him hissing, his strangled grunt, then the thump of his fist hitting the wall motivated me. I took my time with it. There was no rush for me. Liked the way his ass slowly accepted my hardened manhood with little resistance. He was still so tight that I could tell that this still belonged to me. He would never let another man take him the way I did. I pressed my chest against his back as my hands rose to hold his against the wall.

I bit his earlobe as our bodies moved in sync. Nobody moved the way Michael and I moved when we were joined like this. We were all in. Held nothing back. I was in control of him, and as always, that made me crazy. Gave me an insane sense of pleasure. Both of our fists hit the wall at the same time.

"Fuck, Michael. Why you making me do this?" I asked him.

My mind keep flashing that warning sign that told me we were heading down the road to becoming two of *those niggas,* those down-low niggas whom everybody despised. Still, I couldn't stop, even if I wanted to. I was in too deep.

My hands held his waist as I dipped my hips and found a steady rhythm. The muscles in my ass and in the backs of my thighs strained under the intense workout they were getting. I laid into him with powerful thrusts. Ones that only a man would be able to take. My hands snaked around to join his as he jerked his dick. His dick was heavy. Was one of the things that the women we'd sexed had always marveled at. We stroked his front, while I stroked his back. In tandem we found that climax together. His dick swelled in our hands, while mine swelled inside him. Balls got tight with the need for release.

We were so caught up in the moment that not even the knock on his hotel room door stopped us.

# David

She was mad at me. Sat on the couch farthest from me while she kept her gaze on the scene outside the window. There was nothing going on out there except the Atlanta skyline coming to life.

She'd stood outside Michael's hotel room for a whole ten minutes before I opened the door. I had had to rush to the bathroom, clean myself up, and pull my pants on. One look at my face and she'd known. She couldn't bear the thought of what I'd done and had turned to storm off. I'd chased behind her. Barefoot. Jeans unfastened. No shirt as I snatched her up from behind and forced her back into the hotel room. Other guests had stared at us, wondering if a woman was being kidnapped, but nobody had done anything.

Fucked-up world we lived in. They'd frown at me for being a bisexual male, but none of those same people would lift a finger to help a woman being forced back inside a hotel room by a half-naked man. Michael, too, had managed to pull on his jeans. Hadn't bothered to fasten them. Summer had stared at him for a long time. Had seen the oil glistening on his skin, the same oil that was on mine. Had noticed the heady look of satisfaction on both of our faces, and her breathing had become that of a woman drowning and gasping for air.

Now she was sitting there, stoic and like a stone statue, as Michael and I took turns using the shower. Once he was done, he came back out to find us locked in a loud silence.

Michael leaned haphazardly on the bar in the living room, legs crossed at the ankles as he looked on. "What's up, trouble?" he greeted her.

She cut her eyes at him so hard that if looks could kill, he would have been dead and buried the year before. He chuckled and poured himself a drink. He didn't care one way or the other.

"Fuck you," she answered.

"As soon as you get over yourself, I got a king-size bed we can make that happen on," he teased her.

Summer turned her attention back to me. I wanted to be ashamed of the fact that I'd failed her in a sense. "You had to do it, huh?" she asked me.

"We talked about this," was what I gave as an answer. Weak response. But it was all I had.

"You did it. . . . I was supposed to be in—" she began, but I cut her off.

"I wasn't in the room when you fucked him last."

"You wouldn't answer your phone," she retorted.

"Didn't stop you, though." The look on my face said I was drunk on bourbon and high off sex. If one didn't know what it was to be high off sex, then one had truly never experienced satisfying sex. My locks swung haphazardly around my shoulders as I ran a finger across my nose.

She turned her wrath on Michael. "You had to come back to get you a piece of him, didn't you?"

"Came back for you too," he told her.

"Liar."

"I promise."

"Bullshit."

"I missed you."

I jumped in. "He's lying."

"Shut up, nigga. I know my feelings," he scolded me. "I did miss you, trouble."

"Nigga's lying. He missed your pussy. All he could talk about was your pussy," I told her.

She frowned.

Michael laughed loudly. "So what?" he quipped. Didn't even try to hide that truth. "I still missed her. Her pussy's a part of her."

"You're both such dicks," she said as she shook her head.

"You miss me, Freckles?" Michael asked her.

She could never hide her blush when he called her Freckles. She liked that name. "Missed your dick, tongue, and your mouth. Your dick, tongue, and mouth are the only things about you worth missing."

I chuckled.

He didn't. "Fuck you," he told her.

"David beat me to it," she snapped, then stood.

I tried to grab her hand, but she snatched it away as she headed for the door. I went after her. Rushed to step in front of her before she could get to the door.

"Move, David," she demanded.

"Nah," I answered. "What you mad for? It's okay for you to fuck him, but not me?"

"We were supposed to be together," she said as she got in my face. "You said you would show me. We could take that next step slow. You lied," she said, shoving me.

The push barely moved me, but I was sluggish. That nut I'd released with Michael had weakened me.

"He made me do it," I told her. "Seduced me."

"Say what now?" Michael asked behind us, like he was in disbelief.

"Really, David?" Summer asked.

"He did. Got me drunk and brought me back up here. Remember what he did to you in the movie theater? He did that to me too. Seduced me."

She shifted her weight from one foot to the other and folded her arms across her chest. She still had on her work clothes. I loved when she wore those power suits.

The tan skirt she had on hugged her hips and thighs perfectly. That golden silk blouse accentuated her breasts so beautifully. I tried to reach out and pull her closer to me. She wasn't having it, though. She stood there in those six-inch heels, looking like she belonged in somebody's men's magazine. Ass on point. Thighs and calves looking right.

She tried to move around me. I blocked her path. Michael closed in behind her. Scooped her up from behind and carried her to that king-size bed he'd bragged about before. I watched as he dropped her on the bed. She struggled a bit as he kneeled between her legs. His hands went up her skirt with such quickness, and down came her white thong.

He stopped pulling it down mid-thigh and looked up at her. "Tell me if you want me to stop," he told her as he inched it farther and farther down.

She looked like she wanted to take her heels and drive them through his skull, but she didn't tell him to stop.

"You gotta tell me if you don't want this. Never going to force you to do something you don't want, Freckles," he said once he had the thong all the way off. He tossed it to me, and it was soaked.

"Damn, Summer," I said as I held it and examined it in my hand. I sniffed it and was instantly turned up another notch. I watched as Michael pushed her skirt up farther, spread those beautiful golden thighs, and licked his lips.

"I just opened the gates of heaven," he said before his tongue made a wave against her pussy.

"Ahhh, ayyee," she breathed out.

He took the time to pull back and slip two fingers inside her. Praised her pussy with his fingers before licking her desire again. That one tongue stroke had her back lifting from the bed like she was about to float on air. She still had those heels on. There was something sexy about her legs in the air, thighs apart, heels on. I pushed my jeans down, then walked over to climb on the bed with her. While Michael turned tongue tricks on her love below, I aimed to kiss her lips up top. Instead, she took me into her hand and stroked me. Urged me to come toward her mouth, and she sucked me in. Almost swallowed me whole.

It was my turn to hiss and call on God. Mary Magdalene had to be somewhere in Summer's bloodline. She was too adept at the art of fellatio. Men paid women top dollar to do the shit Summer was doing to me. Even on her back, she was sending fire up my spine with the way she was sucking me off. Had my hands and back looking like D'Angelo in his "Untitled" video as he squealed and reached out to the camera during the climax of his song.

I gripped both sides of her head and pulled her mouth away. "Jesus," I called out. My heart was racing in my chest. Dick throbbing with life.

Michael quickly rid himself of his jeans, then got back between her legs. Her moans grew louder and louder as Michael sucked on her clit. Like her, he took the job of oral pleasure seriously. His face was covered in her juices. Tongue stiff while he moved it in and out of her as if it were a small penis. Every time he flattened his tongue, licked from her opening, and then flicked his tongue against her clit, she hyperventilated. Her back was arched as she gripped the white comforter on the bed. He had her in a zone. Waves of pleasure traveled through her body, and for the first time, I heard her call out his name.

"Ohhh . . . ohh, God! Fuck, Michael. . . . I'm . . . ahh . . . oh . . . I'm coming," she whimpered.

"Then come for me, Freckles," he coaxed her.

I slid off the bed and became voyeuristic as he pleased her. She lifted her hips. Grabbed his face and ground all over it. She came all over his face, and he liked every

minute of it. Told her to keep coming for him. Fuck his
face, he wanted her to do. She clamped those thick thighs
around his ears, and I got joy out of watching him try
to wrestle out of them. He stood and ran a hand down
his face. Didn't do much to wipe her orgasm away. He
crawled on the bed between her legs, ripped her shirt
open, and then her bra. I listened as the fabric tore away
from her body. He took her breasts with fervor as his dick
thrust into her, catching her off guard. He'd eaten her out
so good that she had forgot the dick was coming next.

Her shocked pleasure made my dick harden more. I
thought back to her words. Thought back to her saying
I could show her how I was with Michael, because she
wanted to see. So I would show her. Something in me
got jealous when I saw the unmitigated pleasure written
across her features as Michael worked his hips against
her. I was supposed to be the only man who could take
her there. I owned that beautiful, ugly come face she was
making.

I walked over and got behind him. Centered myself
behind him and watched Summer. There was a look of
sheer apprehension on her features, along with lust and
curiosity. She wanted to see it but was too afraid to admit
she was scared of the pleasure it might bring her.

It was like I was back in my dream. Only this was real.
Summer's look of intense desire and apprehension was
real.

"What . . . what are you doing?" she asked when
Michael stopped moving against her.

He wanted it too. Just as badly as I did. We wanted to
experience the nirvana of him fucking her while I fucked
him.

"Giving you what you want," I told her.

I grabbed Michael by his waist. Aimed my dick at the
opening and slipped deep into him with one hard stroke.

He groaned, jerked inside her, making her back arch. I took him from behind while he worked against her. Like in my dream, the more he made her moan, the more I aimed to make him do the same. The deeper he sank into her, the deeper I went in him. He went at her hard. I went at him harder. The way he was pumping into her made him work his ass so it would bounce back against me. That shit was heaven.

This was heaven . . . had to be to be this damned good.

I kept my eyes on Summer, though. Held her intense gaze. So many emotions were passing between us that Michael couldn't see. He had his head buried in her chest, while I held eye contact with the one woman who had managed to steal my heart. I let go. Showed her every part of me. The parts she thought she couldn't handle, I gave them to her. Said vulgar things to Michael. Demanded he make her come for me, and when he couldn't make her get to that orgasm fast enough, I made him pay for it.

I watched the way her features contorted in ecstasy. That beautiful, ugly come face, which I loved to see her make, was in full effect. She was rocking those thick hips in sync with Michael. He still couldn't handle it. Begged Freckles to stop moving her hips like that, or he was going to come too soon.

I held nothing back. Watched her face when Michael raised his head. He had to stop fucking her so he could handle what I was giving him. When he stopped, she kept going. We double-teamed him. Gave him all he couldn't handle and then some. She wrapped her arms around his neck and brought his lips down to hers. Lifted her hips and threw her pussy at him while I pumped my hips behind him. He was having an out-of-body experience. I could tell by the way he humped his back and moaned into her mouth as she kissed him.

She kissed him. Fucked him. I fucked him. We kept eye contact with one another.

"I'm coming, baby," I told her.

She broke the kiss with Michael. Her breathing reached a fever pitch as Michael growled and thrust frantically into her.

"Come for me, baby," she purred.

"He make you come?" I asked her.

She nodded. "I'm coming again. . . ."

Michael raised her legs higher, cupped the backs of her knees in the creases of his elbows, and rode her hard and fast. I gripped his shoulders and returned the favor.

"Damn it, David," Michael's baritone voice growled.

She screamed out. Michael groaned and grunted. I threw my head back and roared through the cramp I'd given myself as the three of us released simultaneously.

# Summer

Snow was falling in Atlanta. For once, the newscasters had been right. David and I had to get home. Didn't want to be caught in any kind of weather-related traffic. At least that had been the plan, but of course, anytime Michael was involved, anything was bound to happen. Three bodies lay in his king-size bed in his hotel room. Three pairs of legs were intertwined, and four arms fought to hold me close to them. David hugged me from behind as he lightly snored, and Michael had me wrapped up from the front.

Even in sleep it was a tug-of-war between the two of them when it came to me. A girl could get used to that. I watched Michael's face as he slept. Peaceful and serene, like he didn't have a care in the world, but I knew that wasn't the case. David and I had tried to pretend we weren't listening when he had walked into the living room of the suite earlier to argue with his wife on the phone. There was trouble back home, and I wondered why. Wanted to know if the woman's guilty conscience had started eating away at her.

David had told me Michael had informed him that his wife didn't know that he knew she'd cheated with his best friend.

"She didn't question why you two had gone to jail?" I'd asked David, curious.

"He told her we'd gotten into a fight with a group of guys in his condo complex," he'd answered.

"Oh."

That conversation had taken place after we'd laughed about Michael and me having the same ringtone. It was a coincidence, but a funny one, nonetheless. What were the odds of both Michael and I having a ringing alarm as our alert to calls?

To look at Michael's chocolate-covered face as he slept, you wouldn't know his age. You'd think he was a fresh-faced college kid. It was the way he carried himself that told you he was a grown man. The package that hung heavy between his legs, and the way he used it, told you that too. Michael was still an enigma to me. As soon as I thought I had him figured out, he would throw me for a loop again. He stirred in his sleep, like he could feel me observing him.

Michael was the kind of man you held at arm's length. You didn't let yourself get close to Michael, because he'd make you fall in love with him, and then he'd leave you caught out there. No, you didn't get to close to men like him. My mind went back to seeing him and David together. As crazy as it sounded, in that moment Michael had seemed more man to me than he ever had. You had to be a real man to take all of David's dick in a hole that small. Jesus . . . my ass muscles clenched when I just thought about it. Yeah, I had gotten crazy and had thought I wanted to explore that route, but I didn't think I'd be able to handle either one of them taking me that way. Not to mention that as alpha as Michael was, he'd allowed me to see him in a submissive role, which was crazy to me.

Still, I couldn't get over the look of Michael's pain and pleasure. He had looked as if he was about to go mad. A look of unmitigated satisfaction had never been so poetic. Then there was David. . . . I'd finally seen him, all of him. Had been able to see what drove him crazy when it came to Michael. Had seen him when he was his most vulnerable. Had seen his fears. Seen his repressed desires. Had watched his face as his breathing had deepened. His chest had swelled. Arms had flexed, upper body had expanded, as if he had been body bulking. The way his hands had grabbed Michael's hips and pulled him back into him had added to the intensity of the moment. I had thought I would faint when I watched his tongue trace down Michael's spine.

All the pleasure he was getting from the moment, and yet he had managed to make the moment all about me. It was like his stroke had been timed to Michael's stroke. Whenever he'd given Michael satisfaction, Michael, in turn, had given it to me. I'd died and gone to heaven in that moment. And when we all found that orgasmic bliss we'd been searching for, it was the most titillating, sensuous adrenaline rush I'd ever experienced.

Yeah, David and I had to steer clear of any emotions when it came to Michael.

David's manhood was pressing into the crack of my backside as I let my fingers trace Michael's lips. He absentmindedly licked them, like he knew what I was thinking. I dipped my head forward, kissed his lips. His lips were moist; mine, a little dry. So they stuck together for a few seconds as I pulled back. I was in love with his lips.

In love . . .

*Careful of that word with Michael, Summer . . .* , I told myself.

*In lust* . . . I was in lust with all things Michael. His lips were so plush. Thick enough to make you forget he was married when he was busy sucking your pussy lips into his mouth. Lips soft, tongue velvety enough to make you forget that he was going to leave again while he sucked on your clitoris like it was a pacifier. I swallowed slowly, then wet my lips. Leaned forward again, then sucked his bottom lip into my mouth. This time his eyes slowly opened. He was sleepy, but he smirked. Moved his thighs between my legs so that they brushed up against my already sensitive slit.

I'd been caught fondling his lips with my own. Would have been embarrassed if his hand hadn't rubbed my thighs. I would have tried to pretend it was an accident if he didn't suck my lip into his mouth. I could taste the bourbon we'd all shared still on his breath. I was sure he could taste it on mine as well. I could feel my love below coming to life, giving me that agonizing ache from the need to be filled, as Michael's tongue traced the outline of my lips before he searched out my tongue.

I moaned. . . . Couldn't hold it back any longer. My body rolled, which made my ass grind into David. I could tell by the way his hands gripped my waist and he pulled me back into him that he too had been awakened. Maybe their bodies were set to the alarm of my sexual needs and desires. David's hands slipped between my legs as he kissed my shoulder. Moved my hair to the side and then kissed the nape of my neck. I moved a hand behind me to stroke his erection to life. He slipped closer to me. His fingers slid in and out of my wetness while Michael sucked on my breasts.

While the world went about its business, the three of us created our own realm. I jerked when Michael raised my leg and quickly slid down the bed. While David entered me from behind, let his manhood kill me with deep penetration, Michael did what he did best, planted his face in my pussy. Sucked on my clit and licked between my folds as David tried to bury himself deeper inside me. David gave me that choke and stroke. While he used one hand to choke me, he stroked me with fervor.

"Fuck me harder," I begged David while holding Michael's face right where I wanted him to be.

"You like that, baby?" David asked me.

Michael's mouth and tongue worked me over as my hips rolled.

"Oh, God, yes. Please don't stop."

David's voice was raspy in my ear, heady with bated arousal. "I won't. I won't ever stop giving you what you like . . . love . . . want . . . need."

I bounced my ass back against him while he pumped into me. All the while Michael was driving me to the brink of orgasmic insanity with his mouth.

Well into the night, that was what we did. We stopped only to eat and drink. Laughed and joked around about creating our own hedonistic den. Michael called room service and asked for more towels, then placed the DO NOT DISTURB sign on the door.

For hours we went at one another. Me on David. David on me. Me on Michael. Michael on me. David on Michael. Moans and grunts of exhilaration filled the room. Phone calls went unanswered. Texts and voice mails were ignored. We locked ourselves in a hotel room and binged on the drug called sex.

David and I woke up the next morning to find we had been snowed in with the rest of Atlanta.

"Damn. I didn't think it would get this bad," David said as he turned on the TV.

"Me either," I agreed.

I stood in front of the couch in a white bath sheet, with my hair still wet from the shower. While David and I stressed about whether we would be able to make it home, Michael laughed at Atlanta coming to a standstill due to two inches of snow.

"In New York my kids would still be on their way to school, and the expressways wouldn't look like a car lot with cars all over the place," he commented as he ate the breakfast we'd ordered.

"Don't act like you're not from down this way. You know we don't get snow but every once in a while. Nobody was expecting this shit for real," David responded.

I added, "Right. I'm mad that only certain counties had the wherewithal to close down their schools, though. There are children stuck on the side of the highway in the cold. That's unacceptable—"

"Still," Michael noted, cutting in, "y'all let a few inches of snow shut the whole city down."

"It's not about the snow. It's about the fact that the tires are melting it, and then it's turning into ice," David explained, defending our hometown. "I guess since you've been in New York for the past ten years, you consider yourself an expert on driving in the snow."

Michael and David kept talking, while I went back to watching the news. I shook my head at all the people stranded on 75, 85, 285, and I-20. It was a mess. Atlanta had been turned into a winter wonderland, an unwelcomed one, but a white wonderland nonetheless. I walked over to the window and looked out. Saw a few guests trying to get the shuttle bus to take them somewhere, to the airport, I supposed, but it wasn't happening.

I turned around and asked David, "Are we going to try to drive home?"

He scratched his chin. His five o'clock shadow was coming in. "I don't know. Let me walk down and see how bad it is out there first. Not trying to have you stranded on the side of the road and not be able to make it to you," he told me.

"Okay. Hold on, then," I said.

"Why?" David asked.

"I want to walk down with you. I have a bag in the car with gym clothes I can change into," I answered.

He nodded, then stood and grabbed his shirt. I quickly pulled on my clothes from the day before. I looked nothing like the well-put-together businesswoman I'd arrived as. I was as disheveled as a woman could get. David's locks swung haphazardly around his shoulders. His dress shirt was untucked. Eyes were still droopy. Our appearance got curious gazes as we strolled hand in hand down the hall to the elevators.

"What are we doing?" he asked me once we got in an elevator and the elevator doors closed.

I looked up at him as he leaned back against the mirrored wall, and then I went over and stood between his legs. "What do you mean?" I asked him.

"This thing with Michael . . . What are we doing?"

"Having fun. Exploring another realm of sexual satisfaction."

"Are we? Is this for fun, or are we going to make this a habit? Will we do this every time he comes to town? He's opening a shop here. Is this going to be an ongoing thing? We're going to be a married man's mister and mistress?" After he asked that, he quirked a brow, with a bemused expression that made me laugh.

"So you want to stop? We can stop. We can get another hotel room—"

"In the same hotel?"

"We can brave the cold and walk down the street and get another one and stay there until we can get home."

David chuckled as the elevator dinged. We got off, headed outside, where the cold had its way with us. David shoved his hands in his jeans pockets while asking the valet for the keys to our cars. I pulled my coat tighter and tried to duck the blowing wind. David showed the valet our tickets and told him we needed to grab some things from the cars. It was so cold, my ankles felt frozen as I walked in my heels. I was a fan of the cold, but not the freezing kind. David had to hold my hand so I wouldn't fall. We made it to my car, and I grabbed my bag. David had a gym bag in his truck too, so we rushed to get it. We stood at his truck, touching and kissing, until the cold forced us back inside.

"Seeing you with Michael was different," I said to David as we walked into the lobby. I figured we may as well talk about the bisexual elephant in the room. It'd been on my mind all night and since we woke that morning. David hadn't mentioned it, and I figured that was because he was waiting for me to.

"Different, huh? Is that good or bad?"

I glanced up at him. Watched the seriousness on his brown face. There was that vulnerability again. He was genuinely worried about what my reaction was going to be. Wanted to know if I saw him in a different light.

"I don't know, honestly. That look of complete baffling satisfaction on your face when you're with Michael . . . I don't do that for you."

"Is that what you think?"

"Yes. I watched the way your body moved. Watched the way you were into him. The way you touched him. The way you kissed him. You do with and to Michael what I've never known you to do with other men."

"You haven't seen me with other men."

"No, but I've seen you interact with them while they flirted with you. You've told me you don't kiss other men. You kiss Michael, and you're very into it. You're intimate with him beyond the sex."

He shifted his weight to his other foot as we stood off to the side. "Because I know him. We established more than a sexual relationship. We became friends. He's one of my best friends besides you. I was with him back then the way I'm with you now. So, yeah, when it comes to sex with him and me, I was honest with you. I told you it was intense between him and me. It's always been that way."

I was quiet as I looked around the place. There were a lot of angry people. Some were mad that they were going to miss their flight because of the driving conditions. Others were angry that they couldn't make it to engagements they had planned. And there David and I were, talking about his sexuality and how it made me feel. More than anything I would always love and respect him for being open about his sexuality up front. Would I ever get to the place where I wouldn't feel too insecure to be with him? That was still up in the air.

We walked back to the elevators. Got on one with a woman who couldn't keep her green eyes off David. He chuckled at her brazen attempt to get his attention as he held my hand. She was eyeing me with a smirk, trying to rile me up. I was eyeing the man who I'd assumed was her husband since they had matching wedding bands. I'd been friends with David long enough to know what to look for when it came to men wanting him. The blond male with the movie star looks was trying to make eye contact with David too. The man's cheeks were flushed, and his breathing had changed. I laughed low. Looked up at David and saw him watching me.

I was about to say something snide. Something loud enough for the woman and her husband to hear, but David planted his lips against mine and put a stop to all of that. I knew he knew the husband had been watching him. But his kiss put me at ease. Most of the time when people thought of down-low men, they thought only of black men. I knew better.

Once the elevator stopped, David and I stepped off, and I left behind the wife who didn't know her husband was attracted to men. We used the extra key card Michael had given us to let ourselves back in the room. Housekeeping had been by, judging by the made-up bed and the cleaned room, and Michael had left a note that he was in the fitness center downstairs. David and I changed clothes. Got more comfortable, since we were going to be there for a while.

David decided to join Michael in the fitness center. I would have gone, but I was really too worn out to do much of anything else. I lay across the bed and flipped through the channels on the TV. Didn't find anything worth watching. Stopped on *Criminal Minds* and watched the BAU catch demented killers. Had a lot on my mind. I thought about my parents and decided to call my mother.

"This is twice now that you've called me without me having to call first," she greeted. "If you and David are fighting again, I'm officially coming there to kick your behind, because I know it's your fault yet again," she joked.

"Ha-ha, Mama. No, we're not fighting." I laughed.

So did she. "So, what's going on? You two snowed in?"

"You can say that. We came to visit a friend that had come to town last night and got stuck at their hotel," I told her.

"Oh, I'm sorry to hear that. Well, at least it's at a hotel, and not on the side of the road, like all those people stuck out there."

"True," I said and then got up the nerve to ask her what I really wanted to know. "Mama, may I ask you something?"

"Sure."

"How is it to love a man like Daddy?"

"I'm not sure what you mean," she said. The noise, the clanging of the dishes going on in the background, stopped.

"Daddy being bi . . . his sexuality and all. How do you love a man like that?"

"No matter your father's sexual preference, Summer, he's still a man. I love him the same way I would a straight man. Your father is really no different to me."

"Did you know he was into men when you first met him?" I asked.

"No, not at first. There were some things that happened," she said, then stopped talking and sighed, like she didn't want to relive whatever those things were. Finally, she added, "There were some things that happened that forced him to tell me the truth. Times were different back then."

"So you never had a problem with him being sexually attracted to men?"

"I did at first. But John gave me security over time. Proved that he could be faithful. He talked to me about his sexuality a lot. Never hid his feelings from me after that big mess we had happen before."

"He cheated on you with a man before?" I asked her.

There was a long pause; then she cleared her throat. "That will have to be a story we'll have to discuss another day. One that I'm hoping we can—" She stopped talking abruptly, then squealed.

"Mama, you okay?" I asked her.

"I have to go. This is your father calling in. Been waiting on his call all morning. I have to go. I love you. Talk later," she said in a hurry, and then she was gone.

She left me with more questions than answers. I sent a text to her cell and told her to tell Daddy I loved him and missed him more than anything. Told her to tell him I watched *Sons of Anarchy* to see Jax so I could pretend it was him I was watching on TV. I tossed my cell on the table beside the bed and then focused back on Shemar Moore chasing a man with a gun. I didn't even know I'd fallen asleep until my phone started to ring. I didn't know why I hadn't changed that stupid ringtone yet. It had been the same since I'd purchased the new phone a little over a month ago.

I rolled over and snatched up the bloodcurdling, earsplitting device. "Hello," I yelled into the phone.

"Um . . . hello?" A little girl's voice sounded on the other end.

"Yes, hello," I replied, eyes still closed, still half asleep. At first I thought it was my brother's daughter. She was always shy, even on the phone.

"Daddy?" the little girl inquired.

I sighed and frowned before sitting up. I looked at the phone to see who it was and saw the name Gemma. *Gemma?* I looked at the picture on the phone, then had to rub my eyes a bit. That little girl looked so familiar. I knew that face. Knew those eyes. Knew that smile. And it was then that I knew the phone wasn't mine. I quickly hung up and then tossed it on the bed. The phone rang again, and I backed away from the bed like it was trying to harm me.

Oh God, I'd answered that man's phone. His daughter's eyes staring up at me from her photo started to haunt me. I grabbed both phones and then the room key card. I made a beeline for the fitness center.

# Summer

"No, Gemma. I left my phone in the fitness center, and a nice lady found it, then turned it in to the front desk," Michael lied to his daughter.

He was standing wide legged in the hotel room, looking over the Atlanta skyline as snow fell. I could tell it bothered him that he had to lie to her. I had seen it in the way he frowned at me when I told him what I'd done. Saw in the way he sighed and shook his head from time to time as he spoke with her.

"Hopefully, I'll be able to get to the airport in a day or so," he said, then turned to look at me. It was more like he was staring me down. "If MJ is bothering you that much, Gemma, tell your mother. What do you mean, he doesn't listen to her? Look . . . go get your brother and put him on the phone. . . ."

Michael and I kept eye contact as he spoke on the phone. David had taken his flash drive down to the business center to print out some forms for work. After seeing how bent out of shape I was, he'd asked me if I would be okay before he walked down there. I'd told him I would be, and that was how Michael and I had ended up in his room alone.

"MJ, you have to stop bothering your sister just for the hell of it, okay? She has a major test in science coming up and really needs her time. So let her be. . . . I don't care that she's ignoring you. She has to study. . . ." Michael chuckled. "You don't get rewarded for doing what you're supposed to do, MJ, but if you behave, we can talk about it. . . . Okay. I love you, too, MJ. Put your sister back on. . . . Okay, I spoke to him. You should be fine now. I love you too. . . ."

He hung up his cell. Slid it in his pocket. He wouldn't be fool enough to leave it lying idly about again. I'd be careful when I heard my ringtone again, even though I'd changed it. I'd never been one to want to break up a man's home, even if it wasn't so happy.

"I'm sorry, Michael," I began. "I was sleeping and jerked awake. Just grabbed the phone and didn't think anything of it until it was too late." I'd already explained that to him, but I felt the need to explain—more like defend—myself again.

"It's whatever. Be more careful next time. Don't want my daughter thinking I'm doing something I shouldn't be."

"But you are."

He frowned, hard. For the first time Michael looked at me with disgust and not lust. The man who hadn't been able to keep his hands off me sexually looked as if he wanted to toss me from the window of the presidential suite.

"She doesn't need to know it. Gemma is very smart for her age. She could test to be a Mensa if she wanted to. She isn't stupid by a long shot," he spat at me.

"I said I'm sorry, okay?"

"Whatever, Freckles," he said as he stalked over to the minibar in the room.

David walked back in the room. Phone was glued to his ear. I swallowed hard and stared at him. My eyes fluttered a bit. Lips turned down in a scowl.

"As far as I'm concerned, and I'm being truthful, Chad, I wouldn't really care if the judge threw the book at him," David said as he spoke to my boss. "He threatened his wife in court. No way Judge Prichard or Atlanta District Attorney Dixon is letting that go. Up-fucking-hill battle at this point," he remarked, venting.

I turned back to study Michael. His whole body language had changed. From the moment he'd stepped foot in ATL, he'd been as smooth as silk and as slick as oil. He'd been in control. At least until now. Now he looked as if he was about to fall apart at the seams.

I couldn't get his little girl's face out of my head. I took in Michael's features, his eyes, lips. I remembered his devilish, sly smile. It shouldn't have been surprising that his daughter looked like him. I shouldn't have been surprised that she had his eyes, nose, lips, smile, dark chocolate complexion. No, none of that should have surprised me. And it wouldn't have, had the little girl looked like Michael and not like an exact replica of David.

Gemma, as Michael had called her, didn't have any of his facial features. She didn't have Michael's eyes. She didn't have his smile. She didn't have his lips. Gemma had David's eyes. She had David's smile. Even down to the dimples in her cheeks, she was him. The little girl looked exactly like her father. Suddenly, my breath hitched. My eyes watered, and I felt like the walls were closing in on me. The little girl had the smoothest chocolate complexion I'd ever seen. And with box braids hanging down her back that were similar to David's locks, it couldn't be denied that she had his DNA.

The pained expression on Michael's face confirmed it. He'd known I'd seen her face as soon as he yanked the phone from my hands. I'd found his weak spot. Found the secret he didn't want to be known. I needed air, needed to be outside of that room so I could breathe. As crazy as the situation was between David and me, there were certain things that kept me sane. There was a reason I was so content in the game he and I played.

I knew that he would never love another woman as he did me. I knew that even when he gave in to his sexual desires and found sex elsewhere his love for me kept him from getting emotionally attached to anyone else. But . . . David had a child. A daughter, whom Michael had been raising as his own. David had a secret that he didn't even know about.

Suddenly, I was angry at Michael's wife. No way she could look at her daughter and not know she belonged to David. The similarities were too strong. Not only had she cheated on her husband with his best friend, but she'd also committed the ultimate act of deception. I quickly made my way to the door.

"Hey, where you going?" David asked in a rushed whisper as he moved his cell from his ear.

I gave a faux smile. "Going to the lobby to see if they have some orange juice," I lied with ease.

He smiled, walked over to me, kissed my lips, and then handed me his wallet. Told me to take money or his bank card to get what I wanted. I did what he asked. Smiled again when he kissed me, then made my way to the lobby.

I didn't know how long I'd been sitting there when Michael took a seat in the cushioned chair across from me. He hadn't showered or changed out of his workout attire. I looked over at him, though my vision was blurry. I couldn't explain why I was crying. Why my heart felt as if it was being violently ripped from underneath my rib cage. Guessed love did that to you. Wondered if that was what David felt each time I rejected him.

"I knew as soon as she opened her eyes in the delivery room," he told me in a grave voice. "I'd seen those eyes enough to know."

"If you knew from the beginning, why not say something?" I asked, my voice shaky.

"In hindsight I can say I knew. Then there was this feeling in the pit of my stomach, which I ignored. As Gemma got older and started coming into her personality more, I really knew."

"And she's never said anything? Your wife, I mean."

Michael turned his lips down. Leaned forward and pressed his elbows into his knees. "Nope. I told you. She's Mrs. Perfect. She and David would have been a perfect match. They can do no wrong and are always the victims. Their shit never stinks. Fire never burns," he said in a huff, grunted, and then sat back in the chair.

"Is that what you came here to tell him the first time?"

"That was the plan."

"This is what you meant when you said God got the last laugh?"

"Pretty much."

"Are you sure your son's yours?" I felt the need to ask this. I needed to attack the character of the woman who'd gone and given the man I loved his first child.

"MJ is mine."

"Are you sure?"

Michael gave me a look that said he was still annoyed with me. I watched as he pulled his phone from the left pocket of his sweats. He slid his thumb across the screen. Scrolled through what I was assuming were photos and then offered me his phone.

There was Gemma again. This time she was standing next to Michael, the man she thought was her father. Again, she rocked boxed braids. Gemma even wore glasses, like David. Gave a wide smile that accentuated the dimples evenly placed on her cheeks . . . like David. The blood in my veins heated up. A little boy, as chocolate as a Dove ice cream bar, sat atop Michael's shoulders. Michael Junior was a fitting name to give the boy, as he looked exactly like Michael. From the honey-colored eyes to the sly fox–like grin on his face. Like his father, the little boy looked like he was up to no good. They even had the same haircut, only the little boy had a crop of tight coils instead of a low-cut Caesar. There was a fourth person in the photo. Well, her shadow was there. I could see from her shadow that she was the one who had snapped the photo of her happy family as they vacationed in the Bahamas. I knew that because of the big sign behind them.

"He's mine," Michael reiterated.

I passed his cell back to him. Didn't say anything for a long while. I couldn't. I watched as people trolled by. Kids ran through the lobby as their parents yelled for them not to. Saw an elder white couple kissing and holding hands. An interracial couple headed to the fitness area. A white woman's belly swollen with life. Saw another man, who looked to be the black man's twin rush to meet them, with his pregnant white wife in tow. Black men were sure to breed themselves into extinction.

I curbed my thoughts. Old issues of being rejected by the black boys at our predominately white school started to ride me. It was funny how when something caused you great pain, you started to think of all the other things that had caused you grief as well.

"Are you going to tell him this time?" I asked Michael out of the blue.

I turned to find that he had been in his own little world. He snapped his head around at me like he'd only just remembered I was there.

"I don't know," he answered honestly.

"Why haven't you said something all this time?"

"Don't want to break up my family. Gemma knows me only as Daddy. Thought about what it would do to my son and daughter if they found out their mother had been an easy whore only weeks after she married me."

I asked, "So why tell him now?"

"Honestly?"

I nodded. "Honestly."

"At first I simply wanted to hurt him. Wanted to finally have something to get back at him with, like he'd done to me. Wanted him to see that I'd been raising his child for the past ten years and she had no idea who he was. David's big on wanting a family. You know that. All he talked about at times was wanting children and a wife eventually. Later on in life, after he'd gotten his career and his life together. I wanted him to see that no matter what he'd done, I still had the life he wanted, even though he had tried to break it up. I still have my wife. Have my kids."

"What changed?"

"You."

I furrowed my brows. I knew that what Michael felt for me had everything to do with what I could give him sexually, and that he felt nothing more. So his answer confused me.

"What? I don't get it."

"When I saw you on his Facebook page, I saw the way he held you like you belonged to him and only him, and then I saw the way he looked at you when I got here. Saw the way he held you, even though he claimed you two weren't together. I saw, for the first time, the way he loved somebody that wasn't me. He loves you now like I loved my wife then."

I absentmindedly scratched my head. Swallowed down his admission of using me like the nasty bile it was. "So you used me. You got to have who David loved, as he'd had who you'd loved."

Michael didn't nod in agreement and didn't shake his head in denial.

David's words echoed in my mind. *If you throw it at that nigga, he's going to catch it, then toss you back in the dugout.*

"The only difference between what I did and what David did is I gave him the option to object."

"So I was another way for you to get back at David."

He gave a one-shoulder shrug. "If that's how you want to take it."

"I'm going to tell David about his daughter."

"Not his daughter."

"The hell you say."

"He may have donated the sperm, but she'll always be my daughter."

"He would have been there, had he known."

"I don't doubt it."

I'd never been racked with such emotions as the ones I experienced as I sat in the lobby of that hotel. I watched as the snow continued to fall, and like the world outside, my insides turned cold. Michael had all but told me I'd been a married man's plaything for him. Wondered if he felt that way about David too. Wondered if he'd been using David simply for the satisfaction of it and nothing more. I laid a hand over my chest to ease the pain I felt. I'd talked David into going down a road he'd been adamantly against taking.

I suddenly realized Michael was a victim in all of this too. On one hand, he'd been every selfish thing David had warned me he was. On the other hand, he'd raised a child who clearly wasn't his without ever letting it break him down. He had to look at his daughter every day and know that biologically speaking, she didn't belong to him.

"Where you going?" Michael asked me when I stood.

"To tell David we should get another hotel room," I said before I walked off.

I headed back to the elevators. Waited patiently until the doors of one of the elevators opened, and then I stepped in quietly. Before the doors could close, Michael stepped through them. Neither of us said anything for a while, and then Michael spoke up.

"I know right now you're thinking I'm some dog-ass nigga, but I'm not. I did what I had to do for the sake of my family." His deep baritone coated my skin in that closed space.

"Okay. And you using me to get back at David?"

"If I apologized for it, would it make you feel any better? I know you see it as something wrong, but we both know that you and I would have ended up sexually involved, anyway. As soon as we laid eyes on one another, it was set in stone."

I tilted my head to look up at him. "And you're so sure of this?"

He caged me between his arms against the mirrored wall. "Yes, Freckles, I am."

"Really?"

"I know your kind. You know I'm a dog, and yet you love my pedigree."

I shook my head. He was beginning to sound like the Michael I'd met at Strip. Like before, his scent seduced me. I shook my head to clear it. "Still doesn't mean it's not fucked up—"

"I'm sorry," he said, cutting me off. "But I'm not sorry for fucking you. I'm sorry for sometimes thinking about how good your pussy tastes and for wanting to fight you because of it. I know that shit sounds crazy, but look, my wife was the only woman I was with for nine years in our marriage. I started cheating on her a few months ago with a girl who works in my auto shop. And still, no woman has ever driven me to the brink of insanity with her sex like you do. I don't even understand why David allowed me to taste you or touch you."

"Because he knows you can never have me like he does."

"And you know this for certain?" he asked me, pressing his body closer to mine.

"I'd bet my life on it. . . ."

For the rest of the ride up, he gazed down at me, and I stared up at him. Neither one of us said anything. I couldn't lie and say being that close to him didn't bother me. It did. As mixed in my emotions as I was at that moment, I was clear about one feeling. Lust. The lust I felt for him was still strong.

The elevator dinged, and I rushed off. Michael snatched my wrist and pulled me back to him.

"Let me tell David about Gemma," he pleaded with me.

"Why? So you can see the hurt on his face when he finds out he's missed ten years of his daughter's life?"

"No. I want to tell him because it's something I should have done a long time ago but was too selfish to do so. Because he'd want to know how smart she is. How much like him she is. She's getting older, and sooner or later, my excuse for why she's the only one with brown eyes in the family is going to wear thin. . She's already asked me and I lied to her. I don't intend to lie to her again."

"Okay. I respect that. As long as you know that if you don't tell him, I will. So if you leave here and do not say a word about it, I'll tell him, and whatever happens after that happens."

"Fair enough," he said.

I meant what I'd said. If Michael didn't open his mouth, as bad as it pained me that another woman had had David's child, I would tell him. He needed to know. I knew what family meant to him. I knew that in the end, after all the bullshit, he wanted a family. He wanted a wife, and he wanted children. He wanted to leave a legacy. Wanted his children to know that he would never abandon them, as his parents had done him.

I was trying not to let my feelings get the best of me. Trying to keep a strong face in front of Michael. Didn't want him to see that his revelation was eating away at me on the inside. But Michael was no fool. No matter how David and I may have lied to ourselves and sometimes to those around us, anybody with eyes could see that I loved him and he loved me. So when Michael wrapped his arms around me and cradled my head against his chest, I held back the tears no longer.

I knew the logical thing to do, especially since I'd accidently answered Michael's phone, would be for David and me to go to another hotel or at least get another hotel room. But when it came to Michael, we'd thrown logic out the window as soon as he touched down in Atlanta. Michael was our green and red Kryptonite. He weakened our resolve when it came to saying no, and then recharged us and pushed us into overdrive once we got into sex with him.

What I did do was push the fact that I would never bear David's firstborn to the back of my head. I absorbed the pain of knowing that David had shared his seed with another woman and had given her a life that should have been reserved for me.

What happened once we got back to the room wasn't what should have happened. I should have forced Michael to tell David about his daughter. I should have said no when David cornered me as soon as I walked back into the room. Should have objected to him wanting to see Michael's face between my thighs again. I should have pretended as if I didn't like the way he demanded I kiss him. When he sat back on the couch, legs wide, dick standing at attention, that slight curve saluting me, I should have stopped it right then, but I didn't.

# David

For the next two days Atlanta was shut down. The mayor and the governor were getting dragged through every media outlet out there for their response, or lack thereof, to the snowstorm that hit the city. Not too much changed inside Michael's hotel room, though. The one thing that I'd always remember from our time together was the night before, when Summer had perfected her skills at fellatio on me. Michael had got down on the opposite side of her. Just as I'd been about ready to explode, he'd placed his lips on the other side of my dick and kissed Summer. The shit was so sensual. The way he snaked his tongue out to join Summer's tongue while they French-kissed the head of my manhood had the muscles in my stomach clenching so tight, they burned.

Michael kept direct eye contact with her as they kissed around my head. When she puckered her lips and placed them against my head, he did the same, while kissing her. The come that slowly oozed out of my head was thick, creamy, and white. Testament to a good diet. Michael snaked his tongue out, caught the first batch on the tip of his tongue. Summer leaned forward, opened her mouth, and let Michael tongue feed her the children I'd never see grow up. She sucked his tongue like it was a pacifier, and once she was done, she lapped up the rest from her fingers, then from my quickly fading erection.

Day in and day out, we were all together. Woke up together. Went to sleep together. Woke up in the middle of the night to Michael and Summer exchanging heated words like angry lovers. Watched from the archway separating the living room from the bedroom as Michael tried to talk Summer into not being mad at him. It wasn't lost on me that he was naked and she was semi-naked. He had to have been for some time, since his erection was aimed right at her. Her nipples were hard, as if moments before he'd been stimulating them.

They went from combatants to lovers in a matter of seconds. All it took to calm her down was his lips pressed firmly against hers. I didn't know what was going on between those two. But I'd noticed the tension between them since she'd answered his phone. I chalked it up to him being upset about his daughter possibly telling his wife that some woman had answered her father's phone.

Once his lips touched Summer's, she was putty in his hands. He used one arm to lift her from the floor and settle her around his waist. She had on only one of our shirts—I wasn't sure which one of our shirts it was—no underwear. Since he was already in his birthday suit, it was easy for him to slip right into her. I rolled my shoulders, cleared my throat, and gave my manhood a slow stroke to calm down the excitement I felt.

Summer's head was buried in his neck as he slowly lifted her and brought her back down. Michael's hand roamed up and down her back. He was holding and caressing her like she was his wife. My upper lip twitched in annoyance. His hands massaged the nape of her neck, then came up to firmly grab a fistful of her hair. He was all in control at that moment. He was the puppeteer; and she, his willing puppet. Once she realized I was watching them, her eyes widened, but she was too far gone to care that I'd caught them. Her thick and creamy excitement was coating his dick. Each time they moved against one another, a fresh coat glazed him.

Michael was groaning, growling, moaning . . . especially when she start gyrating her hips back into him. I saw the moment she switched up the game and took control of him. Now he was her puppet. She took him down to his knees. There was a bow in his back while she worked him over.

I chuckled as I walked farther into the room.

"What the fuck you laughing at?" he barked at me. Sweat dripped down his temples. His brows furrowed, and there was a look on his face that said he was immersed so deeply in pleasure that it was painful.

"You. Laughing at the way she always takes you down. You look like you're confused. Like you don't know whether to toss her off you or let her keep going," I said to fuck with him.

"Kiss . . . my black ass, motherfucker."

I threw my head back and laughed while I poured myself a shot of bourbon whiskey, then downed it in one gulp. Summer bent backward until her back was arched on the floor. Those beautiful caramel hips never stopped grinding, though. Michael gave a guttural grunt as he jerked forward. He sounded as if the wind had been knocked out of him. He braced himself between her thighs, both of his palms flat on the carpet on the sides of her head. He bit down on his bottom lip, growled, and then pumped into her like he had a point to prove.

Summer's purrs and whimpers told me that she was being satisfied just the way she liked it. Michael attacked her breasts with his mouth as one of his hands slid down her stomach to put pressure against her pelvis. Both he and I laughed low when she bucked against him. Her eyes rolled to the back of her head. She was there. Orgasm overload. He soon followed after her. Releasing all he had into her.

Once he was done, he removed himself from her body. Semi-hard dick slapped against his thigh with a light thud. He sat with his back against the couch. One leg folded underneath him and the other raised so he could rest his elbow on his knee. Her glaze still covering him like a second skin. I slipped between her legs. Placed my mouth on her clitoris, fingers inside her, and made her come again. Licked her like she hadn't just had an orgasm that had turned her into Linda Blair. Made her squirt for me. Right in the middle of her raining down on my face, I eased up, caged her between my arms, and slipped right back inside her.

My intent wasn't to come myself. I simply liked the way it felt to be inside her. Loved the way she was still so tight and wet, even after Michael had loved her in the middle of the floor. She knew me well enough to know what I was doing. She went from the wanton married man's whore to the woman who appreciated what it was to be loved by a man who belonged solely to her.

I was face-to-face with her. Kissed her gently. Told her how good she felt. Talked loud enough for her to hear, but low enough so that Michael couldn't. When her thighs closed in around my waist, her arms around my neck, and she reciprocated the feeling, for the first time in eight years I felt her love for me.

From that moment on, there was something different about the way Summer paid attention to me. Normally, I spoiled her. Made it my business to make her feel like she was the only woman in the world for me. For those days we were locked away in Michael's hotel room, she made it her business to show me how much she really loved me. Not that she didn't normally dote on me, but this time . . . this time she did it like she wanted me to know that if I asked her to tell me yes once more, she would be more than willing to.

***

"Looks like the roads are being salted. Valet downstairs told me it is pretty safe to drive if the vehicle has the wheels for it," I said as I walked into the room.

Michael looked up. He was dressing, as he had a meeting with the couple he was supposed to buy the auto shop from. All black, from his shirt to his wing-tip dress shoes. Only thing that wasn't black was the platinum designer watch adorning his left wrist.

"Yeah? Good to know. The guy called me about the shop. Said that he could meet me down in Little Five Points so we could get this thing moving," he said. "Gotta get back home soon, too, before Sadi puts me out of my own house."

I chuckled. "She call you again while I was gone?"

He shook his head. "Nah, but she isn't answering when I call, either, so I'm sure that's not a good sign."

I walked into the bedroom to see Summer still laid out in the bed. She was on her stomach. Right leg bent, left leg straight. Her mouth was half open, and she was breathing deep, giving a light snore. Her hair was framing her face like a lion's mane. Her ass was inviting, like the softest pillow. I had a good mind to jump back in bed with her, but I knew I needed to see how the drive was back to her house so I could be sure she would make it home safely.

"She still knocked out?" he asked me when I walked back into the living room.

"Pretty much," I answered. "I'm going to check out the drive back to her place, then come back to get her."

"Y'all going home today?"

"I figure we should, since you have to get back home soon. Would hate for Sadi to turn angry black woman on you."

He laughed, and so did I. We both knew Sadi could turn into that angry black woman in a heartbeat. I'd seen her do it a time or two before all that shit went down between Michael and me. She may have been educated by the best, but I'd seen her pull out a blade and get down with the worst of them. She had a ghetto side to her, which she hid very well.

"She's been on my ass since the first time I came out here. No idea why. It's not like I left evidence of my dirt."

"Women's intuition, bruh," I told him. "She's not stupid by a long shot. All women have this radar, this alarm that goes off in their head when the man they love steps out on them."

He screwed up his face as he lotioned his hands. "She didn't even act like this when she walked in on my secretary at the shop, sitting on my desk in my office."

I chuckled, then shrugged. "I don't know what to tell you. Better try to fix it before it turns into hell in your home."

"Shit, to be honest, for the past two years or so, it's *been* hell."

"Care to elaborate?"

"I don't know, man. Shit changed in my home overnight, it seems. Her firm merged with another, and there was a lot of stress on her. Since then, she's been like a different person sometimes."

"And you sure she ain't cheating?" I asked him.

"Nah. Trust me, I looked for it, too," he answered.

With that, I walked into the bedroom to shake Summer awake. Summer's eyes fluttered open.

"I'm going to see if it's safe for us to drive home," I told her.

She gave me a light smile and nodded. "Okay. I'm getting up."

"No, you're not," I said. "Stay here until I get back."

"You sure?" she asked after a yawn.

"Yeah. I should be back in no time."

"Okay."

"You love me?" I asked.

Her smile widened. "Yeah . . . I love you."

My smiled widened. "So, when we get home, we can get the answer to that question?"

"Most definitely."

"Y'all can cut all that lovey-dovey shit out now," Michael interrupted from the bedroom doorway.

"Hater has never been a good job reference, Michael," I said to him, then leaned over and kissed Summer's lips.

Standing up tall, I straightened the waist of my slacks. Made sure I looked presentable enough to walk out. I tied my locks back into a ponytail, then moved out of the bedroom. Glanced behind me to see Michael crawl on the bed beside Summer. She giggled when he slipped his hand between her legs. She stopped when he started to tongue her down. I took him in as he lay there and massaged her pussy like he hadn't been worried about his wife finding out he was cheating. Once he'd gotten enough of his touching and feeling, he stood. Adjusted his dick, then blew another kiss at her.

"Wash your hands, nigga," I joked with him.

He walked around me. Slid the fingers he had had inside her across my lips, then chuckled while he kept walking. I licked my lips, while Summer shook her head and turned over. Michael and I left Summer to slumber in peace, then took the elevator down.

"You know we can't keep doing this, right?" I asked Michael when we exited the elevator. It was more of a statement than a question.

By the way he smirked, I could tell he knew what I was talking about. Still, he asked, "Doing what?"

"You know what I'm talking about. Me, you, Summer, we can't keep doing this."

We walked past other guests of the hotel, catching the occasional stare from men and women. The white woman and her husband from the elevator the day before spotted me again. The wife gave a megawatt smile when she saw Michael. She gave us both a glance that told us we could see what her mouth was about if we wanted to. She was more Michael's cup of tea, though. I tended to like my women with color. That wasn't to say that I hadn't fucked a white woman a time or two. I had. I just preferred my women with color. Michael was a pro lover. He didn't have a preference when it came to women most times. Although I'd seen him with more black women than any other kind.

While the wife was busy eye hustling me and Michael, she had no idea her husband was doing the same. Michael and I looked at one another, then chuckled. The husband was neither one of our cups of tea. Couldn't remember a time when we'd fucked a white boy. I was sure there had been such a time once, but it wasn't memorable.

"Like I was saying, this has to end," I remarked.

Michael walked out the entrance ahead of me. The cold air made me want to curse Mother Nature. I pulled my coat tighter as Michael did the same. There wasn't a whole lot of traffic on the road. But enough to let us know we could drive.

"Why? I'm enjoying myself."

"That's the problem. We all are, and a bit too much. I've gone against my rule of helping you be one of those down-low brothers we once hated so much," I explained to him after we handed the valets our tickets.

"It's just you, David. Not like I'm making a habit of this shit. I cheated on Sadi, but not with dudes. I'm not controlled by my sexuality."

"That's not the point. The point is, you're doing it now, and you're doing it with me. We've gotten Summer involved in this. You know how we used to be. This could take on a life of its own, and the last thing I need is for us to go down that road again. If sex were a drug, we'd be in rehab to this day."

He looked over at me. "You make it seem like it was all bad."

"I never said that."

"I hear you."

"What does that mean?"

"It means I hear you."

My phone rang and stopped whatever I'd been about to asked him. One of my partners was on the other end, asking me if I could get to the office for a few minutes. Since it wasn't too far from the hotel, I told him I could.

"You ever think about how what you did with Sadi could have an effect on my marriage, my family life after all these years?" he asked when I'd ended the call.

To be honest, I was sick of talking about it. All I'd done was have sex with her. I hadn't carried on an affair that he didn't know about. I'd fucked the woman once. And while Sadi might have a problem getting down and nasty in her marital bed now, she had had no problem showing me another side to the game.

"To be honest, no, I haven't. I didn't think that it would, since I threw dick to her only once," I told him.

"Threw dick to her, huh?" he repeated, then shook his head. "Guess we even now, since I've been throwing dick to Summer." His facial expression changed. Turned into that same dirty look I'd seen when I showed up at his condo to brag about fucking his wife. I didn't like the way he'd thrown Summer into the fray. Like she'd been something for him to do to get back at me. The valets pulled our vehicles around.

"So you had sex with Summer as some kind of way to get back at me?" I asked.

"Let's just say, now I know the thrill you got behind fucking Sadi."

"Michael," I told him, "I'm going to need you to not do this shit right now. Most importantly, though, there will always be a difference between Summer and Sadi, okay? Sadi fucked me without a second thought. Summer had my permission."

"Summer ain't your wife," he snapped at me.

It was my turn to chuckle. "Yeah, whatever. Doesn't change the fact that the woman you loved bust it wide open, with no fucks given about the vows she'd taken."

With his lips turned downward, he turned to me after snatching his keys from the valet, who backed away quickly. He moved his tongue around in his cheeks. "You know what? I'll take that, David. I will. You know, you and Sadi probably would have made the better match for one another. You two are quick to accuse people of being exactly what you are. Got such a problem with people holding a mirror up in front of you."

"Don't take your issues with the wife out on me, Michael. We don't have to keep doing this. It's kind of like playing ring-around-the-rosy. One minute you're cool, and the next we're back to this shit."

He shrugged. "It's all good, David. Sometimes it gets to me. Not like I can snap at my wife for the affront."

"And that's my fault?"

He walked off to get in his rental. I followed.

"In the end," he said after tossing his briefcase on the passenger seat, "in the end, David, all three of us will need more than an apology to make up for the past ten years of lies."

"What?"

I didn't know what he meant by that last statement. Nor was I too fond of the tone in which he'd said it. I didn't get a chance to get him to elaborate, though. He got in his car and drove off before I could ask him what he meant. I sighed, tipped the valets for both of us, then headed to my office.

# Summer

Between bouts of sleep, I got up and took the DO NOT DISTURB sign off the door so housekeeping could bring more clean towels. I couldn't keep my eyes open for too long. Had been tired as all get out over the past two days. Probably because Michael and David had barely let me rest. I hadn't been sexed the way I'd been over the past few weeks in my entire life.

Michael and David had been gone for about two hours when housekeeping arrived. I didn't even bother to get up when housekeeping knocked. Just yelled for them to come in.

"Work around me," I told the Spanish chick when she came into the suite.

"Okay. My name is Marissa. It's no problem if I turn on the vacuum?" she asked.

"No. No problem at all, Marissa."

"Okay."

She went on about her way. I heard her humming as she cleaned. My phone buzzed. I laughed at the text Michael had sent me.

I responded, You don't miss me. Stop lying.

I tossed my phone next to me and closed my eyes again. Wasn't surprised when he responded to my text.

I do. I know you're still thinking about what I told you the other day. I was being honest, but that doesn't mean I don't appreciate the time spent.

I rolled my eyes and then texted him back. You mean the time spent having sex?

No. Not just the sex. Everything.

You know I don't believe you, right? I texted back.

LOL. I know. Still, regardless of the bullshit, you've left an impression that I won't soon forget. On some other shit, though, what size shoe do you wear?

I cleared my throat and then turned onto my back. Even if I did believe Michael was feeling something for me, that didn't negate the truth in the words he'd spoken days before. Didn't take away the fact that for the past ten years, he'd kept David's daughter away from him. Late in the night, when both men had been sleeping, I had gone through Michael's phone and had sent a picture of Gemma to my phone. Then I'd erased any trace of my invasion of privacy.

Why do you want to know that?

Tell me, woman, and stop being so difficult, he texted back.
A size nine. Did you tell David yet? I texted Michael.

Thanks. No.

I didn't respond to him after that. He and I had had an argument about that in the middle of foreplay. I'd jumped off his lap and demanded he go in the living room and tell David. Would have probably kept arguing had he not had me so heated that I could already feel him inside me. I wondered how long the three of us could keep up this little game we were playing. How long could we continue to fuck and suck one another into oblivion? How long would I be able to take seeing David and Michael together? Those were the questions running through my mind as I drifted off to sleep again.

I was awakened by someone's face between my thighs. Didn't take but a second for me to realize who it was. I had already been dreaming about sex, anyway, so I welcomed his tongue. He hadn't even bothered to take his clothes off. He had fallen face-first between my legs and had woken me up the way any woman would love to be awakened. A few seconds later, the other man walked in. He positioned himself on one side of my other lover. Joined him, and they took turns lapping at desire. I looked down to see their tongues working together, in sync, like they were dancing the tango. With one of my legs over a shoulder of each of them, they lifted my hips from the bed. One lick. Two licks. Three licks. Four. One after the other, they took turns driving me up the wall.

Once they had finished their midday snack, David pointed toward a bag of clothes he'd gone out and purchased for me.

"Didn't get a chance to go to the house yet. Chad and Sai wanted me to come to the office for a quick meeting," he said.

"Everything okay?" I asked him.

"Yeah. The ADA wanted to meet with us to talk about a possible plea deal."

"Oh, okay."

I pulled my tights on and then the long sweater that fit more like a tunic. Michael pointed to another bag in the room with two shoe boxes in it. He told me he saw the combat-style boots as he was leaving Little Five Points and remembered the ones I'd had on when we first met at Strip, so he bought them for me. Bought the others because he liked the way my ass and thighs looked in heels. I quickly finished dressing, as I was eager to get out of that room. I was beginning to get cabin fever. I pulled my hair back into a tight ponytail, then grabbed my purse and my cell.

After David and Michael changed into more comfortable attire—David in jeans, a polo shirt, and a pair of Jordans, which I had rarely seen him wear; Michael in cargo-style sweats and a long-sleeved tee that hugged his upper body—we headed out. Walked around Little Five Points for a while. I guessed a lot of people must have been feeling cabin fever too. Even though it was still more than a little cold out, the eclectic neighborhood was very crowded. Different styles of music collided. Alternative lifestyles were put on display.

Michael and David kept their distance from one another. There were times when I literally felt put in the middle of the two of them. Michael wouldn't walk next to David, so he would usher me into the middle, between them. I knew what was bothering Michael. Could tell by the way spoke to his daughter when she called. When I asked to see his phone so I could look at her picture again, he didn't object.

"When do you leave?" I asked him.

We'd stopped at Bang-On, a custom T-shirt design store. David was at the counter, while Michael and I stood around, looking at the shirts on the wall.

"Day after tomorrow. Have to do some last-minute banking stuff for the new shop, and then I head out," he answered.

"You plan on telling him before then?"

"Yeah."

For some reason, I didn't believe him. I could see the conflict all over his face. Knew that he didn't really want to open that can of worms.

"I guess I never stopped to think about how hard this is going to be for you," I said.

He shrugged. "It is what it is."

I noticed that all through Michael's phone were pictures of his kids. I had to admit that I was looking for photos of his wife too, but I found none of her. There were photos of Michael and his children, but none of her and the children. There was definitely something going on with them.

After leaving the T-shirt shop, we headed to Front Page News to grab a bite to eat. Left there and headed to Atlantic Station. By then some of the tension had eased. David and Michael were talking. Jokes were floating around. Laughter was in the air. David and Michael took turns kissing me, while curious people gawked. Affection floated around, enveloping me in a cocoon. Then the three of us were holding hands again. Lots of touching. Went back to Strip for the hell of it. Ordered a round of drinks and kicked back. Everything was back to normal with the three of us.

"Are we still going home today?" I asked David after Michael had gone to the bathroom.

"That's the plan, unless you don't want to," he answered.

I shrugged and glanced around the place. "I don't know. Should we?"

"I think we should. Not trying to have another verbal fight with Michael about shit that can't be changed."

"You two have words again?"

He nodded. "Same shit. Different toilet."

I hung my head. Everything in me wanted to pull my phone out and show David what probably had Michael feeling like he was. I didn't know who to blame for the situation. Yes, I did. Well . . . I knew who I wanted to blame. I wanted to blame Sadi. She was the reason behind this madness. She should have kept her legs closed, being a married woman. I didn't care how many would call me hypocritical for my judgment of her. It could have been simple jealousy, but I didn't care.

I leaned in closer to David. He already had his arm wrapped around my shoulder. He knew what I wanted. Turned his head and gave me his lips. Our tongues danced around. Moved in sync until we found that high we were looking for. His other hand snaked around my waist. That light squeeze he gave told me he was nearly in a state of arousal. Or it could have been the huge bulge swelling in his pants. Either way, I got as close to him as I could. Let my hand massage that beautiful gift from the Mandingo gods.

"You better stop, before you make me forget we're in public," he told me in a low murmur against my ear.

I glanced around bashfully, then smiled. "I don't think you have it in you" I told him.

He eased my legs open, then placed one on top of his. His hand cupped my sex. Gripped it. Massaged it. Spanked it lightly.

"You want to take that bet?" he rebutted.

My head almost fell back, as I was in a blissful state. He chuckled. I gave a womanly moan, then tried to hide my obvious aroused state when the waitress walked back over with our receipt. For a minute, I wished we were back at that underground sex club, where David's hand on my pussy wouldn't have bothered the waitress. The waitress back at that sex club would have stared openly and appreciated David's display of wanting me so badly that he didn't care who watched as he gave in to carnal desires.

But, alas, this wasn't the underground sex club. David moved his hand. Used the one he hadn't had on my sex to take the pen the waitress had left and sign the receipt. He was ambidextrous. Could use his left hand as well as the right one. We joked about it often. I always told him it was why he was so good at using both his hands during foreplay. Some men knew how to do only one thing at a time when it came to foreplay. David could use his mouth and both hands at the same time while getting you to the point of orgasmic ecstasy.

By the time Michael came out of the bathroom, we were ready to leave. He left the tip since David had paid the bill, even though David had already left a hefty tip. Judging by the way Michael was looking, I could tell he had spoken to his wife again. His face was twisted. One minute he looked as if he was in deep thought, and the next he looked like something stunk to him. He walked out ahead of us in silence.

We hopped into David's truck and headed back to the hotel. Skipped the valet for the time being and found a secluded area in a nearby parking deck. David wanted me. Told me he had the urge to take me from behind as we drove. But he wanted to do it in public. Exhibitionist style, with the threat of getting caught being our aphrodisiac. We ignored Michael in the backseat. He was trying to keep his voice level as his wife antagonized him about the bitch who had answered his phone. He kept telling her the same lie he had told his daughter. She wasn't buying it.

"I can make that happen," I teased David.

"Yeah?"

"Yep."

Michael hung up his phone and lay down in the backseat. He'd had one too many shots of sake. Once David parked, I hopped out of the passenger side of the truck. Walked to the back and opened the door. I saw when David exited the truck. Anticipation sent shivers up my spine. I was already wet because he'd massaged my clit through the fabric of my tights as he drove. I dipped my head into the truck, poked my ass out so it pressed into David's erection. I gave a little bounce, because I knew he liked that kind of thing.

We didn't really have time for foreplay. David knew this, so he slid my tights down over my backside. Admired my ass for a minute with a little spank worship. I massaged Michael's bulge through his sweats. Watched his eyes open slightly as he took in what was going on. I urged him to lift his hips so I could slide his pants and underwear down. Michael's dick sprang out. Slapped down on his stomach and bounced again.

My nails dug into his thighs when David penetrated me from behind. For a second, I couldn't even remember who I was. David was stretching my walls. Forcing me to accommodate his length and girth. I hissed loudly and then let out a stifled moan. Michael watched on, then eased down so he could easily slide his excitement into my mouth. It was hard for me to concentrate, since David was being anything but gentle. He smacked my ass so hard, it echoed. All anybody had to do was step off that elevator and they would get an eyeful of my ass, and of David beating my insides up.

He was mean to my pussy. Was giving it to me like he owed it to me. Hands gripping my waist, nails digging into my skin, he pulled me back into him over and over and over again, until my knees buckled. When I was too weak to stand, Michael pulled my arms and helped his best friend get a better angle. With no hands, I sucked his dick into my mouth and let him control the motion. Michael pumped his hips up and down. My saliva soon coated his dick. His groans sang to me. Gave our illicit freak fest a more melodic sound track.

"Shit, Summer," David growled behind me.

"Look at me, Summer," Michael coaxed me.

I lifted my eyes so I could see him.

David told me, "I'm coming, baby."

I moaned louder, rocked my ass back into him harder. The truck shook and bounced under our weight. I sucked

Michael. David fucked me. Michael let my arms go, grabbed my ponytail, and let his seed trickle down my throat. He sounded like he was struggling to speak. Like his words had gotten garbled in his throat and all he could do was sing a chorus of ahs. David pulled back. Pulled me from inside the truck, turned me around, then told me to lie back on Michael. He lifted my hips and roughly slid back inside me.

I'd never been fucked as good as David fucked me in that moment. Michael was palming my breasts, pinching my nipples, and just so he wouldn't be left out of the action, he maneuvered from underneath me. Kneeled on the seat and leaned over me so his dick dangled in my face. Sixty-nine position, but he wanted only sixty-eight, and I would owe him one. While David stroked me, Michael sucked on my clit. I couldn't handle it. Couldn't take the clitoral stimulation and David's frantic thrusts at the same time. My hips bucked and muscles in the bottom of my stomach clenched as I caught David's thrusts and threw it right back at him. I squirted so hard, had an orgasm that was damn near blinding.

# David

Everything was going good. Summer had spaghetti legs again. Couldn't stand straight after what Michael and I had done to her. We all sat in my truck, fixing our clothes, which we'd twisted and mucked up, so when we walked back into the hotel, we'd be presentable.

Summer ranted about needing a shower. Said she couldn't function with my jism damn near running down her legs. I laughed. She giggled. Michael had returned to being silent in the backseat.

"You okay?" I asked him.

He made eye contact with me in the rearview mirror and gave a head nod. "I'm chilling."

"What does that mean?" I said.

"Means I'm cool," he said nonchalantly.

I let it go. If he said he was good, then I'd leave it be. I pulled out of the parking deck and headed on to the hotel. A few minutes of silence and a traffic light later, Summer picked up her phone. Judging by the way her fingers were working, I could tell she was texting. A few seconds later, Michael's phone chirped. Summer glanced at me to find me looking at her. She nervously moved her hair from her face, then laid her head back against the seat.

"What was that?" I asked her.

She cleared her throat, then asked, "What was what?"

"Between you and Michael, what's that?"

She turned her lips down and shrugged. "You mean in the parking deck? You were there."

I chuckled. "You know that's not what I'm talking about, but okay."

I looked in the rearview mirror again to see Michael with a smirk on his face as he typed away. A few seconds later, Summer's phone vibrated, but she tried to hide it from me. Michael chuckled, kept looking at me in the mirror, and then leaned back. Earlier, I'd noticed how they would isolate themselves and talk to one another. Summer had had his phone a couple of times today. I hadn't said anything then, but now it annoyed me. It was something I'd make mention of later.

We made it back to the hotel and headed up to Michael's room. While Summer prepared to shower, Michael and I sat in the living room and watched the news. I could tell something was on his mind.

I asked him, "You going to talk about what's bothering you or what?"

He grabbed a beer from the fridge, then tossed me one. "Marital issues."

"You're flying back home the day after tomorrow, right?"

He nodded, took a swig of his imported brew. "Yeah. I ain't looking forward to it. There used to be a time when leaving and coming back home to my wife and kids was the highlight of any trip. Now I look forward to seeing my kids."

"Damn. Shit between you and Sadi that bad?"

"Yeah, it's crazy. It's funny how shit seemed to change overnight for us."

"How so?"

"I told you, man, a few months after that merger, things went downhill for us. She started coming home stressed. Lost a few cases, which sent her attitude over the top. It ain't been the same since."

I sat my beer down, pulled my locks back into a pony-tail, then pulled my shirt off. The room was more than a little toasty. I could tell housekeeping had stopped by, as it was cleaner than we'd left it. Mostly, Summer's stuff had been tidied up. Neither Michael nor I made messes when we dressed, and if we did, we cleaned up as we went along. Michael looked to be deep in thought. I kind of felt bad that his home life seemed to be falling apart. But then the other side of me, the side that still held a grudge about how we'd ended, felt some kind of joy over his misery.

In hindsight, I knew Michael and I never could have really been together the way I had fantasized. In the end both he and I wanted a wife and children. Michael never would have been satisfied with just me. He was one of those bisexuals who had only sex with men. He'd never date them or be in a relationship with them. To be honest, even though I'd tried the relationship thing with men, I was probably more like Michael than I cared to admit.

Still, with Michael, I'd been different. I'd wanted to travel that relationship road with him. I'd wanted to see what it would be like for him and me to be more than the magic we created with our sex. If I was honest, I'd say that he and I had our own kind of relationship. The kind where he and I used sexual intimacy to run away from the demons chasing us. He had his issues with his family, and I had my own issues. Still, we didn't let sex rule us. . . . Well, in a sense, we did. I chuckled inwardly, thinking back to the good times we'd had. The highlight of those times would always remain how we protected ourselves and how we were honest with women about our sexuality.

"Have you tried to talk to Sadi about it?" I asked him.

"Shit, man, talking to her lately is like staring a pit bull in the face with raw meat hanging around your neck. I don't know what the fuck happened to my marriage, David."

My friend sounded dejected, like he didn't want to be having this conversation to begin with.

"You two try counseling?" I asked him.

He shook his head. "Nah. Hadn't thought about it really."

"Well, there you go. Another avenue to travel."

We both looked up when Summer opened the bathroom door and walked out naked. She smiled as she passed the doorway. There he and I were, talking about ways to help him fix his marriage, as if he hadn't been cheating with Summer and me the entire time he'd been in Atlanta. It was comical. He and I continued talking, stopping every so often to watch Summer put on a show of oiling her body. She had walked into the living room after drying off and had placed a towel on a chair. Now she sat there, naked, as she moisturized her skin.

I'd always loved that she didn't let the fact that she was plus-sized determine her perception of her beauty. While her body shape complimented her weight beautifully, and she exercised faithfully, she wasn't America's standard of beauty. However, she never let that keep her in a box.

I got up to use the bathroom, leaving Summer and Michael alone. I could hear him asking Summer why she wasn't going to law school. That was a conversation she and I had had plenty of times. She was smart enough to do so, but I guessed she didn't want to.

Once I was done seeing a man about a horse, I changed into some sweats to get more comfortable. Saw Summer's phone lying on the bed and remembered that text she'd sent to Michael earlier. I had a tug-of-war inside my head about whether I should go through her phone. I decided to satisfy my curiosity. Picked up her phone, put in her security code, and browsed her texts. Found the ones between her and Michael. To my surprise, they had been talking a lot more than I'd thought. He'd even told her he was falling for her. She'd told him he was full of shit. He'd LOLed and said he was serious.

My face frowned a bit, and my heart settled into my stomach. I kept scrolling through. Saw the nude pictures he'd sent her and the ones she'd sent him. I shouldn't have felt any kind of way about it, but I did. I knew when I'd opened that Pandora's box and taken a bite of that forbidden fruit that I was playing with fire. Michael had that effect on people. He had the power to embed himself in your DNA, code the strands with remnants of himself, and then pull away.

He had been wooing Summer like he'd done me way back when. I read the late-night messages and the early morning greetings he'd been sending her. The nigga couldn't have been too worried about his home life, seeing that he had been so busy trying to get Summer on his team. Yeah, he'd been texting me too, but not nearly as much as Summer. I chuckled at the irony of it all. Summer had asked Michael if he'd told me something. He'd responded no. Told me what? I thought.

I knew from experience that sometimes the satisfaction wasn't worth the curiosity that killed the cat. So I left well enough alone. Placed her phone back where she had left it, and walked out on the snooping party I'd been having.

Later on that night, the rain decided to roll in again. The three of us lay in the hotel bed. Summer in the middle, as always. She was fast asleep. Michael had the remote in one hand, his dick in the other. Moments before, Summer had pleased us both orally. Had taken turns making each of us speechless as we stuttered in singing her praises. We, in turn, had introduced her to another side of satisfaction. Had taken her on wave of anal pleasure. She'd lain on top of me while both Michael and I relaxed her enough for him to penetrate her there. First, I let her guide me into her sex. She did so with ease. Taking all of me that she could at first, then working her muscles to take all of me in to the hilt. She leaned forward until her breasts were on my chest. Her breathing was heavy. I could tell she was nervous.

"Go slow," I told Michael.

"No shit, Sherlock," he responded in his typical sarcastic fashion.

He'd been so busy admiring her backside that I didn't really think he would hurt her at all. He was too fascinated with it to hurt her. He poured oil in his hands and massaged her ass until it seemed to glow golden. For a minute, I got jealous that I wouldn't be the first to take her there. My hardened muscle jumped inside her. She took in a sharp breath, then returned the favor. Raised her head to look at me.

"You scared?" I asked her.

"Not really. I don't think I am. More nervous than scared. Both you and Michael are well endowed, so . . . I'm worried that he won't fit."

I smiled at her. Her light voice was heavy with headiness. Michael crawled behind her. Our thighs touched since he was between my legs, and it made me look up at him. He'd focused in on her spine. Was licking a trail from the nape of her neck down to the dip in her back. He then spread her cheeks, took his tongue down between each globe. Summer almost bucked off of me. I wrapped my arms around her as she moaned and squirmed.

"Fucking, fuck," she murmured against my lips. "Jesus . . ."

I watched her eyes roll in the back of her head. She was so gone that she dropped her head forward so hard, it knocked against mine.

"Ayyyee, s-sorry . . . so . . . ohmigod . . . s-sorry, David," she stuttered.

"It's okay," I assured her.

I was fighting the feeling myself. With her bucking and jerking, she was creating friction. I was deep inside her womb, so anytime she moved or quivered, my manhood grew and expanded.

"Shit, Michael," she fussed while his tongue worked her over.

His face had disappeared between her ass cheeks, and she was in heaven. Michael's big hands kneaded and palmed her juicy lobes as he spread them apart and flicked his tongue up and down, in and out of her anus. He smacked her ass while he pleased her that way. Moaned like it was he who was being stimulated orally.

Summer was so into it that she started riding me. She was so wet . . . so wet and tight. My eyes were threatening to roll. I almost forgot that I was supposed to be helping her to relax. My hips rose, and I matched her bounce with a thrust of my own. Summer's orgasms seemed as if they always belonged to me. Her love rained down on me before Michael even got to show her the other side of pleasure.

She whimpered, leaned in to kiss me, like she always did when she needed to catch her breath. Michael grabbed the lubricant from the nightstand. He talked to her as he used his finger to penetrate her. We both did. He told her that she was running the show. I kept kissing her lips. Made her comfortable enough so that when his head was aimed at her entrance, she didn't flinch. Michael caged us underneath him. I knew when he slipped inside her, because her breath hitched.

"Shit," she said aloud.

Michael was gentle. Kissed her neck, shoulder. Placed kisses around her shoulder blades. I kissed her cheeks. Placed my lips against her eyes, mouth. Made her give me her tongue as he slowly inched his way into her. I could tell he was bringing her alive in another way. She tried to speak and was able only to stutter.

"Tell me when," he told her. His voice was low. A gentle tone that said he wanted her to be as pleased with his performance as he wanted her to be satisfied.

She nodded. "That's . . . that's enough for now."

Michael's face was a mask of pain and pleasure as he worked his hips gently. Bit by bit he gave her just enough to handle. Summer's eyes watered. Michael's breathing was labored. My dick was pulsating. We'd sandwiched her between us. Gave her double the fun. Double the pleasure. Michael's thighs created friction with mine as we loved her. Summer was so gone. Asked Michael for a little more, then quickly recanted when she knew she'd taken on too much. He pulled out a little. Stopped stroking and placed kisses against her back again.

"I want to come," he told her. "But not before you do. Will you come for me?" he asked her.

He made eye contact with me as Summer nodded. Kept watching me while he rode her. She sat up. Michael sank back on his haunches. I had to break eye contact because of the way she was riding me. I shut my eyes tight, as if doing so would stave off the intense need to let go and coat her walls with my DNA.

"Come for me," she coaxed me.

I told her, "I am, baby. I am."

That was the cue she needed. "I'm there, Michael," she said.

"You're coming for me?" he asked in return.

She nodded. Rocked her hips against me. Threw her head back and leaned into him. My hands caressed her waist. Slid up to massage her plentiful breasts. We all moaned in synchronized harmony. Michael's facial expression was intense. He was into the moment like he'd never experienced it before. Like he was never going to experience it again. I knew that feeling. Summer's vaginal walls were the stuff of legend, but the other pleasure orifice she owned had never been touched. It was tighter. Gripped Michael snugger and made his pleasure ten times more riveting.

"Jesus, this feels so good," Summer whimpered. "Feels so damn good. Shit."

This had to be what heaven felt like. We were in our own little slice of heaven. Burning with intense desire and satisfaction, like we owned it all. Not many people got to say they got a chance to be free and open with their sexual proclivities, but the three of us did. And we rode that wave of ecstasy until the wheels fell off.

Before I knew it, the TV had started watching us. Michael had joined Summer in a peaceful slumber. All of us were tired out from our adulterous affair. It had been fun, no doubt, but Summer and I had to get back to the real world. The world that didn't involve Michael. We had to get back to the unanswered question. To the what-ifs and the hopes of us being together. Summer and I had to get back to what we once knew. We had to get back to the uncertainty that was our relationship. I fell asleep with thoughts of Michael's and Summer's texts to one another on my mind.

A knock on the hotel room door awakened me a few hours later. Michael and Summer didn't even stir as the rapid knocking continued. I hopped up, grabbed my sweats, and threw them on.

"Who is it?" I yelled from the living room.

"Housekeeping."

I frowned, trying to remember if we'd phoned down and asked for anything before falling asleep. I couldn't recall. Grabbed my glasses and headed to the door. It didn't dawn on me to think before snatching the door open. Didn't even think to look through the peephole. I was one who didn't like to be awakened out of my sleep so abruptly. I snatched the door open, ready to give the housekeeper a piece of my mind. I was prepared to let the scowl on my face scare whoever it was enough that this person would never wake a guest like that again. But what I wasn't expecting was the woman standing at the door.

"David?" she inquired, then gave me the once-over.

There I was, standing at the door in only sweats that hung low on my hips. No shirt. Eyes droopy. And I smelled of Summer's sex.

"Sadi?"

"What the hell are you doing here? Where's Michael?"

I'd never been a man to be left completely without words, but in that moment, I had none.

# Summer

I knew something was wrong before she even stormed into the bedroom. Maybe my internal fight-or-flight instinct had kicked in before I even laid eyes on her. I could hear her voice in my head. I thought I was dreaming. It took me a minute to realize I wasn't. I woke up to somebody talking to me. Michael didn't have emerald-colored eyes, and he didn't have blond hair.

"Huh?" I asked her once my fog started clear.

"I asked you what the fuck you were doing in my husband's hotel room," she spat out at me. She stood there, with a look on her face that said she was ready to fight, if need be.

I looked to my right, where Michael had been lying, then at David, who had rounded the corner.

"Michael actually let us use his bed, because he couldn't sleep," David lied. "We came to visit. Got stuck here when the snow came."

My eyes took in the Michael Kors handbag hanging from the woman's arm. Saw the way her blond tresses fell over her shoulders like Paul Mitchell had hooked her up. The threads she had on for sure told she wasn't some random woman. The big rock and the wedding band on her left ring finger made it clear who she was.

She looked from me to David, then back to me. There I lay, naked as ever, in the bed in her husband's hotel room. She gave David the once-over. Let her eyes linger on his body for a second too long. I could tell in that brief moment she was reliving the time they'd had together.

"So why the hell didn't he answer the door?" she asked him.

David glanced toward the bathroom. "I guess because he's in the bathroom. That's why I opened the door."

I slowly sat up in the bed, then pulled the white sheet up to cover my nudeness partially. I wondered if the woman could smell her husband's sex throughout the room. Michael was all over me. His scent had meshed with David's and had created an aroma that was intoxicating.

Even if I'd lied and said I honestly didn't know who her husband was, the fact that she had Michael's name tattooed on her shoulder would have been a dead giveaway. The infamous Sadi had traveled to Atlanta to see if her husband was being unfaithful. Michael had mentioned how smart Gemma was, so I knew there was no way she wouldn't tell her mother about the woman who had answered her father's phone. I didn't care what lie Michael had told her.

I heard the water come on in the bathroom and wondered if Michael had gone in there because his body had told him to or because he'd heard his wife at the door. I wondered if he had jumped up from the bed like a scalded dog and had run for the hills. Wondered if he had forgotten about what the three of us had shared, had let it go in the wind, and had rushed into the bathroom just so his wife would be none the wiser about his adultery.

I didn't know if Sadi was buying David's story. She rushed over to the bathroom door. Slapped the palm of her hand against it in rapid succession about three or four times.

"Mike!" she yelled as she beat on the door.

*Mike.* She called him Mike, not Michael. She was familiar enough with him, comfortable enough to call him Mike. The same name she'd called him when she scolded him about being so familiar with himself the last time he was at my house. There was no doubt Michael had heard her, but he didn't respond to her.

"Open this damn door, boy! I know you hear me," she yelled.

*Boy?* My brows rose, I frowned, and I looked at David. He, too, had a frown on his face as he studied her. I slid from the bed, no longer caring about my nudity, as Michael opened the door. The look on his face showed his disdain for his wife. He scowled at her like she was his enemy instead of the woman he was supposed to love and cherish. David moved around the room to help me find the dress that I'd discarded long ago.

"What are you doing here?" was all Michael asked his wife. "And I've told you over and over again about calling me boy. You want to keep being disrespectful, then we both can travel that road," he told her, then brushed past her shoulder.

He'd put on pajama pants and a T-shirt. Didn't look as if he'd partaken in the best sex he'd ever had. Didn't walk like he and I had sixty-nined while David had loved him from behind. He walked like a man who had the weight of the world on his shoulders and yet found a way to keep his shoulders squared and his eyes assuming.

"Well, maybe if you were acting anything more than what I called you, we wouldn't have this problem. Who the fuck answered your phone? And don't tell me that bullshit lie you told Gemma!" Sadi threw her words at him.

Michael took a deep inhale, looked at David, then glanced over at me. He stopped abruptly and looked intently at me, like it was the first time he had been privy to my nudity. I almost blushed under his heated stare, but just as quickly as he gazed at me as if he'd never seen me before, he turned his head.

David tossed me his dress shirt since we couldn't find my dress quick enough.

"What the hell are you doing here, Sadi?" Michael asked her again.

"I told you," she replied snidely. "Who answered your damn phone, Michael?"

No matter what she called him—Mike, boy, Michael—it all sounded the same coming from her. Sounded as if she had a bad taste in her mouth anytime she uttered his name.

Michael frowned hard as he turned around to look at her. "You left my kids in New York to fly all the way out here to ask me who answered my phone?"

Sadi tossed her handbag on the bed, put her slender fingers on her hips, and pursed her lips. "You're damn right I did," she proclaimed. "This makes the second time, the second time whoever the bitch is you're sticking your dick in has answered your phone when you've been out here."

I glanced at David. David looked pointedly at me.

"I don't know what you're talking about. You're overreacting," Michael snapped at her.

"Don't act like you don't know what I'm talking about!" Sadi screamed. "This bitch answered your phone not once, but twice. So that tells me you know exactly what the fuck I'm talking about."

For all of that top five college education she had, her vocabulary had been reduced to profanity in her anger. I hadn't answered Michael's phone twice, so that must have been some other woman. I stared up at Sadi for a minute. It was like looking at Poppy Montgomery in the flesh. The only difference was Sadi was curvy. She made Ice-T's wife look like a plastic Barbie. I would have never guessed Michael was married to a white woman. His children's complexion gave no indication of it.

"Come on, Summer," David said to me. "Let's give them some privacy."

"No, you don't have to leave, David. You can stay around and witness the mess that is what we call a marriage these days. I'm sure he's filled your ear on all he could about me," Sadi said. "Did he tell you he's screwing the slut in his Staten Island shop too? I know he is. Anytime I go to the shop, the bitch stares me down like I have the problem."

I took David's cue and rushed from the bedroom to get my stuff together. While David and I packed up, Michael and Sadi had a war of words in the bedroom. I kept glancing at David. He'd told me Michael and Sadi had an almost perfect marriage. I guessed the *almost* part was showing. The mood was a sobering one.

We heard when Sadi chuckled and said, "I can't believe this, Michael. Not only are you fucking the girl at the shop in Staten Island, but you find a way to come all the way to Atlanta and screw another bitch too? What? Am I not nasty enough for you?" she asked her husband with disdain. "Does whoever she is do all the nasty shit you like?"

"You didn't have to come here to do this."

"Like hell I didn't. I figure since we don't talk at home, this would be perfect timing, and I don't have worry about curbing my tongue because of our children. Now you tell me what the fuck is going on, or I'm going to proceed to show my entire white ass," she yelled, threatening him.

"Talk at home? Are you serious? When I do try to talk to you, you act as if I'm bothering you or some shit. Always snapping, like just my presence annoys you."

"Maybe if you weren't so busy looking for sex every-where else, you could see what's right in front of you."

Michael sighed and shook his head slowly as he stalked into the living room, where David and I were. "Sadi, stop. I don't want to do this here."

David quickly tossed me my coat after I pulled on the boots Michael had bought. Anytime Sadi mentioned Michael's other women, it felt like an attack on me. Granted, I was one of the women she was referring to, but her words were sharper than a double-edged sword.

Sadi followed behind Michael. "You mean you don't want to do it in front of David? No, I'm not going to stop," she quipped, with a neck roll that looked like she was going to hurt herself. She charged at her husband. "I'm not going to stop," she growled through gritted teeth as she swung at him. "Not going to stop until you tell me why!"

Michael grabbed her wrist, shook her as he yelled at her. "You put your hands on me again, and you're going to get very familiar with what it's like for a man to lay hands on you. Now, I said stop."

Sadi didn't listen, though. She tried to kick Michael. He picked her up by her arms like she weighed nothing and tossed her on the couch behind him. He dropped down, caging her in like a predator. His face was so close to hers, it almost seemed as if he was growling at her.

"Twice. Twice now you've come to Atlanta, and twice this bitch has answered your phone!" Sadi said to him. Her face was red, but she had no tears in her eyes. Just heated anger and resentment.

"She didn't answer my phone twice," Michael said, refuting her claim.

"Oh, so another woman answered your phone at four o'clock in the morning last time you were here? Damn, Michael, how many sluts does it take to make up one of me? How many to curb that nasty appetite of yours?"

I was standing there with a "deer in the headlights" look. Couldn't believe what I was seeing. I didn't know what to think, didn't know if I should have turned away from the couple's quarrel. I blinked slowly as David grabbed my hand and pulled me away from the madness. We left the suite with our bags and walked in silence to the elevators.

As other guests passed us in the hall, they looked from us back to the room we'd exited, as they could hear Sadi yelling too. They were curious. Wanted to know if I was the other nasty bitch Sadi was accusing her husband of screwing.

David held my hand tighter as we rushed into the elevator once it opened. He was protecting me. Guiding me away from the scene of the crime.

"We should have left earlier," he said to me.

"I wasn't expecting that."

"Yeah, neither was I."

"She always been that way?"

"In my opinion, yes, she has. She hides it well."

I looked at my reflection and saw how disheveled I was. David's shirt hung on me so loosely, I looked box shaped. I realized my tights were on inside out, and I still smelled like Michael. Both his and David's scent lived in my skin. My eyes were red and puffy. Lips swollen.

"Yeah, you look like you've been fucked," David said to me.

I looked at him in the mirror. We held eye contact for a long time. Our silence lingered loud around us.

"You say that like you weren't one of the men who fucked me," I responded.

"If that's how you take it."

I tilted my head, confused about his mood. "You mad?"

He shook his head. "No."

"So what's with the attitude?"

He looked away briefly, then back at me. "You didn't tell me how much you and Michael had been communicating over the past few weeks."

"I did too. I told you we'd been texting and talking. Told you he told me he wanted to come back to see us."

"Didn't tell me about the nudes."

I swallowed as I ran a hand through my hair. "Didn't know I was supposed to run a play-by-play of all our conversations," I said, then stopped to think. "Wait, you went through my phone, David?" I asked, a bit perplexed.

He didn't respond. That gave me my answer. I gave a light laugh and shook my head. Panicked inside about the fact that he had possibly seen the picture of Gemma.

"I can't believe you went through my phone," I said aloud to him, but I was actually talking to myself mostly. "Can I see your phone? Am I allowed to see what you and he talk about? Am I allowed to see the shit you send him?" I quipped.

My annoyance that he'd invaded my privacy was clearly visible in the way my voice shook. When David reached into a pocket of his sweats, pulled out his phone, and held it out for me to take, I shook my head and tsk-tsked.

"I got nothing to hide. Never hid anything from you," he said calmly.

I spun around and glared at him. "I wasn't hiding shit from you. I didn't think you would care that he and I had been speaking."

David simply stared at me. The only indication of his anger was the way his eyes narrowed. Those chocolate pupils dilated, and his eyes got darker.

"That's what you get for thinking," he finally said.

I shook my head and turned back around. "This makes no sense. We're both fucking him. You're okay when he's fucking me in front of you."

I needed to defend myself. Couldn't bear the thought that maybe he had seen the picture of the little girl who was his daughter, and was mad at me for knowing about it and keeping it from him.

"It's not the fact that you two have been talking. It's what he says to you and what you say in return," he retorted.

"Like what?"

"He's falling for you, huh?"

I shrugged hard; my shoulders bunched up to where it looked like I had no neck. "I can't control his feelings."

"But you could let him know that he needs to back the fuck up."

I didn't have words for a comeback in that moment. I was speechless. In a sense, David was right. Michael had been telling me stuff, saying things that he shouldn't have been saying. He had a wife, and I—no matter how much I denied it—was in love with David. We shouldn't have even been toying with the idea of Michael falling for me.

"David . . ."

"Take my phone," he told me.

I backed away. "I don't need to. I trust you."

"Take it," he demanded.

"No."

"Take the goddamned phone!" he yelled at me.

I jumped back. I'd never seen him that way before. The elevator dinged and saved us from going somewhere we'd never been. I rushed off as an elderly black couple walked in. We weren't even in the lobby, where we were supposed to get off, but I had to get away from the lunacy. I quickly walked past other guests. I could feel David behind me. Knew it was he who snatched me from behind and pulled me toward the stairs. I tripped over my own feet as he did so.

I was starting to think that Sadi showing up had drudged up old feelings that David had for Michael. Not to mention that my own guilt was eating away at me.

I let him lead me down two flights of stairs before I jerked away from him. I stopped. "What in the hell is wrong with you?" I asked him. "What's all this really about, huh? Sadi being here got you feeling some type of way about you and Michael again?"

He didn't say anything. Just glared at me like he wanted to fight me.

"Tell me! Is that it? Still in love with Michael? So much so that his falling for me puts you back in that old head space of when you lost him to Sadi?" I spat out, instantly regretting it.

David balled his lips as he shook his head. He gave a chuckle that meant he was not amused, a chuckle he resorted to when he was upset. "You don't get it, do you?" he asked. "I'm laying all this shit out for you, and you still don't fucking get it."

"Get what!" I yelled at him. "All of this because you saw that Michael and I have been texting, sharing nude pictures, and that he has feelings for me?"

"And what about you, Summer? Do you have feelings for him?"

I sighed. Took a deep inhale and exhaled loudly. "It's not what you're thinking," I admitted.

"This bullshit," he mumbled, then started down the stairs again.

"David," I called as I followed him. "It's not like that. I like him in the sense of having a crush. It's silly. I'm not . . . falling for him the way he is for me."

David kept going. "Yeah, whatever, Summer."

"I promise. I put that on everything."

"Yep. It's cool."

"David?"

"I said it's cool. Let it go."

"But—"

He whipped his head around to look at me. "Summer, I said, 'Let it go.'"

There we were, fighting again, when hours before we had been lovers doing what lovers did. I trekked behind him in silence until we made it to the lobby. We walked out of the stairwell and startled a few people who were walking by. I still looked like I had been fucked, I was sure. And judging by the way a few people side eyed my appearance, I was sure they were thinking the same thing. When David and I reached the lobby doors, he held a door open for me. I thought about what could be going on in Michael's hotel room. Wondered if he and the infamous Sadi were still fighting.

David's phone rang as we walked outside. He looked at it, then handed it to me. I took the phone, thinking that maybe my mother or sister was calling. Sometimes when they couldn't get me on my phone, they would call David's phone. But to my surprise, it was Michael. I sighed, shook my head, and picked up.

"Yeah?" I answered.

"Where's David?" Michael responded.

"He isn't in a talking mood," I said.

"Oh, I see. You left your phone, Freckles," he then said. There was no life in Michael's voice. There normally was. The Michael I'd met wasn't on the phone.

"You okay?" I asked him.

He didn't respond right away, but when he did, all he said was, "Have you guys left?"

"No."

"You coming to get your phone?"

"Michael . . ."

"Come get your phone, Freckles," was all he said before hanging up on me.

I didn't say anything right away. Passed the phone back to David.

"I left my phone upstairs," I told David.

Without uttering a word, he turned and walked back into the hotel. We were silent as we hopped back on the elevator. He stood opposite me as the elevator slowly made its way up to the floor on which Michael's hotel room was located. Once we got off, we made the walk of shame down the hallway toward his room again. David stood behind me as I knocked on the door. He sat our bags down and folded his arms across his chest as we waited.

The lock turned in the door, and though I'd expected Michael to open the door, it was Sadi who did so. She stood there in almost nothing. Her face and eyes were red. I couldn't tell if she had been crying, but there was a bruise on her neck that stood out to me. I kept looking at it because it was identical to the one I had on my neck, courtesy of Michael. It was almost in the exact same spot too.

I could see her pink nipples through the thin fabric she had on. The little negligee—I guessed I could call it that—stopped where her thighs made a V, and if she moved the wrong way, I was sure I could see where she had birthed her children. I was still panicked. *Her children* . . . David had gone through my phone. Had he seen the picture of Gemma? Was that why he had been so upset? Did he suspect, by looks alone, that the little girl was his, the same as I had?

David was a very smart man, a member of Mensa, so I was sure he would have been able to look at Gemma and see the spitting image of himself. Suddenly, I was angry again. Angry at the woman standing at the door, looking like she and Michael had fought, then fucked. She looked as if she had been taken in the spur of the moment. Looked as if the red pussy-hugging tights she'd had on had been ripped off as Michael flipped her over. And right before he'd roughly slid into her, he'd bit down on her neck and left his mark.

Just as he'd marked me earlier, he'd done the same to his wife. Shit. How long had we been gone before they turned their fight into a roughhouse fuck session? I still had the remnants of his semen in between my thighs, and there he was, fucking his wife like it had all meant nothing.

"Michael said this belongs to you," she said, so unenthused she was.

I held my hand out, and she all but shoved my phone into my hand. "Thank you."

"Yeah, I guess," she responded. She looked past me and spoke to David. "I'm sorry about my attitude earlier. I have to deal with a lot when it comes to Michael, and lately, shit has been rough at home. I'm sorry."

"It's nothing," was all he said.

"Okay. Well, how have you been?"

"Living. You know how it goes. Cases, clients, and more cases," he replied.

She smiled. "Tell me about it."

They threw legal jargon around, while I stood there and felt as if I was having an out-of-body experience. I stared at the woman. Had never been sexually attracted to another woman, but there could be no denying that Sadi was sexy. She knew she was. She knew she had everything that any black man would ever want, just like she had to know that she was talking to one of her children's father. No way she could look at David and not know he was Gemma's father.

I came back into the conversation as she was telling David how great the merger had been for her law firm. She kept telling David that her firm and his would be perfect candidates for a North and South merger.

"I don't see Lowery, Hall, and Lowery merging anytime soon," he told her.

Sadi was smiling wide, like she'd won the lotto. "Well, I mean, if you guys ever decide or start to think about it, keep us in mind."

I'd been studying David during this conversation, and not once had he smiled. I'd moved to the side a bit so I wouldn't be standing in between the two of them as they spoke. Sadi's body language said she wouldn't be opposed to David fucking her like the wanton slut she was advertising herself to be.

"Will do," he told her. "We have to get going."

She looked over at me, and I smirked a bit. "Where did Michael run off to?" I asked her, just because.

"He was speaking to our children, apologizing to our daughter for letting his whore answer his phone," she said with a sneer as she looked at me. "He's in the shower now."

As she talked, her eyes lingered on the passion mark Michael had left on my neck. I kept looking at the identical one on hers. We both made eye contact again and gave forced smiles.

"I hope everything is okay between you two. I hate to see married couples who seem to be so in love come to such a place of discord," I said.

David tsk-tsked, chuckled, and shook his head. He mumbled, "This shit . . ."

Sadi asked him, "What did you say?"

"I said, I agree," he lied with ease.

"Oh. Well, trust me, we may fight, but neither of us is going anywhere," she assured us. "As you can see, we always find a happy medium," she continued, hinting around at what we already knew. She and Michael had indeed fought, then fucked.

David told her, "That's a good thing, then."

"David, I didn't know that you were serious about anyone. Michael never made mention of her," Sadi said.

The way she said "her," it was as if I was an after-thought. Like she could see why David hadn't mentioned me, if there had indeed been a reason.

"Michael never makes mention of a lot of things, Sadi," David said.

I laughed low. Tensions were high. Sadi kept staring at my neck.

"In any case, I see you two are madly in love. I've called housekeeping to change the sheets, as Michael said he heard you two going half on a baby. You don't have kids yet do you, David?" she asked him.

I didn't give him time to answer. "We should go," I said abruptly.

David looked sidelong at me but didn't object. "Yes, we should. Nice seeing you again, Sadi."

"Trust me, the pleasure was all mine, as it has always been. Maybe next time I visit, you and I can catch up on old times," she suggested.

David picked up our bags. "I don't think that would be a good idea, Sadi. Not unless Michael is around to join in on the conversation."

"Well, maybe this time when we talk, he can be. I've always wanted to talk to you two at the same time."

Sadi had a look in her eyes that said she wanted to go there with David again. David cleared his throat. Looked at me to see if I had picked up on the sexual innuendos being thrown around. I had, but I wouldn't snap like I wanted to. Not yet, anyway.

But just to be a bitch, I laughed too, then said, "Girl, let me tell you, having them in the same room, talking, is everything. You have to be on your A-game to hang in a conversation with both of them. I loved talking to both of them at the same time. Going to be sad to see Michael go, but, alas, I understand that he must get back home to his family."

I smiled wide as I waved, and then walked away.

"Tell Michael I'll holla at him later," I heard David tell her.

By the time he caught up to me, I'd made it to the elevators. I looked down the hall to see Sadi standing there, scowling at me. I smiled my friendliest smile and waved at her before stepping onto the elevator.

"Did you have to go there?" David asked me once the elevator doors had closed.

"Me? So it was okay for her to basically give her pussy to you while her husband is in the room?"

"Oh, you mean, like you did with Michael while I was in the same room?" he asked sarcastically.

I tilted my head and looked at him.

"Oh, I see," he said.

"Whatever, David."

"Yeah, whatever, Summer."

I got quiet for a moment. Had started to think about Gemma. It made me wonder if David had ever seen the little girl. I mean, I knew he hadn't seen Michael in ten years, but did that mean he hadn't seen the children?

"You ever see their kids?" I asked him out of the blue.

"What?" he asked.

"I was wondering if you've ever seen pictures of Michael's kids."

"Saw a baby picture of Gemma. Michael's sister showed it to me a while back."

"Oh."

"Yeah."

"Does she look like him?"

He tilted his head and looked at me, then shrugged. "She looked like her mother in the picture I saw. Why? You want his baby now too?"

I had to remember he didn't know my real reason for asking. He had no idea that I wanted to know if he'd been able to see himself in the little girl.

We rode the rest of the way down in silence. Got to his truck and still said nothing to one another. My car was parked on the other side of the lot, so he was going to drive me to it. I needed to get home to shower and clear my head. I had to get away from the madness and accept the fact that David had a child and that the mother was married to Michael.

As we got in the truck, my phone buzzed.

Michael had sent a text. Don't leave, it read.

I glanced at David. He was looking at me.

I responded, Why? You're busy fucking your wife. Why do we need to stay?

David cranked his truck and we pulled out.

Michael responded, She's my wife. I don't say no to her. We were fighting. I found a way to calm the storm. You mad?

Fuck you.

Again?

Kiss my ass, Michael.

You were barely able to handle it the first time.

Whatever. Your wife was trying to get David to screw her again.

You're lying.

No. I'm not.

Yes, you are.

Okay.

Just stay. Let me say good-bye the right way.

I shook my head but didn't respond to Michael. He was either fucking with me or in real deep denial about his wife still wanting a piece of David.

David's phone chirped. He stopped the truck. Looked down at his phone and then handed it to me. I hadn't wanted to look at his texts before. This time I did.

Michael's text to David was the same as mine. Don't leave, he'd texted.

Why? I sent back, as if I was David.

Just stay. Let me say good-bye the right way.

I shook my head. I didn't respond and started to scroll through David's texts. There were plenty from Michael. They'd even exchanged a nude flick or two. According to Michael, he was starting to get those old feelings for David back as well. "Falling for David," was what he'd told him. The only difference between me and David was that he had told Michael that rekindling that old thing between them was never going to happen. He had told Michael that his heart belonged to me, and that wherever his heart was, his body would be also. I got a sinking feeling in the pit of my stomach.

David pulled into a random parking spot as I read through his phone. He propped a fist under his chin, with one hand on the steering wheel, while he stared straight ahead.

He already knew Michael. Had been warning me about the man he was since before he stepped foot in Atlanta. Everything Michael had been telling me, he'd been telling David. Not that it mattered. I was lying. It *did* matter. Whether I wanted to admit it or not, I'd started to feel something for him . . . and it was more than a crush.

"We should stay and let him say good-bye," I said to David.

He looked over at me. "I think we should leave well enough alone and go home, Summer."

I turned to him. "I want to say good-bye."

"Text it."

"Face-to-face."

"Bullshit."

"Because I want to say good-bye?"

"Because you want to see if he will stand in your face and lie about falling for you."

"And?"

"Been there, done that. Let it go."

"I want to say good-bye."

"We should go."

"I want to see him. Want to say my farewell face-to-face."

David sighed and shook his head, but we didn't leave.

# David

Summer was my strength and my weakness. She gave me that extra push when I needed it. Then there were those times when she would cause me to do things that I knew I shouldn't be doing in the first place. Like now, I knew we should have been halfway to her place already, but so that she could do whatever it was that she felt she needed to do, I'd stayed. I'd do anything for her. Even go against my own set of principles to please her. I knew she would do the same for me. Wasn't sure if that was a good thing or not.

So as we sat in the Ham Bar at the InterContinental Buckhead, I kept my nerves in check. Felt back in that old head space when it came to Michael. I shouldn't have reached out to him. Shouldn't have invited him down to *talk*. I should have left well enough alone. In hindsight, I saw the mistake in what Summer and I had done.

When Michael and Sadi walked into the restaurant, they spotted us sitting at a table in the far right corner. I didn't want a booth. A booth would have been too up close and personal for me. So the table was fine. Sadi had changed into a body-hugging black catsuit and a sweater. On her feet was a pair of boots similar to Summer's. This wasn't lost on either woman. Summer gave Sadi the once-over. Sadi did the same to Summer. Her eyes lingered on the boots Summer wore.

Summer, too, had changed. She'd pulled on one of the shirts I'd purchased for her earlier. It pushed her breasts up perfectly. Showcased the perfectness of them. Sadi had tits, but she didn't have the breasts that Summer did. Summer had pulled her hair back into a neat ponytail. Lip gloss made her perfect full lips shine. Sadi had just showered. Both Summer and I still carried the scent of satisfied lovers. Michael strolled back to the table with his usual flair. Once again, he was in control of the room. Had everyone under his spell . . . as he wanted it. If he could have things his way, we'd all be back in his hotel room, having a foursome.

That wouldn't happen, though. Would never happen. I could see the trouble from a mile away. We'd never get to know what it was like for the four of us to play in the Garden of Eden together. There was room only for one snake, one man, and one woman.

"Thank you for staying. Sadi and I wanted to apologize for the way we aired our differences in front of you two. That's not the way we do things," Michael said once he'd sat down. He was talking to Summer. Had locked his eyes on her. She gave him something of a smile, then picked up her glass of water to take a sip.

"It really wasn't any of our business, which is why we left the room," I said.

"We appreciate it," Michael answered.

"Yes, we do, and we wanted to buy you guys a round of drinks to make up for it," Sadi added.

"That isn't necessary," Summer told her.

"We know, but we want to do it, anyway," Sadi said and then flagged down a waitress.

I chuckled inwardly. Sadi had turned her heated anger all the way down. Guessed all it took was a little dick to quell all that rage.

Once the waitress got there, Sadi ordered a round of bourbon and then asked for glasses of water for herself and Michael.

"So, Summer, how did you and David meet?" Sadi asked once the waitress had gone.

"Lenox Square."

"Oh, is that where you work?" Sadi's question insinuated that she expected nothing more of Summer.

"It would be, had I not screwed David and got my current job," Summer answered snidely.

Michael laughed. Summer smiled. I shook my head. Sadi looked appalled for a brief second, then caught herself.

"She didn't have sex with me to get a job," I said, clarifying the matter.

"Was only joking," Summer quipped. "I work for Lowery, Hall, and Lowery."

"Oh, so you're an attorney as well?" Sadi quizzed.

Summer shook her head. "No. Paralegal."

"Oh . . . I see. Couldn't quite get through those years of law school, huh?" Sadi asked. "I understand. It's not for everybody. You have to have drive to tackle that law degree."

Summer gave a faux smile. "True enough. I'll give you that one."

"David, I must say, I'd always expected you to end up with another lawyer on your arm," Sadi told me.

I shrugged. "I'm more than satisfied with Summer."

I placed my arm around Summer's waist. Held her close me as her spine stiffened. Sadi was treading on thin ice. Summer's mother had told me how back in high school Summer had to be extraordinary to get the same recognition as the white girls. She couldn't get just an A. She had to get an A+, or it wouldn't matter. Had to excel in everything, which really didn't make it that much easier for her to be accepted by her counterparts. I could tell by the way she had stopped talking and had started to guzzle down water that she was trying to control her anger.

The rest of the time at that table was tense like that. Sadi kept finding ways to throw slick insults at Summer. Summer kept finding ways to dodge them. Michael and I chimed in from time to time as soon as the claws started to show. I didn't have too much to say to him. He knew that. Didn't try to make conversation with me. Instead, he focused on Summer. He knew that his saying anything to Summer would rattle me. So he kept their conversation flowing. Saying things that he knew he shouldn't have been. He and I made eye contact from time to time. Let our silence speak for us, but there was something else in Michael's eyes. Something that I couldn't pick up on.

"You sure you're okay, Michael?" I asked him, just because.

"Yeah, I'm good. You?"

I nodded. That was the gist of our conversation for the moment. In the back of my mind, I knew that if Sadi weren't around, things would be different. Things were always different when she was around.

Summer excused herself to make a phone call. She'd been texting underneath the table the whole time. Michael had been texting too, but he'd been obvious. As usual, Sadi couldn't see the forest for looking at the trees. I couldn't say I was all that surprised when Michael found a way to excuse himself too. Using the bathroom was his excuse. Sadi and I were left there to talk.

"So are we going to talk about what happened between us after all this time or no?" she asked me once the coast was clear.

"I'm perfectly okay with leaving it where it is," I told her honestly.

"Michael still doesn't know," she said.

I shook my head at her ignorance. She had no idea of what I'd done moments after leaving her bed all those years ago. Had no idea that I'd taken her thong as evidence to show Michael what I'd done. I'd left her apartment back then with her scent all over me, just to show Michael how she hadn't loved him enough not to let me bust a nut inside her walls. She'd liked every minute of what I gave her. Had liked when I roughed her up. She'd liked it when I gave her more anal sex than she could handle. Sadi had begged me to fuck her that way. I thought she had liked it more than the vaginal penetration. I had given her all she could handle and then some. Had eaten her pussy so Michael could smell it on my face. Yeah, I'd been one of those dirty niggas back in the day.

"How do you know?" I asked her to keep up the facade.

"Trust me, he has no idea. If he did, he would try to kill you."

"Me? Why not you?"

"Because he loves me too much," she stated so matter-of-factly.

I kept playing along. I asked, "So what are you going to do if and when he does find out?"

"He won't. I have all my bases covered."

"That's good to know."

"Does she know about us?" she asked me.

I knew the "she" Sadi was referring to was Summer. I had to decide if I wanted to lie or not. I decided to keep all my ducks in a row. So I lied.

"Nah, she doesn't know."

"Do you think she would care, anyway?"

I shrugged. "I don't know."

"Have both you and Michael fucked her?"

"What?"

"Did you and Michael fuck her?"

"Why would you ask me that?"

"Because I want to know. So answer me."

"No."

"Have you ever left them alone?" she asked.

"Once or twice."

"So how do you know?"

"I trust him. I trust her."

"I wouldn't be so sure. You gave her the passion mark on her neck?"

I feigned ignorance. I knew very well what she was referring to. Had seen Michael place it there. "What passion mark?"

"The one she keeps trying to hide with her hair and the collar of her shirt . . . on the left side of her neck. I'm just saying, you might be surprised by what you find if you dig a little deeper."

I frowned a little bit, since Sadi and Summer had a passion mark in the same spot. Sadi was so busy trying to make me see Summer as some highfalutin jezebel that she didn't see her own reflection. The waitress brought the bourbon, and I took mine to my mouth. Needed it to keep my cool in this situation. Then I leaned forward and clasped my hands together on the table in front of me. The place wasn't as busy as it would normally be. There was little noise—only the clinking of utensils against plates—to distract us.

Sadi swung her blond hair over her shoulders. Removed her sweater and revealed a set of perfect C-cup tits. She was beautiful. There would never be any denying that. To me, she wasn't beautiful in the same sense as Summer. She met America's standard of beauty. Sadi was attractive in the sense that she could make a man's dick hard for no other reason than her body. Summer was more than that. Everything about Summer turned me on, from the physical to the mental. Her hair, her eyes, the way she smelled, the way she rocked back and forth when she was angry, the look on her face when I said anything to make her blush, the way she bit down on her bottom lip in anticipation of the love we would make, the way she took the time to educate herself on the things she didn't know. Only if I looked at Sadi's body did I get a rise. Nothing else about her turned me on.

"I had to come out here. You know why?" she asked me.

"To see if you could catch Michael in the act of cheating?"

"That and to see you. Even if you hadn't just happened to be in his hotel room, I would have found a way to see you. Not for sex or anything, although it would have been nice, but to see you and talk about some things."

"Things like what?"

"There has always been something about you that I've been infatuated with. I can't really explain it. There is something in the way you carry yourself. You are confident, but not overtly so. It's like you know you're the shit, but there is no need to broadcast it, because it speaks for itself. You're comfortable with not being the life of the party. That night when we all met, both me and Jessica were hoping you would come over and talk to us too."

Jessica was Sadi's younger sister. Built like a brick house, as Sadi was. But Jessica had come up by having a baby with a man she thought was going to the NFL. Instead, he decided not to go to the draft. Jessica's son's father and I hung around in the same social circle. So I knew him quite well. And although he didn't go into the NFL, he still made smart investment choices with his money. So Jessica had gotten what she'd wanted all along, to have a baby with a rich black man and to become a millionaire.

"Is that right? With the way you two were all over Michael, I would have thought differently," I commented as I thought back to that night. I ran a hand through my locks as Sadi tried to charm me with her inviting smile. Sadi and Jessica had been on Michael like stank on shit.

"I mean, yeah, come on. Michael was . . . is fine as shit, and out of all those women in the room, he came for me. I've always wondered why you didn't."

"I wasn't interested," I told her flat out.

For a second, she looked taken aback. Like she couldn't believe that a man would not be interested in her. "I wish you had been. I'd probably be Mrs. Hall now, instead of Mrs. Pinnock."

I could only laugh and shake my head at it all. It was comical that she was so certain about what she'd said. This was the woman whom Michael had played me to the left for. I had to wonder if he had any idea of what the fuck was going on in her head sometimes.

Sadi laughed too, because she was assuming that I was okay with that idea in some way. I wasn't, and I never would be. At that moment I thought about what could be taking Summer so long. Engaged Sadi in more small talk so she wouldn't start to question Summer's and Michael's long absence. Even when Michael was being an asshole, I still had his back. Love made you do shit like that. Same with Summer. I didn't want Sadi to run up on her and try to confront her about Michael. Unconditional love made you do shit like that.

I excused myself for a bit and walked outside. I made my way to the parking deck to see if maybe Summer and Michael had found their way back to the place we'd all loved in the day before, but I got nothing. Moved back inside, took the elevator up to his room. They weren't there, either. For a minute, I started to think I was paranoid. But then I thought better of it. I knew the two people I sought. Knew them better than I knew myself. I went into the stairwell. Even when Summer was trying not to make a sound, she made sounds. Whimpers. The kind that women made when the sex was so good, a blip of a sound was all they could make.

As soon as I hit the second flight of stairs, I saw them. Summer was facing the wall. Ass arched back perfectly as Michael yanked her head back with a fistful of her naturally golden blond hair. I could see the glaze from her sex each and every time he long stroked in and out of her. Her black tights had been pulled down around her flawless round mounds. Michael's right hand squeezed and smacked her right cheek as he worked. He was grunting. It was the kind of sound a man made when he was deep in the throes of passion. The kind where he didn't care if the woman made him sound like an animal. All he wanted to do was keep stroking. The sound reverberated around the small but narrow place. If anyone were to come down the stairs, they would no doubt see and hear them.

I walked farther down the stairs. Made enough noise for Summer to jerk and stop her frantic thrusts back into Michael. She looked around like she was about to be caught by her "old- time religion" Christian parents. He, too, stopped. Looked around to see if anyone was watching them. He was shielding her. Had placed a protective arm around her waist, locking her to him . . . her back to his chest. The look on his face said that he was prepared to fight if someone encroached on his territory. I knew that look. Knew what he was feeling. Summer did that to the male species. I stayed hidden. Once Michael was sure nobody was coming, he pushed back into her again. Summer's thighs quaked as her nails scraped against the concrete wall.

"Damn, Summer. Shit," Michael moaned. "Why you making me do this?" he asked her, his lips pressed against her ear.

"Don't stop. Shut up and fuck me. Don't stop," she ordered, encouraging him.

"You still mad at me?" he asked, toying with her.

She didn't respond. Mad at him? What did she have to be mad at him about?

He rocked his hips. Dipped his legs and hit a spot that made her all but scream out. He cupped his hand around her mouth. "Still mad?" he asked her again. "Fuck you, right? That's what you said to me. I'm giving you what you want. Still mad at me?" He sucked her neck. Brought his hand from her mouth, slid it between her legs, and stroked her clit, then confessed to her, "You make me feel some type of way, Summer."

She didn't respond to him. She was having an orgasm. Her mouth was at half-mast and her eyes were shut tight as she moaned in satisfaction. My dick was pressing against the fabric of my sweats. It was time for me to leave. No way could I walk back into civilization with the obvious erection pressing against the fabric of my sweats. I pulled my sweater down. Buttoned the peacoat I had on and hoped it hid my arousal well. I left Summer and Michael to their stolen moment of ecstasy and exited the stairwell.

"You find them?" Sadi asked, with an accusatory look in her eyes. She was walking down the hall moments after I came from the stairs. A few seconds sooner, and she would have been close to finding her husband in a precarious situation.

"Find who?" I asked, like I didn't know what she was asking.

"Michael and Summer."

I pulled my locks back into a ponytail. Her eyes traveled down to my dick. "Was I supposed to be looking for them?"

"I . . . I thought you would. They've both been gone a long time."

"Summer's on the phone with her mom."

"How do you know?"

"She's in my truck."

She pulled a set of keys from her pocket. "I came to find you because you left your car keys." Her eyes said she was calling me on my lie. I wouldn't let her know she'd caught me.

I took my keys. "Thank you, but Summer has her own set of keys."

"To your truck?" she asked skeptically.

"Yes."

She shook her head and tsk-tsked. "Yeah, okay."

"You really think I'd be this calm if I thought Summer was fucking Michael?"

Sadi shrugged. "I don't know. Michael told me the stories of the way you and he used to toss and flip women."

"That was then."

"What's so different now?"

"Marriage."

"And?"

I laughed, because the look on her face told me she was very aware of her husband's sexual appetite.

"Summer isn't fucking Michael," I told her. Technically, I didn't lie to her. Summer wasn't fucking Michael at the moment. He was fucking her.

We made our way back to the Ham Bar. Talked about nothing and everything. A few minutes later, Summer came walking back in slowly. Even though she had the phone to her ear as she was telling her mother she would call her back, I could tell Michael had touched her. She was barely walking. Was almost stumbling as she made her way to her seat. Her ponytail had been to the right when she walked out. Now it was to the left. She plopped down and blew out steam. Her lips were swollen. Nipples were still hard. She was missing the top two buttons from her shirt, and her freckles were more visible. She'd been fucked. A quickie, but enough to get her that last hurrah with Michael that she needed.

"I hope everything is okay with your mom," Sadi said. "Took you a while."

Summer attempted to smile. "Yeah. She's fine. We like to talk. Run our mouths about nothing and everything at the same time."

"Oh, I know how that is. Did you see Michael out there anywhere?" Sadi asked Summer. I saw something change in Sadi's features. The atmosphere suddenly felt cooler.

Summer shook her head. "No."

"He left right after you did."

"So?"

"So did you happen to run into him . . . Freckles?" Sadi said.

Summer's head jerked back. Sadi smiled, like she was about to reveal something Summer wanted to keep secret. I cleared my throat and leaned forward, then leaned to the side to look at Summer. A part of me wanted to see how she would handle this situation. It could have been my jealousy from seeing that she had to have Michael one last time. She just couldn't let go without that last hit.

"Don't call me that," Summer told her.

"Why? Isn't that what Michael calls you?"

"I don't know what you're talking about."

"Sure you do."

"No. I don't." Summer's whole face had turned red. She started rocking back and forth like she was Miss Sophia from the *Color Purple*.

"I saw he liked a few of David's pictures with you in them on Facebook, and now I know why. Does David know you're fucking his best friend? Does David know about the naked pictures you send my husband? I looked through my husband's phone. You never had your face in shots, but he calls you Freckles. Has the woman in the naked pictures saved in his phone under 'Freckles' I find it funny you have freckles, so don't lie, either," Sadi said. Then she turned to me. "They've been exchanging messages since the first time he was here. That's why I asked you if you were sure they hadn't had sex. It was her who answered his phone. As soon as she opened her slut mouth, I knew it was her. Did you know?"

I wouldn't answer her question. Wouldn't tell her that not only did I know Michael and Summer were fucking, but that I had fucked him too. I'd fucked all three of them. Sadi was treading down a road on which she would be the only one with egg on her face in the end.

Summer was about to respond when Michael came walking back into the establishment. He cast a smirk in my direction as he slid a hand down his chest and abs. He rubbed his hands together like he was Birdman from Cash Money.

"If I were you, Sadi, I wouldn't travel down this road," Summer told her coolly.

"Don't threaten me," Sadi responded in kind.

I didn't let on to Michael that he was walking into a shit storm. The smug look on Michael's face disappeared when he heard the women's exchange of words. He was no longer the ringleader of this circus.

"That's not a threat, I assure you," Summer retorted. "Stop while you're ahead."

"Or what?" Sadi snarled.

"You have two very beautiful children, Sadi. Gemma's the oldest, right?" Summer said.

Something passed between the two women. Whatever it was, it was enough for Sadi to turn her lips down in a scowl that made Summer bristle. I knew that throwing kids into the mix was a low blow, but I didn't know why she was mentioning Sadi and Michael's kids.

I stood, then pulled at Summer's arm, which she snatched away. She had something to prove now. Wanted Sadi to know that she, too, knew something she wasn't supposed to know.

"Summer, get up. Let's go," I told her.

"No! Since Sadi wants to throw stones at glass houses, let's," Summer huffed.

Michael stepped in. "Summer, stop."

"No. Fuck that," Sadi quipped. "Don't tell her to stop. Let her keep going. This is what happens when you cheat on me with trash."

We had an audience. People were watching on in curiosity as a live episode of *Cheaters* played out in front of them.

Michael's features contorted. Aggravated, he ran a hand down the waves on his head, then blew out steam. "Sadi, why are you doing this? For what reason do you have to do this?" he asked her through gritted teeth.

"Because you're fucking this spotted-face black bitch and you have the nerve to act as if you have no idea what I'm talking about. Only trash would—"

"I told you I wasn't cheating on you, and you still insist on doing this shit!" he fussed, interrupting her.

"And what about the tramp at the shop in Staten Island?" she asked him.

Not to be outdone with the insults, Summer thundered, "Only trash would what? Fuck her man's best friend?" Whatever Sadi had been about to say got caught in her throat. "Keep going, Sadi. Please keep going," Summer snarled, daring her.

Sadi cast a treacherous glance at me, then looked back at Summer. I could tell Sadi wanted to call Summer's bluff, but something Summer had said stopped her. Michael kept cutting his eyes at Summer. Something between them was going unspoken.

"You think anything you're going to say is going to rattle me? Think just because you try to bully me into silence that I'm still not going to call you on your shit?" Sadi asked her. "The fact of the matter is, you're still"—Sadi

stepped around the table—"fucking my husband, bitch!"
She swung at Summer. The slap caught Summer's cheek
before I could pull her back.

Sadi swung twice more but missed, as Michael had
grabbed her, and I had Summer. Sadi's second and third
blows caught me in the back. Summer struggled in my
hold. Tried her best to get at Sadi, but I had seen enough.
Had remained silent long enough. As I held her, Summer
kicked her legs like a child would if she was having a
tantrum.

"David, let me go," she pleaded. "I didn't put my hands
on her, and she fucking hit me!" she all but screamed.
"Please let me go."

"No. Chill out, and I mean it. Calm down, pick your shit
up, and let's go," I told her sternly. "I told you we should
leave, but you had to come back and prove something to
yourself."

"What does any of that have to do with her fucking
hitting me?" Summer snapped at me.

I put her down, turned her to face me. I didn't let her go
though. Michael tried to calm Sadi. He had her wrapped
in a bear hug too. There we were, ex-lovers, now referees
to the women in our lives. Sadi's chest heaved, and no
matter how I felt, it was clear they loved one another.
Michael spoke to her calmly, and she nodded at what he
was saying. She was apologizing for embarrassing him.
Sadi's handprint look liked it had been stitched to the
side of Summer's face. Water trickled down Summer's
cheeks.

The manager of the Ham Bar came over to me and
Summer and asked her if she wanted him to call security.
She declined. He then walked over and told Michael that
he and Sadi had to leave. I looked down at Summer, who
was glaring over at Sadi.

"She fucking hit me, David," Summer said again. "She hit me," she kept saying, like she couldn't believe it.

"You fucked her husband," I told her.

"So. Bitch hit me. Snuck me."

"You fucked her husband."

"So did you. She didn't hit you. She hit me!"

"She doesn't know I stuck my dick in her husband. She knows he stuck his dick in you. Your karma."

Summer's breathing was rapid and harsh. Like that of an asthmatic gasping for air.

"Let me get my phone and purse so we can leave."

"You're chill?"

She nodded.

"You sure?"

"No."

"You're not going to go swinging, right? We're going to leave this time, right?"

She nodded.

"This is done?"

"Bitch slapped me!"

"Summer?"

"What?"

"Is it done?"

"Yeah."

I slowly uncoiled my arms and let her go. "Get your stuff."

Her phone and purse were on the floor near the table. Michael was grabbing his wife's sweater and her purse. Summer stalked over, then kneeled to pick up her things.

I saw it all happen in slow motion.

I called out to Summer. Tried to rush in to pull her back. Before I could, Sadi gave a running punt kick like she was the star kicker for the Atlanta Falcons. Blood splattered as Summer fell back on the floor. Sadi had delivered a kick that knocked Summer's head back.

# Summer

Before I could figure out what was going on, one of her feet connected with my face and my head fell back against the floor. I heard the screams of other patrons, but all I saw was flashes of light behind my eyelids. My eyes fluttered open as I heard people scream some more and chairs dance around. Something hot burned my eyes as it dripped rapidly into them. David called my name, but I felt as if someone was pulling me in and out of consciousness.

"Sadi, what the fuck!" I heard Michael yell. "Why did you do that? Are you out of your damned mind!"

"I almost smacked the shit out of a woman," I heard David tell Michael. "You better get her the hell up out of here!"

"Don't threaten my wife!" Michael snarled in return.

"Fuck you! I let her get away with that shit twice now. I won't again."

Just moments before, Michael and I had been sexing like crazed high school teenagers, and now he stood there, defending his wife. As his wife had sat next to him, he'd texted me and asked me to meet him in the lobby, because he wanted to talk. Wanted to say good-bye properly. I'd told him to follow me to the stairwell. Knew from being there earlier with David that it would be a safe spot. We never did get a chance to talk. Not verbally, anyway . . . We talked without words. Did the kind of talking that Sadi had hinted at earlier, when she all but told David he could have her.

"Maybe I am out of my mind, but you're not going to disrespect me in my face, Mike. It's one thing to have your whore all the way across town and to fuck her in the business I helped you to build. It's another to walk your black ass back in here, smelling like this cunt," Sadi said calmly.

She was calm. She had kicked the piss out of me, and yet she was placid. Seriously, I thought I'd felt urine trickle down my thighs after she kicked me. David was talking to me. I could hear him, but I couldn't see him. It was all a blur.

"Summer, baby, talk to me," he said.

Took me a minute to get my bearings. Even longer to see the emerald-colored eyes glaring at me. I sat up with the help of David. He pulled his shirt off and placed it against my eye to stop the blood from trickling down. I sat there for a moment. My whole world was still spinning. Sadi's look was a smug one. She stood there with her arms folded across her chest.

People had surrounded me. Many of them were asking if I was okay. The manager was back to tell me that this time he was calling security. An elderly black man rushed over to help David out as he tended to me.

"Are you okay, sweetie?" a woman asked me as she handed David napkins.

I couldn't nod my head or anything. I was too dizzy to do so. "You can call security!" Sadi yelled. "She's about to need them in a minute since she's fucking my husband!"

The eyes of the woman who'd joined in helping me widened. The look on her face went from apologetic to accusatory as she gave me the once-over. I could spot a hurt woman from a mile away. It was obvious that she'd been hurt by a man in the same fashion as Sadi had. It was written all over her face. She turned her lips down as she walked off.

David helped me to my feet with the help of the elderly black man. I staggered and stumbled a bit. Spotted Sadi across from me.

She placed her hands on her shapely hips as she inhaled and exhaled hard. Water was in her eyes, but she shed no tears. She looked like a woman who still had some fight left in her. An angry black woman trapped in a white woman's body. I wanted to ask her why she felt the need to be so holier than thou. How in the hell did she justify being so angry at me when she had been lying for ten years? The woman staring me down didn't look like she wanted to talk, though. And I, for one, wasn't in the mood to talk, either. That bitch had given me a running punt kick to the head. I dropped my purse I'd never been confronted by an angry wife. No matter how many married men I'd had sex with, not one wife had come to confront me.

David had told me not to retaliate. Had kept me from putting Sadi on her ass when she attacked me the first time. It put me back in a space and a time when my parents told me to turn the other cheek. When the white girls at school would pick on me, talk about my hair and my features, my thick lips, my freckles, and my high cheekbones, my parents would always tell me I had to be bigger than they were. Well, I'd run out of cheeks to turn.

I'd taken so much shit when I was a kid and throughout my teenage years from girls like Sadi that there was no way in hell I was going to let that bitch kick me and get away with it. Not to mention that I kept looking at her and imagining her walking around, carrying David's child once upon a time. Thought back to all the insults earlier. Remembered her look of longing and lust when she looked at David. . . . Before logic kicked in, I rushed that Amazon. Dodged David, who was trying to grab me. I almost fell because of my head spinning, but my adrenaline and anger kept me afoot.

Even though he tried, Michael couldn't hold me and his wife. It was my turn to deliver a kick, and when I did, it landed right in her pussy. She toppled over, and as I tried to get around Michael, I grabbed a handful of her hair. Delivered a punch that knocked that smug look right off her face. That was the only hit I got in, though. As angry as I was, I couldn't come between a man and the woman he loved. Michael shoved me backward, and I fell hard on my ass again. His eyes had a look that told me that just as David had felt like putting Sadi on her ass for kicking me, he was seconds away from doing the same thing to me. I watched from the floor as he grabbed his wife around her waist and headed toward the exit. I could only imagine that he was taking her to the suite where he, David, and I had all been intimate all those days.

I saw a blur moving past me. Had forgotten David was still there, because in my anger all I had thought about was knocking the shit out of Sadi. His face was contorted, like he was seconds away from snapping. Before I could get up, David rushed at Michael. The punch he threw almost leveled Michael. Michael dropped Sadi to the floor.

"You have to be out of your fucking mind to put your hands on her like that!" David shouted at Michael.

Michael picked himself up, threw a punch at David that rocked him. I saw when the anger in David took over his common sense. Had seen him get mad only once before. He'd had to defend my honor in that situation as well. I'd never seen him get as angry over anything or anyone else. I was his weakness. I was his strength. He'd told me that many times.

David, wait," I pleaded as I rushed behind him.

He didn't hear me, though. He was on a mission. Traded punches with Michael until Michael grabbed him. Tried to pick David up and slam him down, but it didn't work. David had been in hostile situations for years, before his education had afforded him the luxury of leaving it all behind. All the fight he had in him was street level. He was a street fighter who had perfected the art so well, he could fight with an aggression that would put the most skilled of boxers on their asses. This time was no different. Michael didn't win the last fight they'd had. He wouldn't win this fight with David, either.

I tried to rush in and grab David's arm as he charged Michael again. Sadi's eyes widened as she watched on. The manager had said, "Screw security," and had yelled to the bartender to call the police. The elderly gentlemen stepped in between Michael and David. Got punched a few times but managed to get them apart with the help of the manager.

"David, stop!" I yelled. "That's enough. They've already called the police, baby, please," I cried.

He spit blood on the floor. He was still angry enough to kill a motherfucker, but lucid enough to hear my voice. Only when David looked down and saw the tears in my eyes did he stop. He breathed like he was spitting fire. His eyes watered; lips were turned down in a scowl, like he had something foul in his mouth. Michael's face was bloodied. I turned away from him. Too embarrassed to look at the mess David had made of him.

I didn't want David to go to jail. I didn't want to go, either, for that matter, but David had much more to lose than I did. I couldn't stand the thought of him losing all he'd built for himself because of what was happening. There we were, four educated people acting like we had nothing to lose. I grabbed my purse, my phone, David's keys, and hurriedly walked behind David as he left the bar. One of the hostesses led us to a bathroom for employees, where David snatched his ripped T-shirt over his head, then punched the bathroom door so hard, his hand started to bleed.

I jumped at the sound. He was silent. Silent and deadly. For a while, all he did was stare at me in the mirror. He looked at the gash over my eye, which made me take notice. I was still bleeding and had forgotten about my own injury. My eye had swelled. That I could feel. I walked over to the sink, where David was, grabbed a paper towel, and tried to wipe the blood from his lip, but he moved his head.

"Go stand over there," he demanded.

"Let me help you," I said. I was nervous. My voice was shaky because of the edginess in his voice. He was pissed, and this time I knew nothing I could say would change it.

"Get the fuck over there, Summer. Just move. Move away from me."

"I didn't mean for this to happen."

"You just had to go there—"

"She fucking kicked me in the head!" I said, cutting him off. "One slap I could let go, but she kicked me in my fucking head, David. Look at it!"

"This shit is always about you. The past eight fucking years have been about you and the bullshit you've taken me through. Everything I am, everything I've become in the past eight years is because of you! When are you going to make anything about me, huh?" he snapped at me.

His voice was so loud, I was sure people could hear us through the door. Tears burned my eyes, the injured one more so than the other. Maybe I could have let it go and let David take me away from the madness. But she had slapped me, and then she had kicked me. Kicked me like a kicker kicked the ball when his three points were all that was needed to win the Super Bowl.

"One has nothing to do with the other, David. I'm not going to let anybody keep harming me physically and just take it. I'm not," I replied, defending myself.

"One has everything to do with the other, because one wouldn't have happened without the other," he fussed, then shook his head as he spit blood in the sink. "I don't know why I let you talk me into this shit. I don't. I knew where the fuck it would end. I knew it."

My heart started to beat rapidly as we studied one another. I kept my thoughts to myself. There was nothing I could say that would change anything. Did I feel bad for trying to knock the shit out of Sadi? No, I didn't. If I could have, I would have mopped the floor with her ass, but I hadn't got the chance to. The same man who treated me like the ground I walked on should be worshipped anytime he saw me was the same one who had defended his wife. He did what any husband who loved his wife would do. But I did feel like crap about placing David in the middle of the mess.

I slapped the tears away from my face and instantly regretted it. The pain was almost unbearable. I gritted my teeth, then cussed under my breath. David winced when he ran a hand along his left side, where his ribs were. When Michael had tried to slam him to the floor, a chair had caught David's side. Even though Michael was taller, thicker, and had more muscle mass, David was the stronger man, especially when he was angry.

I slowly made my way over to him, tried to help him again, but to no avail. He told me to take care of myself and not to worry about him. I tried to explain to him my position again. It wasn't my fault that Sadi had gone there first.

None of it mattered, though. When the police finally arrived, they didn't care which one of us had started the altercation. Two lawyers, a mechanic with three years of law school under his belt, and a paralegal all went to jail.

# Summer

Five hours later, I walked out of Fulton County Jail. I had no words to explain what had transpired. We had been charged with disorderly conduct and disturbing the peace. I didn't even know where it would leave me and David. . . .

David had bailed me out. My boss and his twin brother were there. They talked to David as we all walked to his truck. I remained silent, as if I'd been Mirandized again. I could only imagine that David had placed the call to them. They told us that they would meet with us at the beginning of the following week, once they had a clearer picture of the actual charges being leveled against us. David thanked them. Opened the passenger-side door of his truck for me to get in. Once I was strapped in, he walked around to the driver's side.

We drove all the way to my house in silence. He didn't say a word to me as he unlocked my front door and held it open for me to walk in first. Ever the gentleman, even though hours before he'd acted like a caveman. Had banged his chest to let Michael know he was never to touch me in a way he didn't approve of.

David followed me upstairs. We stopped in my bedroom, and he removed something from my top drawer. Helped me to undress before he did, then went to my bathroom to start the shower. Still, there were no words between us. We got in the shower, and he washed me up. Took his time with me. I took my loofah sponge and did the same to him. He was bruised. Ribs looked purple and black. He also had a bruise under his eye to match my swollen one. I kept avoiding looking at his left hand. Kept my mind off the question I was soon going to have to answer.

"I've had time to cool down," he said in a calm voice. "Can't really blame anybody for this but myself."

I didn't say a word. I just listened to him as he spoke.

"Never again," he said.

The water created a song of rain around us. Tears burned my eyelids. I knew what he was talking about. Didn't need to question where this conversation was going.

"This is the first and last time," he continued.

"Okay."

"All of this. I did all of this for you." His voice was heavy. Burdened.

"I know."

"Never. Again. I've already given you all of me. Even when I thought there was no more to give, I found a way to give you more. Is this enough, Summer? Huh? Was this enough?"

I nodded as I bit down on my bottom lip. Tears mixed with the droplets of water and rolled down my face. Made the stitches above my eye sting when I dropped my head.

"No. Hold your head up and look at me. Look at me. Look at what you made me do," he demanded.

I raised my head slowly. Looked up at the man whom I'd put through eight years of hell because of my insecurities. I'd had time to think while locked in that holding cell, too. Thought about the shit I'd taken him through in the name of me. I'd been selfish, very much so. I'd felt entitled because I knew he loved me, was in love with me, and would never go anywhere. I'd taken advantage of that.

"I'm sorry, David."

"I don't want your apology. I need to know if this is enough. Is it enough? What more do I have to do? Tell me now. Tell me so I can start doing it, because no matter what, I won't leave you alone. I won't let you go. So, I'll jump through three rings of fire. I'll run through hell, drenched in gasoline. Tango with the devil, grab the hem of Jesus's garments, and curse him to hell, all for you. All for you, I will. So tell me. Tell me, how much more of my soul must I sell to have you, all of you?"

My breath hitched, and in that moment, I was at my lowest. I knew I couldn't explain how I felt upon hearing the pain in his words. I didn't have enough apologies to soothe the ache. I'd driven this man to a place he didn't want to be, because I was insecure. How many women had done that? How many women had made men snap, go to lengths and extremes that they never would to prove their worth?

I couldn't handle his honesty, so I'd made him pay for it. Many women begged men to be up front and honest with them, and in the end, they proved that they couldn't handle the truth. How many women in the black community could really handle their black man admitting that he was attracted to men, just as he was to women? Even when I thought I could, I couldn't and didn't.

"This is enough," I said through shaky breaths.

I looked down at David's left hand again. Looked back up to see tears running down David's cheeks. I honestly didn't know if they were tears or water, but the fact that he looked as if he was crying was enough to crush my heart.

"I'm so sorry, baby. I'm sorry for everything. I apologize for making you pay for your honesty. I'm sorry for making you feel as if you had to hide who you are to appease me. I'm sorry for Michael. Sorry for asking you to reach out to him. Sorry for inviting him in so easily. I feel like shit for making you go against your principles. I apologize for dangling that piece of forbidden fruit in front of you and making you become the kind of man you despise."

I was breaking down. Apologizing to him for all the black men, the bisexual black men, who felt they had to hide because there were those of us in the black community who would ostracize them if they showed us who they truly were.

I laid my forehead on his chest as he cupped the back of my neck and pulled me closer to him. We stood there under the water and let it wash away our sins. I was his Eve. He was my Adam. My left hand connected with his. I let my finger brush against the piece of platinum and gold that encased his ring finger. We weren't friends. We'd never been just friends. From the moment he stopped me in Lenox Square, our destiny had been fitted in the stars.

His thumb stroked my left ring finger. Only, the band that matched his wasn't there. He shook his head, disappointed, but he didn't stop holding me. He didn't let me go. I let his hand go and hugged him like I never had before. I held him like he was the man who loved me unconditionally. I hugged him like he was my husband . . . because he was . . . my husband.

# David

Eight years ago, I met the woman whom I eventually married. I said in the beginning that she friend zoned me, because after all the shit she took me through, that was what it felt like. That first date, when I told her I was bisexual, she did more than hold my hand and smile. She told me that none of that mattered to her, because her mother and father were both bisexual. She told me she wanted to know me. She wanted to know the man who had damn near chased her down to give her his contact information.

Took her three weeks to call me, but when she did, we both fell in love, with no pretenses. Lived life like it was a storybook romance. Got married six months later. Took that honeymoon trip to Aruba. Made love like we were the only people who knew how to do it. For the first few months after we got married, everything was the way any marriage was when two people were madly in love. We were in love, dangerously so, and didn't care who knew it. Her family accepted me with open arms. She gave me something I had never had, family. We loved like we never would again.

Then her insecurities started to show. Any man who looked at me for too long rattled her nerves. Anytime I spoke to any man, she felt like there was some kind of hidden message in the greeting. We started to have arguments, which turned into shouting matches. She accused me of cheating on her. Told me that bisexual men couldn't be faithful and were controlled by their dicks. Started searching my phones and e-mails. I had to get rid of a lot of male friends with a bisexual orientation. Life in our home had become a war zone. We were strangers in our own home, combatants. The honeymoon was over.

She moved out. I let her. Got tired of the back-and-forth. Was annoyed with the fights and arguments. We decided to separate. Were headed to divorce court until we found a happy medium. We started dating again. I was more sensitive to her insecurities. She tried harder to be accepting of my sexuality. We became friends instead of lovers, then lovers and friends. Changed the status of marriage and tried things a different way.

I told her about Michael after she asked me about the other side of my sexuality. Told her the stories of the escapades he and I had gotten into. She wanted to know more about Michael. Wanted to know what it was about him that made me speak about him so passionately. I filled her in. Told her he was the one man whom I'd loved. No matter how many men I'd been with, only Michael had had my heart at one point in time. I told her the two of them had that one thing in common. But I didn't tell her that Michael and I had been intimate.

As fate would have it, Michael responded to me after I reached out to him. The thing was, if Summer hadn't told me to reach out to him, I probably wouldn't have. Against my better judgment, I did it for her. I knew as soon as I saw them together what would happen. I'd always allowed her to be free in her sexuality. Never hindered her. She didn't give me that same freedom.

I started having sex with other people only after we separated, because she told me she had. I'd yelled, screamed, cussed, and fussed, but alas, she'd done it. She had used it against me. Said the fact I'd gone out and had sex with other men proved her point.

Yet married men had always been her Kryptonite. All married men except me, her husband. At least, that was what it felt like. She was okay with the other women. Her soul burned when I told her that men, too, were a part of my sexual escapades. Still, we remained . . . friends. Then, two years ago, she stopped having sex with other men . . . and me. Said she needed to get her mind right and really work on us. Since she was running the show, I went along with it. Anything for her, I'd do.

She told me she wanted to see me with another man so she could accept it. Didn't want it to be some random man. Said he had to be somebody with whom I had a connection so she could see the passion in the sex. Thought Michael being with me would be our first time together sexually.

I told her that Michael was married and that there would be no way I'd go there with him unless his wife knew about it. She'd been okay with that, and then, without warning, she'd changed her mind about wanting Michael to come down. Said she really wasn't so sure she could handle seeing me with a man. I told her that was fine. I never wanted her to do anything she was uncomfortable with. Fate once again stepped in, and Michael decided to fly in, anyway. The rest was history.

I loved Summer. I loved her on her terms, never on mine, but it was still without conditions. No matter her insecurities and her faults, I fought to keep my wife and my marriage. I would do it all again if I had to, but this time, I would do it without inviting Michael into our bed. Michael had never been good for me. He had also been one who I would have gone out my way to satisfy, and I had at one point. But he had walked out on me. Walked away from me for the woman who was his wife. Michael had never loved me. It was one sided, unless it involved sex, men, and women.

Summer walked out of our home, but she didn't walk away from us. She kept fighting and trying as hard as I did. Family and friends often looked at us and shook their heads. They didn't understand the method to our madness. It wasn't for them to understand. Summer and I didn't know our biological sperm and egg donors. She had foster parents who loved and nurtured her the best they could. I had had the system to raise me. The system had almost made me another statistic, but I had refused its offer.

In the beginning, she had never really and truly opened herself up to me. Had never let go. Not with sex. Not with love. Not with herself. Eight years and another man later, a man whom I had genuinely loved at one time, she saw that it wasn't about the sex with men, as she'd thought. It took me eight years. Eight damn years to get her to be as open with me sexually as she was when Michael joined us. Eight years for her to allow me to be who I was. Eight goddamned years to get her to this point, and then I had to share her. It angered me. I couldn't lie. I felt like all the work I'd put in had been for her to slap me in the face with it.

But I couldn't lay all the fault at her feet. I had to take responsibility for it too. Had to own up to the mess I'd made of us too. She'd been right in a sense about every-thing. Reaching out to Michael had proved that there was that part of me that still needed to be sated. I'd gone and done what I'd said I'd never do. I'd told her that I never would, but I knew deep down inside what I was walking into. I'd used her as an excuse to do it. So even though I was in my feelings, I wouldn't lay all the blame on her, because in the end, she was still here. I was still here. Neither of us was going anywhere.

\*\*\*

I picked my wife up and carried her to the bed we had once shared with Michael. I dried her off. Placed kisses all over her body. Wanted to make love to her, but I wouldn't. Not in the bed that had been tainted by our other lover.

I walked over to her dresser and opened the top drawer. On top of our wedding picture lay her wedding band. I picked it up and walked over to kneel in front of her.

"It's time to come home now," I told her. "Say it."

She was still in tears. Couldn't stop crying as she looked at the ring in my hand. I didn't take her hand in mine. She had to want this as much as I did.

When she held her hand out to me, I slid the ring back in the place it was supposed to be.

"Yes."

"Yes, what?"

"I want to go home," she said to me.

So we went home, to our home. Not the house she lived in, but to our home, a place Michael had never been. There was a reason I wouldn't let Michael into my home. That was because it was home. I would never let another person into our home. I had never moved out. Had never left, because I'd known that one day she would come back home. Took us eight years to get it together, but we did.

That night we made love. Despite the bumps and the bruises on our bodies, we climbed that stairway to heaven. In our bed we created magic. I got to know my wife like a man did in the biblical days. Explored her body like I never had before. Took her over the edge, jumped off behind her, and then put her over my shoulders and climbed back to the top so we could do it all over again.

A few weeks later, Summer and I would exchange vows again. Her family would be there, and so would all our friends. The female minister would look on with raised eyebrows as we repeated a new stanza to our vows.

I stated, "Coke on her black skin made a stripe like a zebra. I call that jungle fever. . . ."

"You will not control the threesome. Just roll the weed up until I get me some . . . ," she continued.

"We formed a new religion. No sins as long as there's permission . . ."

Together we ended it, saying in unison, "And deception is the only felony. So never fuck nobody without telling me."

Later that night, she told me she had something she needed to tell me. We had gone to the doctor a few weeks before for her annual exam, and the doctor had alerted us to the fact that her IUD had fallen out. The doctor couldn't tell us when it had happened exactly, but he knew for a fact that she was six weeks to eight weeks pregnant. She wasn't showing, but we both knew a baby was in there. I could see subtle changes in her appearance, like the swelling of her nipples, which were sore. Her skin glowed, and her freckles were more visible. Whatever she had to tell surely couldn't be more emotionally confusing than that news.

She walked into the front room and sat on my lap. Tears were in her eyes, and I had to wonder what it was that she had to tell me that had her so emotional. She had her phone in her hand.

"I've been keeping something from you since we saw him last," she said.

We didn't mention Michael by name. Referred to him only as "he" or "him." Nothing more. He hadn't called us. No text had come through. In typical Michael fashion, he'd packed up and left, all in the name of Sadi. Only this time, I was okay with that.

"Talk to me," I said, encouraging her.

"I should have done this a while ago, but with everything going on, I couldn't . . . didn't really know how to."

"What is it?"

She looked down at her phone and started scrolling through her text messages. It kind of annoyed me, especially when I saw that she still had one from him, even though we'd both agreed to let that part of our lives go.

She slowly held the phone up so I could see. I remembered the argument we'd had about me going through her phone. Remembered her asking Michael if he had told me something. I took the phone from her hand and adjusted my glasses. Looked down at a little girl who, if I didn't know any better, I'd say looked like . . . me.

"Who is this?" I asked her.

"Michael's daughter . . ."

I scratched my chin. Ran a hand through my locks and frowned. No way could what I was thinking be true. "You sure?"

"He's been raising her as his daughter."

"So this isn't his daughter?"

"Not biologically, no."

"So . . . I mean, I don't understand," I said, lying to Summer and to myself. "Sadi and Michael adopted?"

She shook her head, and the tears in her eyes rolled down her rosy cheeks. "Nah, she's Sadi's biological daughter."

My left leg started to shake. Heart was threatening to explode in my chest. "How . . . how old is she?"

"Had just turned ten before Michael got here."

I moved my glasses so that they sat atop my head, used my index finger and thumb to rub the inner corners of my eyes. Sat there doing the simple math in my head.

"She's your daughter, David," Summer told me quietly. "He has known for quite some time. Sadi doesn't know that he knows, or she thinks he's too stupid to know, but yeah, he knows. He was supposed to tell you, but I guess with all the shit that happened, he said, 'Fuck it.' I told him I would tell you. Told him that no matter if he walked away without telling you, I would," she explained and then huffed like she was choking on her tears. Her voice shook with each thing she said.

I pulled her closer while she sat on my right leg. Wrapped my arms tighter around her waist, because I could see and hear the pain in her voice. I stared at the little girl's picture like she was an enigma. Gemma looked exactly like me. Summer's body shook with her sobs. I didn't know what I was feeling, if it was anger or nervousness. I didn't know what to feel. The little girl was ten years old. I had a daughter.

Summer continue to tell me about the conversation she'd had with him. Told me how he'd originally come down here to tell me about Gemma so he could hurt me. "So, yeah . . . David, you have a daughter. A ten-year-old daughter," Summer said languidly. "Your firstborn."

I didn't have to hear her say it to know she was crushed by the thought of someone else having my child. We'd talked about children. Had talked about the gender we wanted our first child to be. Had made plans for our first child. But she could no longer give me my first child, and she was hurting because of it. She'd given me my first real family. I'd been her first love, the first man she'd ever loved. The first man who'd ever loved her. But she wouldn't bear my first child. . . .

I locked the phone in my hand. Wouldn't let my daughter go. Wrapped my wife in my arms and held her. I didn't want her to see the tears in my eyes when I told her, "I'm sorry, baby. I'm sorry."

She nodded, tried to say it was okay, but I knew it wasn't.

"Shhh," I told her. "I'm sorry."

I was apologizing to my wife and to the daughter I hadn't known I had. I'd missed a whole damn ten years. She had already developed her personality. She was her own person. I'd missed first steps, first words, first days of school, first tears, first everything. I went from being regretful to angry, then back to sorrowful. My emotions were all over the place. The one that stayed with me no matter what was the desire to confront Michael and Sadi. Why would they do that? Why keep her away from me? What was the reason for the madness? I had to know. Needed to know.

Summer sat with me as I dialed Michael's number. I got his voice mail. I tried every number I had, including his shops in New York, and got the same message each time. He wasn't there. I called Sadi. Had more luck with her.

"Hello, David," she said as soon as she answered.

I put the phone on speaker, laid it on the table so Summer could hear. "What's up? Are you busy? I wanted to talk to you about something."

"I was, but I can make a few minutes for you. Hold on."

Summer's face had turned into a frown. She'd never gotten over Sadi's assault. She still had a scar over her eye to show for it. We could hear Sadi ordering people out of her office in the background.

"Okay, talk to me," Sadi said once she got back on. "But first, I need to apologize about what happened—"

"No need," I said to cut her off. "Charges were dropped. We've moved on."

"Oh, thank God. That's good to know."

"Yeah, but, look, I need to ask you something."

"Ask away."

I didn't want to beat around the bush or waste time. "Is Gemma my daughter?"

"Wh-what?" Sadi asked like she couldn't or didn't hear me.

"Gemma, is she my daughter?"

There was silence on the other end of the line for a long time, and then . . . she hung up. She hung up on me without a yes or a no. But her nonanswer was the answer I needed. Didn't matter, though. She didn't have to answer me.

I looked at Summer, who had stopped crying, but her eyes were still puffy and red. "We have to go to New York," I told her.

"I know," was how she responded.

I didn't understand why God had decided to go this route. I wanted the chapters of my life with Michael and Sadi, all the madness, to be done. I wanted it to end, but I guess the Most High had other plans. I'd never get why Michael and Sadi would keep my daughter away from me. I would never accept what they had done. As Summer stood next to me as I fought for the right to see my daughter, to get to know my daughter, I would have a hard time forgiving the man who used to be my best friend and lover, and his wife.

But seven months later, when Summer and I would be in the delivery room and our son would be born, we'd know what it was to fall in love all over again. As the years passed, we'd remember why we hadn't given our first son my name. His honey-golden eyes, his dark chocolate skin, and his sly fox–like grin would give us the answer.